Contents

Subterranean Towers

Subterranean Towers

◆

A Father–Daughter Story

Irina Eremia Bragin

iUniverse, Inc.
New York Lincoln Shanghai

Subterranean Towers
A Father–Daughter Story

iUniverse, Inc.

For information address:
iUniverse, Inc.
2021 Pine Lake Road, Suite 100
Lincoln, NE 68512
www.iuniverse.com

ISBN: 0-595-31136-9

Printed in the United States of America

Acknowledgements

I wish to thank my mother, Regina Eremia Kortz, for her courage, devotion, inspiration and support throughout my life; my father, Ion Eremia, for entrusting me with his prison manuscript, *The Subterranean Tower*—from which Chapters I, III, V, VII, IX, XI, XIII, XV and XVII were drawn; Joanna Bujes, for helping me translate material from my father's manuscript used in Chapters I, III, V and VII; Ashley Lewis, for her enthusiasm for the story; Corona Machemer, who began editing the manuscript while at Knopf and continued to work on it as an independent editor; Jon Dorf for the final editing of the manuscript; Wendy Tokunaga for forcing me to get it out. I am deeply grateful to my husband Ronald Bragin, who has been my editor, translator, cheerleader, partner and friend from the time we met; my lovely children Andy and Lauren for the joy they bring me; my brother Sorin, who has shared with me our difficult childhood and has been a devoted son to my father and a loving brother; to Aunt Pupi and Uncle Jack, who helped us survive in Romania, start a new life in America and have supported me in every way always, and Cousin Dinu, who made growing up in Romania sweeter.

Introduction

Reunion on a Different Planet

The man in the black suit and wide-brimmed hat now walking hesitantly up the ramp from customs looks Romanian. Is he my father? Should I run up and hug him? I press through the throng gathered to meet the Pan Am flight from Bucharest.

"*Bine ai venit*!" I hear a voice behind me, and another woman runs up and kisses the man in the black suit on both cheeks. My mistake terrifies me. What if I don't recognize him? Twenty-five years ago when I said good-bye to him, I was not yet twelve years old, a frightened little girl on her way to a new land. Even then, I had barely had the chance to get to know him, for he had been arrested when I was five, released from prison when I was eleven, and less then nine months after that, was sending his family off to America, where he, himself, might never be allowed to go.

Suddenly I spot him. There's no doubt in my mind, it's him! The round, warm, familiar face, the luminous blue eyes now sparkling with tears, my blue eyes, my children's blue eyes.

"*Bine ai venit*!"

"*Bine te-am gasit*!" Traditional Romanian greetings: "It's good to see you." "It's good to be here." His familiar voice pushes memory back, beyond the bewildered eleven-year-old girl shrinking fearfully from the emaciated man with missing teeth who had suddenly come again into her childhood as suddenly, as inexplicably as six years before he had vanished from it. His voice awakens memories of a time before his disappearance and all the questions, rumors, doubts; a time when a little girl competed with her big brother for a larger share of their father's chest, where they rested their heads as he crooned "Somnoroase Pasarele" ("My Sleepy Little Birds"). Now a parent myself, I too have sung "Somnoroase Pasarele" to my sleepy little birds as I kissed them and rocked them to sleep. My young son and daughter, who had dozed off during the long wait, are now staring up, bewildered, at the stranger who must be the grandfather they have never met.

I embrace him, trying hard not to cry. My brother, Sorin, rushes to my father and hugs him next. Less demonstrative than I am, he has stood calmly beside me, waiting, but now I notice that he, too, is struggling to hold back the tears. How does he feel about the man who abandoned us because he would not abandon his beliefs?

◆ ◆ ◆

I was five and Sorin was seven in September 1958, when my father was arrested for an act of conscience that destroyed our fairy tale childhood. Before the night of his disappearance we had lived a charmed life. Our old, stately house and its large, beautiful garden, with its pear, apple, apricot and quince trees, remains the Paradise Lost of my memories. I remember red rose bushes and white butterflies. I remember a hen, Albuta, who used to lay a fresh egg for my breakfast every morning. And I remember running to the gate to meet a tall man wearing a white jacket with epaulets, medals and shiny gold buttons who would lift me up, up, up and kiss my cheeks. His moustache tickled me and made me giggle. Then one morning he was not there at breakfast to walk me to kindergarten and kiss me goodbye. My mother said he would be back soon, very soon. I believed her even when we had to leave everything and move in with my grandmother, and even later when children pelted me with snowballs and called me "convict's daughter," and still later when my best friend told me that her parents wouldn't allow her to play with me anymore because my father was a criminal. "You're a liar!" I shouted at the closing door.

When my father did come back, I was eleven years old and had become accustomed to living without him. I had learned not to think about him, not to ask questions. I had become a promising swimmer, trained to someday represent my country in the Olympics. I wore the red kerchief of the pioneer around my neck. On national holidays, I sang fervently along with the rest of my class:

> Romania, my beloved country!
> Hallowed in words and in deeds!
> In good and bad times I belong to thee
> 'Tis for you that I plant my young seeds!

I was not prepared to hear that my father had been sentenced to twenty-five years in prison for writing a satirical political allegory called *Gulliver in the Land of Lies.*

◆ ◆ ◆

When my father fell in love with my mother, a young actress whom he first saw on stage, he was a general, a rising star in the new regime. A career officer who had joined the anti-Nazi communist underground during World War II and one of the few well-educated members of the Communist Party, he became Vice Minister of Defense in 1952, a position he shared with Nicolae Ceausescu, his co-Vice Minister. Unlike Ceausescu, my father could not tolerate the injustices that were so apparent to him: the growing impoverishment of the Romanian people, the loss of individual rights, the terror, the lies, the arrests, the executions—injustices for which he, as a member of the regime, felt responsible. Ousted from his post for expressing his outrage, he proceeded to write *Gulliver in the Land of Lies*, which he tried to smuggle out of the country. Caught, he was condemned in 1959 at a secret trial to twenty-five years in prison. My mother might have gone to prison too, had my parents not gotten divorced only weeks before my father's arrest, in anticipation of this possibility. Then, in 1964, all political prisoners were granted amnesty, an overture by Romania toward the West.

◆ ◆ ◆

My first encounter with my father was an accident. My mother, who met with him at my grandmother's house (it is from there he called her, having been unable to find us at our old address), was so shocked by his condition and worried that we'd be frightened, that she decided our reunion should be put off several weeks to give him a chance to gain a few pounds.

But fate willed otherwise. One afternoon, I happened to go to the park with a friend and found a place on a nearby bench, next to a thin, bald man with missing teeth, who looked at me piercingly as I sat down. He asked me my name and offered me his bread roll. I grabbed my girlfriend's hand and ran away. I wouldn't tell her why.

An hour later, the toothless stranger knocked at our door. I could see him through the keyhole. My brother was at school and I was alone in the house. Still, I let him in. He reached out to hug me with two long, thin, bony arms. I turned away.

◆ ◆ ◆

The first time I allowed my father to hug me was nine months later, at the airport, when we said farewell for what we thought might be forever. During that short and painful interval, we had finally almost managed to overcome the barriers erected by the six lost years. Once again my father had told me stories, sung me songs and recited poems that he had composed himself in that dark, terrible place. My brother, too, had warmed up to Neclo—our old nickname for my father—and begun playing chess with him as in the old days. But just as we were becoming a family again, the Romanian leader, Gheorghe Gheorghiu-Dej, who had been liberalizing the country's policies, was suddenly reported dead and Nicolae Ceausescu named his successor. My parents foresaw disaster. "Me, they'll never let out, but perhaps you and the children can go," my father told my mother. She was Jewish; he was not. We could try to take advantage of the newly expanded Jewish emigration quotas. My mother applied for us to join the rest of her family who had emigrated to California. My father signed a form giving his consent. "There's no future here for you, children," he tried to explain to us; we were reluctant to leave behind our father, our friends, our schools, our sports teams, our lives.

As our plane began to board, I finally consented to give him a kiss—his first and last kiss from his eleven-year-old daughter.

◆ ◆ ◆

How do you "catch up" after twenty-five years?

◆ ◆ ◆

True, since I came to America, my father and I have maintained a correspondence, sharing important moments, thoughts, impressions, feelings. Our mutual passion for literature has contributed to our intimacy. From the age of thirteen, I have sent my father my essays, poems, short stories, sections from my dissertation, screenplays, and chapters from my novel. My father taught himself English so that he could understand and critique my literary efforts.

Still, there is so much we do not know about each other. Can the life events of twenty-five years be squeezed into letters? On my side there is junior high school, high school, the years of adjustment to a new language and culture, college, marriage, graduate school, screenwriting, buying a home, remodeling, the birth of two children, teaching, writing. On my father's side, there are long years of loneliness and longing for absent children; a second marriage; humiliating, underpaid work as a ghostwriter; hard years of struggle to regain the right to publish under his own name; finally, a published historical novel, followed by three more; cold winters with minimal light or heat; long food lines, angry crowds, the battle for bare necessities; and one recent terrible bout with depression, a recurrence of post-traumatic stress syndrome late in life, from which he may still be recuperating.

How do you overcome the barriers between such different worlds? What will this man, who has been through so much, suffered so much, think about my life? I am, like all my friends, a baby boomer trying to raise perfect children while pursuing a career and running for good health. I share, I must admit, the habits, preoccupations, problems and obsessions of my American-born contemporaries. I have become so assimilated that most people can't even detect an accent. How will my father be able to relate to me and to my children? Will our worries seem to him petty, our problems trivial? Will he approve? Will he understand?

◆ ◆ ◆

"A beautiful dream!" he exclaims as we enter Sea World. My father has been dividing his time between my brother's home in Marina Del Rey, our home in Cheviot Hills, and trips around Southern California. My husband, my children and I have taken him to San Diego for the Memorial Day weekend. He is delighted by everything. Baby Shamu's acrobatics, the little packages of sugar, cream, mustard and ketchup available to everyone at the food stands, the simulated earthquake on the Universal Studios tour, the endless, well-stocked shelves at Vons Market, the opulent mansions of Beverly Hills, the magical efficiency of the McDonald's drive-through, the quick-service gas stations, the clean bathrooms—all equally amaze him. "No one back home would believe this," he keeps murmuring, describing the long food lines waiting in freezing weather for small, rotten potatoes, soup bones and pork fat, the only food available in Romania for the past few years. "This is a different planet," he sighs. "Everything here is available to everyone, not just a select few."

Like the old emperor in a fairy tale he used to tell me as a child, my father "laughs with one eye and cries with the other." He is glad when he sees the high American standard of living, but he is sad when he compares it to the Romanian people's misery and deprivation. "Romania was such a wealthy country, so rich in natural resources, and now, look at us now…"; tears well up in his eyes. Hungry, cold, suspicious, Romanians, who were once known for their Latin joie de vivre, hospitality and good humor, are now often angry and bitter, my father tells us.

"Americans are happy people," he says, as the audience laughs and cheers at "The Sea Lion and Otter Show." As tireless as my children, he doesn't want to miss anything. He's in excellent physical shape. He tells us that he swims regularly and goes mountain climbing. His proud, military bearing and powerful, athletic build make him look taller than his height and younger than his years. His deep-set blue eyes are soft and wistful, the dreamy eyes of a writer. They laugh and sparkle, and his face lights up in childish merriment as he feeds the seals, chases my children, eats hamburgers and French fries. But just as he begins to enter into our light, abundant world, I enter the dark world of his past. While he laughs, I cry.

At the Bahia Hotel beach, my father helps my son, Andy, to build a tall tower out of sand. Farther back, I lie on a chaise longue and read the excerpts my father brought with him from a memoir he wrote in his mind while in prison and only recently set to paper. I see my father, alone in his dark cell, counting the footsteps of the guard who comes to peer at him every five minutes. Then he climbs up on his prisoner's stool and strains his neck to catch a glimpse, through the bars of his tiny window, of the tops of several poplar trees, and through them a patch of sky. My father is not allowed to talk to anyone or do anything. During his solitary fifteen-minute walks in the prison courtyard, he must keep his eyes fixed on the ground and under no circumstances look up at the sky. "I thirst for the sky," he cries in one of his poems:

> From my dark cave
> From my deep grave
> Under sheets of ice
> Under waves of fog
> I miss endlessly
> That blue infinity
> How I thirst…thirst for the sky.

This last line echoes through my mind all the next day as we visit the Hotel Del Coronado, take a harbor cruise, pose for pictures with my husband and children. I'm inhabiting two worlds: the light, bright world of a California vacation, and the dark, tragic world of the Romanian prison. That afternoon, while my father and children splash in the pool, I lie on another chaise longue reading the chapter titled, "The Coughed Prayer":

> It was the third day of Christmas, St. Stefan's Day, my father's name day. Lost in my happy memories, I didn't notice at first the loud coughs in the cell next door. It was my neighbor, the Catholic priest, the only prisoner among us granted the right to cough out loud—he suffered from tuberculosis. I realized that his coughs followed the Morse code signals we used to communicate with each other through knocks on the wall. I deciphered a short cough, a dot, followed by a double cough, a dash. The priest was using his special privilege to convey a prayer to St. Stefan, on behalf of us prison slaves. He repeated his prayer twice, and I finally understood it: "Saint Stefan, you, the first martyr of Christianity, listen to our fervent prayer, destroy our chains, and deliver us from our torturers. Amen."

A wet little hand touches my cheek and startles me.

"Why are you crying, Mommy?" asks Lauren, my little girl.

"The sun's in my eye, darling." I wrap her in a towel, hold her shivering little body next to mine and wonder: Was it worth it? My father was robbed of our childhood. We were robbed of our father. Was he aware of everything he was risking when, at the height of a brilliant career, married to a wife he loved, raising two children he adored, he stood up and spoke the truth? Because he could not bear the injustices suffered by others, we, his children, went through childhood without him. My brother and I were the price of his courage. Wasn't this price, perhaps, too high? And in the end, what had he achieved? There were no flashing camera lights or TV reporters waiting to greet Ion Eremia when he arrived at Los Angeles International Airport, only two children who had grown up without him and two grandchildren who had never met him.

◆ ◆ ◆

On our way to the Wild Animal Park, my father, sandwiched between my two children, radiates happiness. "I'm a very lucky man," he suddenly says. "I was born on a lucky day." My husband and I are amazed. We are both thinking about my father's six years of psychological torture, about the loss of his children, about the cold, hunger and fear endured in the hell Romania became in the last decade of Ceausescu's reign. I think of the nightmares and depressions that plague my father and will continue to plague him for the rest of his life. I think of Primo

Levy and Jean Amery, both Holocaust survivors, both suicides. "The injury cannot be healed: it extends through time and the furies...perpetuate the tormentor's work by denying peace to the tormented," Primo Levy wrote. "Anyone who has been tortured remains tortured. Anyone who has suffered torture will never again be able to be at ease in the world, the abomination of the annihilation is never extinguished," wrote Jean Amery. I share my surprise with my father, and he surprises me further by telling me that he was able to find happiness even in prison, for it was there that he discovered himself as a writer.

As we near the Wild Animal Park, it begins to rain. We find ourselves in the middle of a storm and have no choice but to turn back. "Oh, no!" my children cry. I'm disappointed for them and for my father, too. He was so anxious to see a place where animals are not kept in cages.

"Don't cry!" he tells my children. "Is good! California has drought. Your earth is thirsty!"

◆ ◆ ◆

"I have come to believe that the greatest happiness in life is the happiness of making others happy," my father tells me, shortly before he decides to go back to Romania. I suddenly remember how, twenty-five years ago at the Bucharest airport, before he said goodbye to my brother and me, he held our hands tightly, unwilling to let go, even as he tried to cheer us up: "I know this will be your first time on an airplane, but don't be afraid. You'll rise above the clouds and fly like the birds over the ocean. And then you'll get to America, where you'll grow up to be everything you want to be."

My father has gotten to America too late to start a new life. He feels useless here. In vain my brother and I try to reassure him. "No, I have consumed enough of your time and energy. You have your obligations, your families, your work." Then he looks at me significantly. "Finish your novel. Make it as good as it can be." I will never forget the answer I received from him when I was in college—in response to a letter in which I told him that what I really wanted to be was a writer. "My darling, I was in my mid-forties, and in difficult circumstances, when I came to the same conclusion. You must not silence that voice within you that is crying to be heard, or as you yourself sense, there will always be a part of you that will remain unfulfilled." Several years later, he encouraged me to turn down the opportunity to work-for-hire as a Hollywood screenwriter, dismissing the financial advantages as not worth the compromise with what ought to be a writer's true goals: "Aim high. Aim for the best in yourself. Aim to create literature that will outlast you. Never settle for anything less."

It is for the sake of his own writing that my father is impatient to get back to his native country. He has important work to do. He is searching in the archives of the secret police for the manuscript of *Gulliver in the Land of Lies.*

Despite his appreciation of his children's domestic happiness and material comfort, my father is by no means blind to the problems of Los Angeles life. He notices the economic disparity between the east and west sides of town; he notices the homeless, the congestion, the smog, the fast-paced, pressured life his children lead, and the materialistic, commercial culture in which his grandchildren are growing up. "Take your children to see mountains, forests, rivers and lakes. Let them breathe fresh air, run freely through the meadows, notice the beauty of birds and flowers. They'll come to love life with every fiber of their being," he advises me. Already, he misses his beloved Carpathian Mountains and the shores of the Black Sea, where he spent his boyhood swimming like a fish.

He leaves me the excerpts from his prison memoir and promises to try to mail me the rest. He hopes things are improving back home. A month after his departure, the manuscript arrives in the mail. The mass of thin sheets of Romanian paper fills me with dread, curiosity, resentment. Why must I do this? Should I not be devoting my precious free hours between teaching and children to completing the novel I was working on before my father arrived? I let his manuscript sit on my nightstand and ignore it for a while, until finally, cautiously, reluctantly, I pick it up. Then, in spite of myself, I fall under its spell.

A man sits on a stool in a dark cell for sixteen hours a day. He must not lean his back against the wall. He must not talk—even to himself. Every five minutes the piercing eye of the jailor scours his tomb-like cell. This, he has been told, will be his life for the next twenty-five years. How will he keep from going mad? I watch him, this Robinson Crusoe of the mind, as he learns to survive in the wilderness, as he protects himself from the beasts who threaten to devour him, as he begins to sow his arid island with the fertile seeds of his imagination. As I read, my thoughts often wander far from his cell to the little girl he left behind, and to her mother and brother—the convict's family who were made to suffer the consequences of his intransigence. Like her father, she, too, countered loneliness and deprivation with fairy tales, fantasies and dreams. Like many children who grow up in hostile environments, she used her imagination to create a world of her own. The gates open, and memories flood in.

Suddenly I imagine writing my own memoir and placing it next to his, juxtaposing my memories and his. Alternating, in parallel chapters, between my father in prison and his daughter in the greater prison outside his prison, our book will capture the missing years of our relationship and reclaim through art what was stolen from us in life.

Excited, inspired, I struggle for several hours to make the overseas connection. When I finally reach him, he returns my enthusiasm. It is by writing, he observes, that we have defied time and distance and maintained our closeness through all these years. In our joint book—not two disparate memoirs, but a single, seamless text—we will stand side by side forever. Art will undo life!

1

Ion: The Demonic Eye

Solitude is a torment not threatened in hell itself.

—John Donne

I hear the steps first, slightly dragging. A few more seconds and the iron socket stuck in the door's oak hide flicks open its lid and is filled with a cloudy, luminous orb, filigreed with blood.

The Eye.

It hunts me down. It finds me. It tears into me. It stabs through the light of my eyes into my brain.

It examines my face. It touches my hands and my feet. It searches my room, my convict's chair, the iron bed behind me, the straw mattress, the bars on the window. Then the bloody Eye suddenly draws back, the lid shuts over the iron socket and darkness falls.

In exactly five minutes, the steps sound again. Again the iron lid flicks open. Again the Eye scours, searches, retires.

After another five minutes, it reappears.

The Eye, the Eye, always the Eye.

During the night, it fixes upon me, still unwavering, traps me in my sleep and turns my dreams to nightmares.

What has the Eye to do with me? Why does it follow me? What does it want from me?

Clearly it wants to see whether the four torments—hunger, cold, immobility and solitude—are having their full effect.

It appraises my body to make certain that hunger has sufficiently hollowed my cheeks and clouded my eyes.

It ascertains that my teeth chatter as they ought and that my hands tremble like leaves do before they fall.

It checks my hands and lips to ensure that I am manacled into immobility and muzzled into silence. I am not allowed anything that would lighten the leaden moment. It is not permitted that I write a single word—even a scratch in a bar of soap. I cannot knead the few bread crumbs or whatever shreds of food I can salvage from hunger into another form. What might that form mean? I cannot twist a straw.

I cannot move my lips to murmur a verse, nor hum a tune to transform this unending oblivion into a snatch of ordered time; not even a momentary respite is permitted. The hands that have forged tools and the lips that have shaped words, transforming the dumb beast into a man, here remain frozen. The hands may only be used to carry food to the lips. A bit of gruel or corn meal mush—just enough to fuel the consciousness of suffering.

The Eye also wants to see that I have not closed my eyes to shut out my view of the scabrous wall of my cell or sunk all the way into the sleep that would allow me to forget the hunger and the cold and make the immobile solitude in which I live slip by more quickly. It examines the bedstead to see that I have not dared to lean against it; I am forced to spend seventeen hours a day sitting on a stool with my back bent, unsupported. If it finds fault with my posture, it will be delighted to subject me to additional punishment.

The Eye checks my gaze to see whether it is fixed upon the void and whether the pupils have dilated like those of madmen, or whether they are haunted by visions, as has happened to some of my brothers in suffering.

Finally, the Eye checks on my bed-sheet, ensuring that I have not concealed it in the hope of transforming it—in the dead of night, when supervision is less fierce—into a noose that would slip neatly around my neck.

Because I am not permitted to die.

2

Irina: Witches

At night, from under my quilt I hear angry voices, shouts, arguments:

"YOU MUST STOP TALKING! YOU'RE DESTROYING US!"

"THE TRUTH! I WILL TELL THE TRUTH!"

"THE CHILDREN! WHAT ABOUT OUR CHILDREN?"

"THE PEOPLE! I WILL NOT LIE TO MY PEOPLE!"

"WHAT IF THEY TAKE YOU? WHAT IF THEY TAKE ME?"

"DIVORCE. WE'LL GET DIVORCED. THEY WON'T TOUCH YOU IF WE GET DIVORCED."

I turn to my brother, awake in the bed next to me. "What does that mean, 'divorce'?"

"Shut up! Go back to sleep." He knows, but he won't tell me.

I'm afraid to sleep. They keep chasing me, the witches, up chimneys, over rooftops, on broomsticks through the air, where I am flying with bird's wings. They chase me through all the rooms of our house, where I search desperately for my parents. Finally, I find one or the other and run for protection toward comforting arms. I am greeted by a cackle, black claws, sharp teeth. I am staring straight into the eyes of the witch.

I wake up screaming and throwing up. I throw up all over my pink satin quilt. Night after night I throw up.

At first my mother is patient and understanding. She takes my temperature, makes me tea or lemonade, gives me aspirin, calls the doctor in the morning. After a while, she just changes the sheets, opens the windows, covers me up with the red satin quilt that we save for special occasions. I continue to get sick every night, even after my father and I switch rooms and I sleep with my mother in the big bed.

My mother loses patience with me. She grows irritable and begs me to please, please stop doing this. Not every night. I cannot possibly be sick every night. She can no longer bear it. One night she spanks me. Afterwards, I hear her weeping softly into her pillow. I want to run to my father, but he doesn't sleep in our house anymore. He went away to the Soviet Union. On a trip, my mother says. She says Neclo will come back soon.

We are standing in front of our door after school holding our book bags. The key doesn't fit in the lock, and we can't get in. They must have changed the lock, my mother tells Sorin. Who did this? Why? I don't understand! I want Ancuta, my big baby doll. How will I get her? I cry!

We go to my grandmother's house. Omama's house is warm and full of good smells. I sleep at the foot of Omama's bed. I stop throwing up.

3

Ion: Theater Of The Absurd

In its darkness and bleak isolation my prison resembles Chateau d'If in *The Count of Monte Cristo*. But I am no Edmond Dantes, no victim of historical circumstances, thrown into captivity by unlucky chance or through the self-serving machinations of a jealous rival—a neighbor who coveted my apartment, a colleague who wanted my job, a former mistress looking for revenge. Nor was I on the losing side of political upheaval or a target of persecution. On the contrary, I was one of the winners, conquerors, beneficiaries. I am where I am by my own free choice—to the extent that our choices are ever truly free and not the consequence of all that has gone into making us what we are.

The knowledge that I had a certain degree of control over my fate would afford me some satisfaction, were it not tinged with guilt. I made my choices—but those I love most, my wife, my children, must also now suffer the consequences of my actions. The Securitate—our secret police—came for me one rainy night in the fall of 1958. Out-thundering the thunder, they tore the massive oak front door of our house from its hinges and caught me unprepared. Weeks before, after the typescript was completed, I had buried the original, handwritten manuscript of my novel in the cellar and piled carrots, potatoes and onions on top of it. The evening of my arrest, however, I had dug it up in order to give it the next morning to a trusted relative, who had convinced me that he had found a more secure place for it. Was the timing of his offer a coincidence?

Gina, my wife, was even less prepared than I. At first, she thought the men were robbers and begged them not to harm the children. They brandished a warrant for my arrest and a search warrant and began systematically ransacking the house.

"What are they looking for?" she asked me, terrified. I didn't answer. It was too late to explain. I hadn't told her about the novel because I didn't want her to be held responsible. Besides, she wouldn't have approved. Her career had already been ruined along with my own. Never would she have risked further damage to our lives and the lives of our children.

It hurt me to look at her. This was not what she had envisioned that evening, nine years before, when I waited outside after the play with a bouquet of red roses and told the beautiful young actress with amethyst eyes and hair the color of ripe wheat who performed with such sensitivity and passion that I found myself irresistibly drawn to her. Nor could she have imagined, on that clear summer evening in the garden, at her parents' house, when I proposed (in the old-fashioned way, on bent knee), and she accepted, that one day she would be left alone to fend for our two children, the disgraced family of an enemy of the state. But then the young officer who spoke to her so eloquently about becoming partners in the realization of their dreams had felt he was on top of the world, a key architect in the building of a new and just society.

In less than an hour, the security police found the manuscript. My children were sleeping in their room. I was allowed only a few seconds to look at them. The chessboard with the game my son and I had started that evening was still on the night stand. My daughter would wake up expecting to hear the end of the story we had begun together before she fell asleep. What would their mother tell them in the morning? I could not say "goodbye." Handcuffed, I was led out of the house.

For a year, I was in custody at Malmaison Prison in Bucharest, while the secret police held their inquest and I held mine. Alone in my cell after each day's relentless interrogation, I subjected myself to my own grueling self-examination. Could I have made other choices, done differently than I had done?

Three years before, I had been General Ion Eremia, co-Vice Minister of Defense, along with my political rival, Nicolae Ceausescu, of the People's Republic of Romania. Like all members of the new ruling elite, I lived in a mansion confiscated from the old and had a staff of servants and orderlies at my disposal. If I chose, I could dine every day on truffles and pheasant and caviar purchased in shops the general public knew nothing of. But every day, I drove in my limousine past long lines of desperate, frightened people, starving people, endlessly waiting to buy a few soup bones or a piece of cheese at stores whose shelves were bare. I could have chosen to bury my nose in the very important papers on my desk, to mind my own business, as my wife said. But how could I? I, who had once seen myself as a key architect of a brave new world, had become one of the architects of a state that was not so different from the concentration camps we had liberated during the war.

Gina begged me to keep my mouth shut, to think of our children, to think of her. So many had been arrested, so many had disappeared. Why flirt with self-destruction by speaking out? What could I possibly hope to accomplish, anyway?

But I didn't see myself as a Don Quixote, a romantic fool tilting at windmills. I was co-Vice Minister of Defense, a general, a war hero, a party member since my youth. My colleagues, some of whom were close friends, were the leaders of the nation. Surely, I reasoned, they must be experiencing the same doubts, feeling the same pain I was. My brother Gica, with whom I always shared everything, encouraged me. He, too, was outraged, but not being in as high a position as I was, felt helpless. Convinced that unless we changed our course, our country was headed toward disaster, I began to share my perceptions and voice my concerns.

The result of my candor was that one morning when I came to work I was suddenly called to a special meeting, headed by Emil Bodnarash, the Minister of Defense (who had always liked and supported me), and told that I was accused of disloyalty to the party and of spreading lies about our government. Bodnarash offered me a chance to redeem myself by making a public confession that I had been led astray by the "capitalist lies and propaganda" I had heard on Radio Free Europe which was, of course, banned. I refused.

The consequences were immediate. I was dismissed from my job and forcibly retired from the army with no pension. My wife, who was by then one of the leading actresses of the National Theater of Bucharest, was also dismissed. No one associated with such as I could be allowed to appear on the stage. All my brothers and sisters were demoted.

Still, I was not thrown out of my house (perhaps through the intercession of Bodnarash), and I was given work as a "commercial inspector," a job that consisted of having to "catch" various employees in markets and restaurants in the process of watering the wine or "stretching" the ground meat, common practices among people living in want who could only better their lot by cheating. It was humiliating work, and after a few months I resigned and tried to support my family by "ghostwriting" books and articles for those who wanted the credit but lacked the talent.

Despite everything that had happened, this turned out to be an exhilarating time for me. I was no longer a liar among liars. And my sporadic work enabled me to be with my children. Sitting on a park bench, watching them as they played, I conceived the satiric novel that became *Gulliver in the Land of Lies.* After returning from the Houyhnhnms, Gulliver undertakes a new voyage to a strange realm called Kukunia. Here the inhabitants live in poverty, misery and terror. Nevertheless, they are expected continually to declare that they live in a perfect state of bliss and to provide daily proof of their endless love and gratitude toward their beneficent leader, The Great Granit. I got more satisfaction from writing this book than from anything else I have ever done.

I finished it in the summer of 1958 and showed it to my older sister, Agripina, a schoolteacher. She liked it and found me a typist. My brother Gica also read it and helped me get in touch with a mutual childhood friend who was an officer in the commercial navy. He was to mail it from any Western port to a Romanian exile, a former schoolmate who now lived in Paris, where we hoped it would get translated and published. This, however, never came to pass. From the attitude of the policemen when they found the handwritten original on the night of my arrest, it was clear to me that they had also come into possession of the typescript and that now they could establish beyond any doubt the identity of its author. The typescript had been intercepted, or perhaps surrendered by someone I trusted. On another rainy autumn day, almost exactly a year after my arrest, I finally faced a secret military tribunal along with Gica, Agripina and the unfortunate typist. Poor woman! She had thought she was earning a few extra pennies by typing a children's book. And I thought I was protecting her by not telling her otherwise. The authorities, however, decided to punish her anyway. I had walked into the courtroom proud of my *Gulliver*, with no regrets about anything I had done. But when I saw the poor typist and then my sister, Agripina, who turned her head to have a glimpse of me after a year of separation and was kicked and cursed by the guard, I felt stabs of guilt. Since my arrest, I had not seen my mother, my wife or my children. How were they holding up? Were they, too, being cruelly punished for my crimes?

My trial was theater of the absurd in its purest form. The prosecutor accused me of betraying my country by writing a book of lies about the Communist Party and its leaders. Yet at the same time, he contended that "Granit" was easily recognized as Stalin, that "Gitlej" was clearly President Gheorghe Gheorghiu-Dej, that "Pikiriki" was Nicolae Ceausescu and that "Kukunia" was Romania.

"Anyone reading your book would know immediately that you are speaking about our party, our country and our leaders!" the prosecutor shouted.

"How would anyone know who or what I am talking about if my portrayals are false?" I asked. "If my characters and situations are so realistic as to be immediately recognizable, my book must have captured some well-known truths. Are you trying to punish me for telling the truth?"

My answer came in the form of the maximum sentence: twenty-five years at forced labor for betraying my country by intending to publish an anti-communist novel. My brother was sentenced to fourteen years, my sister to seven and the typist to five.

The next day I was shipped in a special police van to the infamous Jilava Prison on the outskirts of Bucharest, where I was to be incarcerated temporarily until a permanent prison was decided upon. My journey to that nether world lasted no more than an hour, during which I could see nothing, but after a year of being buried alive, it was a delight to me, and I absorbed with all my other senses the smells, the sounds of men on earth. Once again I heard the shouts and laughter of children, the high, velvety tones of women's voices, the grave, sonorous voices of men; I listened to the music of the small orchestras that played in the outdoor cafes and savored the tumult of the city, which seemed to me as harmonious and joyous as a symphony. Even the complaints and threats of old men addressed to those who forced them to stand the live-long day, waiting for a bit of gristle or rancid cheese, were music to me. The breeze and the scent of fresh grass and meadow flowers also reached me as we passed the outskirts of town and then the silvery sound of bells, the mooing of cows, the bleating of sheep, the shepherd's playful flute. Now I was traversing the valley that lay between the capital and its ancient defense outposts. We traveled another half hour through the valley where the hay had been freshly mowed, then left the paved road and headed up a cobbled lane. A few moments more, and the way changed to a final, abrupt descent. The police van stopped, the key turned in the lock, and the hoarse, broken voice of the guard intoned:

"Hey, you! Get off! You've arrived at your 'hotel'! Hurry, or I'll give you a real reason to limp!"

I emerged, climbed down the steps of the police van and put my hands to my eyes, blinded by sunlight. When I could see again, I looked curiously around me. I was in a defensive trench, facing a high wall of burnt brick in the middle of which was a stone plaque: JILAVA PRISON. I proceeded through the door and entered a courtyard paved with flagstones and surrounded by a group of barracks with shuttered windows. Here I witnessed a scene straight out of Dante's *Inferno*.

Twenty men, facing each other in two rows leading to the prison doors, formed a sort of Gothic arch with knotty clubs held above their heads. Smiling and joking, they were waiting for a slowly approaching convoy of men who looked more like walking corpses.

"These are the next guests of cell zero, dumb-shit!" the guard informed me, his face like that of a boy anticipating a good trick. "That's where we'll keep 'em chained 'til the execution, or 'til they get the answer to their appeal. You'll see what a treat our boys have in store for 'em!"

After a few moments, the ghastly convoy entered the tunnel of clubs. The condemned stooped their shoulders and bent their heads, attempting to protect their faces. The sound of wood striking flesh, accompanied by the satisfied curses of the guards, was amplified by the stone walls of the fort. The victims struggled to remain on their feet so as to pass more quickly thrôugh the arch, but one after another, they fell and were forced to crawl across the flagstones toward "cell zero." Their trail was threaded with rivulets of blood.

Now the guard took me through subterranean tunnels to the prison's storeroom, where he made me trade my clothes for the coarse, striped garb of the prison inmate. Then he led me down a series of damp, rancid corridors to a heavy, doubly ferreted, oak door. He opened it, releasing a wave of stale air and the odor of urine and feces, and thrust me inside.

I found myself in a room filled with bunk beds and skeletal creatures—nearly eighty, I later learned, that had been built to accommodate a platoon of thirty. They studied me in silence, trying to figure out who they had to deal with: a new victim of the communist tribunals or an informer. After a few minutes of this inspection, I broke the silence and presented myself:

"How do you do! I am General Eremia, condemned to twenty-five years of forced labor for attempting to publish an offensive book."

A middle-aged man with a distinguished and friendly face came toward me and offered me his hand. "I am Dr. Victor Costinescu, in charge of this cell. Welcome, if it is possible to welcome a man into prison." We shook hands, and I greeted the other prisoners as well. Then, not sure of what to do next, I stood embarrassed next to the cell chief. He took my arm and whispered, "Let's find you a place to sleep in this luxurious resort."

"I am used to all kinds of accommodations," I replied.

"Have you been arrested before?"

"I'm a rookie," I quipped, "except for a year's custody in Malmaison."

The 'voice of the people' led us all through there. Malmaison is the antechamber of Jilava and Jilava the antechamber of the various prisons waiting to be assigned to us, to each according to his needs.

While we were talking, I felt someone touching my shoulder. I turned and found myself looking at an old school friend, Dumitru Roiu, or, as he signed himself, D. Roiu, from which came his nickname, De Roi—the king. I knew him as an honest man, and I was not at all surprised to find him in prison. It turned out that Dr. Costinescu was his uncle and had been arrested for hiding De Roi, who was wanted for having helped another friend who was wanted…

"Someday our 'wolves in sheep's clothing' will get their due!" I promised them vehemently.

"I hope you're right, but in the meantime we've got to survive this place," the doctor said. "The prison is full of informers. They come cheap: a few more crumbs of bread, an extra slice of polenta. We'll point out the ones we know, but there are others. Make sure you never complain about anything. The guards here will beat you to death!"

I assured the doctor that I had already had some experience with informers during my year-long imprisonment at Malmaison. He was relieved, and we started our sorry search for a bed I could sleep in. We finally found a free space, two feet wide.

"We are so crowded, we can only sleep on one side," the doctor whispered. "Forget about turning over."

"If I can't turn over, I won't worry! I'll sleep like a log," I joked.

I didn't laugh that night, however. After struggling for hours to sleep, I woke up in the morning with an agonizing cramp in my side and a longing in my heart for my munificent concrete bed at Malmaison, three feet wide. Which proves, as Einstein said, that everything is relative.

The room in which I found myself, Roiu informed me, was reserved for political prisoners with long sentences—fifteen years to life. As politicals, we were treated with much greater brutality than the inmates of other sections of the prison. Beatings were the order of the day and were dispensed at a guard's whim: for speaking above a whisper, for a few straws found under one's bed, for "lack of respect," for "hostile remarks," for whatever other offense a guard cared to invent when he got bored and wanted entertainment. We were beaten on the spot with the guard's belt or taken to a special room, forced to lie face down on a table, and beaten with a broom handle across the back and buttocks.

But the punishment in which cruelty, mockery and humiliation found their fullest expression was the "sack race"—a "sporting event" in which some guards participated while others watched. The "contestants" were forced to hop with sacks tied around their legs. Their "coaches" spurred them on with clubs. The "spectators" cheered, booed, laughed and applauded. The last to reach the finish line was beaten mercilessly until he fell down flat—to the great amusement of the "fans." The faster "runners" were forced to run another lap, and then another, until they too fell, one by one, under the unceasing blows.

For a while I managed not to give my jailers any reason to punish me. I swept meticulously when my turn came. I was careful about what I said. I muffled my laughter. I controlled my anger. I whispered. I kept silent. More than the physical pain, I feared my reaction to the humiliation of punishment: if they hit me, I'd hit back and end up getting myself killed. So I contained myself on my own account; eventually, however, my outrage at an incident involving another prisoner overwhelmed caution.

Among my cellmates there was a young man of surprising innocence. He was around twenty, with deep-set eyes and extremely delicate features. His hands, especially, seemed to have been carved by some Renaissance sculptor, so long and graceful were his fingers, so pale and diaphanous the skin. He paid unusual attention to his hands: morning, noon and night he massaged them for hours at a time, flexing his fingers and practicing rapid, precise movements across an invisible keyboard. For he had been a gifted pianist, winner of several international competitions.

When his turn came to sweep the room, he held the broom gingerly, as if he were holding a bunch of thorny roses, terrified that he might hurt his hands. This made him appear ridiculous, and some of the other prisoners made fun of him. To help him, Dr. Costinescu had proposed that we excuse him from sweeping. Unhappily, the prevailing view was that all prisoners were equal and must share equally in the cleaning chores.

I liked him, sought his friendship, and managed to gain it quickly because I shared his passion for music. We whispered for hours in a corner of the room about Beethoven, Mozart, Liszt, Chopin, Brahms, Enescu, Rubinstein...We never spoke about politics. When I tried to broach the subject, I realized that he wasn't interested and didn't understand the first thing about it. I wondered how this naive boy had wound up a political prisoner. Finally, I wrested from him his secret:

He had been engaged to the daughter of his piano teacher. She was a beautiful girl, but insanely jealous. She attended all his concerts and carefully surveyed his admirers. When he so much as gave an autograph to a woman, she went wild. After winning first prize in a piano competition in Paris, he began corresponding with the young female pianist who had taken second place in that same competition. Their correspondence was exclusively concerned with their music. As the young man had nothing to hide, he made no effort to conceal these letters from his fiancée. She found them and in a fit of rage, went to the local collective. Making use of a conversation she had witnessed among their circle of friends in which several had remarked upon the gross ignorance—even illiteracy—of their communist leaders, she denounced all the participants, including her lover.

The secret police arrested everybody. With the exception of the young man, all the accused had indeed criticized the regime, and confessed their guilt without too much hesitation. They got off lightly. However, the pianist, indifferent to politics, hadn't contributed to the discussion and refused to admit any guilt. Consequently, he received the harshest sentence, since his crime was aggravated by his attempt "to lead inquiry and justice into error." Now I understood why the young man sought to preserve his hands, although in the world in which he found himself, their delicacy was of no use. His hands were his hope.

One day, when it was the pianist's turn to sweep the room, the guard looked in and spied him going clumsily about his task. Outraged, he stormed into the room convinced that the pianist's manner of sweeping was a form of mockery.

"You goddamn lazy bastard!" the guard screamed at the frightened boy. "You call this sweeping?"

The poor pianist froze. Finally, he whispered, "I am a pianist…I'm trying not to hurt my hands."

"You're protecting your paws? Ha! Ha! Ha! What did you say you were?"

"A pianist."

"You mean you bang on the piano for grub and booze in the beer halls?"

"No, sir. I don't play in beer halls."

"So where do you play, little fart?"

"In concert halls, on the radio…"

"You mean you're a 'classy' musician?"

"Sort of…"

"Trying to spare your hands, huh?"

"Yes, sir."

"You dumb shit! What do you think you'll be doing in your next prison? Breaking stones for new roads! Digging in the fields! The calluses on your hands are gonna be bigger than walnuts."

"I'll be careful, sir…"

"You stupid asshole! Someone's got to break those hands in for you. I think I'll do you that favor right now." He wrested the broom from the boy's hands and commanded, "Stretch 'em out!"

"I can't, sir," the young man whispered.

"Are you crazy? You want twenty-five laps in the sack race? Stretch 'em out!"

"I can't, sir!"

"You mother fucker! I'll teach you to obey me!" And the guard began hitting the pianist with all his might, aiming for his hands. But the pianist held his hands tightly to this chest, protecting them with his body so that the blows fell every which way across his head and back. The cell resounded with them.

Too indignant to care about the consequences, the rest of us began to shout in unison: "Stop hitting! Stop hitting! Stop hitting!" Our voices reverberated and, perhaps frightened, the guard backed off. He was about to leave the cell when the officer in charge entered, enraged at the commotion, and sent the pianist off to solitary for refusing to obey an order.

Perhaps I should have known better, but I could not keep quiet and shared my outrage with my cellmates. Among them there was an informer who repeated my words to the guards. The next day, the guard who had beaten the pianist—we had nicknamed him "Gorilla"—came into our cell again. At once there was deathly silence.

"Which one of you assholes is Eremia?" he raged. No one answered.

"Cell chief, where is the son of a bitch?" Gorilla roared again.

The doctor looked about the room, pretending to search, but said nothing.

"I'm asking for the last time, you bastards!"

"Here sir," said one of my cellmates, pointing to me. Gorilla stared at me, his face so red with rage I thought he'd explode, and bellowed: "Why didn't you answer, mother fucker? Are you so scared you shit in your pants? You weren't scared to talk behind my back, were you?"

I looked him in the eye and kept silent. If military school had taught me anything, it was that cowering before bullies only spurs them on. They'll advance when they sense weakness, retreat when they detect strength.

"Son of a bitch! Are you deaf?"

I answered him in as calm a voice as I could muster: "No, sir, but I am not accustomed to being called names."

For an instant, Gorilla remained frozen in place, disbelieving his ears. Then in one leap, he landed next to me and raised his fist to strike. Somehow I managed not to lower my eyes, not to cringe. Instead, my eyes met his, and a miracle happened. It was his eyes that avoided mine. His fist fell. I suppose he thought I was mad, and that, if he hit me, he might die with my teeth in his jugular.

"You'll rot in your own shit in the tower," he said at last, then wheeled left and stomped out of the cell.

Following my run-in with Gorilla, the prison bosses concluded that I was a dangerous element and should be isolated. I was transferred from the common cell to the secret section, that is, to one of the fort's solitary cells, a few meters underground. These were small, narrow cells, more like closets than rooms, with moldy, putrid walls. The floor of mine was awash in slime, with small islands of algae floating here and there. A dim light kept the cell in semi-darkness and gave it the feel of a tomb or medieval catacomb.

When I next saw the light of day, the guard who came to get me held his nose in disgust. "Where the hell did they get this mummy?" he asked nobody in particular. And indeed I must have looked and smelled like Lazarus. I had been buried alive for three weeks. Still, when I finally saw the sun shine, there flickered in me the determination to survive my incarceration, to live to denounce what I had witnessed before some human tribunal. The sun itself seemed to demand it, as Plato realized when emerging from the cave of false prophets.

With curses and blows I was led away to the storeroom, where I was told to hand over my penal uniform and given back my old clothes. I gathered from this that I was to be transferred to another prison. Next, I was taken to a workshop upon whose rafters were arranged chains attached to cuffs of various sizes. A squat anvil took up the middle of the room. Near it was a hammer worthy of Hephaestus. It was not the god who approached me, however, but a swarthy man of middle size. With a deft, judo-like maneuver, he laid me flat on the floor; then, taking my foot, or rather the bone that hunger had left, he fitted a cuff over my left leg. He inserted the bolt in the hole and with a fierce hammer blow flattened it into the cuff, which sank into my flesh. He did the same with my right foot. Then he lifted me into the air and handed me to the guard "ready to go!" The guard commanded me to walk, which I attempted to do only to trip and fall. The guard and the smith laughed. With difficulty I stood up, took a few steps, stumbled again but without falling, and finally managed to reach the truck that was to take me to the railroad station. The guard pushed me up under the tarp, then bound my eyes.

I was not to catch a single glimpse of the city after the prison's dark rot. Just as during my journey to Jilava, I had to content myself with smells and sounds. This time, however, I was tortured by the hope that, by some chance, the truck would pass near my house and that my children would be playing outside and I would hear them.

Needless to say, nothing of the kind happened. But I could not stop myself from hoping until I heard the clatter as the truck approached the marshaling yards of the Bucharest North station. The guard took off my blindfold, lifted me easily into the air, then landed me, not so easily, on the sidewalk. From there, I lurched to the coach reserved for transporting prisoners. Amazingly, it was comfortably fitted; it even had a private bathroom.

Assembling the train took about an hour. Through the cracks of the blind, I could see the whole world. I envied the men sitting on the benches, waiting for their trains. Although they did not seem and could not be happy, at least they were not on their way to prison; they were not followed, they were not beaten, they were not mocked.

In a while, the train began to move. Soon we reached the Grant Bridge, which resounded with the cheers, songs and whistles of tens of thousands of soccer fans on their way home from the Giulesti Stadium. It was Saturday afternoon. The men were off work and, forgetting their grinding worries, were still reveling in the game they had just seen. Then we left behind the suburban gardens of the capital and passed by fields and mountains so green that my eyes, deprived of this particular color for more than a year, widened with enchantment. I had nearly forgotten it as I had forgotten the sun's face, which now blushed and bled toward the horizon. Below, in the empire of green, the russet harbingers of autumn danced in a mad race with the wind.

The night brought with it a full, silver moon and then a lake in which the moon also found itself. And I was straightaway plunged into remembrance of the summer nights I used to spend with school friends, young lovers of pranks and poetry. We were engaged in an old ritual of my native Constanza: bathing under a full moon. It was a tradition we observed without fail. After splashing near the shore, the better swimmers headed out to sea. From there, we looked back upon the silvered mansions of that city built upon the rocks—the rocks that, according to legend, were the children cast into the sea by their mother, Medea. Then we would swim back, eager to recount our exploits to the younger boys left on the beach.

One night we swam out to sea while pulling a small rowboat in which we had stored our clothes. Sated with swimming, one by one, we climbed into the boat and were paddling lazily along. Suddenly we heard behind us a chorus of women singing.

"Those are sirens! Don't turn your head or you'll go mad!" cried my friend Mihai, the best in our class in Greek and mathematics.

"You really think it's sirens?" I asked.

"Although they say that the Greeks were as courageous as they were boastful and that all their myths were only a pack of lies, it is undoubtedly true that whoever turns to look at Sirens will lose his mind," Michael assured us, with all the authority of his "A" in Greek.

"That's the way it is," seconded another. "Where there's smoke, there's fire."

This being the case, no one turned his head. But the sirens sang more beautifully than ever, and I began to worry that some of us would be unable to resist the temptation. Then I had an idea: a way to look at the sirens without turning our heads. For some reason I carried a mirror in my coat pocket. I raised it to my eyes. Yes, there could be no doubt. These were sirens, naked as Eve and beautiful as Helen. After admiring them for a long time in the moonlight, ignoring my friends' impatient and envious cries, I finally passed the mirror around so every boy could see the dangerous sight without losing his mind.

A short while later, the sirens dove into the sea and disappeared. Had they caught on to our trickery? We decided to meet again the following night. But the next evening we could find no trace of the enchantresses. "We were wrong…" one of us said at last. "I heard my dad say that there were some opera singers touring in Constanza and that they went on a swimming escapade last night. We were such idiots! We might as well have looked at them straight on. They weren't sirens, just sopranos."

"Impossible! They were too slender to be opera singers!" argued Michael, who was not only terrific in math and Greek but also attended the Opera frequently.

Remembering this now, on the train on the way to the prison where I was to serve out my sentence, I smiled. To this day, I do not know whether my friends bought the story about the sirens and my ingenious solution, or whether, due to their youth, they simply had not dared to face a woman's nakedness. As for me, I had really believed the stories told by ancient Greeks and old sailors and had used the mirror in good faith. I have always been easily seduced by myths and fairy tales.

The moon continued to scatter its silver light until dawn, when the train entered the marshaling yards of the station, Riminicu-Sarat. It shone upon the special coach that was uncoupled and pushed by a locomotive into the prison yard of my new abode: "a disciplinary prison with a strict regimen of solitary confinement." I was led first to the ironmonger, who rid me of my shackles, and then through a large, square hall framed by layer upon layer of cells, to number five on the ground floor. It contained a single iron bed, a sign that I was to be the cell's sole occupant. The walls were damp, and the floor was made not of wood, as in the communal cell at Jilava, but of cement. The authorities had decided that I would spend the next twenty-five years here. If, that is, I managed to live so long.

4

Irina: Before the Nightmares

Sunshine floods the little room where I am awakened every morning by our rooster's crowing (cucurigu-gagu! cucurigu-gagu!). I run to the window and survey our beautiful garden, with its roses and lilacs, its pear, apple, apricot, cherry and quince trees. "Pui, pui, pui!" I hear fat Nasha, our maid, call to the chickens she must be feeding, and I hope that our hen, Albuta, has laid an egg for me. Unmindful of my brother, asleep under his blue quilt, I burst out the door and tiptoe into my parents' bedroom, where my mother (we call her Giunica) is applying the last touches of makeup at her dresser, that treasury of mysterious bottles and jars of cream, of powder puffs and hairpins, curlers, ribbons and combs. I surprise her into a delighted laugh as I crawl into her lap, and she hugs me tight and covers me with kisses.

"Why are you up so early, Galuska?" she says, nuzzling me under my ear, making me giggle. Her soft, white skin smells of violets. She cradles me for a moment like a baby, pretending to give me a bottle, then stands up and sets me down. She is tall and slim and very graceful, magnificently dressed in a silk print. It is cinched tightly around her tiny waist, the skirt puffed by a crinoline. I want to crawl under her full skirt, hold on to her leg, make her take me with her wherever she goes. I follow her into the kitchen, where Nasha is finishing up her breakfast of scrambled eggs with sausages and onions. For us, Nasha prepares food my mother considers healthier: French bread toasted on a fork over the gas flame, thin slices of cheese, tomatoes, cucumbers, green peppers, and my fresh egg, soft boiled for exactly three and a half minutes. My mother prepares my father's strong Turkish coffee, to which she adds a thick layer of cream she skims from the top of the pot of boiling milk, and my brother's dark, sweet cocoa, which only she knows how to make to his taste. We sit at the stately dining room table. Through the large windows and French doors that open onto the terrace, light bursts into the elegant dining room, bathing us in sunshine.

"Good morning, my two beauties!" My father comes into the room followed by my brother, his shadow. (When Neclo is home, the two are inseparable.) He kisses my cheek and my mother's hand. He sits next to my brother, who is a finicky eater (unlike me, who loves everything), and promises to tell him the story of how he beat Ceausescu at chess, if only Sorin will eat the last bites of his toast. Chess is their passion, and when Neclo is home, he spends hours at the chessboard with my brother while I keep track of the captured pieces. Sometimes, if the game takes too long, I sneak up behind my brother and give him a hard push, causing him to fall forward and knock down the men. Everyone thinks Sorin is smart because he can play chess. But I am faster than he and can run and hide under my parents' bed before he can catch me and pay me back for ruining his game.

I crawl into my mother's lap, eat some of her bread and butter and insist, though it is late and she has to go to her rehearsal, that she tell me the story of "Chucha, the Little Chocolate Girl" who lives among her little chocolate girlfriends in a chocolate kingdom that lies hidden at the bottom of a village well. I love this story, which Giunica has made up with my help. She tells it to me once, and I want her to tell it to me again. But Madame Olga, our French tutor, has arrived with her *"Bonjour mes enfants!"* This means it is time for my parents to go to work and for my brother and me to go to our French lesson. I clamp my mother's arms around me and refuse to let her get up. She kisses me and explains that it is very late, that she is expected at the theater, and that I must be a good girl and go to my lesson. But I stubbornly hold her down, clutching at her hand, her sleeve, her hem, and cry and stamp my feet. "Don't go! Don't go! I won't let you go!"

"*Oh, la, la! Monsieur le General,*" Madame Olga says to my father, who looks concerned. "*Elle est une petite actrice.*" My soft-hearted father is so easily moved by my tears. "*Allons nous! Allons nous enfants,*" Madame Olga cries, "*Allons voir si la rose/qui ce matin avait declose/a robe de poupre au soleil/Et son teint au votre pareil...*" she chants as she marches us through our garden, making us pause and admire each flower, each tree, the name of which sounds even more delightful in French than in Romanian.

Delicate and lady-like, Madame Olga is Russian, and my mother says she used to be a duchess when she was young. Though she has lived in Bucharest for a long time, she still speaks Romanian with a thick accent. Madame Olga's husband was killed during World War I and her son during World War II. She gives French lessons to several other children on our street; she has to support her mother, who was also a Russian duchess in the old days. My brother, who reminds Madame Olga of her lost son, is her favorite pupil, a "brilliant boy," she says. I don't know what she thinks of me.

We sit on our veranda and listen to our teacher read to us from a pretty book with a picture of a little girl with long, blond hair on the cover. Quickly, I get confused.

"But who is talking now?" I ask, after the little girl, Alice, wonders, "Do cats eat bats? Do bats eat cats?" and then someone else speaks.

"The narrator, of course," Madame Olga replies, surprised by my question.

"Who is he?" I insist.

"Lewis Carroll, who wrote the story."

"But where is he? Can Alice see him?"

"No! He wrote the book more than a hundred years ago! He's dead but his words live on."

"But how can he be in the story if he's dead?" I want to know.

"Quiet!" my brother shouts, demanding that Madame Olga go on with her reading. She begins: "Alice felt that she was dozing off…"

"But I want to know about Lewis Carroll!" I interrupt again.

"*Oh, la, la! Tu es impossible!*" Madame Olga exclaims, giving up on me and sending me out to play.

I love to run in our garden, climb the trees, gather fruit. I love the hard, green, sour apricots before they ripen and their even harder seeds, which we crack in doorways to get at their soft, white centers. After the French lesson, my brother rides his bicycle and I my tricycle on the broad sidewalk of our street, which is lined with pretty houses ("villas" my mother calls them) and shady poplar trees. Many of the fathers in our neighborhood work in the same place as my father. They, too, have big black cars driven by drivers in black brimmed hats.

My brother's friends, Bogdan, Milu and Mircea, join us in a game of cops and robbers. They would like to be rid of me, but I tag along, threatening to call Madame Olga and have them sent home if they leave me out.

At one o'clock, Nasha serves our main meal of the day: *Ciorba* (a sour meat and vegetable soup made with borscht), *sarmale cu mamaliguta* (stuffed cabbage with polenta) and *clatite cu dulceata* (crepes filled with preserves) made from our own rose petals. After lunch, I nap while my brother and Madame Olga read more of the story of Alice, undisturbed by interruptions from me. I wake up just as Frau Gemma, our very tall, very fat German tutor walks in to replace Madame Olga, who goes to give lessons to her older pupils, now coming home from school.

Frau Gemma walks slowly and breathes heavily. When she sets her great body down, her large behind breaks through the wooden chair on our veranda. We laugh and laugh while Frau Gemma struggles to free her round posterior from the square frame.

French I speak fluently, but German I resist. Instead of *der tisch* for "table," I insist on saying *das pish*. My brother is amused. "You! Das pish! Come here!" he yells, summoning me to collect the crayons he claims I've left scattered all over the floor.

Tonight, it is my father who rescues us from Frau Gemma's long, German fairy tale of which I understand not a word. Unlike our tutors, Neclo does not read to us but makes up our bedtime story himself. He lies in bed between Sorin and me, and we snuggle up close to him, each struggling to get a larger share of his chest, where we lay our heads, as he spins out a marvelous tale about the Romanian hero, Popa Stoica, and his adventures fighting the Turks. Now and then he stops and invites us to contribute our own imaginings to the story. As we get sleepy, he sings our favorite song, "Somnoroase Pasarele" ("My Sleepy Little Birds"). No matter how hard I try, my brother manages to stay awake longer and whisper his secrets to my father, while my heavy eyelids close.

One evening, my father takes us to see my mother perform in a play. My beautiful mother has always seemed like a queen, but now she really is dressed like one, and lives in a palace. I want to run up and join her on her throne, but my father holds me down and whispers that I must wait until the play is over. I fall asleep, and when I wake up I am lying across my mother's lap, surrounded by kings and queens who are talking and laughing and drinking champagne. Everyone is congratulating Giunica for a wonderful performance. I hold on to her fiercely and shout at them to go away and leave us alone. Don't they know that she is my mommy? Everyone laughs. "She's feisty like you, Gina," one of the lords says.

◆ ◆ ◆

Sundays we walk to Parcul Stalin, which is not far from our house. This large, beautiful park, with its manicured French gardens, its sculptures and statues lining the paved walkways, is for me an enchanted land. First, we go to the children's playground, where Sorin and I pose for pictures on the bronze turkey and duck at the entrance and then run to the swings and see-saws. We always stop at the open air children's library and sit at a wicker table poring over story books. Later, we walk to Lake Herastrau and rent a row boat. Sorin and I take turns helping our father row. We stop for dinner at the Pescarus, an outdoor restaurant on the lake. It is always very crowded, and there's a long line of people waiting to be seated, but the waiter takes us immediately to one of the tables closest to the lake. There is an orchestra and a dance floor where I, along with the other little girls, twirl around and around, pretending to be ballerinas, while the adults are still eating or waiting to be served. Then, as it gets darker, the real dancing begins. While my brother and I munch on the precious American peanuts our parents have ordered for us, a rare delicacy which we carefully count up and divide, my parents dance. Tall, slim, blond and nimble, they move together gracefully around the dance floor like Cinderella and Prince Charming in the illustration from my book of fairy tales.

Perhaps even more than our Sundays at the park, I love our Sundays at Omama's house. Here we join my mother's family, her parents, brother and four sisters (a fifth lives in Israel), for a sumptuous five-course meal. My grandmother makes golden chicken soup with plump matzo balls, sweet, savory stuffed pike, chopped chicken liver, roasted lamb, garlicky, crunchy roasted goose, sweet apple strudel and honey cake. "Eat, my little one, eat." My mother protests, for she always worries about my weight. Galuska, or "little matzo ball," is my nickname because of my love for my grandmother's galuskas, and also my plump, round figure.

At my grandmother's house, we are showered with attention by our uncle and aunts. We call each by a nickname: Jaculica is my Uncle Jack, a chemical engineer who often travels abroad and brings us fantastic toys that don't exist in Romanian stores, like my big doll, the size of a baby, and Sorin's electric train. Aunt Pupica ("little kiss") reads us fairy tales, while Renica ("little Rachelle") tells us "true" stories from our mother's childhood. Coculeana ("little one"), whom everyone says looks like the American actress Kim Novak, has given us the best present of all: Cousin Dinu, now two years old, who crawls around the dining room after us and is more fun than any toy. Opapa, our grandfather, plays cards with us and is always full of jokes and tricks. When she isn't cooking, Omama, a beautiful tiny woman with thick, blond hair falling in waves down her back, clear blue eyes, and milky white skin, follows us around giving us adoring looks and stuffing us with treats. Omama's house is noisy, lively, crowded, full of laughter and good smells. Here we can make mountains out of pillows, trains out of chairs, boats out of carpets. The last time my mother got mad at me, I filled up a suitcase with clothes to run away to Omama's house.

◆ ◆ ◆

This summer we must leave the city, for our doctor has frightened my mother with news about a terrible disease, "polio," which is spreading among little children, "killing some and crippling others." If you catch it, my brother says, you'll never walk again. Our parents take us to the mountains and Omama and Aunt Renica take turns staying there with us. Every day, we hike a little way up the mountain to a meadow where the shepherds bring their sheep. We gather wild flowers, which my grandmother weaves into colorful crowns for us. Sometimes we hire a horse and cart and ride along the dirt roads, where peasant children play barefoot among the cows and goats. Omama and *Renica* stuff us with fresh berries and sour cream, *casha* and *urda* (sweet cheeses made from sheep's milk), lamb chops, roasted baby chickens and fried trout. Our cheeks get so round that, when our parents come to get us, they almost don't recognize us anymore! "Is this a girl or a peach?" my father cries, as I run, barefoot, down the road to greet him.

For the last three weeks of the summer, our parents take us to Mamaia, a resort on the Black Sea. The sand is fine and soft, the water clear and warm. Every morning we walk to the beach and set up our cort, a tent made from bed sheets and wooden poles. All day Sorin and I splash around naked in the water while our parents lie in the sun. Sometimes Neclo joins us in the water and pretends he is a shark. My brother and I take turns swimming on his back. Then Giunica joins us and, holding hands, the four of us form a circle to jump the waves. "*Valu! valu! valu*!" I yell as each wave approaches, and we jump high and catch it before it breaks.

◆ ◆ ◆

"Where does the snow come from?" I ask Opapa, as we watch, through my bedroom window, the snowflakes dancing like white butterflies. I have the flu, and my grandfather is sitting with me while my brother is outside, building a snowman with his friends. I wish I, too, were out there, making snowballs out of the soft white powder, or being pulled by Opapa on my shiny new sled. But my nose is running and my eyes are tearing, and my mother has ordered me to stay in my room with my grandfather, as far away from my brother as possible. "One sick child at a time," she says.

"The snow comes from God," my grandfather tells me. "God makes it snow."

"How does he do it?"

Opapa scratches his head and smiles.

"He pushes a button."

"What button?"

"A white button. God sits on his throne behind a large desk full of buttons. When he wants it to rain, he pushes a brown button. When he wants the sun to shine, he pushes a yellow button. Now he's pushing a white button."

"Will he push it for a long time?" I ask, hoping that the snow will outlast my illness.

"Of course! It is only the beginning of December."

When I tell my brother what Opapa has said, he laughs.

"There's no such thing as God. God is a concept men invented to help them exploit other men."

"How do you know?"

"My teacher told us. And I'll tell you something else. Old Frosty doesn't exist either."

"That's a lie!" My brother must be teasing me, as usual, I think. Everyone knows that Old Frosty visits good children on New Year's Eve with a sack full of gifts! Still, I am worried. What if my brother is right?

◆ ◆ ◆

Everything changes during the long, cold winter. Frau Gemma stops coming to give us German lessons. Nasha leaves one morning and does not come back. Omama, Opapa and Aunt Renica come at different times to sit with us after Madame Olga, too, leaves. Mr. Ionescu, our next door neighbor, who always took his hat off whenever he saw my father, no longer says "hello." And my father does not go to work anymore. He stays home and plays chess with my brother and tells us stories. My mother no longer works in the evening. She is no longer in any plays. I am glad to have her home, but she is sad.

A week before New Year's, my father's mother, whom we call Bunicuta, invites us, as always, along with Neclo's brothers and sisters, to her house for a special meal. Here we have sour cabbage rolls instead of the sweet ones Omama makes, roast pork instead of roast lamb, cheese instead of apple *placinta* (a pastry) and *cosonac* (a round, tall coffee cake filled with nuts and raisins) instead of honey cake. Unlike Omama, Bunicuta has white hair and wears no lipstick or nail polish. When she talks about a neighbor's child who died of polio, she makes a "cross sign" over her chest. Omama never does that.

All through dinner, my father and Uncle Gica whisper to each other. My mother must think they're being very rude, because she keeps looking at them angrily, the way she looks at Sorin and me when we start kicking each other under the table. Then my father and Uncle Gica get up and go in the other room. They are gone for a long time and are still not back when Bunicuta serves the dessert and coffee.

"State secrets?" Giunica asks Neclo when he finally reappears. She is very angry with him, I am sure.

◆ ◆ ◆

Every afternoon, now that the snow has melted and the flowers are blooming again, my father takes us to the park. We swing on the swings and play in the sand, while he writes furiously in a thick, red notebook. He uses the gold fountain pen my mother gave him for his birthday, covering page after page with small letters in blue ink.

"What are you writing?" my brother asks him.

"A book. A children's book," my father replies.

"What's it about?"

"It's about Gulliver."

"The one from *Gulliver's Travels*?"

"Yes," my father says.

"Will you read it to me after you finish it?"

"Yes," my father says.

"And to me too?" I ask.

"To you, too," he promises.

Sometimes my father has visitors during the day. When a friend comes to see him, the two men walk around our garden with their hands clasped behind their backs, talking in low whispers. My mother does not like these guests, particularly Uncle Gica. Whenever he comes, my mother gets angry. I gather that she is angry about what my father and Uncle Gica say to each other while they pace up and down our yard. I can never hear what they say, but for some reason my mother thinks that other people can.

"You must stop talking!" I hear her pleading with my father one night. "Think of me! Think of the children! What will happen to them?"

I toss and turn in my bed, unable to sleep. After a while I go into the kitchen, where I find my mother alone, staring out the window. I whisper that I would like a glass of water.

"Why are you whispering?" she asks, concerned. "Is your throat sore?"

"I am afraid to talk," I whisper. "I don't want anything bad to happen to us."

My mother bursts out laughing. She laughs and laughs, and after a while I can't tell whether she is laughing or crying.

I stand in the doorway, staring at her.

"Go to bed, Galuska," she bids me. "It's late."

I lie in my bed, afraid to shut my eyes. Last night, witches and warlocks appeared in my dreams. I am afraid they will come again tonight.

◆ ◆ ◆

We have been living at my grandmother's house. I have always liked it here, but now I am waiting for my father to come back from Russia and take us home.

"Why did he go there?" I ask.

"He has important work to do."

"Did he take the bus there?" My grandmother lives half a block from a bus stop. I like to watch the people get on and off. I wonder where they come from and where they are going: To Russia, where my father went? To Germany, where my uncle buys us beautiful toys? To Africa, where elephants and lions live?

"No, Irinika," my grandmother explains. "Russia is very far away. People can't travel there by bus.

"Then how did he get there?"

"The train," she says, and sighs. She does not like it when I ask her questions about my father. No one does.

My brother, who has been quietly building with blocks, suddenly gives his castle a swift kick. He walks out into the backyard. I follow him.

"Where's Russia?" I ask.

"In Europe," he says, picking up a ball and kicking it hard against the wall.

"Is Europe far away?"

"We live in Europe, stupid! Europe is a continent, not a country."

"Did our father have to ride on the train for a very long time?"

"I don't know!"

"Does he live in a house in Russia?"

"Why are you asking me all these dumb questions? Leave me alone!" Sorin runs off and disappears, and though I search for him everywhere, I can't find him.

My brother is constantly running away from me now. I want to catch him and make him tell me what he knows. He knows everything. Last night, I overheard

Aunt Renica tell Aunt Pupica: "Sorin knows everything. His mother explained it all to him. He understands, just like an adult." What is it that my brother knows? What is it that he understands?

◆ ◆ ◆

My very smart brother has done something very stupid. He told his teacher what no one was supposed to know. He told her that we are living at Omama's house. From behind the closed doors of my uncle's study, I hear my mother screaming at him. "You must not tell anyone anything! Anything! Keep your mouth shut!" I hear a loud thud. My mother has smacked Sorin.

I feel sorry for him. My mother has spanked me only twice in my life: once when I crayoned our dining room walls after she had them freshly painted, and the second time when I kept throwing up in the middle of the night. (She must have thought I was doing it on purpose.) This is the first time she has ever hit my brother. Sorin is now crying in a way I have never heard before: he makes high, shrieking sounds like the wails of a siren. I run to the bathroom and practice locking my lips together in front of the mirror.

◆ ◆ ◆

"Please, God," I pray, "don't let anything happen to my mother." I am at Omama's house, staring out the window, my nose pressed against the glass. I am waiting for my mother to come home. I count each bus as it stops and lets out a handful of people. I search for her face among the hunched black raincoats, beneath the hurrying, black umbrellas. Where is she? Why is she late?

My grandmother promises me there really is a God. She prays to Him every Friday night when she lights candles, covers her hair, closes her eyes, and moves her lips silently. I now pray to Him that my mother is alive, that no bus has crushed her, no stranger stabbed her, no lightning struck her, no witch poisoned her, no dragon eaten her.

I have counted five buses already. If she doesn't get off the next bus, I am sure she is dead. My tears cloud my vision. Suddenly, I see her amid the dark, wet mass pouring out of the bus, a radiant flower among weeds in her white rain coat and matching white rain hat. She carries a white umbrella. My beautiful mother! Alive! I burst out the door and run toward her and throw my arms around her waist and bury my face in her dress and cry.

"Where were you? I was so worried about you."

"My silly little Galuska, you're getting all wet!" she says reproachfully. "You know I'm looking for a job. Sometimes I have to wait for a long time. The buses are crowded. The lines are long. I'm all right. You must not worry about me."

But I can't help it. I am afraid. In the middle of the night, in the bed where Giunica, Sorin and I now sleep together, tightly squeezed against each other, I wake up. I examine my mother's face, then put my head over her heart. My brother has told me that if your heart stops beating, you are dead. Is my mother's heart still beating? I strain and strain to hear.

5

Ion: Literary Music

A harsh winter! The bitter cold, the hunger, the solitude, the silence have plunged me into depression. Hungry, I lose my appetite. Lonely, I lose faith in myself and interest in my surroundings. My thoughts turn to suicide. I fear that this is the beginning of the end—the end of my sanity, the end of my being. How can I halt this headlong rush toward madness and death?

I aim my thoughts toward that island of light and happiness—my home, my children. But the threadbare blanket of memory fails to comfort me. It is not enough.

I must do something! I must find something that will occupy me and distract me from morbid obsessions. I must speak, if only in a whisper, or lose my voice altogether and surrender to the wildness that awaits me.

I feel the need to sing. In the past, this has been my instinctive reaction to moments of stress. I have never attempted to analyze this involuntary impulse but merely submitted to its command: to sing out loud or in a whisper, depending on the circumstances, until my soul regains its balance. I must do so now.

I begin in a low murmur, one of my favorite melodies. The peephole flickers open. My spies, confused, are doubtless trying to ascertain whether I am talking to my neighbors or losing my mind. Whatever they decide, punishment awaits me. Speaking is forbidden. I must stop. I cannot stop. I must sing.

It is 6:45 in the morning. A deafening high metal whine pierces the air, the sirens summoning workers to the factory near the prison. They ring from 6:45 to 7:00 every morning and from 3:00 to 3:15 every afternoon. I am saved! Under cover of their shrieking, I can sing loudly enough to hear and admire my own sound. For a while, I treat myself to morning and afternoon concerts and manage truly to enchant myself. After all, I get to be both the performer and the audience! When the winter wind howls, I indulge in longer performances, broadcasting to the unhearing world all the lieders, arias and folk songs I can remember.

My free concerts don't last long. One morning, carried away by my own enthusiasm, I forget to turn down the volume. When the wind dies down, my guard, who has for some time suspected something, is thrilled to finally catch me. He lets me sing on while he goes to fetch the officer on duty so he can really nail me this time. The result: three days in solitary, a punishment which, in the dead of winter, may well lead me to join the celestial choir.

Solitary is created by removing the straw mattress from my iron bed and reducing my daily food ration to four ounces of bread. To sleep three nights upon the bare metal grill, just over the icy concrete floor, almost certainly means pneumonia and death. What possible resistance can my body offer? But where, then, can I sleep? There is no other place. I put my brain to this ultimate test of survival. Finally it offers me a solution: I must not sleep at all.

But can I go without sleep for three nights? I must nap as best as I can. Exhausted, I scrunch up, knees-to-mouth, fetus-like, on my convict's stool. I doze off, but minutes later, I dart up, as if shocked by a live wire. My back has accidentally touched the iron bedstead. To touch the bed, or lean against it to support your back while you sit on the stool during the seventeen hours when you are supposed to be awake, is a punishable offense. Conditioned by terror, I have acquired this defensive reflex. I jump up and pace my icy cage, but after a few hours, drained by cold, hunger and fatigue, I'm once again forced to sit on my stool. I curl up like a porcupine to avoid the possibility of touching the bed should I fall asleep. And indeed I sleep. How long I don't know, since I wake falling headlong to the floor. I get up and again begin to pace the length and breadth of my cell. Toward daybreak, drunk with exhaustion, I fall asleep while walking, or more precisely, stumbling. To avoid breaking my neck, I begin to recite poetry, and thus manage to stay awake for a few more hours. Finally reveille is sounded, and I realize that I have made it through an entire white night.

I nibble on the dry bread crumbs I saved from "dinner." With the morning light I find myself a little stronger and my eyelids a little less heavy. I continue walking and reciting to keep awake. As I murmur to myself the verses I memorized as a child, my thoughts wander to my children. Suddenly this strikes me as the strangest thing in the world, that I can do two things simultaneously, recite poetry and at the same time reminisce about my children. After twisting my brain for some time, an effort that manages to abolish sleepiness, I conclude that the impression that I am thinking simultaneously about two different things is false. Perhaps my different thoughts, like the notes of a Bach partita, chase each other along at different speeds, merely giving the impression of simultaneity. I try an experiment to test my theory: reciting poetry in a whisper while counting my steps, reciting it in my mind while counting my steps. I discover I am right: I lose track of one or the other. But I am mentally exhausted. I have two more days and nights—to get through. I must find something that requires less mental energy than verse, something that will carry me along. A song? But it was singing that got me into this mess. To be caught singing again would be perceived as adding insult to injury and punished even more harshly. Yet sing I must, if I am not to sleep or slide off my chair or support my back against the wall or scream! I can make no move that does not lead to punishment.

I decide to sing softly, too softly for anyone to hear. After a while I find myself singing without making any sound at all. Perhaps I have done so before in my life without noticing it. Now I am aware that I am producing music solely in my mind, yet music that is ruled, like its sonorous sister, by pitch, phrase and melody. I begin to like this silent music, which now engages me completely.

I proceed to sound out in thought my favorite melodies. I begin with easy, short pieces, those I had sung under the protection of the factory sirens and the howling wind: arias, folk songs and lullabies learned from my mother. I sing them with the same pleasure as when I sang them aloud.

No longer constrained by the fifteen-minute blare of the sirens, I can now experiment with more complex compositions. Unhindered by the limitations of my voice, I can reproduce the sounds of violin, cello, woodwind, piano, and treat myself to entire concerts as often as my heart desires. Now, in succession, I recreate in my mind: the *Ballad* of Ciprian Porumbescu, Chopin's *Intimite*, Schubert's *Serenade*, Grieg's *Solvegslied*, Puccini's *E Luceman Le Stelle*, Di Capua's *O Sole Mio* and Gunod's *Ave Maria*. The minutes and hours slip by.

I learn! I learn! My desperate situation teaches me that I must preserve the integrity of my mind: my life depends upon it. From performing silent music, I proceed to another mental exercise, which suits me even better: composing poetry. The first love of my life—"what thou lovest fair remains"—now becomes my new intellectual challenge, my new passive activity. I remember Ovid, like me cast out, imprisoned, and his *Tristes Epistulae es Ponte*, the outpourings of a stranger in a strange land—as it happens, Constanza, which is my land, too.

My first poem grows out of my agonized yearning for my little ones, whose faces haunt me awake and asleep. In the beginning, it stutters forth in the classical form of the late nineteenth century that I studied in school and employed in the verses I composed in my youth. But this feels outmoded, and I reach for other rhythms, experimenting with different forms—I have time enough—until I create a form that is mine, within which my ghosts can assume a proper shape, within which they emerge as me. As I.

Come, children, again,
Stealthily, tonight,
Late, when jailers sleep
Late, when hunger wakes
My infinite yearning
Dissolving these walls of stone.

Trace the moon's secret path
To my cell. Come again,
Hand in hand; unafraid
To gather together
These precious hours
For the guards are asleep.

Bring to this desolate place
The sunlight upon your face
Your voices, the murmurs of spring
The rushing rivers, the birds' sweet hymn
In your hands, two budding flowers,
Moist with dew and April showers.

I walk in the deserted yard. I walk with my head down. I walk with my head down not because I am sad but because the slaves here do not have the right to gaze at the sky during their fifteen-minute walk in the prison courtyard. The authorities have had the foresight to create this rule. We must not look up, we must not cleanse our eyes of our gray walls with a clear expanse of sky. If we dare, from under lowered lids, to glance up even for a moment and strive to catch a glimpse of the Carpathian eagle, the sentinel on the prison's high wall rings his bell. The guards grab us, drag us to our cell, and reward us with three days of solitary.

Out of respect for the regulations, and because I know better, I keep my head down as I walk. Obediently, I glue my eyes on the brown dirt, stifling my aching need to glance at the sky and delight in the freedom of birds in flight.

I long for a country of blue
For its azure wildness,

Cleansing, transparent,
Infinite. I cry
To dart up, like an eagle
Fearlessly, to soar high
I thirst, I thirst for the sky

Buried in a grave
Swathed in sheets of ice
Hidden in a cave
Under rocky cliffs
Under waves of fog
I pine for my horizon
In this crypt of clay
I dream about the day,
Its heat, its golden light,
Entombed in frozen night,
Endless, formless night

I long, wing torn,
Still long
To fly
Long endlessly
For the blue eternity
I thirst, I thirst for the sky

As verses multiply beyond my capacity to remember, I feel that I am losing the battle between memory and imagination. What would I not give for a piece of paper and a pencil stub! But a pencil stub is seen here as a stick of dynamite, paper as a terrorist conspiracy against humanity. We are subjected to regular, painstaking searches. First, they inspect the cell, centimeter by centimeter: the bed, the coverlet, the pillow, the mattress, and every crack and crevice of the wall. Then we are undressed, and every fold of our garments and underwear is carefully examined. The body is made to yield its secrets: the hair, mouth, ears and anus. There is much insistence on the latter, the guards reveling in our humiliation.

If they find even a cigarette paper, they administer the maximum punishment. The offender is clubbed into unconsciousness. This punishment is earned also for being caught "conversing" with a neighbor, through either speech or Morse code. Many a night I have been awakened by the harrowing cries of men paying the price for these mortal sins! When I was in Jilava, my friend Roiu told me that the renowned scholar, Istrate Micescu, the greatest civil law specialist in the country, had been killed in captivity. The reason? He had been caught with a few scraps of paper on which were written some critical remarks about the prison regime.

Still, I write poetry. I write in my mind and record in my memory. My soul revels in it, my mind drinks from it as from a clear spring, my body feasts on its pure energy.

◆ ◆ ◆

The sunlit days of May are upon us. Though in my tomb the cold oozes from the walls and lingers still, I can hear the twittering of sparrows and swallows. Outside, the grass clings tighter to the earth, the sap flows sweetly in the trees, and the leaves glisten in the sun. I am sick of my cracked gray walls and the muddy icicles still hanging from my window. I long for the green of meadows and forests, the green of the hills and the mountains. Where can I find a patch of green? When I first arrived here a year ago, after my unshackling, while I was being processed and admitted, I observed a splendid garden filled with flowers and shrubbery in the administration courtyard. I have not seen it since, nor will I ever see it again. In the prisoners' courtyard, no blade of grass pierces the sand and gravel. No tree, no climbing bush is visible beyond the walls surrounding our yard—not one living thing to disturb the uniform grayness of our lives.

One morning, during our spring cleaning, I am handed a dust mop and ordered to clean the cobwebs from the ceiling and windows of my cell. To reach the ceiling, I must climb up on my stool. When I happen to glance out the window from this position, I see in the distance several treetops, sporting their leaves as ostriches sport their feathers. I count seven, poplars, I think. Swathed in wisps of clouds, this small green island seems to be floating in a frothy sea. I have not experienced such happiness since my journey here from Jilava. Then, my feast lasted only twelve hours. Now, I promise myself, it will be my daily dessert.

I prepare to wage a Homeric battle, which I christen, "the battle for the seven poplar tops." I know that my guard checks on me every five minutes. Sometimes he turns around after spying on my neighbor, hoping to surprise me in some act of disobedience, like leaning against the bed. He has never returned in the middle of the five minutes, however, and I calculate that I have three to four minutes to enjoy my green island—the time it takes me to count to two hundred. By following this rule I'm able to climb upon my stool whenever I feel like it. The urge comes quite often: it is the only way the hapless creature of the dark and the damp can take part in the festival of spring.

I savor my daily treat for some time without mishap. One day, however, a new guard, who is either more clever or less organized than the others, returns halfway through my safe interval and catches me in the act. This costs me three days of solitary. I live the three days entirely in the power of gastronomic obsessions accompanied by the concert of my innards, the symphony of my stomach. I live by solemn oaths to keep within my hourly allowance of bread, which I devise by crumbling my daily ration of four ounces into small heaps to correspond to the hours of my punishment. But even during this time, I will not surrender my enchanted isle. It has become as much a necessity as food and drink.

I now take every precaution. I listen intently for the faint sound of boots, muffled to conceal the guard's approach. As soon as I hear it, I jump off the stool and sit down like an obedient schoolboy with my hands folded in my lap. Before long, I become adept at hearing him coming from quite some distance. I'm now unbeatable in the "battle for the seven poplar trees."

Still, I often feel the pull of depression. Now and then a great sadness overwhelms me. Regrets cloud my reason, and I am tempted by the certainty of despair.

My heart is a drop of venom
Which feeds my soul its bane
A sponge soaked with poison
Potion of grief and pain
My heart is a bloody scab rent
In relentless torment

My soul's an Inquisitor's Jew
Torn by rack and by screw
An Arab to be slaughtered
By camels, drawn and quartered
My soul is a serf on the spit
Food for dogs in the street

My life's a devil in a sack
That I must carry on my back

A wretched hag, a spiteful nag
In summers, sweating, I must drag.
A cup of wine and curare,
Sipped slowly, with a smile
Sweet poison, stay a while!

I recite these bitter lines to myself again and again, for several days. They fill me with satisfaction, allay my suffering, soothe me, save me.

6

Irina: The Convict's Daughter

"Move away from the window, darling," my grandmother begs me. "You've been sitting there long enough."

I'm watching the rain pouring down, soaking the blanket of red and yellow leaves now covering the ground. God must keep pushing the black button, for it has been raining day after day. The trees have been stripped bare. The birds have flown away to the warm countries. "You see, in autumn the swallows all fly to the warm countries…" I know this from "Thumbelina," a story I make my mother read to me every night and which I now know by heart. I whisper my favorite part to myself: "Goodbye, you lovely little bird, goodbye and thank you for your beautiful singing last summer when all the trees were green and the sun was so bright and warm. Thumbelina laid her head up against the bird's breast. Suddenly, she heard a kind of thumping inside. It was the bird's heart. The bird wasn't dead; it had been lying numb and unconscious and now, as it grew warm again, it revived. Thumbelina brought the swallow some water, in the petal of a flower, and the bird drank it. When it felt stronger, the swallow told Thumbelina how it had torn one of its wings on a bramble and theretofore couldn't fly as fast as the other swallows when they flew far, far away to the warm countries."

"Is Russia a warm country?" I ask Omama.

My grandmother sighs. "For the love of God, child, move away from that window! Come and sit next to me and watch me sew. Someday, you may need to know how to sew, though, God willing, you'll grow up to be an important person, a great doctor, or a famous scientist and you'll have a maid who can do your housework. Still, it doesn't hurt to know how to darn a sock."

"Is Russia a warm country?" I ask again, refusing to move. I like looking out the window.

"No, darling, Russia is very cold now, even colder than here."

"Then where are the warm countries? Where do the birds go for the winter?" I insist. For I know that Thumbelina flew there on the back of the swallow. The swallow saved her from the mean mole who wanted to marry her and keep her shut up, underground, forever. In the warm countries, it is very beautiful: "The sun shines there more brightly than it does here, and the sky looks twice as far off. On walls and slopes black and white grapes grow, in the woods there are lemons and oranges; the air smells sweetly of myrtle and curled mint, and the most delightful children dart about on the roads playing with large gaily-colored butterflies."

"Maybe the birds migrate to California," my grandmother says. "It is warm there year-round. My brother Hershala lives there. And my sisters, Deborica and Lizica. In California, people walk around in shorts all winter long. And they lie on the beach in their bathing suits, eating oranges and bananas and sipping coconut milk." For a minute Omama takes her eyes off Uncle Jack's sock and stares dreamily into the distance.

Every New Year's Day, my brother and I have found several plump, juicy oranges wrapped in red cellophane among our presents under the New Year's tree. Once, my father brought each of us a banana. I try to conjure up its heavenly taste, so light, so soft, so sweet. I have never tasted a coconut, but Sorin says it is the most delicious fruit in the world. You crack it open and drink the magic milk, a sweet, rich potion that makes you strong, like Tarzan, a little boy left alone in the jungle who grew up on nothing but coconut milk.

I wish that I, too, could fly on the back of a swallow to the warm countries. Or even just to our old house. The ground there must be covered with fallen ripe red apples, now brown and rotting, unpicked. I miss my house. I miss the garden, the fruit trees, the flowers. I miss Milu, Mircea and Bogdan. I miss my father. My mother is out, looking for a job. My brother is at school. My grandfather is standing waiting to buy our food.

I watch the raindrops jump in circles in the puddles on the street outside my window. The sidewalks on Omama's street are not as broad, the houses not as fancy as on our old street. Here, the days are slow and long and hard to fill—much harder than before. I have nothing to do but follow Omama about and watch her cook and clean and sew and mend.

I watch the water flow like a stream through the gutters, and I think about Thumbelina asleep, floating down the river on the leaf where she was placed by the ugly frog who stole her away from her home on her mother's table, away from the beautiful water-filled plate where she used to sail on a tulip petal with two white horsehairs for oars.

"Irinika, God love you, don't make me ask you again!" My grandmother's voice, usually gentle and soothing, is now growing irritable. "Get away from that window! The neighbors will see you and start asking questions."

The neighbors! Everyone here worries about them. The neighbors must not know that my father went to Russia. The neighbors must not know that my brother, my mother and I are staying at my grandmother's house. The neighbors must not know what my relatives say to each other at the dinner table when they huddle their heads together and whisper. If anyone raises his voice just a bit, he is immediately reprimanded: "Shhh! The neighbors! Shhh! They'll hear you."

How do the neighbors hear you? I wonder. Through the walls? Do they stick their ears to the walls of the house and listen? Do they sneak up to the windows in the dark and peer inside through the cracks in the blinds?

I move away from the window and lie on the bed. I leaf through the worn-out pages of "Thumbelina" to my favorite picture. The tiny girl is looking at the blue sky through the hole that the mole has made in the roof of the dark passage. Though I can't read, I know each word under the picture by heart: "Thumbelina felt so sad. She was never allowed to go out into the warm sunshine. Every morning as the sun rose, and every evening as it set, she stole out to the opening and when the wind parted the ears of corn so that she could see the blue sky, she thought how lovely and bright it was out there…"

"Can't I go outside?" I ask Omama. "Look. It has stopped raining." At first my grandmother hesitates, for she worries about the wet and the cold and the neighbors, but I persuade her, tears gushing, that I will stay safe and dry and clean in the backyard. Patiently, I suffer myself to be swathed in sweaters and scarves and even agree to wear my galoshes.

I leap down the stairs and jump through the puddles and poke in the mud with a stick. I find an old glass jar and fill it with wet leaves. I run back and forth between the backyard and the front yard and climb on the gate.

Across the street from my grandmother's house is an empty lot, a mound of earth that the children use for sledding during the winter. The mound was once a house, but during World War II, my brother says, the Germans dropped a bomb on it and blew it up. I see another little girl there, digging in the ground with a soup spoon. Her name is Mariana. She is six years old, and she lives two houses down from my grandmother's house. She shows me how to make mudcakes, which we decorate with red and yellow leaves, gravel and weeds.

Suddenly Mariana's mother comes running from across the street. She is angry because she has been calling for her daughter out the window, but Mariana has ignored her. She is angry because Mariana's clothes are filthy. She turns to me and asks, "And you? Who do you belong to?"

I glance at my feet, covered with wet dirt. I remember my promise to Omama to stay clean and dry.

"Little girl, what's your name?"

"Irina," I mumble.

"Irina what?"

I can't answer her. I'm not allowed to answer when an adult asks me questions. "If anyone asks you anything," my mother has instructed me, "say, 'I don't know.' You are just a little girl. You are not expected to know. Little children must always answer, 'I don't know' when strangers ask them questions."

I try to say, "I don't know," but I choke on the words.

"Don't you know your last name, little girl?"

Mariana looks at me, a contemptuous smile on her face. I'm a big girl, and I don't even know my own last name. But that's not true. I do know my name and I know how to spell it and I know how to count to one hundred, too. I wish I could show them all that I know, but I must keep quiet.

Mariana's mother keeps staring at me. "Aren't you living at the Abramovicis'? Aren't you Mrs. Abramovici's little granddaughter?" Her small, brown eyes pierce through my jacket, sweater, blouse and undershirt. Can she see my heart, beating like the heart of the swallow?

"I don't know," I whisper and wish I could disappear through a hole like the mole and the field mice. I'd like to run back home, but then they would see where I live. It begins to rain again, but I don't dare cross the street to Omama's house until my friend and her mother are gone. I'm so ashamed. Mariana must think I'm very stupid. Will she ever play with me again?

◆ ◆ ◆

"Regina Eremia! Regina Eremia! Where is Regina Eremia?" shout the loud-voiced men who ring our doorbell and wake me up, startled from my deep early morning sleep. I sit up in my bed and look around the room. My eyes meet my brother's. "She's in the shower," he whispers, pulling the covers up to his chin.

"Bombonica! Bombonica!" Omama bursts into the bedroom, disheveled and shivering, as she tries to hold her unbelted blue robe together. To Omama, my mother is "Bombonica" or "little candy," her nickname from childhood, to her friends "Gina," to my brother and I, "Giunica." But the harsh, male voices keep calling: "Regina Eremia! Regina Eremia!"

Finally she comes out of the bathroom, covered only by a towel, her shower cap wet and still dripping. "They want you to go with them for questioning! May God give you strength, health and wisdom!" my grandmother cries, clasping her hands together. She begins chanting in Yiddish.

"Please, mama!" Giunica says in the same tone she often uses to scold my brother and me. "Offer them a coffee and a piece of strudel and ask them to wait until I'm dressed."

My grandmother sighs and walks out.

My brother opens his mouth to say something, then changes his mind and closes it.

Giunica chooses a dress carefully from her suitcase, lays it neatly on a chair, and begins taking the curlers out of her hair. I jump out of bed and wrap my arms around her waist. "Where are you going?" I ask her.

"Please, Galuska, let me finish here. I'm in a hurry."

"Where are they taking you?" my brother asks from the bed, in an unusually high, squeaky voice.

"To an office downtown. They just want to talk to me. Don't worry, I'll be back soon."

She slips into her dress, styles her hair, powders her face, perfumes her wrists, and, to appease me, dabs some perfume under my chin. When she is ready, she lifts me up and kisses me, then bends down and kisses my brother. Then she straightens herself up, tall, slim, elegant, and after a final, approving glance in the mirror, walks out with proud, determined steps.

All day I follow Omama around, holding on tightly to her skirts. She does not object, and lets me roll out the dough for a new apple strudel, grate the apple, mix the nuts and raisins and taste the delicious, sweet filling. As she works, Omama keeps moving her lips in prayer while glancing up at the ceiling. Is there a little hole in it through which she can see God?

In the afternoon, Uncle Jack comes home earlier than usual and takes my brother and me for a walk "downtown." I love to walk at this time of year when the ground is covered with dry leaves, which I crackle under my feet. I love the hustle and bustle of Bucharest's center, the cars, streetcars, buses, the crowds of people gathered at stop lights, bus stops and in front of stores. Bundled up in their black overcoats, men and women waiting in line pass the time chatting, joking and teasing each other. Sometimes arguments flare, sudden angry outbursts, and they begin to shout, calling each other funny names, wishing each other funny things using long phrases I have been told never, ever to repeat. After the numbing, shushing silence shut up in the house, I love the shouting crowds.

"Hey, you, with the long ears, since when did you get ahead of me? Go back to your place, you donkey!"

"Bite your tongue, you frog-eyed witch!"

"Cut it out, comrades. You're fighting over nothing. Is there any sense in fighting over who'll get nothing first?"

My brother and I poke each other in the ribs and giggle as we pass by this quarreling queue. As we go on down the crowded street, I invent a game. Whenever I see two adults together coming toward me, I refuse to go around them, but squeeze in between them, forcing them to separate. Usually, they're good natured about this. "*Schmeckero*!" ("little trickster!") they shout after me, trying to pinch my cheek. I escape them and laugh, delighted with myself. My brother, however, is embarrassed and hangs back, refusing to be seen with me. "Stop it!" he yells at me, but I refuse. I'm having too much fun.

Uncle Jack takes us into a pastry shop, and we wait in a long line for a free table. Why was it, I wonder, that when my father took us here before, we never had to wait, no matter how long the line?

When our turn finally comes, I order my favorite, a scoop of peanut ice cream, and my brother his favorite, a *jofra*. Uncle Jack orders a cup of Turkish coffee with *caimac*. He sips it slowly and still has a lot of it left when Sorin and I are finished. "How about another round?" our uncle offers. "No," my brother says. "I want to go home and see if Giunica is back."

"She may not be back yet," Uncle Jack tells him. "You're a big guy; you can certainly put away two jofras, can't you?"

Sorin reluctantly agrees. I don't have to be asked twice. I forget about everything, immersed in the smooth, soothing, world of peanut ice cream. I swish it around and around in my cup until it turns into liquid, and I pretend that I, too, am drinking Turkish coffee like my uncle.

Before we leave, my brother remembers that my mother loves hazelnuts, which are hard to come by, and insists that we get her some. When we get home, we run breathlessly up the stone steps to my grandmother's flat, fighting over who should carry the bag of nuts. "Giunica! Giunica!" we yell. Our Aunt Coculeana opens the door.

Omama is in the dining room, praying over her lit candles.

"Good shabbas," she says, when she sees us. "She's not back yet." Tears roll down her cheeks.

Coculeana hugs us.

"Your mother will be back soon, don't worry." She winks at my brother. "Tonight I'll put you to bed and tell you the story about Ileana Cosanzeana and

Mos Condoi." This has been his favorite story ever since he was small. But this time Sorin doesn't want to hear it.

I start howling. I am sure the loud-voiced men have taken my mother away. They have taken her away on a bus, or on a train, someplace far away. My mother is gone. She is gone, and she will never come back. She is gone, and I will never see her again. I cry and cry until I have no more tears. I cry until I fall asleep in a chair, my head buried in my hands on the dining room table.

Much later, through my blanket of sleep, I hear a chorus of whispers. Gradually, I awaken, prick my ears, and try to make out what they are saying. They are talking rapidly and using long, boring words that I don't understand: "interrogation," "denunciation," "declaration." It sounds like the men wanted my mother to say something she did not want to say. They kept shoving a piece of paper under her nose, and she kept shoving it back at them. Finally, they gave up but then, as she was about to leave, they told her that she should "never expect to appear on stage again."

My grandmother's voice bursts out, loud and clear, waking me completely.

"The beasts! The monsters! As if they need you to denounce him! They do what they want anyway. May they all rot in hell! May their names be blotted out!"

"Hush, Mama! The neighbors! Shhh!"

"The bandits! The criminals! May all of your suffering fall upon their evil heads!" My grandmother's voice now cracks and breaks into a sob. I jump up from my chair and fly into my mother's arms. "Giunica! Giunica!" I yell.

"Shhh, Galuska! You'll wake up your brother," she scolds me. But when, hand-in-hand, we go into the bedroom, we find my brother sitting up, his red, puffy eyes wide open.

"Giunica!" he cries, "You're back!"

"Of course I'm back! Didn't I tell you I'd be back?"

Sorin digs under his pillow and takes out the bag of hazelnuts, which I had forgotten all about.

"Look what I brought you," he tells her proudly.

"Me too!" I shout. My mother thanks both of us, puts the bag on the night stand, and promises to share it with us tomorrow for breakfast. Then she gets into bed and squeezes into the middle, between Sorin and me, holding our heads close against her chest.

"Sing us 'Trestioara de pe Lac,'" I beg her.

"No!" my brother objects. "I want you to sing 'Somnoroase Pasarele.'"

"Now you know I can't sing that!" She sighs and kisses his forehead. Then she kisses my forehead.

"My two rays of sunshine," she whispers.

Tonight, I know we are safe.

◆ ◆ ◆

Great puffs of snow transform the muddy mound across the street into a shimmering, shiny hill where sleds can slip and slide. My nose pressed to the window, I watch the neighborhood children go down, pell mell, feet up, head down, falling and rolling, stumbling and tumbling into the soft, squeaky new powder.

"I won't wait! I can't wait! By the time Sorin gets home, the snow will have melted," I cry. "Please Omama, please let me go. Please, please, please!"

Omama relents, and bundled up like a mummy, I spring out the door and fly across the street to the dump that was once a house that is now a hill. I have no sled, no skates, no wooden board; still I climb the mountain, my boots sinking into the soft whiteness. I fill my hands with snow and toss it in the air and catch it in my mouth. It's fresh and cold and tastes like vanilla ice cream, only less sweet.

At the top of the hill, two boys and a girl are rolling a mound of snow into a giant ball. The girl is Mariana, the kid who lives two houses down from us.

"We need charcoal for the eyes!"

"And a carrot for the nose!"

"And a broom for the hand!"

I slide down the hill on my behind and run back to Omama's house, where I know there is an old broom used to clean the courtyard on the porch behind the kitchen door. I grab it and run back holding my trophy, triumphant.

"Look, I got a broom!" I tell the girl, Mariana, who lives two houses down from us. Proudly, I hand it to her, my offering, my admission ticket. She grabs it and tosses it back down. It rolls all the way to the bottom of the hill and sinks into the snow.

"Why did you do that? We need it!" one of the boys yells. Mariana whispers something in his ear. He gasps and looks at me with horror and disgust, as if I am some kind of freak. Is she telling him that I don't know my own last name?

"Your father's in prison! Your father's a criminal!" the boy suddenly blares at me.

"Little criminal, go away! You can't play!"

The three dip their hands in the trunk of the would-be snowman and make snowballs which they begin tossing at me, while chanting in unison:

"CON-VICT'S DAUGH-TER GO A-WAY!
LIT-TLE CRI-MI-NAL YOU CAN'T PLAY!
STAY A-WAY! STAY A-WAY!"

I sob into the darkness of Omama's lap. She runs her fingers through my long hair and croons: "Your father's in Russia. On important state business. They don't know what they are saying. That's how children are. They lie. They say mean things. Your father will be back soon. Real soon." Omama's lap is soft and warm. I suck on the soft fold of her skirt. It smells of cinnamon and vanilla.

"My angel, for the love of God, stop crying, you'll make yourself sick, Irinika, it's not good to cry like that. Children can lie, children can be mean, oh, so mean."

Animals can be mean, too, I think. The frog was mean. The field mice and the mole were mean. The cockchafers were mean, too. They lied. They said Thumbelina was ugly. "Ugh, she's got only two legs. And she hasn't any feelers. Ugh! Isn't she ugly!" they said. But that was not true. Thumbelina was very pretty. And in the end, she flew to the warm countries and met the handsome little prince who fell in love with her and married her and changed her name from Thumbelina to Maia. And they lived happily ever after.

Mariana was lying. She was still mad at me because she got muddy and her mother spanked her and I wouldn't tell them my name. My father is a hero. He is a general in the Romanian army. He is in Russia on important state business. It is cold in Russia now, and all the birds are gone. My father will be back soon, real soon. He will come back again, and take Sorin and I home to the house with the fruit trees, and we will make up stories again, and snuggle up against his chest again, and he will sing us "Somnoroase Pasarele" again. And this time I will keep my eyes wide open and make sure Sorin is the one who goes to sleep first.

I bury my head in my grandmother's dark, woolen skirt. I close my eyes. I fly on the back of the swallow, high up into the air, over the mountains of eternal snow, to California, where the flower fairies greet me with a set of wings.

7

Ion: Superior Intelligences

Every morning, as soon as I wake up, I turn over another leaf in my imaginary calendar. I refuse to relinquish the sequence of days, months, years, and allow myself to wander, confused and baffled, upon the stormy ocean of time. In large, black letters, I record each new day.

Today, May 27, 1961, is a red letter day in my mental calendar. Last night, I managed to break through the deadly silence of my cell. Last night, I discovered another human being. Our fingers tapped messages on the thick wall that separates us. Our brains deciphered the code. We spoke.

Many a night after curfew I have sat up listening, with ears made keen by practice, to the muffled taps on the cell walls. It did not take me long to realize that these were messages sent by one convict to another through a prison adaptation of the Morse code alphabet. However, being accustomed to the normal convention of long and short beeps I learned in the army, I needed time and practice to learn the prison "dialect." Even after I understood the signals—one knock, a dot; a double knock, a dash—I had to train myself to make "conversation" quickly. During the day, I rehearsed by tapping messages in the Morse alphabet on the edge of my chair. At night, I began to tap messages to my neighbors. But here I had another obstacle to surmount: the distrust of my fellow prisoners. How were they to know I was not an informer?

Last night, for the first time, the neighbor on my left has decided to answer my insistent calls.

"Now I can understand you perfectly," he tapped.

"Me too," I replied. "My ear is finally attuned to this Morse-through-the-wall."

"Haven't you ever been in a common cell, where the other prisoners could teach it to you?"

"Only briefly. I've been alone most of the time."

"Here, all of us are alone. This is a maximum security prison. We even have our own railway line!"

"What is your name?" I asked him.

"I prefer not to reveal personal details that can be used later as evidence that communication has taken place. I'd rather spare myself a bad beating."

"All right. Then we'll have to remain nameless. Let's use numbers instead. I'll be "Five"; you be "Six," I suggested.

"So be it, Five. Goodnight."

The long months of practice, the painstaking effort of transmitting each thought, letter by letter, word by word, and the dull pain in my finger mean nothing compared to my delight in this newfound speech. My first human conversation in over a year and a half! Today I celebrate. Today I declare a holiday.

◆ ◆ ◆

"How long have you been here?" I ventured, during my next communication with Six.

"Since March of 1960...How about you, Five?"

"Since November of '59," I tell him. "Do you have any news from the outside?"

"Bad news. The triumvirate of Dej-Ceausescu-Draghici continues to provide slaves to build their canal between the Danube and the Black Sea, especially from among the intellectuals. In these labor camps people are dying like flies. The price of dissent has also risen: a minimum of fifteen years for criticizing the government. At Jilava I met a couple of high school boys who got fifteen years at hard labor for reading some satirical verses about their Young Communist leaders at a party."

"So you were in Jilava, too?"

"Yes, I think all of us start there, but only *la crème de la crème* end up here."

"Do you know any of your other neighbors?" I probe.

"Yes. Above me is the distinguished philosopher, Constantin Noica, who got a heavy sentence along with several other professors for maligning the government."

"I've heard of him," I say. "He is perhaps the greatest classical scholar in Romania."

"And he is still producing, even here. He is just now in the middle of a treatise on Socrates, Anaxagoras, Democrit, Plato and Aristotle."

"And how is he coping with our misery?"

"The isolation doesn't bother him as much as the other conditions. He has plenty to keep him busy, but he's in poor physical health."

"I'm sorry to hear that. But I'm grateful to you for the precious information you've given me. You're a good man, Six."

"And how do you know I haven't turned 'rat' in prison? How can you be sure I won't sell you for an extra bowl of soup?"

My neighbor, I surmise, is trying to teach me a lesson in prudence. I reciprocate with a lesson in logic: "Men of that sort, dear Six, are not incarcerated here to begin with. Didn't you, yourself, say that we are *la crème de la crème?*"

"You're probably right, Five. Still, enough said for now. Goodnight."

This second conversation lasted for over an hour, for we are forced to stop at every flutter of our birds of prey. Still, I am content. Along with his bleak tidings, my neighbor has also brought me the assurance that I'm not alone. The knowledge that there are others like me, both here and "outside," lifts my spirit and strengthens my resolve to resist.

"I think we can both relax now," I say, opening my third conversation with Six, and I tell him, in brief, the story of my crime and punishment. Then I invite him to do the same.

"My case is a little different," he replies. "I got twenty years for anti-social and obscurantist propaganda."

"And what exactly does that mean?"

"It means that the authorities didn't know precisely why they didn't like what I had to say, so they got rid of the problem by getting rid of me."

"Can you speak a bit more plainly?"

"I'm afraid it's rather complicated. I'm a professor of mathematics, formerly the chief astronomer at the Observatory in Bucharest. I developed certain theories which my superiors found offensive, and which may take too much time, effort and risk, for me to explain to you now."

"No risk, no gain, my friend."

"I prefer not to gain a broken back."

"Please, go on," I beg. "I'll prick my ears. I've been training them for some time, and I assure you, my hearing has now become as keen as a dog's. At the first hint of footsteps, I'll knock twice and you'll know to stop."

"All right. I'll take the risk," he finally decides. Then he taps me his story: "I happen to believe in the existence of superior intelligences on other planets in the cosmos. According to my calculations, around one-half of one percent of all the stars in the universe have planets where life can be sustained. My calculus of probability demonstrates the likelihood of more than five hundred million milliards of habitable worlds. Furthermore, I am convinced that life forms that inhabit some of these worlds are superior to those found on earth."

"What exactly do you mean by life forms?"

"I mean forms of superior intelligence capable of organizing matter and benefiting from movement, nourishment, growth, development, reproduction, memory, thought..."

I interrupt him. "I believe that man himself is the highest such form of temporal intelligence."

"You're wrong," taps the astronomer. "As a mathematician I can prove to you that the likelihood that man represents the apex of intelligent development has a probability of one in five hundred million milliards—a near-zero probability."

"And what is the relationship of your superior intelligences to us, inferior earthly creatures? Do you contend that they created us?"

"No. Life is a manifestation of a cosmic principle. Wherever suitable conditions exist, life appears. But the way through which man evolved into the sophisticated, complex creature he now is could not have occurred simply through mutation and natural selection. The probability of that is no better than the likelihood of someone winning the lottery three times in a row. Man's evolution had to be programmed, organized and manipulated by the superior intelligences of other planets."

"Why can't you admit that these superior intelligences inhabit our own planet, even our own two prison cells?" I retort. "After centuries of speculation, science has still not managed to prove the existence of other forms of intelligent life. Until we have such proof, why not give man the credit for being the supreme miracle of the universe?"

"Because this is conceit, pure conceit, similar to primitive man's belief that the sun revolves around his small village, which is at the center of the world. I find your view insufferably provincial, my dear Five."

"And I find yours insufferably condescending, my dear Six. Which is not to say that I don't uphold your right to express it. And I even understand why the authorities found it dangerous. After all, if the Party is omnipotent and omniscient, what business has a man to suggest that its dominion and intelligence are not only limited, but inferior?"

"I'm glad that you understand this at least, my friend."

With that we ended our discussion, for by now our fingers were numb.

◆ ◆ ◆

Since this conversation, with its curious commingling of science and theosophy, I have been thinking about my father, a lover of science, and my mother, a devout Christian and lover of poetry. They were both children of country priests, but we grew up, thanks to my father, in a liberal and tolerant atmosphere, completely open to the views of science. In his youth, my father had been sent to learn his craft from an older brother who ran a machine shop in the port of Braila. It was there that he came under the influence of socialist teaching, as socialist circles were fairly widespread in Romania from the end of the nineteenth century on. Under their influence, my father not only studied the socialism of Marx and Lasalle but also widened his humanistic education, particularly in social studies and history. In time he became a knowledgeable man, well respected by his fellow workers in the port of Constanza, where he set up house following his marriage at the beginning of this century.

He fell in love with the daughter of a priest from a neighboring village. Judging from the wedding pictures, the young couple was very attractive. My mother loved music and poetry. She had a beautiful voice and could sing nearly all the songs of her time, which I can still hear today, because she sang them to me often. And she could recite numerous ballads and poems. In fact, she was, and still is, a poet herself. She makes up verses without the aid of pen or paper, memorizes them, and then recites them when occasion calls for it. Even now, in her eighties, she composes poems to soothe friends in need. In her youth, she used her great facility for improvising verse to amaze and enchant us children.

I have been thinking about her and her hard life after her husband's death. My father died trying to rescue people from a tragic fire; a hero, he was mourned by the entire city of Constanza. But did anyone ever acknowledge my mother's more quiet heroism, her brave struggle to raise a houseful of fatherless children, alone? Over the past few days, I've been composing a poem in honor of my mother and of all women, who seem to me to be, by far, the stronger of the two sexes. Now I have the pleasure of tapping it out to my astronomer friend:

We bear the weight of maternity
In the name of immortality
And the burden of eternity
Yet some joke about our frailty

Laughing, dismiss our humanity
Lightly, like their paternity.

"Very clever," my neighbor taps back, "but I don't much care for the message. I don't happen to share your high regard for women."

"That's not surprising," I remark. "Mathematicians traditionally have not hit it off with the opposite sex. As the courtesan told Rousseau following an unfortunate encounter: '*Lascia le donne, studia la matematica*!'"

"No, my friend, this doesn't apply to me. I have a very different reason for disliking women."

I invite him to elaborate.

"Have you ever run into the famed Wanda, the interrogator working for the security police?"

"I haven't had the pleasure," I confess.

"Pleasure is hardly the word. You should thank your lucky stars you never did have to deal with her. I, unfortunately, did."

"I had no idea women are used to interrogate men."

"This is a woman of special talents. Wanda began her career in the security prison at Timisoara. She soon became famous for her particular method of interrogation, which worked with even the most stubborn subjects. Word of her success reached the powers that be, who, in recognition of her worth, moved her to Bucharest."

"What does she do?"

"A variation on an old theme, dear Five. An innovation added to an ancient method of torture: whipping a man's testicles."

"And what is the innovation?"

"Imagine this: you find yourself in the torture chamber, face to face with a beautiful woman, half naked, wearing a minuscule slip and parading about seductively. When she realizes that the optimal conditions have been achieved and you are fully aroused, she begins to beat you over your testicles."

"Monstrous!" I shudder. "How on earth did she come up with such a horror?"

"Who knows? Maybe she's a psychopath. Or a born sadist."

"Or maybe she's getting even for the way she's been treated by some man," I venture.

"Are you trying to defend her?"

"Not at all. I'm just trying to explain her behavior. Obviously, that she is a psychopath is the most plausible explanation."

"The even worse psychopath is the one who put the whip in her hand," the astronomer says.

"True," I agree. "So you see, you have no reason to hate women after all, my good friend."

"I would think my story would cure even an innocent like you of your romantic illusions."

"One woman does not all women make," I quip. "I'll never forget who brought me into this world and through what pain." And so I put an end to our conversation about the worth of women.

◆ ◆ ◆

It is, according to my mental calendar, June of 1961. Although it is now warm, the walls of my cell, which face north, are just beginning to thaw. Finally, my crypt warms up. It warms up perhaps too much for a man used to shivering during the year. The quickening heat has reached even into the cracks and crevices of my cell, adding some spiders and a multitude of flies to the roster of winter survivors. The spiders have already spun their webs across the window gratings through which the sun beckons the careless, smaller flies to liberty and death. I have no idea how or why the larger flies got in here. The superior intelligence that inhabits this cell is an avaricious creature who never lets fall the smallest crumb of bread. Still, they refuse to give up hope, attempting to wear away his vigilance and break down his stubborn defenses with their daring aerial maneuvers. Their greed is matched only by their libido. They mate in midair and navigate in tandem. This is the moment in which I have recourse to the scorpion's tactics: I kill them in their ecstasy. What else can I do? I am acting in self-defense. We are enemies in an undeclared battle for survival. It is not the microscopic bits of daily rations that I begrudge them. No. But I fear the diseases they carry, because illness here is met only by the indifference of our temporal masters and the mercy of God.

When I am not hunting flies, I make music. I have my ample repertoire of romances, lieders, serenades, madrigals, sonatas, and arias. No one can stop what no one can hear. I have given up the foolish desire to hear my own voice. I do, however, look foolish to the guards, who mistake my attempts to beat time and conduct my concerts for the tics of a madman. So there is music, silent music that fills the daily pyramidal silence and without which I would go mad, indeed.

And yet, since even this cell is part of a larger universe, there are times when the silence is broken by unexpected intruders. Last night I woke in the middle of the night to the sound of an exquisite song. I sat up, like a man invited to partake of a divine mystery, and listened 'til the break of dawn:

An upstart flute beckons
The tender woodwind follows
Then the sweet murmur
Of the harpsichord
And music falls like rain
Upon sleeping lovers

Enchanted they follow
The slippery trill of the pan pipe
The guitar's pulse quickening
Their swift dance steps
And the grass sighs softly
Under their naked feet

The nightingale's song
String by string
Note upon note
Races toward morning
When dawn reddens the cheek
And lovers at last can sleep

I have heard the nightingale before, in happier circumstances. But never has her song seemed closer to symphony—to a music so rich and inclusive that there is not one figure or phrase that does not fit perfectly within the harmonious whole. Some say that birds have stolen their music from man, that mere animals cannot possibly rise above imitation. And yet, having listened to this veritable symphony half the night through, it seems to me now that it is the nightingale who first created our celestial music, and we who have stolen her art.

I cannot sleep after the marvelous nocturnal concert, although there is at least one hour left before the shrill wake-up call. But the unexpected music, along with the scents of a summer's night, awaken a flood of memories. Once again, I see the sweet, eager faces of my children, begging me to tell them just one more story before we come in from our garden, where they sit, listening to me, on warm summer evenings. After "Hansel and Gretel," my little ones issued a decree against all fairy tales. "What father would leave his children in the woods to be eaten by the wolves?" they protested. So we began making up our own stories instead—happy stories in which the good acted justly and no one got hurt in the end.

Where are my children now? Since the night of my arrest I have had no news of them. They were sleeping when I was taken away. What did they say the next day when they saw I was gone? And the next day? And the day after that? And what did their mother tell them to restore their peace? Are they healthy? How do they get by? Oh God!

I find myself on my knees, my hands raised in prayer, weeping and imploring the one my mother has taught me would give us our daily bread, the one I begged to make my mother well when she was sick, the one I implored to end my father's suffering when he lay, burned alive, in the throes of death. I whisper to myself prayers thought long forgotten—for the health and happiness of my children, for the well being of all those who now care for them, for my wife, my mother and myself, miserable being. May He whom I have for so long forsaken, forgive my transgressions, deliver me from bondage, and enable me to see my loved ones again. Amen. I cannot live without God.

8

Irina: Rose Buds

"Twenty lei for the two bunches, lovely lady. Where else will you find such beautiful gladioluses, whiter than the whitest snow on the highest mountaintop?"

"Twenty lei is too much," says my mother, grabbing our hands and starting to walk away. She is haggling with the Gypsy woman in the flouncy, flowery skirt, who sits on the steps of the old church with her basket, over the price of the bouquets we must bring, as my mother says is customary, to our teachers on our first day of school.

"All right, fifteen then, my princess, and this for the sake of your emerald eyes and your two beautiful children, may they grow up as straight and as tall as two pine trees."

Again my mother pretends to walk away, and again the Gypsy woman rushes after her, grabbing her sleeve.

"Let it be ten, then, I'll take ten, for the sake of my little ones and their empty tummies. But hurry up, dear lady, for I see a cop coming around the corner."

She sticks the bill inside her big bosom; with one hand she gathers up her long skirts (three of them, I count, in red, yellow, and green), with the other hand her flower basket, and she dashes across the street, barely avoiding being hit by a bus.

"Why is she afraid of the policeman?" I ask.

"She's breaking the law," my brother says.

"What law?"

"Don't you know anything? People aren't supposed to sell things. Only stores. State stores. We're communists, not capitalists," my brother explains, irritated, as usual, by my ignorance.

But I'm still confused. Everyone buys flowers from the Gypsies, and roasted pumpkin and sunflower seeds, and popcorn at the park. Are all of them breaking the law? Should they be arrested and put in jail?

"Come on, don't dawdle, or we'll be late," my mother prods us, quickening her already quick step.

I forget about the Gypsy woman in my excitement over my first day of school. I have been waiting for this moment forever. For so long it seemed as if my seventh birthday would never come, and every weekday morning I'd have to sit back, ignored, while my mother, grandmother, and aunts fussed over my brother—his uniform, his boots, his jacket, his lunch, his books, his homework—sending him off, like a hero to battle, with interminable wishes of luck and health: "May you have a healthy, happy, productive day, and learn well, so, God willing, you'll grow up to be a great doctor or a famous scientist and bring honor to yourself, your family and your people!"

Now, finally, it is my turn. I have my own bookcase and pencil case (it smells so sweetly of pinewood) and a pen with a shiny, sharp point, and a bottle of blue ink, and a set of coloring pencils and a notebook, and a cheese and tomato sandwich for my lunch. I'm wearing the black and white checkered dress with white pinafore that for years I've admired on other schoolgirls. My long blond hair is braided and tied with crisp white ribbons; a third white ribbon I wear as a headband, also part of the uniform. I prance down the street, a big girl, a school-girl.

According to my brother, Ion Luca Caragiale is one of the biggest schools in Bucharest. The children and their teachers are gathered outside in the large courtyard, divided into groups according to grade. My brother runs off to join the third graders, while my mother and I search for the sign with my teacher's name—Comrade Pana ("feather"), a nice name, I think, imagining a graceful, birdlike woman. Comrade Pana ends up being bigger and heavier and older than I had imagined. If she looks like a bird, it is a hawk she resembles most, I think, noticing her beaked nose and narrow, close-together eyes.

"Don't go!" I beg my mother, clinging to her hand. She squeezes it, reminding me to give my teacher the flowers, along with a hug and kiss.

Comrade Pana accepts my offerings, throwing my gladiolus on a bench along with the other bouquets.

"Please stay," I whisper again in my mother's ear.

"I'll wait until you go in, but that's it," my mother answers. "I can't afford to be late for work, you know that, darling."

I know how hard it was for my mother to find work, and how important it is that she hold on to it. Giunica works in an office now. She adds up numbers and subtracts numbers and writes down long lists of numbers in big, thick notebooks. I know that she likes being in plays much more than counting up numbers, even though she wants to hide her disappointment from us. She doesn't want us to feel sorry for her, but I can't help it; when I think about how hard she tried, I feel like crying for her. Every night, for a long time, she practiced in front of the big, oval shaped, Austrian crystal mirror (Omama got it from her own "omama"), the different parts for which she would try out in the morning; a queen, a princess, a partisan, a worker, a peasant, a maid. Then the next day she would come home, sad and disappointed. "No use, no use, no use, even when they want to say yes, they must say no," she would complain to Omama. One day, she came home very happy. A theater "director" did hire her. She would work at a children's theater, she told Sorin and I, in that gay, excited voice I hadn't heard for a long time. She would make plays about animals, and fairies, and witches, and sorcerers and little children. And the two of us could go with her every Sunday and see the plays for free! Giunica grabbed our hands, and all three of us twirled around and around the room, laughing and singing. But the very next day my mother went to work and came back home a very short time later. She looked so unhappy. After that, she stopped looking for acting jobs. But even other kinds of jobs were hard to find. After a long time, a friend of Aunt Coca told her that he knew someone who worked in an office. One evening my mother went to this person's house with a beautiful bottle wrapped in cellophane that my uncle had brought back from Germany. The next morning she started working in the office where she must hurry to now, for now, she must never, ever be late.

"We cherish thee, Romania, land of our fathers..." the children, the teachers and the parents begin to sing, as our red, yellow and blue flag is raised. The words to our national anthem are so beautiful, they bring tears to my eyes. I squeeze my mother's hand. I'm still not ready for her to leave. The principal of our school, a short man with glasses, stands in the middle of the circle of children and speaks in the microphone. We are the hope and promise of our land, he tells us, the budding flowers who will bloom into "hard working, dedicated citizens, future communists, devoted to the struggle of the working classes to build a just and equal society in Romania and throughout the world."

My class is large and spacious and smells of chalk. The walls are freshly painted, and covered with pictures and slogans. "Workers of the world, unite," my teacher tells us one slogan reads. "Long live the Socialist Republic of Romania," says another. "Long live our brothers and sisters in the Soviet Union," reads a third. Then she tells us about the men in the pictures on our classroom wall: the man with the hand over his heart next to the big, red, flag, is Lenin, the father of our great Revolution. The man with the long bushy beard who looks like a werewolf is Karl Marx, another one of our great fathers. Marx and Lenin are dead, but the man with the fat, round face, Gheorghe Gheorghiu-Dej, is alive. He is the President of our country. The other men with stern faces in gray suits are members of the "council of ministers" of our great socialist state: Ion Maurer, Emil Bodnarash, Nicolae Ceausescu..."

"I know him!" I want to shout. "My father used to beat him at chess, and Nicu, his little boy, once chased my brother around the table with a steak knife. And some of the other men, I know them, too. We were at their house. They pinched my cheek. I used to play with their kids. I open my mouth, then close it again. I must keep it shut.

Our own names are called in alphabetical order, and we are assigned to our benches, two by two. My "benchmate" is a small, dark skinned boy, whose name is Florin Dimeica. I wish I sat next to a girl, but I know that "D" comes before "E" and there is no girl with a name beginning with "D." Comrade Pana tells us that we must get used to being called by our last names, for we are big children now. We must also learn to sit in our seats, quietly, and raise two fingers if she asks us a question and we know the answer. Otherwise, we must not speak unless spoken to, and we must sit up straight, and hold our arms folded around our chests.

"And this big book," she says, pointing to an enormous, thick notebook which covers half her desk, "is the 'Catalogue.' Here all your names and your grades, as well as my comments and observations about you will be recorded." She looked at us with narrow, piercing, hawk's eyes. "Every three months your parents will be called to school for 'conference' night. They will sit in this classroom, in these desks. I will open the catalogue and I will read out loud, in front of everyone, your names, grades, and my comments about your behavior and performance. If you work hard and obey the rules, your parents will be proud of you. If you are lazy and disobedient, your parents will be ashamed of you." I fix my eyes on the blackboard. I fold my arms tightly over my chest. I will not move.

◆ ◆ ◆

"I've never been so humiliated in my life," my mother tells my grandmother the night she comes back from the conference.

I keep my eyes shut and pretend I'm asleep. I'm afraid to breathe. Can they hear my heart beating?

"What did she say?" my grandmother asks, dismayed.

"'Eremia is unfocused and undisciplined. I often catch her not paying attention.'" My mother is now imitating Comrade Pana's harsh, raspy voice. I shiver, feeling as if my teacher were in my room, standing over me, shouting in my ear.

"'She dreams in class. Her mind wanders. And she is a very clumsy child. Her handwriting and her drawings are disgraceful. Very, very messy!'" My mother sighs. "You can imagine how I felt in front of all the parents. And I'm not used to this at all."

Of course not, I think, my face burning. Sorin always gets a glowing report: "an exemplary student," "a brilliant mind," "the best in the class." A ball of tears is pressing hard against my throat. I want to cry it out, but I can't. I sink my teeth in my pillow.

"An evil witch!" Omama exclaims. "May her nasty mouth dry up and her wicked tongue shrivel! The old bat hates her for some reason. Such a good, smart, sweet child, God bless her!"

I stifle the sound, but the tears flow, drenching my pillow. My dear, kind Omama. She always takes my side. She always knows the truth.

"She's got to try harder, mama," my mother answers her, in a firm, impatient tone. "She's got to shape up. It will be hard enough for my children as it is. They have to be the best, and even better than best."

But it's not fair! It's not fair! I want to cry out. I am the best reader in the class. I stand up straight and tall and read smoothly from my primer. Nobody can read like me, not even Popescu, the best at everything. And I recite poetry with expression, the way I've heard my mother when she was rehearsing for her roles. I don't like math and find it hard to keep my mind still when the teacher writes numbers on the board, but whenever she booms, "Eremia, how much is three plus six plus nine plus eight or five plus seven?" I always give her the right answer, no matter how hard she tries to stump me!

In art and handwriting I try so hard! I want so badly to make my letters straight and neat. But the ink blots. The paper tears. The lines are crooked and misshapen. Comrade Pana yells at me, and slaps my hand.

"You clumsy child! Look what a mess you've made!" My fingers shake. And I can't copy right. I can't make the picture on my sheet look like the picture in the book. The crayons slip, the colors slide, my hand makes circles instead of squares.

I'm afraid of Comrade Pana. When she gets mad, her face gets red and puffs up like a tomato. Her eyes bulge out like onions. "Eremia!" she bellows, "copy that page over again!" My eyes cloud. The letters leap and jump. I pretend they're alive, a family, a mommy and a daddy, a grandma, a nanny, aunts, uncles, cousins, small children and little babies. "Can't you make them even, you stupid girl? Look at this 'A': a dwarf! And this 'L': a giant!"

The class laughs! She is so mean! So mean!

But she's not mean to everyone. She's never mean to Georgescu, or to Manescu. She loves Doina Manescu. Her father's chauffeur drives her to school in a big black car. Even when she stutters and stumbles over easy words in our primer, Comrade Pana has a smile for her. The teacher never shouts at her the way she shouts at me or at my benchmate, Dimeica, who never knows his lessons. Dimeica has dark hair and dark skin. The children say he's a gypsy. "*Tsiganule,*" they shout after him. Does his mother sell flowers or popcorn on street corners? "You idiot! You bird brain!" Comrade Pana yells at him when he stands up, blinking at the blackboard. Yesterday, the teacher grabbed him by his black curls and dashed his head against the board. I was surprised his head didn't break or bleed. He's got a hard head, a wooden head, Comrade Pana kept screaming at him. I wonder if I have a hard head. Or would mine crack open and spill out, my brains splattering over the blackboard? I toss and turn. I wish I could fall asleep and never wake up. I don't want to face Comrade Pana in the morning.

◆ ◆ ◆

Outside the children are laughing. They are hiding and seeking, chasing and tagging, tossing and catching.

"I-RI-NA! I-RI-NA!" calls Mariana, beckoning me to come out and join the game. Rodica, her other friend, is sick with the flu and I'm the only other seven year old girl on the block.

"I'm doing my homework!" I yell out the window and return to the kitchen table, where I bend down over my notebook and try to make my letters neat, tidy and neat.

My mother did not scold me this morning when we sat down to breakfast and my brother asked her what our teachers said about us, last night at the conference. After congratulating Sorin on his glowing report, she fixed her large, green, serious eyes on me. "You, too, are a smart girl. I know it, and I am sure your teacher knows it, too. But you must pay more attention in class and write more neatly in your notebook."

"But I try! I try!" I moan.

"I know you try, but you must try harder. If handwriting is difficult for you, you must take more time with it, darling. You must work at it twice as hard as all the others. You must never settle. You must always do your best to be the best at everything you do."

I now try my best to lift my pen up and bring it down in a straight line. I try my best to make the loops and swirls as smoothly as I can. But my "A" comes out too fat! And my "H" too skinny! My "L" is too tall, and my "S" too short. Exasperated, I tear out the page and start again. But this time I dip my pen too long into the ink. It makes a big blot. I try to scratch it out and make a little tear which turns into a large hole. Again, I must rip up the page. My notebook's getting thin. Comrade Pana won't like it. I begin again. I'm very careful this time. I strive to make each letter the same size, and to leave even spaces between each word. But just before I reach the end of the sheet, the pen tip picks up a speck of dirt which leaves its smudgy track along the last half of the page. I want to tear the notebook and my hair!

"For God's sake, my child, why are you crying so? What's the matter?" Omama is standing over me, looking at me with eyes full of pity.

"I can't do it! I just can't do it!" I sob, desperately.

"My poor, sweet darling, you're breaking your little heart over this. Here, let me help you."

Omama takes off her apron and pulls a chair next to me at the table. She puts her warm, soothing hand over my hand. Then she gently guides my hand with her hand. My pen glides across the page. The letters dance in even, perfect lines.

◆ ◆ ◆

Proudly, I hand my notebook to Comrade Pana the next day, who glances at it as she picks it up. Suddenly she stops dead in front of me. Her face puffs up. Her eyes bug out.

"Who did this?" she blares at me.

"I did," I squeak.

"You're lying. You didn't write it. Who wrote it?"

"I did. I wrote it," I whisper. Tears are streaming down my cheeks.

Comrade Pana grabs me by the scruff of my freshly starched, white collar (Omama sat up late last night to iron it!) and drags me in front of the room.

"Admit! Admit right now, in front of your classmates that you cheated on your homework and lied about it!"

"No," I say. "I didn't."

"Very well, then. Prove it. Sit down, right at my desk, so everyone can see you, and write here, in this notebook, exactly the way you wrote at home."

Everyone is silent. Everyone is waiting. I dip my pen in the inkwell. I start the first letter. The tears are dropping on the sheet, turning my lines into blue waves. But I try my best to do my best. The teacher stands over me. I can see her shadow on my sheet. I write and cry and write some more. Endlessly, I write. Finally, she grabs the notebook from me. She holds it up, ink dripping, for everyone to see. Then she holds up the other notebook.

"Children, do you believe that the person who just now did 'this,' could be the same person who yesterday wrote 'that?'"

A chorus of voices answer her: "Noooooo!"

"Eremia!" she orders. "Go to the blackboard."

I go to the blackboard.

"Now pick up some chalk."

I pick up some chalk.

"Now write: 'I…"

I begin to write: "I…"

"'Admit!' Come on, write, 'I admit!'"

I stare at her, my chalk poised in mid-air. I stare at my teacher, the hawk with the beak. Suddenly my hand darts back, and with a quick, sharp motion, it hurls the chalk against the blackboard. It smashes to pieces and scatters on the ground. My feet sprout wings and fly me to the door. But a shocking, shrill pain holds me back. Comrade Pana has grabbed hold of my ear. She is holding my right ear between her thumb and forefinger, and she is pulling, pulling with all her might, pulling and twisting, lifting me off the ground, trying to tear my ear off.

◆ ◆ ◆

"I'm gonna kill her!" says my mother. "I'm gonna kill her".

"That nasty old witch!" cries Omama. "May her wicked hands wither and fall off!"

"Tell her that your husband still has friends in high places," shouts Aunt Coca. "They'll know just how to fix her!"

"Old Army friends," adds Uncle Jack, seething with rage.

"I'm gonna kill her!" says my mother. "I'm gonna kill her."

◆ ◆ ◆

I shake in my seat, watching my mother, who held my hand all the way here this morning and promised that no one would ever dare to touch one hair of my head again. She is talking to Comrade Pana. Everyone is silent. My mother's face is dark and threatening. Her eyes are blazing. She looks fierce and terrible, like that horrible woman, Medea, whom she once played, the Greek woman who killed her own children to punish her husband. Comrade Pana looks scared. She takes a step back. My mother is telling her, yes, I'm sure she's telling her, that she will do something awful to her. She will cast a spell on her. She will send Comrade Pana a poisoned garment that will burst into flames when it touches her skin and turn her into smoke. In the middle of the night she will creep into the teacher's house, find her in her bed, and plunge a knife into her heart.

Comrade Pana does not look at me or talk to me for the rest of the morning.

At lunchtime, the principal comes into our classroom. He tells me to pack up my books. He leads me into a different classroom.

"Comrade Vlada, this is your new student, Irina Eremia," he tells her. She points to an empty seat in the back of the room.

"Sit there for now," she says. "Later, I may move you elsewhere."

◆ ◆ ◆

I sit down, relieved. Maybe this new teacher won't hate me.

"Twenty lei for the two bunches, lovely lady. Where else will you get such fresh, fine roses, finer than a newborn's soft, pink skin?"

"Twenty lei is too much," says my mother, grabbing our hands and starting to walk away. We're bargaining over the price of the bouquets of roses my brother and I must bring, as my mother says is the custom, to our teachers at our end of the year assembly.

"All right then, I'll sell them for fifteen, for the sake of your two handsome children, may they bloom, like these rose buds, into fresh, beautiful flowers."

My mother makes the bargain, for we're in a big hurry. I'm very excited. Both my brother and I know we will receive prizes today—it said so on our report cards. My brother, as usual, came in first in his class. He'll get a certificate and three books. I came in third in my class. I'll also get a certificate but only one book. Still I am grateful I came in third and not fourth, for only the top three students get prizes.

We sit at the back of the crowded auditorium. The flag is raised. The national anthem is sung. The principal goes up to the microphone and makes a speech. We are the hope and promise of our land, he tells us, the budding flowers who will bloom into "hard working, dedicated citizens, future communists, devoted to the struggle of the working classes to build a just and equal society in Romania and throughout the world." Then one by one, the three top students in each class are called up to the microphone. The principal shakes their hands, gives them a certificate and a present. He begins with the sixth graders, then the fifth, the fourth…

"When you go up," my mother whispers to my brother, whose class is now being called out, give your teacher the bouquet of flowers and thank her for a wonderful year. And you do the same thing," she tells me. The third prize in my brother's class goes to a girl, Michaela Lunganu. The second prize to another girl, Ioana Iliescu. And the first prize—my heart starts beating, as my brother stands up, goes to a boy, Mircea Statescu! Not Sorin Eremia! My brother gasps. My mother looks stunned. Mircea Statescu gets his handshake, his certificate, his present, and smiling, gives his teacher his bouquet of flowers.

"He was second! I was first! And Lunganu was only honorable mention!" my brother says, a bit too loudly, for several people turn around and stare at us.

"Shhh!" my mother quiets him. "There must be some mistake. We'll get it straightened out."

The second graders are called. Then the first graders. First Comrade Pana's class, and then my own. A boy gets third prize. A girl second. And another girl first. I get nothing. The ceremony is over.

"Let's go home," says my brother, hiding his face in his collar.

"No!" says my mother. "Come with me."

She drags us by the hand to the front of the auditorium where the principal stands, surrounded by smiling teachers, holding their bouquets of roses. My mother pushes her way through the group and taps the principal on the shoulder.

"I must talk to you, comrade," she tells him in a firm, hard voice. He looks up at her, surprised.

"Make an appointment to see me Monday at my office," he tells her.

"No! Now!" says my mother, her eyes on fire. "Or I'll make a scene, right here, in front of everyone."

Nervously, he follows her outside to an empty, isolated spot, under a poplar tree. My brother and I cower behind her.

"What is the meaning of this, Comrade Director? Is this a way to treat young children?"

The principal feigns surprise.

"What's the problem, comrade Eremia?"

"My son's report card states he was first in his class. And my daughter third. Why were they not awarded their prizes?"

The small man looks up at my mother, who is towering over him, an incredulous expression on his face.

"Prizes? You really expect your children should get prizes Comrade Eremia? Be glad that they're allowed to attend our school at all. Be glad if they manage to stay through the seventh grade. Don't even dream about high school!"

My mother turns her back to him. She grabs our hands. We walk away. I feel worse for Sorin than for myself. He was first. I was only third. He is crying, and he never cries. When we get home, he throws his roses on the floor and tramples them. Unlike me, Sorin never has temper tantrums. But this time, he goes wild.

A little gray lady stands in the doorway, holding a parcel wrapped up in newspaper. She looks familiar, but I don't know why.

"Does the Eremia family live here?" she asks in a thin, timid voice.

"Why Madam Borcea!" exclaims my mother, from over my head. "Come in. Come in."

"Madam General," the old lady says to my mother. "I'm sorry. So sorry." Her eyes fill with tears. Then she looks around the room. "Where is he?" she asks.

"Sorin!" my mother shouts. "Look who is here to see you!"

Then, I finally realize who she is. Comrade Borcea! Sorin's teacher.

My brother staggers in, his eyes fixed on the floor.

"I brought you something, darling," his teacher tells him, handing him the package.

"I can do it!" I yell. "I know how to open it!" My brother watches me, indifferent. I take out three books and a certificate. "It's yours! For the first prize!" I shout.

My brother looks at it and smiles between his tears.

"Thank you, Comrade Borcea."

"That's so kind of you, madam," says my mother. "You've made all the difference."

The teacher shakes her head and sighs. "It's so unfortunate! So unfortunate! How things have changed. I'm relieved to be retiring this year." Then she looks at my brother and smiles.

"I want you to know, Sorin Eremia, that in my forty years of teaching, I have never had a student brighter than you."

Sorin runs out for a moment and returns with the bouquet of roses. But they are my roses! He trampled his! I try to decide whether to object or not.

My brother hugs Comrade Borcea and gives her the flowers.

"Thank you for a wonderful year," he tells her.

"Wouldn't you like a cup of coffee and a placinta?" my mother offers. "We just made a fresh batch."

"No, thank you, Madam General. I must rush home. My husband doesn't even know I'm here. I'll tell him the flowers are from a secret admirer." She beams at my brother. Then she walks to the door, cradling the bouquet like a baby in her arms. I decide to keep my mouth shut. I'm happy I gave her my rose buds.

9

Ion: Dracula's Mob

I wake up to a glorious June morning, caressed by the sun's rays which, despite the guards, have managed to creep into my dark cell. Suddenly the lock to my dungeon creaks, the heavy door opens and my guard bursts in shouting, "Your bags!" I stare at him dumbfounded. Could this be the great moment that I, like every convict, have been dreaming about incessantly? Furtively, I look up at my jailer and seem to discern a subtle smile flashing across his frigid face. I pick up my "luggage"—my striped convict's hat.

I follow the guard's heavy boots through the Milanese hallway, through the desolate courtyard, past the charming little administration garden and stop in front of the clothing warehouse, where I wait for my companion to open the door. A strong odor of mold attacks my nostrils. At the guard's order, I pick up some shabby civilian clothes and shoes green with mold and begin to undress. My body luxuriates in the soft fibers of civilian clothing, which, in spite of their condition, are still infinitely softer and more soothing than the striped prison garb.

I am led out without blows or curses. Two gentlemen dressed in blue velvet suits are waiting for me by an elegant car. Politely, they invite me to step in. One takes the driver's seat, the other joins him in the front while I sink my body in the plush back seat.

Resting my back, stretching my legs, staring freely out the window, I estimate my chances of being granted my freedom at ninety-nine percent! Am I not traveling by car, rather than van, free, rather than in chains, accompanied by civilized human beings instead of sadistic brutes? I allow myself to become totally absorbed in my delightful journey, the beauty of which far surpasses the last one I took, two years earlier, in the van that transported me to Rimnicul Sarat. Now I delight freely in the streets and piazzas of this quaint town, which I once visited and know well. From here we take a paved road that parallels the curve of the Carpathians, and after two hours we reach the city of Buzau. Next, we drive toward Ploiesti, passing beautiful cherry orchards in full bloom and green fields of young wheat.

My companions are pleasant and friendly. Surely, I am being taken to the capital, where my pardon will be granted! Soothed, comfortable, hopeful, I lose track of time. Suddenly we are in Bucharest, and my excitement grows. Any moment, the great miracle will take place, and I will be set free!

Suddenly, I realize that instead of turning toward the road leading to the Interior Ministry, as I had hoped and imagined, the car veers off in the direction of the Malmaison Prison! In one split second, my chances of freedom have dropped to fifty percent. As we pass the Military Tribunal, which is in the neighborhood of Malmaison, and then enter the prison's courtyard, my chances go down to ten percent. As I actually walk through the prison corridor, I still have a very pale hope, which vanishes like a ring of smoke when I am escorted to my new residence: an empty cell.

The bedtime bell rings. Exhausted by the trip and the disappointment, I fall into a deep sleep with no dreams.

◆ ◆ ◆

This morning I am served a real cup of coffee, which is, wonder of wonders, sweet. Then, I receive a visitor: the young and handsome chief of interrogation from Internal Security, with whom I had already had the honor of dealing during the "investigation" before my trial.

He walks in smiling, obviously intent on charming me.

"We are old friends, Mr. Eremia. I want you to know that, leaving our political differences aside, I consider you an honest man and I…"

"Thanks for the compliment," I interrupt him, hoping to temper his enthusiasm a bit.

"As I was saying," he continues, "we are now in a position to truly value your sincerity. Indeed, we are appealing to this very quality in you."

"How can I help you?" I ask him dryly.

"With your cooperation toward the clarification of the situation in the investigation of several of your former friends: Bodnarash, Dusa, Agiu, Manescu, Badescu. You know them well and there is a lot about them you can clarify for us."

"I certainly don't know enough to help you send them before a military tribunal."

"Why are you so impatient and rude?"

"Why are you wasting your time?"

"Why are you slamming the door in our faces?"

"I have never been an informer and am not about to become one now."

"You mean even after three years of not seeing your wife and children, you haven't changed your tune? Why are you rejecting a unique chance to return to them?"

The interrogator is pushing all my buttons. Still, I manage to control myself. "For two reasons. First, because I know nothing compromising about the people you mentioned, and secondly, because even if I did, I would not believe in your generous proposals."

"You will come to regret your stubborn impudence, prisoner!" my interrogator explodes, dropping his mask. "Especially as I have detailed, written declarations that prove your direct involvement in an espionage affair!" He storms out the door.

◆ ◆ ◆

Alone in my cell, I try to analyze the situation. I know that the chief interrogator reports directly to "Dracula the stutterer," and I have no doubt that it is he who is behind this sordid scheme. It appears that "Dracula" is out to get Emil Bodnarash, the biggest fish in the pond just mentioned. Thinking about them, I remember the wise words of a French historian whose name, unfortunately, I have forgotten: "Revolutions are conceived by visionaries, executed by fanatics and exploited by scoundrels." I am not certain whether my old friend and mentor, Emil Bodnarash, qualifies as a "visionary," but I am certain that "Dracula the stutterer," as some of us nicknamed my former colleague, Nicolae Ceausescu, is precisely such a scoundrel.

◆ ◆ ◆

It was my older brother, Gica, who introduced me to the Communist Party. I had always loved and admired him, even though we were very different. In April 1943, he was arrested along with all other suspected communists of my hometown, Constanza, where I served as an officer. An ammunition dump belonging to our German allies was destroyed, and the communists, who formed the only organized resistance to the Nazi collaboration, were immediately suspected. I went to visit my brother in jail. Through the bars that separated us, he whispered an important request: Could I find a way to save the life of another officer, Victor

Dusa, the Communist Party leader of our region, now threatened with execution for setting off the explosion?

Unlike Gica, I had never been interested in joining the Communist Party. Although I had always been attracted by the utopian vision of a worker's paradise, I was infinitely more drawn to the world of letters and ideas than to that of politics and action. I had gone through military school to please my father, who believed that the only way a smart boy from a poor family could make something of himself was by choosing, like Stendhal's Julien Sorel, the "red" or "the black," the military or the church. Gica had been sent to the seminary, I to the military academy. My brother hated the seminary, abandoned the Church and joined the Communist Party. I, however, thought I had discovered a way of following my true calling within the career my father had chosen for me. More than anything in the world, I wanted to write. In 1941, after Ion Antonescu's coup, when Romania entered the war on the side of the Germans, I had been only months away from a graduate degree that would have enabled me to teach history and philosophy at a military academy—freeing me of financial worries while still leaving me the time to chase the stories and poems that were constantly flitting through my imagination.

Although I was not politically involved, I hated the German Nazis and Romanian Black Shirts and was horrified by the atrocities they committed. My brother's request presented me with the opportunity not only to act according to my principles but also to save a man's life. And I succeeded, providing him an alibi by falsifying some army documents to prove that he had been on a military mission in another city at the time of the explosion. After charges against Dusa were dropped (as they were also against my brother and others due to lack of evidence), he became my friend, entrusting me with more underground work for the communist resistance and introducing me to Emil Bodnarash, who was on the party's central committee and who enlisted my help in the conspiracy to overthrow the Antonescu regime. When, on August 23, 1944, Antonescu was arrested and Romania switched sides in the war, joining the Allies, I was finally able to serve as I believed and joined the campaign to liberate Transylvania, Hungary and Czechoslovakia from the Nazis.

I returned to Bucharest in the fall of 1945, a major decorated for valor on the battlefield, a communist rewarded for my efforts for the "underground." I was full of pride, ambition, great hopes and big dreams. Emil Bodnarash, now the Romanian Minister of Defense, gave me a job "according to my abilities." For the first time in my life, I felt that my work suited my temperament. I was put in charge of the "cultural sector of the army"—its newspaper, sport arena, theater and light opera. I was most interested in these last two, as I got to assist at rehearsals, take part in productions and live the full and feverish life of actors, singers, directors and producers. I got to know every performer from the walk-ons to the stars, and it was among them that I met the lithe young actress who would become my wife.

Perhaps because I was one of the few educated communist leaders (Bodnarash and I were the only two high-ranking officers who had graduated from military academies), I was well regarded and was quickly promoted from major, to colonel, to general. In 1952, Emil Bodnarash appointed me as his Vice Minister of Defense, along with Nicolae Ceausescu, my co-Vice Minister. Several of us used to refer to Ceausescu as "Dracula," because he was cruel and sadistic with his inferiors and duplicitous and perverse with his equals; another nickname we invented for him was "the stutterer," because he would stutter and stammer whenever called upon to justify himself.

"Dracula" did manage to hide his claws from his great protector, the President of Romania, Gheorghe Gheorghiu-Dej, who loved him like a son. While in "illegality," the two had served time in the same prison and shared the same common cell. It was there that Ceausescu had managed to get under Dej's skin, shining his shoes, doing his errands, anticipating his needs, convincing the powerful Communist Party boss that his devoted follower was a timid, humble, hard-working and loyal young communist.

In reality, Dracula was a dangerous man with criminal tendencies. He had "made his bones" during the elections of 1946 (fraudulently won by the Communist Party) by murdering the candidate for the Liberal Party with his own hands. At that time the Communist Party, though strong, was not completely in control of the country, and there was a commission for election control. An investigation took place, but its chairman, a man by the name of Florea Dinescu, happened to be a friend of Dracula's and got him off clean. To repay him, several years later, Ceausescu promoted Dinescu from the position of ex-naval sergeant to no less than admiral.

This resulted in my first confrontation with "Dracula." I had happened to be away when this miraculous promotion took place, and when I came back and found out about it I was outraged. At the first military council meeting, I protested. I said that Florea Dinescu is well-known not only for his stupidity and incompetence but also for his shady moral character. Realizing that this may have something to do with "Dracula," Defense Minister Bodnarash invited me to have a few words in private with him. I will never forget the evil look "the stutterer" threw me as I walked out the door. Alone with Bodnarash, I revealed what I knew about Ceausescu's relationship with Dinescu. Bodnarash agreed to help remove the man from his post. He tried, but Gheorghiu-Dej wouldn't hear of this, for his "spoiled child" had insisted Dinescu was worthy of his promotion. Soon, however, I was proven right and Dracula wrong, for the overnight admiral quickly made a fool of himself in front of the entire naval force, giving Dej no choice but to remove him from office. Florea Dinescu was sent to a military course in the Soviet Union, which, to everyone's mirth, he flunked.

Bodnarash warned me that the laugh would be on me, for as a result of this matter, I had made a deadly enemy of Ceausescu. And indeed, soon after, Dracula began to show his fangs. A series of anonymous letters reached Dej, accusing me of various acts of treachery, dishonesty, embezzlement, etc. Ceausescu did not, however, succeed, not at least until I brought about my demise through my own acts.

And now, Dracula is after Bodnarash, the Minister of Defense himself, who may once have been in a position to remove him, but out of a failure of nerve, did not. I consider Emil Bodnarash as one of the few decent men in our government. Unfortunately, we live in a time when, to put it in the words of William Butler Yeats, "the best lack all conviction/the worst are full of passionate intensity." I have always respected Bodnarash, despite his shady past. (It was well-known that he had been drawn, in his youth, during the early thirties, by a woman into committing espionage for the Russians. He had a weakness for hard liquor and beautiful women. While serving an eight year prison sentence for spying, he strengthened his ties with the Romanian Communist Party.) In spite of everything, I found that he had a positive role in our government. He was one of the few intelligent, well-educated men there, a career officer who like me had gone to the military academy before the war, contrary to so many other high officers who had no military education whatsoever but had been promoted because they were communists. He was a dignified man, a man of his word who loved the army and cared about his men. Because of his intelligence and tact, he was highly respected by Dej and had much influence in the government. He used his authority well, gave good advice, helped save many innocent people and in general did much good around him. With great subtlety, he tempered the Stalinist excesses of Dej, Chivu Stoica, Ceausescu, Draghici and other blood-thirsty members of the politburo. He tried to behave as well as he could, given the band of thugs who came to rule our country in the shadow of Stalin.

Still, Bodnarash did not have the guts to stand up to Ceausescu, despite all my efforts to encourage him to do so. One time I came close. It was a late afternoon, in 1954, when my boss invited me to his office to have a private conversation.

Normally a calm man, polite but formal with his subordinates, he surprised me by his distraught, agitated appearance.

"Do you remember," he began, in a nervous, shaky voice, "the meeting I held last week at the military academy with the commanders of our regiments?"

"Sure!" I said, noting that I had never seen the defense minister look so bad. The man was truly beside himself.

"I was seated, if you'll remember, at the head table, between my Vice Ministers, you and Ceausescu, along with Salanjan and Stefanescu. Do you remember what I said when the issue of 'healthy social origin' came up from among the officers?"

"Certainly," I assured him. "The issue was brought up because the men were nervous about their jobs, some of their colleagues having been fired under the pretext that their parents owned land or businesses before the War. You said, and I quote: 'Today, after almost ten years of our socialist democracy, we are no longer concerned about the social origin of our officers. If a man has proven, through time, that he is professional, hard working, honest, capable and loyal to our regime, the matter of who his father was is no longer relevant.' Everyone breathed a sigh of relief, of course."

"That's right. That's exactly what I said. But do you know the message that reached Stalin's ears about my statement?"

"No!" I exclaimed, surprised.

"Stalin was told I said that the Romanian army leadership doesn't give a damn about the social origin of its officers!"

Bodnarash was trembling with anger and fear. For Stalin, such a statement would signify a brazen defiance of his policies, which could lead to the end of the defense minister's career, if not of his life.

After discussing the meeting in detail, both Bodnarash and I concluded that it was Ceausescu who had blown the whistle, for the latter had looked very displeased and angry and began whispering something to Salanjan after Bodnarash made this statement.

"Please help me," my boss asked me. "Write a memo to Dej, detailing the entire content of my statement, how I said that a man's social origin will not be held against him if, in the course of ten years of our popular democracy, he had proven himself to be capable, hard-working and loyal to our regime. Surely when Stalin reviews my entire message, he will find it less objectionable."

"I will," I said, "but in turn, I also have a favor to ask you. I know that Dej has great respect for you and a high regard for your opinion. As soon as you have a chance, tell him that you know that it was Ceausescu who spilled the beans to

Stalin. Tell him what you really think about this man. Tell him that his 'spoiled child' is a dangerous snake. Tell him that one day he will dig his own Papa's grave, stab him in the back, like Brutus stabbed Caesar! Tell him, confront Ceausescu head on, and help us get rid this viper."

"You write your memo and I'll worry about Ceausescu," Bodnarash replied, promising nothing.

I realized then that the defense minister did not have the courage for a frontal attack on Dej's favorite. He was a man who would have preferred to do the right thing—as long as the right thing did not involve any serious personal risk. In the end, he found a way to kill two birds with one stone by removing Ceausescu as Vice-Minister of Defense and promoting him to secretary of the central committee. By this move, he both appeased Ceausescu and kept him at a safe distance.

From his high position, "Dracula" found ample opportunity to do evil. He had always had a passionate hatred for intellectuals, perhaps because he was uneducated and envious, and now he managed to eliminate many of the intelligent people he came across, destroying their careers, sending them to the country to do manual labor or shutting them up in prison, saying that they are "reactionary elements," or "class enemies."

Marxist jargon and mobster tactics—these were the methods also employed by Gheorghe Gheorghiu-Dej, whom Ceausescu studied, emulated and surpassed. Like father, like son. On the surface, the two men seemed very different. Dej, husky, robust, jovial, enjoyed eating, drinking and wenching (many of his state banquets ended up in orgies in the straw-filled little room behind the banquet hall). Ceausescu, lean and hungry, intense and nervous, was an ascetic, a compulsive worker who never cracked a smile or looked you in the eye. But in reality, the two men had much in common: their working class backgrounds, their hatred for Jews, Hungarians and intellectuals, and their ruthless, criminal tactics. It was Gheorghe Gheorghiu-Dej who in the early fifties began the "campaign for the purification of the state apparatus" through the liquidation of "those of unhealthy social origin." He did this not just to please Stalin, but for the same reasons that motivated the Russian dictator: to consolidate his power by eliminating all opposition. A great number of intellectuals, academicians, economists, superior officers, scientists, artists and professors, many of whom had been won over by the party and honestly believed in communist ideals, were fired from their jobs under the pretext that they were of unhealthy social origin and hence not to be trusted. Tens of thousands were sent to dig the canals between the Danube and the Black Sea, where Nazi-like work camps were set up; very few survived the brutal conditions. These men were replaced by Dej's own trusted cronies, who in turn filled more spots with their own friends and relatives.

Soon a clique of incompetents was running the country, but Dej was in a powerful enough position to strike at his key competitor, Lucretiu Patrascanu. Patrascanu was one of Romania's leading representatives after the war, well-respected abroad, and a signatory to the Paris peace treaty. Unlike Gheorghiu-Dej, Patrascanu came from the upper classes, was a doctor in philosophy and a lawyer, an eloquent leftist writer and publicist, the most brilliant mind of the Romanian Communist Party, a man of high ethics and moral conscience. Dej succeeded in having him arrested on trumped up charges of high treason and espionage. Patrascanu was tortured, tried, sentenced and executed based on the false declarations signed by two of his friends who were subjected to tortures of the Inquisition. His trial was enacted by Dej with the aid of Draghici, Pantusa and Dracula and the silence and complicity of all the members of the Politburo. Lucretiu Patrascanu was sentenced to death. Later, Miron Constinescu, a former member of the Politburo, at the time in Dej's good graces (though later also deposed), revealed to me an incident which showed Dej for who he really was. Miron met with Patrascanu while he was waiting to be executed. Here, the old communist leader broke down. After swearing to Miron that he was innocent, Patrascanu begged him to convey to Dej the following message: "Send me to the most obscure prison corner, in the furthest end of the country, where no one will ever hear of me and I cannot possibly be of any threat to you, officially declare that I've been executed, but let me, at least, have my life!" Moved to tears, Miron conveyed this request to Dej. The burly party boss turned red with anger. Jumping out of his chair, he pushed Miron toward the door, swearing at him as was his habit: "Miron, you mother fucking son of a bitch! If I pardon the bastard now, he'll never pardon me later!"

Patrascanu was shot in a cowardly fashion, from behind, while he was taking a walk in the courtyard of Malmaison, at the order of Dej, by the same hit man, Pantiusa, who several years earlier murdered the former secretary of the Romanian Communist Party, and who several years later was appointed chief of the Securitate. Bullies, thugs, hit men, murderers—these were the men who won the struggle for power in Stalinist controlled Romania. True believers like Patrascanu, Marxist idealists with character and integrity, never really stood a chance. Such men very quickly ended up disgraced, incarcerated or dead.

When my interrogator threatened me with being charged with espionage, he knew perfectly well what he was doing: deliberately, he was reminding me of poor Lucretiu Patrascanu and warning me that very soon, I could end up sharing his fate.

◆ ◆ ◆

After two weeks of boiling in Satan's cauldron reminiscing about Dej, Ceausescu, their henchmen and their victims, I am finally summoned to my interrogator's office. This time he greets me with a frown.

"Well, have you had sufficient time to reconsider your position regarding the issue of collaborating with us in our investigation?" he asks me the moment I am led through the door.

"Certainly," I answer, calmly. "And I have nothing to add to what I've already told you."

The interrogator's face darkens, but for the time being he maintains his composure.

"Have you considered that we have signed evidence from reliable sources that prove you committed acts of espionage for France?"

"Yes."

"And what do you have to say?"

"Nothing."

"Nothing is not an answer."

"I don't have another."

"Maybe you'll change your mind when you see our signed declarations."

I decide it wouldn't be a bad idea to see them, so I could at least understand what they had in mind.

"By all means," I tell him, "I would be delighted to take a look."

"You'll have to be content with having them read to you."

"Why? Are you worried if I see your "declarations" with my own eyes I'll recognize them as false? I already know that to begin with."

"You impudent bastard! How can they be false when they contain concrete evidence detailing your espionage activities?"

"The same kind of evidence, I suppose, used to convict Patrascanu. You probably will use the same false witnesses. And the same methods of making them sign their names to lies."

"Yes, indeed! We do have excellent methods! No one can resist them, you know."

"You're wasting your time. None of your methods will work on me!"

"You stupid idiot! You're going to lick our hands, kiss our butts and sign everything we want as soon as we warm you up a bit!" the interrogator shouts.

"Do you have anything else to ask me?"

"You son of a bitch! You have the nerve to throw me out of my own office? I'll teach you, don't worry, how to treat state officials with respect. So you're in a hurry, eh?"

I continue to look at him with disgust.

"I am asking you for the last time. Are you going to collaborate with us, or not?" he bellows.

I stare at him and say nothing.

After waiting a while, he presses violently on his bell and yells at the guard:

"Take the bastard out of here."

I leave without looking at him.

Alone in my cell, I reflect on the well-known tactic used against me by the Securitate: first the sugar lump, then the rod. First they try to soften you up by treating you well and raising your hopes. When that doesn't work, they take out the rod. If you don't bite into the sugar, they'll bite into your flesh. I feel sure that by nightfall they are going to start the process of "warming me up." What methods will they use? Will they hang me upside down like a lamb over a spit? Will they beat me? Electrocute me? Pull out my fingernails?

One thought horrifies me most: I remember the rumors I heard about what was done to Moscony-Sircea, one of Patrascanu's loyal friends and so called "accomplices" when he heroically resisted signing the phony documents: his wife was brought in and tortured in front of him. This, Moscony-Sircea could not bear, and finally gave in. What if they were to do this to me? What would I do?

◆ ◆ ◆

A new inmate is brought in to share my cell. He is a very distinguished looking older man, friendly and talkative. It has been three days since my interrogation, days spent in the terror of my imagination, but nothing has happened to me yet. The man doesn't even have to open his mouth for me to recognize him as an "advisor"—as some friends from military school who took secret service courses once told me such men are called. Recruited from among the weaker convicts, the "advisor" is willing to buy the goodwill of his jailers by playing the part scripted out for him. His function is to strike terror in his cellmate's heart by graphically describing all the horrible things that were done to him when he refused to cooperate. My "advisor" begins to work on me right away. I pretend to believe him and be moved and frightened by his stories.

◆ ◆ ◆

After an entire week of this charade, I am once again called up by the interrogator. He puts a declaration in front of me stating that during the period of time after I was fired from my job and dismissed from the army, I, along with several other "accomplices," were involved in espionage activities on behalf of France. I laugh in his face. He threatens me with all kinds of things. I won't budge.

◆ ◆ ◆

For some miraculous reason, Dracula's men have decided not to torture me. Instead, they are sending me back to the penitentiary. This time I travel in the windowless van, with chains around my legs, accompanied by the usual blows and curses. On my return trip to Rimnicul Sarat, I can think of nothing other than my destination, that "garden of sighs" where three dozen political prisoners (there are thirty-six individual cells) are guarded by a staff large enough to accommodate thousands of inmates. How is it that our regime can allow itself such an extravagance? And what are they trying to gain by their obsessive control?

Within the walls of this prison, I decide, must be gathered what our rulers consider their most dangerous political opponents. They watch us so closely, not only because they don't want us to communicate through Morse code, but also because they would prefer that we don't kill ourselves. Our death might provoke public indignation at home and abroad. They would rather keep our bodies alive but destroy our souls and crush our spirits so that, some day, when we are liberated, we will have been politically neutered.

The brutality of our treatment is a calculated political maneuver. The four perfect tortures to which we are subjected—hunger, cold, solitude and immobility—are part of a "strategy of misery" used not only against those who dare to raise their voices against the group of gangsters who rule us, but also against the entire population, the average man and woman who would not otherwise tolerate their regime. Threatened with the specter of hunger, cold, disease and death, exhausted by the incessant daily struggle for survival, human beings lose their sense of solidarity. Fear, suspicion and mistrust poison personal relationships. Informers are planted among one's friends, colleagues, associates, neighbors and even relatives. Terrorized, people withdraw and live, like the inmates here, in silence and isolation.

Our political strategists have learned from history, and the long experience of enslaving regimes, that slaves don't make good heroes. Had Spartacus not been made a gladiator, but been left to carry stones day in and day out, perhaps he would have never become Spartacus, the heroic leader of the Roman slaves against General Crassus, the greatest possessor of gold in antiquity, who died when King Orodes poured melted gold down his throat to give him his fill of the precious metal. Of men thirsty for gold and slaves, the world has never been short. The "dictatorship of the proletariat" has brought to power a gang of street toughs, greedy for wealth and power, illiterate, inept and lazy, who try to blind and deafen the population with such bombastic phrases as "love for the masses," "popular democracy," "the rule of the people," "the triumph of the working class." They rob, starve and torture the people, twist their hands behind their backs and force them to "admit" that they have never been happier, freer or more prosperous.

◆ ◆ ◆

By the time I reach my desolate old "home," I have worked myself up into a rage. This gives me the nerve to object vehemently to the ugly, smelly, moldy rags, and broken shoes three sizes too small that are now given to me in return for my civilian clothes. No one, of course, pays attention, and I am brutally shoved back into my former cell.

It is still light out and my dungeon, at least, is warm. As if to compensate for the bitter winter, we have been blessed this year with a magnanimous summer. While staring at my four walls, I suddenly realize that one of them has been transformed by the sunlight into a giant screen where I can contemplate, at sudden, fleeting instants, the shadows of butterflies, bumblebees and other creatures belonging to the aerial kingdom. Fascinated, I lose myself in the spectacle of shadows.

10

Irina: Friends and Enemies

They walk together, hand in hand, giggling and laughing. With their arms around each other, they skip down the yard, their hair tossed in the wind. When a boy taunts one, the other sticks her tongue out and makes him chase her, saving her friend. In class, when one doesn't know the answer, the other whispers it to her. At recess, when one gets picked for a game, she always chooses the other. They sit together on a bench, sharing sandwiches and secrets.

Oh, how I wish I had a best friend!

"I'll be your best friend!" Omama comforts me, one day when I come home from school, dejected and sad-eyed. For everyone has someone: Doina has Rodica. Mara has Lucica. Mariana has Natasha. Anca has Lenuta. Diana has Marica. Only Gabriela, whose hands are wet and slimy, is left over—and Mihaela, who can't even read or remember to do her homework.

"I mean a kid, Omama," I try to explain, "a girl from my class, someone I can play with!"

"Play with all your classmates, my darling. Be nice to everyone. Be everyone's friend!"

"You don't understand!" I shout, my face reddening. "I want a special friend. Someone I can count on. Someone I can trust."

My grandmother looks at me, alarmed. "Listen to me, Irinika. Always remember this: you can trust your mother, father, brother, Omama, Opapa, your Uncle Jack, Aunt Pupi, Coco and Rene—your dear ones who are close to you and who love you more than life. But a stranger? A stranger you can never trust."

"But I'm not talking about a stranger," I try to explain. "I'm talking about a classmate—someone I see every day when I go to school!"

"A classmate? Let me tell you about classmates," my grandmother says, her blue eyes filling with sadness. "When my oldest daughter, Eva, who now lives in Israel, God love her, was a young girl, she had a best friend, a very refined Romanian girl from an excellent family. She ate at our house. She slept at our house.

She was like another daughter to me. One day, after the war started, her friend approached Eva and asked her: 'Please don't talk to me at school anymore. And if you see me walking down the street, please don't say 'Hello!' I don't want people calling me a 'kike lover.'"

"What does that mean?" I ask, puzzled.

"Someone who likes Jews. This was a time when almost everyone hated us and wanted to destroy us. One horrible night in Bucharest, the Green Shirts—Romanian Nazis, may they burn in hell—rounded up hundreds of Jewish families, shoved them into the slaughterhouse, and butchered them the way you butcher cattle. In our town, the Greenshirts marched around the streets, shouting, 'Twenty-four more days until the death of the Jews! Twenty-three more days until the death of the Jews! Twenty-two more days until the death of the Jews,' and so on, every day, until the last day, when half-mad with fear, we tried to hide in the cellar, the only place we could think of. But God came to our aid at the last hour; their leader was such a blood thirsty maniac that even Hitler couldn't stand him and had him eliminated. Then another man came to power who had a Jewish mistress, and he let most of us live a little longer. Eventually, he would have had to give us up to be slaughtered, like the Hungarian Jews, had the Russian army not reached us in time. Still, there were plenty of Romanian Jews who were murdered. May the criminals suffer what their victims suffered!"

"But who wanted to kill the Jews? And why?"

"Oh, my precious darling," my grandmother sighs, drawing me close to her and kissing my forehead, making me feel safe again. "These things are hard to explain, and you'll have plenty of time to learn about them when you get older. Right now if I don't start cooking, we'll end up without dinner."

I tag after Omama to the pantry where she keeps her vegetables.

"I will tell you another story about classmates, though," she turns to me again, as I follow her into the kitchen and she starts peeling a large onion. "One day, when your Uncle Jack was in high school, all the boys in his class ganged up on him and almost beat him to death. God alone saved him."

"Why did they beat him?"

"Because he was Jewish! Luckily, it was a cold day, and he was wearing a thick furred vest under his shirt or they would have crushed his lungs. And his teacher, may his heart burst if he's still alive, watched and did nothing. The next day he even reported to the principal that Jack Abramovici, that impudent Jew, attacked all thirty of his classmates and should be expelled. That's why my darling, I tell you, be nice to all your classmates, be everyone's friend. As for trusting, only in your family can you place your trust, and in God!"

Furiously, Omama chops her onion into tiny little pieces. Tears drop down her cheeks.

"Omama, am I a Jew?"

"Yes, dear, your mother is Jewish, which means you are also Jewish. But people don't need to know that. With your blond hair and blue eyes and Romanian last name, no one would suspect it."

"You mean I should keep it a secret?"

"I wouldn't talk about it, my darling, if I were you. They say that it doesn't matter anymore, that we're all brothers now, but deep inside many of them haven't changed, still call us 'kikes' behind our backs, and still blame us for everything! I go to the market, I stand in line, I hear what people say!"

This, then, I decide, will be a secret that I will not share with my best friend, even after I get one. When I find a best friend, I will tell her about the little kitten who shows up at our back door every morning for the plate of milk I sneak out of the kitchen. And I will tell her about the special game my brother and I play every night, after everyone goes to sleep, when we take our flashlights into the long, dark corridor leading to the kitchen, and pretend we're building a secret tunnel to escape from the dungeon where our enemies have trapped us. My brother knows all about prisons and dungeons and how to escape from them from a book called *The Count of Monte Cristo*. I want to read it, too, but Sorin says I'm too young and should stick to fairy tales.

◆ ◆ ◆

Marica Serban is the only girl in my class who is as tall as I am. She is beautiful. Her hair is thick and brown and falls in rich, dark waves over her slender shoulders. She has glowing red cheeks, large, brown, mischievous eyes, and dark, arched, eyebrows (not like mine, two thin, straight, pale lines). Her nose turns up. Her eyes sparkle. Her chin dimples. Her uniform is always neat, her pinafore freshly starched, her white headband gleaming in the sun. She is funny and clever and bouncy. When the teacher calls on her, she always knows the answer. She reads well, with expression, almost as well as I do, and she's even better than me at math. And she has a lovely voice. The teacher always picks her to sing the solos. Marica has long, thin, slender fingers. She is a concert pianist. Every day after school, she walks over to the music academy for her lessons. She wins competitions. Someday, she'll be famous. Why on earth did she pick Diana for her best friend?

Diana has a long face, disheveled black hair which always pulls out of her long, coarse braid, and droopy, dull eyes. She looks like a cocker spaniel. She nods her head at everything Marica says and blinks her eyes and laughs like a seal. When she reads out loud, she stammers and stutters, and when the teacher gives her a math problem, she stares at her, open-mouthed.

Diana follows Marica around like a shadow. She never gets sick. She escapes the flu, the chicken pox, the measles, the mumps! But I keep waiting, waiting for my chance.

◆ ◆ ◆

Because I am the tallest girl, I have the longest legs. I'm the fastest runner in my class. The boys can never catch me. Today after school, the boys are chasing us and catch everyone except Marica and me, who are ahead and keep on running. The boys are yelling. They will pull yellow strands from my hair and brown ones from hers to decorate their caps! Marica and I run faster and faster, and she yells out, "Follow me, let's take my street!"—and we keep on running until we find ourselves in front of an apartment building, and Marica pulls me into the lobby where we hide behind the door. It's a beautiful lobby, with marble floors and an elevator. A man gets off and glares at me. I'm afraid that he will throw us out, but Marica reassures me: "It's O.K.! I live here."

Cautiously, we peek through the glass doors. The boys are gone. We smile at each other triumphantly and say, "goodbye." Once outside, I look at the street sign and realize, with a thrill, that this is also my street. "Aviator Iliescu" is the street where last month, "the movers" (as my mother calls them) transferred our things from our large old house into a small apartment. I have not seen it yet and have no idea where it is. My mother says it's a tiny place, full to the brim with our possessions. "Right now it's a warehouse," she explained, "two tiny attic rooms crammed with furniture. If you see it now, you'll hate it. Wait until I sell some of the furniture, paint the walls, sew some drapes, cheer it up and make it livable, and then I'll take you there."

I walk up and down the street, which stretches for several long blocks, carefully examining each building. There are no homes with gardens here. Only apartment buildings, some of them two or three levels high, others much higher. I decide that Marica's apartment building, small, freshly painted, and ivy covered, is by far the nicest. But I remember my mother saying that our apartment was somewhere way up high, up three long flights of stairs, and that there was no elevator. Which one is it?

This neighborhood is full of children. Boys are playing soccer in the middle of the street. Girls are jumping rope and playing hop scotch. Several small children are playing in the mud. One little girl's dress is torn, and she is sitting on the curb eating a discarded watermelon rind that is crawling with ants. Yuck! Why isn't anyone looking after her?

I can't wait to move. Every evening after dinner at Omama's house, after Giunica bathes us, helps us with our homework and reads us our bedtime story, she goes to our new apartment and works on it. She sleeps there and returns early in the morning to help us get ready for school before she goes to work. Late at night, I miss her and worry about her. "Please take me with you! Take me home!" I plead with her every night. As much as I love Omama, I don't want to sleep at the foot of her bed any more. "Please, God," I pray to Omama's God, the God of the Jews, "let Giunica take us home, and let Marica be my best friend!"

◆ ◆ ◆

The rooms are small. The roof is slanted. Instead of normal windows, there are many tiny square ones all along the wall. That's because this used to be an attic, my mother explains. She has sewn flowered pink curtains which cover up the windows entirely. I find our things from the other house which remind me of our old life: the dining room table where the four of us had our meals, the bed where my mother and father used to sleep, the Persian rug, the crystal ashtrays, the glass vase, the painting of the wagon with the two gypsies that used to frighten me so.

"Why did they keep our things for so long?" I hear my brother ask my mother in the other room.

"To search through everything, I guess…"

"Who?" I break in. "What are you talking about?"

"Nothing," snaps my brother. "Mind your own business."

Always secrets! I hate secrets!

"Did you find Ancuta?" my mother asks me. The baby doll my Uncle Jack gave me for my third birthday. There she is, lying on the bed, her head on my old, embroidered pillow.

"The movers broke one of her arms," my mother explains, "but I fixed it! I even washed and ironed her clothes!"

I grab Ancuta and cradle her in my arms, my poor abandoned baby. I will never let them take her to the orphanage again! From now on, she'll stay with me forever, I swear to her, kissing her red cheeks.

◆ ◆ ◆

When the bell rings, I follow Marica and Diana. I walk behind them through the school yard until Diana goes off in a different direction. Then, I catch up to Marica. "Guess what?" I announce. "I now live on your street."

We start walking together. I tell her about my doll, Ancuta, the biggest doll anyone has ever seen, as big as a baby.

"You want to come over and play with her?" I ask.

"I have to go home and practice my piano."

"Just for a little while," I insist. "I live right down the street from you."

Marica is tempted. Though she is not allowed to go anywhere without permission, she breaks her parents' rules and follows me to my building, which is less than a block away from where she lives, and up the three flights of stairs to our small apartment. When I take my key out of my book bag, she is astonished.

"What? There's no one home?"

"My mother works and doesn't get home until four o'clock. My brother and I have our own keys. He's in the fourth grade. He should be home soon."

"At my house, there's always either my nanny, who takes care of me and my baby brother, or my maid." She is excited at the thought that there are no adults around to tell us what to do.

"Oh, my gosh, she's beautiful," she exclaims when I take her to see Ancuta, displayed in all her splendor on my bed, sitting on the embroidered pillow like a queen on her throne.

"She's almost as big as Ovidiu, my baby brother!"

I demonstrate how the doll's eyes open and close and how, when you turn her upside down, she cries, "Wahhh!" just like a real baby. I let her hold Ancuta for as long as she wants.

"I've never seen anything like this!" Marica exclaims. "Where do you get a doll like this?"

"My Uncle Jack brought it back for me from Germany."

"Do you think that the next time he goes there, you could ask him to bring another doll like that for me? I'm sure my mother could give him the money."

"Sure, when he goes again, I'll ask him," I promise. But since my father left for Russia, Uncle Jack hasn't been on any more trips abroad. Still, there's no reason why I couldn't ask him if he were to go there again.

"I'm so glad you moved here," Marica tells me, as she is about to leave. "My father won't let me play with any of the kids on the street. He says they're little hooligans. Soon, he thinks we will be given our own house with a garden in a nicer neighborhood, and there, he promises, I'll be allowed to play outside."

"I hope you don't move for a long time!" I yell after her, as she dashes down the stairs.

"Me too!"

I close the door slowly, in ecstasy, intoxicated by the sound of Marica's voice, and her laughter.

◆ ◆ ◆

Standing outside Marica's door, waiting for someone to answer the bell, I'm excited and nervous. This Sunday afternoon I've been invited to go with Marica to a concert. Her father's chauffeur is going to drive us there and bring us back. I have never been to Marica's house before. I have never met her parents. I have never been to a concert.

The maid invites me in and asks me to sit in the "salon." Marica's not quite ready yet. The room is large and elegantly furnished. It reminds me of the "salon" from our old house. A big black piano, like the one we sold, sits by the large, opened window. Marica, wearing a red velvet dress, walks in, followed by her mother, a short, plump, attractive woman with dark hair and creamy, white skin. She is wearing an elegant, low-necked, black silk dress. I remember Marica telling me that they are having guests this evening. "*Placintas cu brinza*," I guess, inhaling the rich smells of sweet cheese pastries.

"What a beautiful dress!" Mrs. Serban exclaims, as I am introduced to her. I'm wearing a mauve chiffon dress with full skirts that puff up over a crinoline. It is one of my cousin Zizi's dresses that my Aunt Eva regularly sends us from Israel. Nothing like that, my mother says, can be found in Romania.

Marica's mother seems to think so too, for she examines my dress carefully.

"Where do you get a dress like that?" she asks.

"It was a present from my aunt. I'm not sure where she got it," I answer, trying to be as truthful as possible.

"Irina's so lucky!" Marica tells her mother. Then she continues to chatter on in a different language. She begs her for something. Her mother says, "No." Marica begs and pleads. Her mother refuses. Their voices rise. They argue.

"Stop that damned noise!" a male voice bellows from the other room. A tall, very handsome man with Marica's thick, brown hair, large, dark eyes and dimpled chin walks in, buttoning the coat to his jacket.

"What the hell are you jabbering about in that cursed tongue? Don't you speak Romanian? Have you forgotten I'm home?" His rage makes him oblivious to my presence. Embarrassed, Mrs. Serban tries to make up for his rudeness:

"This is Marica's new friend, Irina Eremia. She's in Marica's class and lives down the street. Marica has seen a lovely doll at her house that Irina's uncle brought back from Germany, and she's been pestering me to find out if we could get one like it for her."

"Germany! Which Germany? East or West?"

"I don't know," I falter.

"What does he do there?"

"He's an engineer. Sometimes, when he travels there on business, he brings us back toys."

"What's your uncle's name?"

"Jack," I whisper. I know from my grandmother that his last name, Abramovici, is a Jewish name, and I have a feeling that Marica's father would not like that.

"Jack what?" Mr. Serban insists.

But at that very moment the maid appears, followed by the driver.

"You'd better go now, girls, or you'll be late," Mrs. Serban saves me from having to answer. "Have a good time, and take good care of each other."

"Thank you, Mr. and Mrs. Serban, for inviting me to go with Marica to this concert. I am very much looking forward to it." Finally, I remembered my manners.

Marica's mother looks pleased.

I feel very important sitting in the front row with Marica, watching the concert. The music is lovely, but I wish I knew as much about it as much as Marica does. She knows the names of the composers and has played some of the pieces on her piano. As she listens, her fingers flutter on an invisible piano key. What happened, I wonder, to the big black piano under the window overlooking our garden in old house? Is another little girl practicing her scales on it now?

After the concert, we go across the street to the pastry shop, and Marica treats us to ice cream and cookies, while her father's chauffeur waits for us outside.

"What language were you speaking to your mother?" I finally ask the question that had been on my mind all evening.

"Hungarian," Marica answers. "My mother taught it to me when I was young but my father hates it."

"Why?"

"Because he doesn't understand a word of it. So he thinks we're telling secrets. We try not to speak it in front of him, but sometimes we forget. Silly, isn't it?"

She tries to laugh. But I know that she is still embarrassed about her father's behavior.

"If your mother's Hungarian that means you are Hungarian, too, right?" I ask her.

"No, not at all! Just because I speak Hungarian doesn't mean I'm not Romanian." Marica seems offended by what I have just said.

I wish I could explain and tell her about my parents: my father is Romanian, but my mother is Jewish which, my grandmother says, also makes me Jewish. I also want to tell her that my grandmother asked me to keep this a secret because many people hate Jews, but that since Marica is my best friend, I know I can share this with her. I am tempted to say all this, but for the time being, I keep quiet. Still, I have a feeling that Marica is the kind of friend you can trust.

◆ ◆ ◆

Diana has found another friend—Gabriela with the runny nose and slimy hands. Marica and I walk with our arms around each other, share our lunches, skip rope together during recess, and stick our tongues out at the boys. All winter vacation long she comes over to my house, and we play together under our New Year's tree. (I'm the only kid on the block Marica is allowed to visit). We gather the newly fallen white powder on our windowpanes, open our tiny attic windows and pelt the street children with snowballs. Laughing, we hide behind the flowered curtains as our victims look around, bewildered. My brother lets us dress up his old doll, Raducu (Ancuta's counterpart), like Old Frosty. We glue a beard on him made out of cotton balls and dress him up in Ovidiu's red sweater. With Raducu in one arm and Ancuta in the other, we take turns pulling each other up and down the street on Marica's new sled. When my mother tells us that we can't afford gifts this year, I tell her I don't mind and mean it. We have our own place now. And Marica Serban is my best friend. I don't need any other presents this year!

◆ ◆ ◆

One morning, before spring elections, my teacher draws me aside and asks me to nominate Marica to be the president of our class. I'm proud of my task.

"I nominate Marica Serban to be our class president," I declare, in a loud, clear voice, "because she is a diligent student, a helpful classmate, and a thoughtful friend."

"All those in favor, raise your hand," the teacher commands.

All hands go up.

"Anyone opposed?"

All hands stay down.

At the school wide elections held in our large assembly hall later in the afternoon, Marica, now our new class president, seconds the nomination of the girl who will become the president of our school: a sixth grader who is also the granddaughter of Premier Gheorghe Gheorghiu-Dej. Marica has only met her once at a birthday party, but the teacher has told her what to say: As a second grader, Marica declares, she considers this sixth grader as a model of the kind of dedicated student, friend and young pioneer she herself would like to become in future years. Everyone claps.

"Those in favor, raise your hands," the principal commands. All hands go up.

"Anyone against, raise your hand." All hands stay down.

I am happy that the student body president is a girl and that my best friend, Marica, got to nominate her. But at the May 1st parade, when all school children march before our country's leaders, I'm suddenly struck by the injustice of it all. The president of our school gets to walk up the stairs to the Central Committee's high platform and give President Gheorghe Gheorghiu-Dej a bouquet of flowers. He smiles, hugs her and takes her on his lap. But he is her grandfather! She gets to hug him all the time!

◆ ◆ ◆

One afternoon, at the end of May, Marica tells me in a very excited voice that she has a secret to share with me. The principal of our school is coming over to her house for dinner. He knows that Marica is a gifted young pianist and wants to hear her play. Marica's parents have told her that she must keep quiet about this so as not to make the other children jealous. But Marica knows that I, her best friend, will be happy for her. And I am.

Marica tells me that Ana, the maid, is preparing a sumptuous feast: meatball soup, roast goose and red cabbage and *clatite* (crepes) with home made cherry preserves for dessert. Knowing how much I love *clatite*, Marica promises to wrap one up in a napkin and bring it to school for me the next morning.

◆ ◆ ◆

I stand in front of Marica's building expecting that we will walk to school together as usual. I can't wait to find out about the principal's visit. And I'm looking forward to my *clatita*! But for some reason, Marica doesn't come down. I get to school late, convinced she must be sick. To my surprise, she's already sitting at her desk, and I get in trouble for being late. During the break, I rush up to her:

"What happened?"

Marica looks uncomfortable and embarrassed.

"My father's chauffeur drove me to school today. He'll be taking me to school sometimes from now on."

But school is only two blocks away. I don't understand. Anyway, I ask:

"Can't I meet you at your house and drive with you?"

"No! My parents want me to go alone," she snaps at me. Then she walks away. Why is she mad at me? What have I done?

"Marica! Marica!" I try to catch up with her. "Did the principal like the way you played the piano for him?"

"Shut up!" Marica's brown eyes are flashing at me furiously. Oh, my God! I have just betrayed her secret. I forgot she had forbidden me to mention the principal's visit. I look around, horrified. But no, it doesn't seem like anyone has heard. We're safe.

"I'm sorry," I whisper in her ear. "I forgot."

Marica ignores me and moves away. She joins Diana and Lucia, who are skipping rope on the grass.

After school she leaves as soon as the bell rings and no matter how fast I walk, I can't catch up with her.

I throw myself on the bed, unable to stop crying. I betrayed Marica, my best friend. It was an accident. But she doesn't know that. I must explain. I must be patient. When she hears me, she'll understand.

Again Marica walks away from me when I try to sit next to her on our bench. I'm left to eat my sandwich alone. After school, Marica's chauffeur picks up Marica and Diana. Where is he taking them, I wonder, sick with grief.

◆ ◆ ◆

"What's the matter with you? What happened? Why aren't you eating?" Giunica wants to know.

I wish I could keep it to myself, but the words gush out along with the tears.

"I'm not at all surprised, my dear. From what I hear, Marica's father is becoming quite a big shot."

"What's that got to do with it?"

"He's an important man now. Too important for us."

"I'm friends with Marica, not her father!"

I lock myself in the bathroom and try to fill the tub so Sorin and Gina won't hear me cry. I end up using all the hot water, and they get angry with me anyway.

◆ ◆ ◆

"Dear Marica," I write. "I am so very sorry. Please forgive me for opening my mouth without thinking. It was an accident. A dumb, silly mistake. I swear that I did not do it on purpose. You are the best friend I have ever had. I'm enclosing the purple dress you love so much. I want you to have it. Please, let's make up and be friends again!" I add my favorite red crayon, my new white ribbon and the hairbrush that Marica always borrows from me. I make a parcel out of newspaper. If this isn't enough, I might even offer her Ancuta. Marica's place is bigger, and she'd never be left home alone. Anyway, I assure myself, Ancuta is only a doll, while Marica is a real friend!

"Have you no pride? No shame? No self-respect?" I wake up to find the dress, the crayon, the newspaper, scattered all over the floor where Giunica, in her anger, must have flung it. She has found the parcel on my night stand and is now having a fit:

"Never, ever beg someone's friendship, or try to buy affection with a bribe! Are you my daughter? How could my daughter humiliate herself like that!"

My mother is very proud. She, too, has friends who won't speak to her. Sometimes, when we walk in the park, we see people whom we used to know, and they avoid our eyes and pretend they've never seen us before. Giunica's back stiffens, her neck stretches up, her head tilts back and she marches on like a soldier at the May 1st parade. Once, when I saw one of our old neighbors on the street and shouted, "Good afternoon, Mr. Salceanu!" before he had a chance to pass us by,

Giunica was furious with me. "When we're together, my dear girl, don't you dare greet anyone until I greet them first!" she warned me.

It is easy for her to be proud. She is all grown up already. She doesn't have to eat lunch alone or walk home by herself or die of shame when no one picks her for a game or wants to hold hands with her when the teacher tells the class to line up, two by two.

◆ ◆ ◆

I write the letter over on a piece of paper in my notebook while sitting on the toilet during our snack break. I put it on Marica's desk before she comes back from jumping rope with Diana. I follow a few steps behind her as she walks home, my letter in her hand. I know she knows I'm there. When she gets to her building, she stops and turns around to look at me. Her face is wet with tears. I fly to her, my arms wide open. But she recoils. I barely catch my balance and manage not to trip.

"We can't be friends anymore. I'm sorry. It's nothing that you did," Marica whispers. I can barely hear her.

"Why then?"

"My parents won't allow it!"

"But why?"

"The principal said your father's in prison. Your father's a criminal. I can't play with you again." Marica runs into her building and slams the fancy door in my face before I have a chance to yell out, "Liar!" Only the doorman hears me.

◆ ◆ ◆

I'm doing my best to fall asleep. But the sheets are rough, the covers keep falling off, and I'm squeezed against the wall.

"What's wrong with you?" Giunica finally asks me.

"Nothing."

"Why are you tossing and turning like that? What's bothering you?"

"Nothing."

"You're still upset over Marica, aren't you?"

"No," I lie.

My mother sighs and sits up. She props herself against her pillow. I can see that she's preparing to make me one of her lectures. I turn against the wall, but there's no escape.

"You, my darling, are a sincere, trusting little creature. Unfortunately, most people in the world aren't like you. The sooner you realize that, the better you'll be able to protect yourself from getting hurt."

"But how do you know who will help you and who will hurt you? Sometimes people can seem one way and then turn out another!" I cry. I want to keep on crying, but I know that if I start, I'll never stop.

"Don't ever rely on anyone beside your family to help you! Yes, it's nice to make friends—believe me, with your looks and charm you'll find plenty as you get older—and you'll be able to laugh with them and joke with them and play ball with them and dance with them and go on hikes and picnics and walks in the park. But confide in them your innermost thoughts and secrets and problems? Never!"

"But why? Are my relatives the only good people in the world? Is everyone else bad?"

"No, of course not. Only most of the time, it's hard to tell who's who. People you think are your friends might suddenly turn around and stab you in the back. But there are also times when people surprise you. I'll never forget that when I was growing up in Braila, we had a neighbor, a police captain, whom we thought was our worst enemy: our families were always fighting over some ivy separating our properties, and I even think we got into a law suit. One day, when I was about your age, I decided to go by myself to the beach at the Danube river. At the time, there were strict laws forbidding Jews from going there."

"Why?" I interrupt her.

"The Nazis were in power. We were not allowed to take trains or boats, go to movies, beaches, parks, museums. If I had obeyed all those rules, I would have died of boredom. It was hot, so I went to the beach. A girl from my school, someone I never knew wished me ill, reported me to a guard. He was about to arrest me. I would have been sent to Transnistria, and no one would have heard of me again."

"What is Transnistria?"

"A concentration camp. A place where many Romanian Jews died during the War. Just as he was about to take me away, my neighbor, the police captain, who also happened to be at the beach, came to my rescue. He offered to take me to the police station himself. But that's not where he took me. He took me to a pastry shop, bought me an ice cream, and took me home. My parents couldn't believe it. Here was a man we had always considered our enemy, and he saved my life! So, no, not everyone outside our family is bad. And most people aren't all good or all bad. But there are situations which bring out the bad in people. Because you can never truly know what lurks hidden behind a stranger's smile, you should never give anyone the power to hurt you. It is one of life's hardest lessons, but one you must learn as soon as you can. Had your father learned it, he would still be here with us, instead of far away…

"He was sent far away because he trusted his friends?" I ask, confused.

My mother takes a deep breath. She is about to tell me something. My heart starts beating. I'm afraid to hear it. "Look, Galuska. There are many things you are still too young to understand. For now, this is all you need to know about making friends: Develop your self, your mind, your interests, your talents, and friends will come to you. Friends will come to you when they need you, and not when you need them. Always show the world your smile, never your tears."

◆ ◆ ◆

I toss and turn, unable to fall asleep. Who are the bad people, who are the enemies who are spreading lies about my father? Who are the false friends who sent him far away? Although I haven't seen him for a long time, I can still remember, when I concentrate, the soft, gentle sound of his voice, as he sang to us: "Somnooorоase…Pasaarele!" When my father returns from Russia, he will put on his white uniform with all his epaulets and medals and walk over with me to the Serbans' apartment. He will ring their doorbell. Marica's father will stand at attention and salute my father. "I'm General Ion Eremia, back from Russia where I have been sent on an important mission," Neclo will tell him, in his strong, deep voice. "Do you know that I could have you arrested for the lies you've been spreading about me?" Mr. Serban will stutter and stammer and shake and apologize. My father will slam the door in his face. Marica will know what a terrible mistake she has made. She will run down the stairs and beg me to be her friend again. But it will be too late. Gently, I will tell her that I have a real best friend now, a true best friend, a friend I trust will be my friend forever. I fall asleep dreaming about her.

11

Ion: The Coughed Prayer

This April, 1962, is the cruelest month of my imprisonment. Since my return to the underworld after my close brush with freedom, I have been fighting a downhill battle against despair. Through the damp fall and icy winter, my state has gotten progressively worse. My former weapons for survival—poetry, recitation, literary music, glimpses of "the green island"—are losing their power to rescue me. Spring, with its normally uplifting signs of renewal, only hurls me deeper into the jaws of depression.

I am tortured by questions and doubts. Was I wrong? Was I foolish to give up my own happiness to fight for the happiness of others? Night after night, I agonize, wide awake, about my wife and children, gnawed by grief and guilt over the suffering I've caused them. I can't eat. My stomach growls but recoils, nauseous at the sight of food. I can't work. My thoughts refuse to focus, but slip and trip and scatter in a myriad of directions. After my white, tormented nights, I can't keep my eyes open during the day. Exhausted, hunched over my stool, I doze off. The guard bursts in spreading blows and curses. I must not sleep! I must not rest my back! Every moment is a torture. One dark thought invades my mind and begins to obsess me: "I must end it all!"

In my more lucid moments, I realize that I'm treading on a dangerous path and that if I don't get off it soon, I will find myself trapped with no exit. I decide to turn to my astronomer friend for help.

"I think I am beginning to go mad," I tap to him. "I can't eat, I can't sleep, I can't work. Every second is a torment, and all I can think about is ending it all!"

"What about your poems? Have you stopped composing them?"

"Don't you understand, man? I can't concentrate, I tell you!" I complain, desperately.

"Be patient, Five. I'm trying to help you. For how long, exactly, have you been incarcerated here?"

"For almost three years."

"And how many poems have you produced thus far?"

For the first time, I add them up.

"Six," I tell him.

"That's not much for three years of solitude and inactivity."

"I suppose not," I admit.

"How many days did you fill up with the process of composing them?"

Again I have to consider carefully. Slowly, I make my calculations.

"Up until now, I would say, between thirty to forty days total."

"That's not much for three years of silence and immobility," the astronomer repeats himself. "What did you do with the rest of your time?"

"Do? What could I do? We're not allowed to do anything! What on earth do you do?" I challenge him, annoyed.

"Mornings I work on my treatise concerning the distribution of the galaxies and the expansion of the universe. Afternoons I teach a two-hour course in theoretical math…"

"You teach math to the other prisoners through Morse code?" I ask him, surprised.

"Certainly not! Do you think anyone here would risk a broken back for the love of mathematics? I teach an imaginary student, of course. Morse code conversations I reserve for the hour after curfew, before going to sleep."

For a minute, my finger remains poised in the air, unsure of what to tap. I am overwhelmed by admiration for this man who has managed to structure his time even in hell.

"Obviously, you are a very disciplined person," I finally reply.

"I have no choice but to be. Only by organizing my activities and creating a strict, continuous, daily routine, do I manage to prevent myself from going mad. And I'm by no means the only one here to do this. Why don't you try, right now, to make up a daily schedule for yourself?"

Moved by his concern for me and inspired by his example, I consent. I gather up all my efforts and try to come up with a plan. This takes me some time, as my torpid mind works at a much slower rate than usual.

◆ ◆ ◆

"So, what have you come up with?" the astronomer presses me an hour later.

"How does this sound: mornings, before breakfast, I'll listen to my 'literary music'—favorite symphonies, arias, ballads and popular songs which I play in my mind. Then, until lunch time I will work on my writing…"

"Your poems you mean?" he asks me.

"Yes, and even some prose, perhaps."

"Why, 'perhaps'? Weren't you put in here for writing a book? That was prose, not poetry, if I'm not mistaken."

"Yes, it was a satirical novel called *Gulliver in the Land of Lies.*"

"So why not write another novel? Something longer than poetry, something that will sustain your interest and concentration day after day?"

"Before my trip back to Malmaison I had been considering something like that myself," I confess. "But I hadn't quite committed myself to it, and then I was taken to Bucharest and after that..."

"Commit to it now! You have plenty of time. And no excuses!"

"All right. Maybe I'll try. What I had in mind was a confessional novel, a kind of memoir, a book, written in the first person detailing everything that I am experiencing in prison but also interspersing reminiscences, essays, meditations..."

"Something in the manner of Marcel Proust?"

"No, something in the manner of Ion Eremia!"

"Excellent! You've got a big ego. That's a very good sign. Go on. I'd like to hear the rest of your schedule. So what do you plan to do after our delicious lunch has been served?"

"I plan to spend half an hour savoring my dessert: 'the enchanting green island' I have told you about. Then, until dinner, I will work on my book," I tell him, committing myself to starting the book on the spot. "In the evening, before curfew, I will spend one hour reciting poetry and another listening to music. After curfew, I hope to talk to you and maybe even my other neighbor, if he ever decides to answer my calls."

"Very good. Your program is richer and more varied than mine," the astronomer encourages me. "And that, of course, is to be expected. I am a mere mathematician, while you are poet, novelist and musician," my neighbor flatters me.

"Your work, on the other hand, has concrete, scientific basis, while mine depends solely on my inspiration," I remind him.

"Neither of us can estimate the value of our work to the outside world. Its principal value is to us, in keeping us alive."

"You're right. I will keep you posted on my progress and even occasionally consult your opinion."

"That, I'm afraid, is worthless. I know nothing about literary matters. In any case, good luck."

◆ ◆ ◆

I feel much better now, after my conversation with the astronomer. How quickly he penetrated to the core of my problem! All my life, from grade school to the military academy, all the long years of military training followed by the many more years of practicing my profession, I have led a structured, organized, productive existence. My daily work schedule was rarely interrupted by anything other than holidays and vacations. But now, suddenly, I am being deprived of a most basic human need: the need to work. It is part of my essential nature, as a homo faber, to actualize myself through purposeful activity. In the absence of such activity, I feel useless, debased, dehumanized.

Up until recently, I have somewhat resisted by creating work for myself. But this work was irregular, sporadic, haphazard. I composed poems to chase away depressive states. I recited the poems of others in moments of crisis. I listened to "literary music" whenever the mood struck me. But I never structured a real schedule for myself and tried to stick to it faithfully day after day.

I am proud of my six poems. But surely I am capable of much more—of a longer project, a book that will enable me to synthesize the incredible experience I am now living. But will I be able to write it without pen or paper? It is one thing to compose a poem, another to structure an entire book. Will I manage to impose harmony and unity on its various parts, or will I end up with a series of disjointed fragments? And is my memory powerful enough to record that much? What if, while working on the second chapter, I forget the first?

My thoughts turn to a time, during my first year of high school, when I was required to learn lengthy biology lessons by rote. I remember how hard it was at first and how I toiled for hours to memorize each lesson, word by word, sentence by sentence. But gradually, after repeated and sustained effort, I managed to memorize my lessons after only one reading. My memory had been trained, and once trained, it did the job much faster. The same thing, I promise myself, will happen to me now. The more I write, the more I memorize, the easier the process will get. Let me get started, let me stick to my schedule, and all the other difficulties will resolve themselves along the way.

What kind of book will I write? In large strokes, I draw up a plan. My book will trace my struggle for survival in hell. It will be loosely structured. Present experiences will be intermingled with past memories, observations, reflections and poems. I don't quite yet know how exactly it will develop. This is a book that is being lived, not invented. The last chapter of my book will correspond with my last chapter of residence in hell. Hopefully, there won't be too many chapters!

◆ ◆ ◆

For over a month I have been working, hour after hour, day after day, on the first chapter of my book. This chapter, which I have entitled, "Theater of the Absurd," covers the events which took place between October 1958, when I was arrested, and December 1959, when I was brought to this prison. It is a very long chapter—around thirty typed pages in my estimation.

Prose is much harder to memorize than poetry. Now I must think not in terms of lines and stanzas, but in terms of sentences, paragraphs and sections of various length and structure. At first the rhythm of my creation was slow, but now my inspiration seems richer, and I'm starting to pick up speed. My guardian angel is my survival instinct which orders my subconscious: "Write, if you care to live!" I write, a gun to my head, impelled by necessity.

I must admit, not without some shame, that so far in my life I have written only when driven by circumstance, rather than by my love of language or my devotion to art. I wrote my first book out of an irresistible need to fight the despotism of communism, and I am writing my second book out of a desperate need to fight madness and death.

And yet, from a very young age, I have loved the melody of words and longed to twist and turn them to give shape to my dreams. But I never had the time. How hard it is for a man to find a month—or even a week—of peace and quiet in his life in which to express himself in one poem or short story!

In high school, where my teachers discovered I had talent and encouraged me to write, I had to cram my brain with math, physics, natural science, geography, Latin, French and German, knowing that out of the six hundred who started only forty would manage to graduate. The rest would get lost along the way, to become postal clerks, railway clerks, bookkeepers, and end up spending their lives at small desk jobs, a fate I was determined to avoid. I was a poor man's son. My father convinced me that at military school I would get an excellent, free education, and an assured, time-honored profession. I was hoping to satisfy my passion for literature after I graduated from the military academy. Unfortunately, my destiny carried me, like a wandering Jew, through a series of different jobs, very few of which were suited to my temperament. I served as an officer at the front, as a building supervisor of semi-permanent fortifications for bridges and highways, as a transmissions officer, as chief editor of the army's newspaper, as director of military sport events, as coordinator of army theatrical production, as construction manager of permanent fortifications, bridges and airports, as general of the Romanian Army, as Vice Minister of Defense… Along the way, I got married, had children, gave lectures, made speeches, participated in conferences, attended social events, etc. Somehow I never found the time either for poetry or for prose. To be honest, I did try occasionally, while on an isolated work site, to compose a few verses, here and there, but the technical and administrative problems which I had to confront never gave me much peace.

Now, in my mid-forties, I had to reach hell, like Orpheus, in order to fulfill my creative dreams. But unlike Orpheus, who entered hell of his own free will to save his beloved wife, Eurydice, I've been thrust here by the Mighty Gods—because one of my songs sounded unpleasant to their most delicate High Ears.

Today I sing for entirely different reasons than those which moved the son of Apollo and Clio. He, of divine origin, made music to delight Gods, men and beasts; his motives were altruistic. I, a mere mortal, compose words for my own pleasure, to soothe and delight myself; my motives are selfish. An ill-fitting admission coming from a man who claims to struggle and suffer for the good of humanity!

◆ ◆ ◆

It is the beginning of June, and I write as if I were possessed. I am writing almost as fast as if I had pencil and paper. My devotion to the Goddesses Calliope and Polymnia is so powerful that sometimes I disregard my schedule and give up on literary music and poetry recitation in favor of working on my book. This state of creative intensity I have experienced once before, when I wrote *Gulliver In The Land Of Lies*. Only then, I wrote in parks, cafes or at home, where my power of concentration was often weakened by all the distracting activities around me. Here, no one can stop me from writing what I want and when I want. I can write even in my bed, after curfew. I carry no burdens. I am free of the struggle for my daily bread, of professional, family or social responsibilities. Other than those moments of painful longing when my thoughts wander to my loved ones, nothing can distract me from my creative task. In a sense I am in a state of absolute liberty. Never in my life have I felt more free. Suddenly my tomb has turned into a tower, a subterranean tower, perfectly isolated from the world of men.

◆ ◆ ◆

Finally, after a long quarantine, the neighbor on my right has decided to give me a vote of confidence and answer my signals. I have been aware of his presence for almost eight months because of his frequent, tumultuous, coughing spells. Inmates here are not allowed to cough, so I suspect my neighbor must suffer from some serious illness. I introduce myself and tell him my story. Then I invite him to do the same:

"With whom do I have the honor?" I ask him.

"With Adrian Sulutiu, former parochial priest and professor at the theological seminary in Blaj.

"How did you get here, father?"

"With chains around my legs, son."

"Same as I did, father."

"All of us have come here with anklets and bracelets, as we are all considered dangerous criminals."

"So what did you do wrong, father?"

"Me? Nothing. The wrong has been done to me."

"How's that?"

"I was condemned to twenty years because I refused to abandon my parishioners and also because I helped a Christian in trouble."

"And who was that Christian?"

"What difference does that make? To me, he was my brother and it was my duty to help him."

"And why did the authorities mind?"

"Because he was not only an anti-communist charged with sabotage but also a Hungarian."

"What did that have to do with it? Twenty years for religious faith and for helping a Christian according to your canonical vows seems unusually cruel, even for our ruthless tyrants."

"Since the man I helped got life imprisonment, I got a sentence close to his. Especially as I cursed my persecutors in open court!"

"Why did you do that?"

"Why not? The judges knew that a Christian priest could not have done otherwise. Yet the prosecutor dared to argue that I shouldn't have helped him because besides being a saboteur he was also a Hungarian and the Hungarians are our enemies, today, yesterday and forevermore, as every Romanian knows."

"And what did you say to that?"

"I said that even though there are plenty of Hungarians in Blaj, I never noticed that they were our enemies. The man I helped had been my childhood friend. That is why he came to me in the first place. If I had been in trouble, he would have done the same for me."

Our conversation was suddenly interrupted by one of the priest's violent coughing fits. I waited for some time and then asked him, concerned:

"Are you ill, father?"

He didn't answer me for a while and then, finally, just as I was about to try again, he tapped:

"I'll be better after I get some sleep, son. Good night. God be with you."

◆ ◆ ◆

We are reaching the end of 1962. From that other world, from which I am separated by great stone walls and guards armed with rifles ready to shoot, I hear the festive sounds, muffled by the whistling north wind and the howling snowstorm, of carolers celebrating the approaching New Year with songs, cheers, yells, cracking whips and ringing bells.

This winter is as merciless as all the other winters that hit these parts. But now I don't care about the wind and the snowstorm or the cold that penetrates deep into the bone. I no longer fear that maddening suffering when despair and depression push me into the arms of non-being. Now I am happy, and my happiness protects me against everything. I am happy because for the first time in my life I am living out my adolescent dream: I am writing, writing, writing…

I write on an imaginary notebook on clear white pages. First I jot down an outline of the chapter I have in mind. Then I work myself up into a euphoric state by "listening" to one of my favorite pieces of "literary music." Then I write as if I were possessed, my imaginary pen dashing madly across the page. The faster I write, the more fertile my thoughts, images and metaphors. I am now able to memorize my text the very first time I write it; my mind registers it instantaneously, like a dictaphone. (After disciplined, daily practice, my power of memorization has grown in a spectacular way). After this agitated state, a calm follows, when I turn my pages back, revise and polish them.

I no longer write, a gun to my head, out of necessity. I write with passion. I write with pleasure. I write from an overwhelming and violent love, a first love, a late love. I am like an old maid who finds out for the first time, from an accident of destiny, the frenzy of lovemaking, the ecstasy of orgasm, the wonder of maternity.

Occasionally I take brief "vacations" from my book and indulge in poetry. My thoughts wander to the first time I fell in love, and to an enchanting night of passion under the stars accompanied by the faraway sounds of a violin:

A violin cries
Under the moon's spell
Sweet tremors
Tender moans
Of passionate turmoil

Its deep sighs
Sadden the zephyr
Bring tears to the rose
And bloody dew
Fragrant and radiant

And all the buttercups
The poppies, the lilies,
The chestnut and oak trees
All join in the cry
In the sizzling heat
Under the blazing sky

The rustling wood cries
Cries until dawn
When dew wets the soil
With pearl-like tears
Of arduous toil

◆ ◆ ◆

The day before Christmas, I receive a call from the priest. This time, he taps the wall very lightly, and I have trouble deciphering his message.

"I can barely hear you, father. Is something wrong?"

"I don't feel well. Today I threw up blood."

"What happened? Did they beat you?"

"Yes. But not now."

"Then when?" This is the first time the priest is willing to discuss his illness with me.

"A while back. During my interrogation."

"And you never got over it?"

"I will never get over it."

"Why?"

"Because they beat me with sacks of sand over my back, which turned my lungs to mush. From then on I have been spitting blood, and once in a while I hemorrhage. Now, because it's so cold I cough, and this irritates my lungs."

"Didn't you ask to see a doctor?"

"Sure I did. But the medical orderly here said that there is nothing that can be done for me, since I have lesions on both my lungs."

"What does he know? Why don't you ask to be sent to a hospital in Bucharest?" I demand, appalled at my neighbor's helpless suffering.

"I did ask, but I was told it would be useless: my lungs are in tatters, and no one can help me. So I wait, patiently, for God to take me. May he forgive those who sped my one way journey—they knew not what they were doing."

"On the contrary, they knew perfectly well. That was their job—to send innocent people to the next world," I remind him.

"Sooner or later, we will all get there. Only the Lord can help us now. Anyway, I did get something for my pain. I am allowed to cough, unlike the other prisoners. But enough about me. What about you? How do you feel, my son?" my considerate neighbor kindly inquires.

"I would be lying if I told you I felt badly, father."

"Then you must be a very strong, healthy man, my son."

"True, father, I have spent much of my life in the fresh air, practicing all kinds of sports, especially swimming and hiking, and I have built up some physical endurance. But I have also been lucky. My interrogators were less brutal than yours."

"Better not speak of luck, son, when describing your condition in hell!"

"To be perfectly honest, father, though this may seem strange to you, lately I have come to believe that one can find happiness even in hell, especially a man like me."

"What kind of man are you, son, that you can be happy here? I should hope that your life outside was no worse than here."

"Of course not, only from a certain standpoint, I do feel freer now than I did before..."

"I beg your pardon, son," the priest interrupts me, with strong knocks this time, a sign that what I said made him blow his top. "What you are telling me is impossible to believe. How can you feel free when you are buried alive?"

"I beg your pardon, father, I didn't mean to offend you. I am only telling you what I feel. Have patience and hear me out."

"How can I have patience man, when I hear such idiocy? What do you take me for?" The priest is now tapping with his fist rather than his fingertip.

"Father, I respect and admire you, and I don't believe in bad jokes. Allow me to explain why what seems like an absurdity to you is perfectly logical to me."

"Don't insist my son. I understand very well. Today you don't feel good yourself. I will pray for your mental health."

"Thank you, father, and please forgive me for making you angry, especially today, when you're ill. I, too, wish you well."

I gave up on trying to convince the poor, suffering priest, and felt guilty for having angered him. Certainly, I had chosen the wrong moment to persuade him that man can be happy even in hell.

◆ ◆ ◆

Today is the third day of Christmas, Saint Stefan's day, a special day for me: it is my father's name's day. It brings happy memories of joyful childhood celebrations, as well as painful memories of my father's death. I loved him dearly. He was a kind, loving man who adored his children and would come home from work every day calling out, from blocks away in a booming voice that everyone could hear, all eight of our names, from big to small. Often he took me with him to meetings and demonstrations. He was a born orator, with a wonderful voice and clear, convincing arguments which always moved and persuaded his audience. His work mates revered him and, during disputes or troubles, turned to him for advice.

On June 9, 1927, a fire broke out among the great vats of gasoline in the shipyard. My father saved the city of Constanza from a catastrophic explosion by locating the source of the fire and managing to extinguish it; in the process he was himself consumed by the flames. He was hailed as a hero throughout the press ("a flower among weeds," according to *Dacia*, the local paper), and his funeral was attended, with much pomp and circumstance, by all the city's workers and dignitaries. Although my mother received a pension from the government, we had a very hard time growing up without him.

Lost in these memories, I almost don't notice at first the cascading coughs coming from the direction of our sterile courtyard, where my neighbor, the priest, must be taking his walk. It seems as if the fierce cold has brought another one of his spells. But no, something different is taking place. I listen intently and realize that this time the priest is coughing in Morse code. I decipher a short cough, a dot, followed by a double cough, a dash. My neighbor is using his "special privilege" (as the only inmate allowed the "right" to cough) to convey a prayer to St. Stefan on behalf of the prison's slaves. He repeats his prayer twice, probably for the benefit of those, who, like me, did not catch it the first time:

"Saint Stefan, you, the first martyr of Christianity, listen to our fervent prayer, destroy our chains and deliver us from our torturers. Amen."

After a short pause, the priest continues:

"Five Ave Four."

This, I interpret as a message addressed especially to me, a signal that he has forgiven me for having irritated him three days ago and that he wants to make up.

It is now my turn to be brought out for my walk. Once in the courtyard, I am struck by a sight that moves me to tears: the freshly fallen snow is stained with a circle of red. The priest accompanied his sermon with his own bloody offerings!

Back in my cell, overcome by dark foreboding, I decide not to wait until evening to find out about my friend. In the five-minute intervals between the guards' observations, I tap message after message to the priest. No one answers. Perhaps he is afraid to communicate with me now. I wait a while longer, then try again. Again, silence. What if the priest is lying unconscious on the floor of his cell in a pool of blood? Desperate, I pound on my door. Now, of course, there is no guard in sight. Finally, someone comes.

"I noticed when I took my walk that the snow was soaked with blood. My neighbor must be very ill. Please, send him a doctor!"

"Mind your own business! And shut up! You're not allowed to talk to me!"

For a week now I have tried in vain to establish communication with the priest. This morning I try again. Another man, who refuses to give me his name, answers. From the vigor with which he signals his letters, I judge him to be young and healthy. He knows nothing about the fate of the previous occupant of his cell.

I am haunted by the priest's tragic act of heroism, performed in silence and anonymity. Last night I dreamt that I was back in my parents' home, on the shore of the Black Sea, in my childhood bed, listening to the sad lament of the waves crashing against the rocks:

In my dream, I hear moans
Deep, choking sighs
Deaf, smothered groans
Dumb, stifled cries

The wind roams among the rocks
Like Ovid, the exile
Its mournful lament
His sad, wistful style

In my sleep, I hear waves
Splashing tears of foam
And the cold, bitter rain
Soon-to-be a storm
That will wash all his wounds
And drown out his pain

12

Irina: The Red Kerchief

In our parts you'll find dense green forests
And lush fields made out of silk
Plenty of colorful butterflies
And cows that give fine, rich milk
Nightingales from foreign lands
Come listen to our shepherd's tunes
Here you'll find songs, and flowers, too
And tears, plenty of tears...

We have a dream, never fulfilled
It is the child of woe
Grieving for it, our parents died
Like their parents, long ago

From days of old
From days gone by
We moan a pain that sears
The desolation of a dream
We water with our tears

"Do any of you children know what causes the people in this poem so much grief, so many tears?" Comrade Crisan, the political instructor at our school, asks us during his first weekly session with both third grade classes. I wish I could answer the question, for I so much want to make a good impression on this slim young man with thick black hair and flaming eyes.

I remind myself what Omama has always told me, that like my mother, I have a golden tongue. Here is my chance to prove it. Bravely, I raise my hand:

"They are crying for their parents to come back," I declare, full of self-confidence.

"From the dead?" Comrade Crisan asks. Everyone bursts out laughing. Sixty students. Two teachers. One handsome party official. I want to crawl under my desk and never come out.

"What is your name?" Comrade Crisan asks me.

"Irina Eremia."

"Children, your classmate, Eremia, is not entirely wrong," he turns to the class. "The people in this poem are indeed crying for their parent, a greater parent even than the one who gave them birth. They are crying for their motherland, Romania, their beloved country, a land that from days of old, from days gone by, has been robbed and plundered, first by the Romans, then by the Turks, then by the Austrian-Hungarians, then by the Germans, and always by their puppets and lackeys—the fat, rich landowners who have sucked the life blood of the Romanian people!"

My face cools off. I'm so grateful to Comrade Crisan for saving me from total disgrace. I make a vow to myself to make him proud of me. I fix my eyes on him and drink up every word.

"Children, you are a very lucky generation! You were born almost a decade after August 23, 1944, the day of our liberation from the Nazi yoke, the birthday of our great socialist state. But before that great day, our people were an oppressed people, a long-suffering people, chafing under their chains. Do you children have any idea what your life would have been like, had you been born not in 1953, but let's say, in 1905, when the verses I have just read to you were written?"

This time no one raises his hand. Comrade Crisan continues in his forceful, yet at the same time, gentle voice:

"You would most probably have been the children of peasants, for the majority of our people at that time lived in tiny villages and were very poor. And do you think that you would have been given shiny new books and notebooks and bright pens and pencils and sent off to school in fresh, crisp uniforms, like you are today? No! You would have been sent off, hungry and in rags, to toil alongside your parents on the rich man's farm. And if by any chance, your empty little stomach cramping from hunger, you had dared to pluck a juicy red apple from the landowner's tree, what do you suppose would have happened to you? The landowner's henchmen would have grabbed you, torn the rags off your back, and set his master's well-fed bloodhounds to sink their sharp teeth into your naked flesh and chew you all up right in front of your mother's eyes."

During recess, I leave my sandwich untouched. Sharp teeth bite into my stomach as I imagine the big black dogs that bite into the soft white flesh of little children. I'm so lucky to have been born after August 23, 1944!

◆ ◆ ◆

In Language Arts we take turns reading out loud a story about a very poor peasant family in the old days. On a beautiful autumn morning, the whole family woke up very excited. Father, mother and their six children were getting ready to go to the landowner's vineyard. The long awaited grape picking day had finally arrived. As they ate their meager breakfast—cold slices of leftover polenta dipped in garlic and salt water, they dreamt about the moment when they would put some of those sweet, juicy grapes into their hungry mouths. When they got to the vineyard, where the entire village was gathered, the fat priest made a speech: "God commandeth, 'thou shalt not steal,' so I and your masters have devised a way to help you avoid temptation." The priest passed around strange, netlike contraptions made out of thin wire. The people stared at them, shocked. "Dog muzzles!" a voice cried out. "That's right!" answered the big-bellied landowner. "Anyone who doesn't like it is free to go home!" No one dared to move. Humiliated but helpless, stomachs hurting from hunger, the villagers put on the muzzles. The youngest boy in the family was given a tiny, puppy-sized muzzle. His nose itched and he couldn't scratch it. He could hardly breathe. He tried to squeeze a grape against the muzzle, sticking his tongue out to suck the juice. Not a drop reached him. His mouth was dry. His tummy ached. I cry for the little boy.

◆ ◆ ◆

"Do any of your parents go to church?" Comrade Crisan asks the class. Everyone is silent. No one raises his hand.

"Come on! I'm sure some of your parents must still go to church and sometimes take you along!"

All hands stay down. But I know that some of the children are lying, for I have heard them talk about going to services during spring vacation and knocking colored eggs against each other on the steps of the church. My father's mother, "Bunicuta," sometimes brings us those red, blue, yellow and orange eggs. Does she go to church, I wonder?

"Good!" Comrade Crisan exclaims. "Young pioneers never go to church, and I know all of you want to become pioneers by the end of the year. The church is the enemy of the people. It was the big-bellied priests who have always helped the fat landowners enslave the poor peasants and workers. If your parents should ever ask you to go to church, you should remind them: 'I'm a pioneer, a future communist. Communists don't believe in lies. Communists don't believe in God. Communists don't go to church."

Comrade Crisan opens up a thick book of poems with a red cover, *Heroes and Martyrs*. As he reads, the words sing like music and burn themselves into my heart. After school, I run to the library, check out the book and read the poem again and again until I have it memorized. The next day I raise my hand in class and tell Comrade Crisan that I can recite "The Party." He invites me to the podium. I try to say each line to bring out its loveliness:

The party is in everything
In that which is today
And in the tiny seed
That will sprout tomorrow
In the babe in his cradle
And in the gray old man
Rocking in his rocking chair
The party is in everything
The party lives forever
Undying, eternal, everlasting

"Bravo!" Comrade Crisan claps his hands after I finish. If only I could throw my arms around his neck, press tight against his chest and hear his happy heart beat!

◆ ◆ ◆

This week we read a story about a little boy who lived in a capitalist country—Italy. His father and mother were both dead. The child slept on the street, in cardboard boxes, and ate out of garbage cans. One evening, an older boy who felt sorry for him told him that he would help him get a good meal. The older boy took him to a rich man's house, where a big party was under way. He led him to the kitchen, where he smelled delicious, mouth watering smells that almost made him faint from hunger. A servant girl gave him a clean, white shirt and a pair of black pants which he had to roll up because they were too big for him. He was then told to carry big platters of steaming roast meats into the brightly lit garden, where elegant ladies and gentlemen dressed like kings and queens were milling around. Almost everyone had a dog on a leash. The trays of food were placed in front of the dogs. This was a birthday celebration for the Duke's pet greyhound! Sweat poured down the little boy's face as he carried in tray after tray. Only at the end of the evening, after the dogs ate their fill, did he finally get paid for his work: he was allowed to eat the dog's leftovers! Tears of joy ran down the boy's face as he gobbled down the precious treat.

◆ ◆ ◆

During our history period, our teacher tells us about a time, long ago, when the Romanian peasants, driven to desperation by hunger and want, tried to rebel against their cruel landlords. Men, women and children with pitchforks, sticks, stones and whatever they could get their hands on tried to fight their oppressors. But the powerful landlords cruelly stifled the revolt. Brutally, in cold blood, they killed men, women and children, old people, mothers with babes in their arms. They caught the leaders of the rebellion and tortured them mercilessly. A big picture in our history book shows us just how they were punished: The leader of the rebellion was chained to a chair made of iron, above a blazing fire. A crown made of red hot iron was placed on his head. With red hot pincers, two torturers were pulling pieces of flesh from his body, while two others were forcing his followers to swallow the bloody morsels!

◆ ◆ ◆

"What's the matter? Why don't you eat your meat?" my mother demands at dinner, catching me pushing aside, disgusted, the chunk of beef bleeding on my plate.

"I just don't feel like meat. Can I have more potatoes, please?"

"No. I stood in line for hours to make sure you children get meat for dinner. What's wrong with it?"

"I just don't feel like meat. Why can't I have potatoes?"

"Do you want to grow tall? Then eat meat. You want to end up short and fat? Then eat potatoes!"

"But you're tall and thin," I protest. "And all you ever eat are potatoes and tomatoes!"

"But I don't need meat anymore. I'm all grown up. When I was your age, I listened to what my mother said and did as I was told!"

"I'll have it later," I promise, to appease her. "Make me a sandwich with it for school tomorrow," I suggest, knowing that I will easily be able to trade it with just about any kid for bread and marmalade.

"Giunica, is Italy a free country now?" I ask her, hoping to get her to think about something else.

"What do you mean?" Giunica stares at me, confused.

"I mean, have they had their revolution yet or are the Italian people still exploited by the capitalists?"

My mother appears to be at a loss for what to say.

"Italy is a capitalist country," my brother answers for her. "Like most countries in Western Europe, it's still behind the Iron Curtain. That means that the exploited masses there are trapped like in a prison and can never come out and see the free, socialist world. You'll learn all about this in geography, in the fifth grade."

My mother sighs and gets up from the table. She looks disturbed. Is she still mad at me about the meat?

◆ ◆ ◆

During music, which I usually hate because my teacher constantly reprimands me for singing out of tune, we learn a song I love. I remember it instantly and hum it constantly. Sorin hates it and chases me around the house screaming that my screeching is giving him a headache. I lock myself in the bathroom and croon to my heart's content:

> My mother is a factory worker
> To clothe our people, she toils all day
> I, along with my little sister
> Try to help, not just to play
>
> We make our beds
> And sweep the floors

We buy the bread
And do the chores

My mother is a factory worker
To clothe our people, she toils all day
I, along with my little sister
Try to help, not just to play

We slice tomatoes
Grind the meat
Peel the potatoes
Bake something sweet

When she comes home
She puts up her feet
Tired but proud
We sit and eat

My mother is a factory worker
To clothe our people, she toils all day,
I and my little sister
Try to help, not just to play

I love this song because the family it describes reminds me of my family. It is a family of three: a mother and two siblings. The mother works all day, and the children are home by themselves. Although the mother comes home tired, she is proud of her work and happy to sit down and have dinner with her two kids.

As I keep on singing it, it suddenly dawns on me how little, by comparison to these children, Sorin and I do to help our mother. We come home from school, do our homework, go down and play, sometimes on our street, sometimes at my grandmother's house. My mother stands in long lines after work to buy milk, bread, vegetables, fruit, meat (when she can find it) or whatever else is available. She cooks, cleans and makes our beds. In the evening, after dinner, she checks on our homework and tests us on our lessons. I decide that my life is not worthy of a future communist.

I make up my mind to model myself after the girls in the song. After school, I sweep the floor, wash the leftover dishes from the sink, set the table, peel the potatoes, slice the tomatoes and even scrub the kitchen floor. I wish I could "bake something sweet," but no one has ever taught me how. When my mother gets home, I show her proudly around the house.

"What came over you?" she asks me.

"I just wanted to help you," I tell her.

"Thank you," she says, not looking quite as pleased as I expected.

In the evening, when she tests me on my history lesson, she is disappointed to find out that I haven't memorized the pages I was assigned to learn by rote. And my math sums came out all wrong. Now I'm too tired, and I don't understand anything she's trying to explain to me. Exasperated, she yells:

"Did I ask you to do my housework? All I have ever asked you is to do your schoolwork! That's your only job! That's your only responsibility!"

Hurt, I start to cry. My mother looks so tired every evening. Her hands shake from carrying those heavy bottles of milk up the three flights of stairs. Other children on our street are sent by their parents to stand in the food lines or to buy the bread or to carry the milk home. But my brother and I don't do anything. We are parasites sucking her life blood. I want to explain, to defend myself, but I am choked by tears.

"It's that dumb song!" my brother suddenly exclaims.

"What song?" my mother asks, puzzled.

"Oh, this stupid song Irina keeps repeating like a broken record: "My mother is a factory worker/She toils for the people all day/I and my idiot sister/We scrub the toilet/And flush the shit away!"

"That's not how it goes!"

"Sorin! How dare you?" my mother yells at him.

Still crying, I recite the now sullied lyrics of my favorite song. When I'm finished, my mother bursts out laughing.

"My Galuska! You're a little romantic, just like your father!" She draws me to her and kisses me. "Listen, darling, I really appreciate what you tried to do for me today. But school is hard. If you want to have any kind of a future, you must do your best to be the best in your class. There is nothing wrong with factory workers, but that's not who we are. I'd rather you do your lessons or read your books than wash my dishes."

"I finished all the books you checked out for me," I tell her, mournfully. What did she mean that I'm a little romantic like my father? Is that a bad thing? I wonder. But then why did she smile and kiss me when she said it?

"You're in third grade now. You're allowed to check out your own books," my brother informs me. Like always, he knows everything.

◆ ◆ ◆

"How old are you?" asks the school librarian, a plump young woman with a pleasant smile.

"Nine. I'm in the third grade," I tell her proudly.

"What kinds of books do you like?"

"Something about children. But something real, not a fairy tale."

The librarian seems to understand me instantly. She comes back with a book called *Little Heroes.*

◆ ◆ ◆

I read! I read! This is a book about real children, brave children, "small in size but great in deeds." All of them lived in that great and wonderful land, the Soviet Union. Some of them fought with the people's army against the white Russians during the Revolution. Others helped in the struggle against the enemies of the people left over after the Revolution. And others, my favorite heroes, fought in the underground with the partisans against the Nazi invaders during World War II. All of them sacrificed their young lives for their country. In one story I find a Jewish child, a little girl who hides with the partisans in the forest next to her village, now occupied by the Nazis. She is caught by the Gestapo in a church where she crosses herself the wrong way, betraying she is not a Christian. They arrest and torture her, but she refuses to betray her comrades. She dies imagining Comrade Stalin putting flowers on her grave.

I read my book day and night, unable to put it down. How I admire the "little heroes"! How I wish I could be like them! They have names like Sasha and Ilia and Pavlik and Serioja and Tania and Katia and Sonia and even Irina. They throw themselves over mines to save the lives of their comrades; they sneak food and medicine to wounded pilots hiding in cellars; they creep into the woods and bring messages to partisan fighters; they lead underground leaders to the homes of traitors and informers; they tell the Red Army where the White Russians are hiding. When they are discovered, they run; when they are caught; they struggle; when they are questioned, they keep silent; when they are tortured, they grit their teeth; when they are shot, they sing the "Internationala."

Only one story in the book confuses me. It is the story of a teenage boy in Russia after the revolution, when communist leaders were struggling to "collectivize" the land. This boy, a young pioneer, was earnestly dedicated to the goals of the revolution. To his shock, he found out that his own father was a *kulak*, hoarding land for himself and selling produce on the black market. Ashamed, the boy denounced his father, who was then arrested and put in jail. The next time the boy went to bathe in the river, his cruel older cousin grabbed him by the hair, and held his head underwater until the boy drowned. The criminal was caught and punished. The dead boy became a "hero of the Soviet Union," remembered by all for his courage and honesty.

I am more disturbed by this boy's death by drowning than by any other death in the book. How can his own cousin have murdered him? I adore my Cousin Dinu, who is two years younger than me and so much fun to play with. That a child could kill another child, and a relative, too, horrifies me. But when I tell my mother the story, she is far less shocked by what the cousin did to the boy than by what the boy did to his father.

"But his father was an enemy of the people!" I try to explain.

"If you thought that I was an 'enemy of the people,' would you denounce me?"

That's a ridiculous question, I think. How can she compare herself to that terrible man!

"No one and nothing is more important or more precious than your own family!" my mother exclaims. "This is a revolting story! An ugly story! That little boy was not a hero, but a monster!"

I keep my mouth shut. Giunica hasn't read the story. She has no way of knowing that Serioja was honest and selfless and brave and sacrificed his life out of love for the people of his town who were suffering because of his criminal father, a cruel man who used their money to get drunk and then beat up his wife. But all of this is too complicated to explain. From now on, I'll keep my little heroes to myself.

◆ ◆ ◆

"I loved the book," I tell the librarian. "I want to read more books about heroes and partisans and people like that. She gives me a book called *The Young Guard*, another thick volume which I devour in a few days. A group of friends, young Kosomol members, vow to resist the Nazi invaders. They manage to communicate crucial information to the Soviet Army, destroy important German ammunition, kill several informers, help a wounded Russian soldier to escape, but in the end, one by one, they are all caught. Brutally tortured by the Nazis, they refuse to betray their comrades. They die with their heads held high, knowing that their suffering was not in vain.

◆ ◆ ◆

I devour book after book about Russian partisans and Romanian freedom fighters, those who fought against the Nazis and those who struggled against the Secret Police in the days of the Czar or of King Carol. I dream that I, too, am a partisan, an underground fighter, risking my life for the Party. I, too, sneak out in the middle of the night and carefully, making sure no one is following me, find my way to the dark cellar where my comrades are gathered. In the early morning hours, I paste communist manifestos on houses and store fronts. Chased by gendarmes, I jump over fences and run to the woods, where I find the partisans who give me my own rifle. Fearlessly, I fight the Nazis and manage to save the lives of all my comrades. I am decorated for my courage and made a "heroine of the Soviet Union!"

I no longer feel lucky to have been born after August 23, 1944. I was born too late. I missed all the excitement, all the battles, all the opportunities for heroism. My life is so dull and uneventful when I compare myself to the "little heroes" in my books. Someday, I decide, I will penetrate to one of the countries behind the Iron Curtain, one of those poor, oppressed lands like Italy, France or America, where workers are still exploited and communists still hunted down by the secret police. I will join their underground struggle, fight with them against injustice, and lead their revolution. If the capitalist secret police catches me and tortures me, I won't talk. To prepare myself to withstand torture, I practice holding my breath for increasing intervals of time. I place my bare feet against the wall heater. I look at the clock. For how long can I tolerate the heat before pulling my feet away?

"What are you doing? Are you crazy?" my brother shouts, catching me during one of my training sessions in heroism.

"None of your business!" I had almost succeeded in breaking my old record of endurance. If capitalist enemies were to catch my brother and burn cigarette holes in his skin, would he withstand the pain, or would he betray his comrades? Someday, when his sister is declared a heroine of the Soviet Union, he'll regret having made fun of her when she was young!

◆ ◆ ◆

As the end of the year approaches, everyone in my class is in suspense. The best students will be made young pioneers while still in the third grade. The rest will have to wait until next year. The worst may not be given the red kerchief until the fifth grade. None of us can wait to be allowed to wear the pioneer's uniform: blue skirt or pants, white shirt, red kerchief. Finally we are told that a decision has been made. Comrade Crisan reads the names of the first group of third graders to be made young pioneers: Marica Serban, Petruc Radu, Mircea Manescu, Marius Ionescu and Irina Eremia. After class, Comrade Crisan stops me:

"You're going to memorize a nice poem for our ceremony, won't you?"

"Sure!" I answer, thrilled. I fly home, carrying my happiness like a banner, a red flag fluttering in the wind. Only the first group of children in a class to be made pioneers are treated to a festive ceremony. Everyone will be there: all my classmates, their parents, other teachers, the principal of our school. I leaf through my book and find a poem worthy of the honor being done to me. At our next meeting, I show it to Comrade Crisan, who loves it and asks me to practice reading it at the rehearsal after school.

In the empty auditorium, Comrade Crisan demonstrates how and when we should walk up, salute the flag, and take our oath. We rehearse singing the National Anthem: "We cherish, thee, Romania, our ancestral land/Many different nationalities live freely under your peaceful blue sky…" Then he teaches us a different song for the occasion:

This is Romania, my beloved country!
Hallowed in words and in deeds!
In good times and bad times I belong to thee
'Tis for you that I plant my young seeds!

Now it is my turn to practice my poem. Comrade Crisan and the other future pioneers sit down, while I walk up on stage with my volume of poetry. This is my moment of glory. Puffed up with pride, I'm ready to soar in the air, like a balloon. I take a deep breath, and read:

My red kerchief
Red for the blood spilled

By martyrs of our revolution
To end injustice and oppression
For the good of our people

My red kerchief
Red for the blood shed
By workers and peasants
The exploited masses
Of our once oppressed land

My red kerchief
Symbol of my solidarity
With the hungry and suffering
The enslaved multitudes
Of far distant lands

My red kerchief
Emblem of a pioneer
A young communist
Ready to shed her blood
For our glorious cause

"Why are you reading this?" a voice booms from the back of the room, before anyone has a chance to clap. It is our principal, who must have walked in unnoticed during my performance.

"Comrade Crisan asked me to…" I answer, confused.

"You are going to be made a pioneer this Saturday?"

"Yes!"

"And you think that you will get up in front of everyone and read from that thick book?"

"No! I plan to have the poem memorized!"

"Why don't you have it memorized right now?"

"I…I…haven't had the time," I falter. What does he want from me? What have I done?

"Shame on you! If you were asked to present a poem, you should know it by now! And look at you! Where is your white head band? And why is your hair cut in bangs? Don't you know the uniform code?"

I know that school regulations require girls to wear white headbands. But my hair is fine and the headband constantly falls off, no matter how many pins I use to hold it down. Lots of girls have this problem, and no one has ever gotten in trouble over it. As for my bangs, which my mother recently cut for me to keep the hair out of my eyes, I had no idea that was against the rules. I stand on the podium, speechless, waiting for Comrade Crisan to come to my rescue.

Comrade Crisan follows the principal to the back of the room. They stand there whispering. The short, fat, ugly principal waves his stubby finger at my young, frightened instructor. What is Comrade Crisan afraid of? What has he done?

"I'm sorry to have to say this to you, Eremia," the principal suddenly breaks the silence, "but we cannot make you a pioneer this Saturday." I look straight at Comrade Crisan. With my eyes, I beg him to help me. He turns his head away.

"Everyone can go home now," Comrade Crisan announces, without looking back, on his way out the door. Glued to my spot on the stage, I watch the "elect," the soon-to-be-wearers-of-the-red-kerchief, leave together, whispering and laughing. I am left alone in the empty auditorium, hugging my thick red book, *Heroes and Patriots*.

◆ ◆ ◆

"For God's sake! What have you done to yourself?" my mother screams, horrified, when she comes home and finds me sobbing desperately in front of the mirror.

I have cut off my bangs—as much of them as I could—with the small nail scissors, the only scissors I could find. I cut them off crooked. What does it matter, now that I won't be made a pioneer! I didn't memorize the poem. I didn't wear my white head band. I had bangs.

"WHY DID YOU CUT MY HAIR IN BANGS? BANGS ARE AGAINST THE RULES! THEY WON'T MAKE ME A PIONEER BECAUSE OF THE BANGS!"

I grab the scissors and try to cut off the stubby strands of hair that stubbornly cling to my forehead.

"Stop it!" Giunica struggles to wrestle the scissors away from me.

"No! Ouch!" I yell, stabbing myself. I watch the drop of blood dripping from my hand, the hand that no longer needs to know how to salute the pioneer's salute or tie the red kerchief. I cry for my red kerchief.

◆ ◆ ◆

"Excuse me, comrade, but if you don't have kids, can I have your flag?" I ask the skinny, freckle-faced young woman who just turned the corner and is walking toward me, smiling.

"Sure dear, you keep it!" she tells me, handing me the red, yellow and blue paper flag. I roll it up and put it in my book bag, which is now bulging with flags, paper flowers, posters and insignias, collected from the adults returning from the parade. Today is my favorite day of the year: August 23, the day when the Romanian people, with the help of their Soviet brothers, were liberated from the Nazis. Today is the birthday of our socialist state. Today is the great parade, when all day long people from all walks of life—from teachers to peasants, from workers to doctors, from soldiers to pilots—all march "shoulder to shoulder" in front of our country's leaders.

I love the festive streets, the pushcarts that sell candy, pretzels, ices, soft drinks and goodies hard to find throughout the year, the returning groups of marchers crowding around the food stands, the children competing for parade paraphernalia, the balloons, the flowers, the fireworks. I love the time at the end of the day, when all the kids on the bloc get together and trade balloons for banners, flags for flowers, candy for insignias. Carefully, I stake out my territory, determined to collect more trophies than anyone else on my street.

I have discovered a trick that guarantees instant success: I don't waste my time with adults who look like parents and who save everything for their own kids. I only approach very young or very old people, who seem more than happy to part with their flags or banners. I cross the street and pass through the Park Lupoica, trying to avoid my competition. As I walk around the statute of Romulus and Remus suckling the she-wolf, I find my brother, sitting on a bench, eating an ice cream bar.

"Didn't you get anything?" I ask, surprised to see him without any spoils.

"No! I've got better things to do than to go around begging for garbage!" he tells me.

"You don't have to beg. Just ask people nicely. If they don't have kids, they'll throw the stuff out anyway. Look how much I got." Proudly, I open my book bag.

"Big deal!"

I don't believe him. He's just making up excuses for not being successful. I make up my mind to help him. This is one thing I'm better at than he is.

"Watch this!" I tell him, and approach a young couple returning from the parade, carrying red flags in their hands.

"Excuse me, comrades," I ask them sweetly, "but if you don't have kids, would you mind letting my brother and I keep your flags?"

"Oh no, dear, sorry, but we do have a little boy at home who also wants them," the man answers. But his wife stops and stares first at me, then at my brother.

"Yes. Of course they can have them," she contradicts her husband. She gives me her flag, then grabs her husband's and hands it to Sorin. Then she whispers something in his ear, and the two rush off in a hurry.

"Why did you have to do that?" Sorin shouts at me. "I didn't want their dumb flags!" He dashes his flag to the ground. I pick it up and put it in my book bag. If he doesn't want it, it's his loss.

"Do you know who those people were?"

"What people?"

"The people you just now stopped like a beggar-woman. That was Aunt Duli and Uncle Aurel, our father's sister and brother-in-law."

"How do you know?"

"Because I know them, stupid. They used to come to our house. We used to play with their son, our cousin Lucica. He sometimes rides his bike up and down our street, but he doesn't remember us anymore."

"I don't remember him either. Or his parents. Still, it was very kind of Aunt Duli to give us the flags. She seems like a very nice woman."

"Yeah! Sure! Very nice!" my brother mocks me. He is making fun of me as usual, and as usual I don't get the joke.

I decide not to let Sorin's bad mood spoil my happiness. I have now added two bright red Soviet flags to my collection. For sure I'll have more flags than any other kid on the block. It's been a good day, a lucky day. I breathe in deeply the fragrant, warm, summer air, revel in the sounds of trumpets, drums and marching bands, and look up at the clear blue sky, expecting to see at any moment the parade's grand finale, the sudden burst of white pigeons and red balloons, soaring freely toward the sun.

13

Ion: From Inferno to Purgatory

I perch myself up on my stool to watch, insatiable, the "green island" and the seven tops of poplar trees which have sprouted buds. It is May 15, 1963. Again, I have survived the winter. Again, the freezing weather is forgotten, and I taste once more the delights of spring: the sun shining through the bars of my window and projecting the enlarged shadows of aerial creatures on my walls, the fragrance of blooming trees, the chirping of birds, the zooming of insects, the rush and ferment of life which vibrates even into my desolate cell.

Soon, I will "celebrate" four years since I have been alone with myself. Only my Morse code conversations, undertaken at great risk, have succeeded, occasionally, in breaking my loneliness. Still, I have managed to provide myself with good company. I have forged myself a world populated by words, images, rhymes, verses, music, memories and dreams. I have felt deep feelings, delighted in the excitement of creation, experienced heightened moments of joy, pleasure and victory. My faith in the beauty and goodness of life remains unshaken.

Since my great turning point last year when I began *The Subterranean Tower*, I have been writing tirelessly. I continue to register what I write instantaneously. I have even learned to "leaf" through my book in my thoughts, stop and erase, correct and revise. It is enough for me to repeat the improved version once, to be able to record it in its new form.

All of this erasing and revising have sharpened my memory even more. To test my newly acquired power, like an athlete working out his muscles, I devote an entire day to reciting verses non-stop, for seventeen hours straight, breaking only for lunch and dinner. Not once do I trip or stumble. Proud of my prowess, I congratulate myself: I'm getting to be as good as the great Romanian actor George Vraca, who held marathon recitations of the poetry of Mihai Eminescu.

Suddenly, a different name creeps into my mind: Stefan Zweig and his story "The Royal Game," about a man imprisoned in solitary confinement who masters chess and plays against himself every hour of his captivity until he goes mad.

Am I not perhaps also headed in that direction? Haven't I already lost my sense of proportion? What if the strain of these prolonged sessions of memorization lead to a "circuit overload" and a mental breakdown? I must restore some balance to my life. I force myself to relax by taking more breaks to contemplate the green island and listen to literary music.

◆ ◆ ◆

"Your bags!" the guard barks, bursting into my cell on a beautiful May morning. Are they sending me to Bucharest for another interrogation? I wonder. Will they pick up where they left off? Will I now be subjected to the torture I escaped before?

Out in the courtyard, I realize that I am not the only inmate to be forced out. The prison is in the process of being evacuated. Thirty-six "living dead" are herded to the train station platform and shoved into a special car with bars on the window. I find myself in a compartment with four other convicts: Vasile Luca, former Minister of Finance; Alexander Jacob, his former Vice-Minister; my friend and co-conspirator, Colonel Ardelanu, and Barsanescu, former leader of the Liberal Party. We stare at each other in disbelief, dazed by our years of silence and loneliness. Regaining our lost voices, we begin to confer about our fate. All of us agree that the prison is being dismantled and that we are being transported elsewhere. Is it possible that we will be granted amnesty? No, that doesn't seem likely. If that were the case, we would have been freed on the spot, not locked inside this prison car. Judging by the train stations we are passing by, it appears that we are on our way to Bucharest. Will we stop there, or be taken elsewhere?

We are equally anxious to talk, to hear each other's voices, to share our experiences with our comrades in suffering. Starved for human contact, we relish this brief respite from isolation. My friend, Colonel Ardelanu and I, embrace each other. He was tried along with me and condemned to twenty-five years for criticizing the government and complaining to some of his friends about the horror of having to serve as prosecutor in Patrascanu's trial, where all of his arguments had been prepared in advance by the Securitate. He looks pale, weak and hungry, but not as broken as the others who have been in prison much longer than we have.

More than by anyone else, I am fascinated by Vasile Luca, the powerful former communist underground leader and celebrated head of the Hungarian minority. He was another victim of Gheorghe Gheorghiu-Dej's thirst for power. In the early days after the war, Luca was a member of the Politburo and Minister of Finance; then, Dej framed him in a trial for sabotage and had him condemned to life imprisonment. I had met Luca when he was in his glory, at a meeting organized by the Communist Party after it came to power. He was a passionate orator, full of life and energy. When he spoke, he kept his forehead up and his head tilted back slightly, while his bright, penetrating eyes looked far off in the distance, toward the "golden dreams of humanity" in which he so fervently believed. Today he is an old, depressed man, with tired eyes and a pale face carved with deep wrinkles. He looks like someone who has been through unspeakable suffering. I sense that he has undergone a tragic transformation, which he tries to keep secret from us because of his pride. His spirit had been crushed. His disappointments have been too great, his sufferings too deep, for him to be able to maintain a high morale in the face of his tragic destiny.

I approach him carefully, trying not to pressure him with too many questions. I begin by offering my own opinion about our immediate future. I try to sound optimistic: The evacuation of our prison signifies, for me, a reaction on the part of our regime to world opinion. We live in the age of mass media. Crimes against humanity cannot remain hidden or unnoticed forever. The world must be putting pressure on our government to free its political prisoners.

My long and optimistic discourse leaves poor Luca unconvinced. He listens to me absently, with bitter sighs and skeptical glances. Still, the fact that after innumerable years of total isolation he is being addressed by another human being, a younger, healthier, more positive man who seems to care about his state of mind, does make a mark. He answers me with a sad smile.

"What you are saying sounds too good to be true."

"I am convinced that I am right," I insist.

"I wish I could believe you, but I don't. My hopes have been raised, and then crushed, too many times."

"This time is different. This time we have a solid basis for our hopes," I argue.

"Believe me, I have told myself the same thing a thousand times already. And then I ended up having my nose rubbed in it every time! You heard everyone else's opinion: we are just being transferred to another prison. One thing's for sure, at least: let them search the country far and wide, they still won't find a worse hole than the one we just left! A deathtrap! An extermination camp!"

I nod, sympathetically, and ask him:

"In all your years of experience, have you ever witnessed the evacuation of a prison before?"

"No, and I've been shut up for many years. But this transfer is no big deal. It's simply a matter of money. To keep such a large staff, for only thirty-six 'guests,' is ridiculously expensive. I'm surprised it took them so long to figure that out."

"Yes, but why do this now, when the international situation has changed in our favor? Isn't that too much of a coincidence?" I press him.

"What do the damned at the bottom of hell know about 'the international situation?'"

"We have detailed news about the release of political prisoners in the Soviet Union via Morse code messages from convicts recently arrived to our prison who listened to reports on 'Voice of America' before their arrest."

"It's foolish to trust such rumors. Some inmates start them on their own, to give themselves courage. Others are merely bragging that they are well informed. If you only knew how many such characters I've come across in all these years!"

"All right," I concede, realizing that it's impossible to turn a pessimist into an optimist. "Still, you yourself admit that we're making a move for the better, since you don't think things could get any worse."

"That's for sure. I've roamed through many prisons but never found one as destructive as Rimnicul Sarat. It permanently ruined my health."

"You don't seem to be sick," I lie to him. "Just tired and disillusioned."

"That's very nice of you, my friend. I wish I could believe you. Unfortunately, my heart tells me a different story."

"You have heart problems?" I ask him, concerned.

"And how! A beautiful pectoral angina. I feel like I have a pair of pliers inside my chest squeezing the life out of me."

"I'm so sorry to hear that! And the authorities won't allow you any treatment?"

"Of course not! What better way to get rid of me than by a natural heart attack?"

"And how did you manage to kill time in prison?" I ask, wanting to change the subject.

"With all kinds of thoughts and Morse code conversations with my neighbors. How about you?"

"The same thing. Only in my case the thoughts took the form of poems or stories," I partially confess, not wanting to risk angering him as I angered the poor priest by telling him that I had found happiness in hell.

"You intellectuals seem to have it a bit easier than men like me. You manage to find more ways of keeping yourselves busy. My neighbor was a philosopher who filled his time by thinking about the ancient Greeks. He tried to teach me, even, about Plato, Aristotle, Anaxagoras and others. But what could I, a simple man who never went past grade school, make of all that? I had once hoped that in 'the worker's paradise' I would make up for my educational shortcomings. I never dreamed to do it through Morse code lectures in prison!"

As we keep on talking, he gradually warms up to me. To lift his spirits and liven things up, I suggest we sing together an old, nostalgic Hungarian song which was a big hit in the 1930s, "Sad Sunday." We begin to sing, and soon the others join in. We repeat the song again and again, and every time we sing it, tears swarm down poor Luca's cheeks.

◆ ◆ ◆

I start talking with Alexandru Jacob, Luca's former Vice-Minister, who was implicated in his boss's trial and condemned to long years of prison, of which he has served about ten. By eliminating Luca, Dej rid himself of a Hungarian. By eliminating Jacob, he rid himself of a Jew. Jacob's parents had been sent to Auschwitz and gassed by the Nazis. Jacob, then a teenager, had hidden with the communist underground and fervently believed, like many other Jewish idealists, that "the new, classless society" would promote "brotherhood among men" and put an end to persecution and anti-Semitism. Like Luca, Jacob was a gifted orator who also happened to be endowed with great beauty and charm. Women especially loved to listen to him and said his dark, swarthy good looks reminded them of Tyrone Powers, in great vogue at the time. He was married to the daughter of a rich factory owner who contributed substantial amounts to the coffers of the Communist Party.

After ten years in solitary confinement at Rimnicul Sarat, Jacob is a shadow of the man he used to be. His cadaverous face is old, his skeletal body bent, his eyes buried deeply in their sockets. The story he tells me is horrifying: For several weeks after he was brought to our "special prison," he received nothing to eat. He was a step away from death, when he was finally given a few spoonfuls of gruel and a bit of sauerkraut. He himself cannot explain how he managed to survive. One of his comrades, incarcerated at the same time, died begging for food, like Count Ugolino, in Dante's *Inferno*. Later, conditions somewhat improved, and he got a bit more to eat, but full, of course, he has never been. Looking at him I realize that his face and body have been permanently ravaged by that early, intense hunger from which the man has never recuperated. No one else looks quite as bad as he does! I tell him that I suspect that international pressure is being exerted on our behalf and that things should get better for us soon. He nods vacantly and looks unconvinced.

Everyone stops talking to admire the enchanting spectacle of the Buzau Mountains and the Istritii Hills at their base. We pass by the vineyards and wineries of the Pietroase, where some of our best wines are made. We pass by Mizil on our way toward Ploiesti. At a stop, we hear a conversation between one of our guards and a group of schoolboys who have come to stare at our train.

"What's in this car with the iron bars?" asks one lad.

"Beer kettles," lies the guard.

"Get off it, Mr. Policeman!" the boy challenges him. "We'd be smelling the beer from miles away! You can't fool us. Everyone knows what's in there!"

"What, smart-ass?"

"Politicals, of course!"

"You're gonna get it, you little bastard! I'll give you something to remember me by!" cries the guard, jumping off the step and chasing after him. Just then the train starts, and the guard has to run after it, struggle to catch up and climb back on. He is accompanied by the children's loud laughter and our silent applause.

"Boooo! Boooo!" the children shout after the train.

Around sunset we arrive at Bucharest's North Station, where we are picked up by vans and taken to Jilava, which serves as a transit prison. The five of us are put together in the same cell. All evening long the door opens and different guards poke their heads in. They want to see Vasile Luca, whose infamous trial was publicized throughout the country years ago. They hurl insults at him. We ignore them.

◆ ◆ ◆

After three days, we are awakened in the middle of the night, brought out to the courtyard, and subjected to the humiliation of handcuffs and chains around our feet. Then we are taken back to the train station and to our old car, which is attached this time to a regular passenger train. By the crack of dawn, we reach the magnificent Prahov Valley and the Carpathian Mountains. Then we enter the Transylvanian plateau, which offers another gala spectacle to us, visitors from the bottom of hell.

This journey I spend much time conversing with the former leader of the Liberal Party. He is a distinguished, amiable man and a wonderful conversationalist, well-versed in many subjects. Though he is, like the rest of us, a "living corpse," his morale is high. Like me, he believes we will be released in the near future, basing his hopes on information received through Morse code which leads him to make political speculations similar to my own.

Our train stops in Aiud, and we are taken to an ancient prison from the time of Maria Tereza. Though a new section has been added to house the multitudes of "class enemies," I am taken to the old wing of the prison, the famous "Zarca" section reserved for those with "heavy sentences." Again, I'm locked up alone. The window of my new cell has blinds, and only its very top part is uncovered. But through it, to my delight, I manage to see a slice of sky. On evenings with a full moon, I'll be able to admire the "queen of the night" to my heart's content. I notice another advantage as well. My floor is made of wood rather than of cement. This means that this winter I'll shiver a little less than in the past—if I'll still be here by then.

◆ ◆ ◆

Today is August 5, 1963, my birthday—according to my birth certificate, but not reality. This is because, eleven years after I entered the world, our ancient Julian calendar was replaced with the Gregorian one, so Romania could be in tune with the Occident. That meant that I was made thirteen days younger, and that my real birthday was moved up to August 18. Since I got married, it is on August 18 that I celebrated my birthday with my wife and children. But my mother, brothers and sisters have always congratulated me on August 5, the day on my birth certificate. I, of course, benefited from all this, as I got to celebrate my birthday twice a year, which I didn't mind at all. Here, in hell, I am also born and reborn. This year I am celebrating the two versions of my birthday in my new infernal residence where a new epoch of my life has been launched: the purgatorial epoch. I am being purified of my sins on my way toward heaven, that is toward freedom, or better said toward being released from prison, since in our unhappy country the second must not be confused with the first. Everything happening here confirms my suspicions that we will soon be let out. From early morning until late at night, the cell corridors resound with megaphone messages encouraging us to confess, renege our sins, beg forgiveness, be penitent. These calls come from men with vague, trembling voices, echoing of disease and malnutrition. It is possible that their owners have plenty of their own sins to repent, for this prison also houses former Nazi leaders who murdered communists along with Jews, led pogroms and committed atrocities.

This circus does have its good side, however. The authorities would not be demanding these acts of penitence were they not trying to pave the road for our release. Obviously, they want to make sure that the returnees will be discredited before all who know them and will never be able to raise their voices or lift up their heads in public again.

I, of course, have no intention of apologizing for trying to expose the terrible outrages committed by this government upon my suffering countrymen. I followed my conscience and spoke the truth—the only thing an honest man in my position could do. I will never regret it. I will never repent it. Whatever they do to me, I will resist.

Even in purgatory I can write. Even in purgatory, I can hold on to my schedule. To celebrate my birthday, I indulge in happy memories of my childhood spent on the shore of my beloved Black Sea, lulled by the music of the waves and the stories of old sailors and fishermen. To escape the ghosts haunting my new abode, I make up, as a birthday present to myself, a poem about the ghosts of my childhood:

I got to know ghosts
As a young boy
In Constanza
Beloved of waves,
Wooed by rocks and sea shells
Charmed city

In the dark fall
Through the thick fog
The tortured souls
Roamed restlessly
Seeking ceaselessly
Their bodies which have drowned

They came from our neighborhood
Our sailors' lost relations:
There was the fisherman, "Calin,"
And his son, "Charlie Chaplin,"
Fun-loving men, who went to sea
And were never seen again

And the sailor, "Artacord,"
Who got drunk and fell overboard,
Wordlessly, he asked me:
"Have you seen my body
With the muscles of Hercules
And the fists of Tarzan?"

And the lovely Constanza,
Whose harsh aunt, Speranza,
Forced her to marry
A rich man in a hurry
Instead of the poor sailor
Who was her true lover

In her pure white gown
She decided to drown
And the wedding broke
This was Neptune's bad joke
He had wanted her body
So he turned it to smoke

I was home alone
Mama had gone to market
To buy fresh fish
From the fishermen
Of Constanza
I stayed behind to catch ghosts

14

Irina: From Competition to Emigration

Ever since my Uncle Jack gave me *The Little Ballerina*, I no longer need to shrug my shoulders when adults ask me the hated question: "So what do you want to be when you grow up?" I am going to be a ballerina, a prima ballerina, like Galina Ulanovna, the great Soviet dancer whose triumphant story I read again and again in my beautifully illustrated book. What a sad childhood Galina had, growing up in Czarist Russia during World War I, studying at the harsh boarding school where she had to practice her ballet steps, on an empty stomach in heatless rooms! Her stomach aching from hunger, her thin legs smarting from the cold, Galina still danced, danced lightly and gracefully, flying across the stage like a delicate butterfly. Her life greatly improved after the Revolution, when her magic dancing brought joy and gladness into the Russian people's hearts, filling them with faith in their society's bright future. Proud of her country's achievements, Galina represented the Soviet Union on stages throughout the world, even making people in capitalist countries laugh and cry and throw her big bouquets of red roses. When I grow up, I'm going to be just like Galina Ulanovna.

Once a week, I walk to the cultural center in our neighborhood, my ballet slippers in my satchel. I love the large, mirrored room, the baby grand piano, the bars along the walls, the shiny wood floor. I love the pink ballet dress Omama made for me out of one of my mother's old chiffon summer dresses, the envy of all the other little girls. I love to get to class early, before the teacher walks in, and tumble across the floor and do cartwheels and somersaults and headstands and hang upside down on the bars like a monkey. Comrade Gruita, who plays the piano, is kind and gentle, but Comrade Petrovna, the ballet teacher, is a mean old witch. "First position, second position, third position!" she orders, in her sharp, hoarse, smoker's voice; "Battement! Tendu! Jeté!" she commands as she walks around the room and hits our feet with her long, sharp baton. My feet get hit quite often, because they always seem to be standing in the wrong position. "Attention! Attention!" she yells.

At home, when my mother is at work, I dance on our old giant dining room table that takes up our entire living room and that I pretend is my stage. I'm Cinderella or Snow White or the Sugar Plum Fairy (ballets I've seen performed at the cultural center) or Juliet or Masha or Aurora or Giselle (danced by Galina and vividly described in my book). I also like to hum my own background music and create my own ballets: I am a princess shipwrecked on a beautiful island. A group of pirates land on the white sand beach and tie up a handsome prince to a palm tree, planning to kill him in the morning. In the middle of the night, I dance by the sleeping guards and quickly untie him. But just as we are about to flee, the pirates wake up and chase us through the woods. Together we dance through forests and fields and meadows. We find the boat with the pirates' treasure and sail away to a golden kingdom where we divide up our treasure with all the people of our land and live happily ever after.

"You're going to break that table!" shouts my brother, catching me in the act.

I lock myself in the bathroom and dance on the rim of the bathtub, pretending I'm an acrobat on a high wire.

Outside, I give dancing lessons to the children on my block. My best students are three sisters, all younger than me, who live in the basement of our building. Because they are crammed, along with their parents, in one windowless room, the girls are always playing outside. I feel sorry for them. I've seen them fighting over a crust of white bread, which to them is a delicacy, or even over a piece of black bread spread with marmalade, the staple of most children around here. Whenever I get chocolate from my aunts and uncle, or cookies from my Grandmother, I try to save some for my little friends, who in return are willing to do anything I ask of them. Dutifully, they line up in front of our building, holding on to the gate as to a ballet bar. In a firm voice, I command: "First position, second position, third position, battement, tendu, jeté!" Then I gallop to the middle of the street and demonstrate my "pirouettes" and "arabesques" and "pas de chats."

One day, a new girl comes out of the ground level apartment and stops to gaze at our little ballet class. I'm surprised to see her, because as far as I know the Dimitrius, the people who live there, don't have any children. Mrs. Dimitriu is a sharp-tongued, middle-aged woman who had a fight with my mother and does not speak to us. It happened one evening, when Mrs. Dimitriu came to our apartment uninvited, installed herself on our sofa and assaulted my mother with all kinds of questions about the neighbors who live next door to us.

"What do you know about Comrade Ionita and his wife?" she had asked my mother.

"Nothing that you don't know."

"Do they have many visitors?"

"Who?"

"Your neighbors. The Ionitas. I'm here to ask you some questions about them."

"I don't know. I get home late and leave early. When I'm home, I'm busy with my children."

"Don't you ever bump into them on the stairs?"

"Once in a while, I suppose," my mother admitted.

"And don't they ever carry in shopping bags or packages or things of that sort?"

"I don't know! I've never looked at what they carry in and what they don't carry in!"

"Why not? Can't you see well? Maybe you need glasses?"

Giunica jumped up, rushed to the door and opened it wide.

"My children are hungry. I'm sure your husband must also be waiting for his supper."

Mrs. Dimitriu's pasty face turned red and splotchy.

"Are you throwing me out?"

"Good evening!"

"You'll regret this, comrade. The party will not appreciate your refusal to cooperate!"

Only then did the door slam shut. My mother, who seemed to have controlled herself so well with Mrs. Dimitriu, took her anger out on us.

"If anyone ever asks you children anything about me, our family, our friends or our neighbors, please act as if you're deaf and dumb, you hear?"

Ever since that day, I have avoided Mrs. Dimitriu. But now, seeing the new girl emerge from her house, "the enemy camp," I'm at a loss for what to do. New children are a rarity on our bloc. She is a very pretty girl, petite and slender. She wears her hair piled up high on top of her head. She seems to be around my age or a little older. Uncertain, I continue to display my pirouettes.

"That's not how you do a pirouette! I'll show you how to do a real pirouette!" the new girl suddenly exclaims. She runs to the middle of the street and twirls around and around in a much prettier figure than anything I have ever been able to accomplish. Then, she lands in a perfect split. My friends and I stare at her, open mouthed.

"Are you Comrade Dimitriu's daughter? How come I've never seen you before?" I finally ask her.

"No, she's my aunt. I'm just visiting."

Then it's all right to talk to her, I decide. She won't be here long.

"Are you going to be a ballerina when you grow up?" I ask her admiringly.

"I'm already a ballerina. I go to the National School of Ballet."

By her tone, I gather I'm supposed to be impressed.

"What's that?"

"You don't know? It's the place where all future ballerinas go to school. In the morning we have regular classes, like everyone else, but in the afternoon we train for the ballet."

"How do you get to go there?" I ask her, fascinated.

"You have to be accepted. Not anyone can go! You need to ask your mother to take you to an audition."

"And if I go to school there, I'll become a ballerina when I grow up?"

"If you're good and don't get kicked out along the way. It's very hard. They get rid of girls all the time."

"Do you like it?" I ask her.

She looks at me with contempt.

"It's not fun and games, you know. That's not the point. We work very hard. But it will all pay off in the end. Ballerinas have wonderful lives. They meet important people. They travel abroad and visit foreign countries. They buy their food in special stores and their clothes in special shops. It's worth all the sacrifices I'm making now, my mother says."

"What sacrifices?"

"Not having much time to play with other children after school. Having to practice until every muscle in my body aches. Never being allowed to touch sweets. They weigh and measure us every month. One girl in my class got kicked out for gaining too much weight!"

I love sweets, I think. It would be hard to give them up. But to be a ballerina, a prima ballerina like Galina Ulanovna, and to dance on stages all over the world, yes, for that I'll even give up sweets!

◆ ◆ ◆

This Sunday we're celebrating my mother's birthday around the big dining room table at Omama's house. I shock everyone by refusing a piece of chocolate torte.

"What's the matter, Irinika, are you sick?" my grandmother asks me, alarmed. Never in my life have I ever refused chocolate torte. This, I decide, is the perfect moment for me to tell everyone the good news. I know that for a long time my relatives have been concerned about my future. Often, I've heard them talking about what "would become of my brother and me" in hushed voices.

I now expect that everyone will be delighted to hear that I have finally made up my mind about what I want to be when I grow up. No one needs to worry about my future anymore. My brother has already said a long time ago that he plans to become a chemical engineer like Uncle Jack. I take a deep breath and make my announcement.

"I'm not sick. I just don't want to eat cake anymore. And I have something very important to tell you. I know what I want to be when I grow up."

All look up at me with smiling, expectant faces.

"I am going to be a ballerina. A prima ballerina, like Galina Ulanovna."

Everyone bursts out laughing. Do they think I'm joking? My voice shaking, I continue to assert myself.

"I am going to try out for the National School of Ballet. The tryouts are next week."

"You've really investigated this, haven't you!" Aunt Renica remarks. "You must know exactly what you want!"

"Of course she knows what she wants!" exclaims Omama. "Irinika is almost ten years old! She knows her own mind! May God grant you success in whatever you choose to undertake, darling, and if you want to be a ballerina may you become the greatest ballerina in the world!" Tears begin to well up in the corners of her eyes. "You have the long, slender legs of a gazelle, and you're as graceful as a butterfly!"

"In my opinion, she looks a lot more like an elephant!" my brother bursts in.

"Who asked your opinion?" I shout at him.

"Believe me, if you don't lose a few kilos, your partner will never lift you off the ground!"

"You shut up!"

"Sorin! Don't be mean! I'll check into it, Galuska," my mother reassures me. "I am convinced that once you make up your mind, you can do anything!"

◆ ◆ ◆

Every ten-year-old in the city of Bucharest must aspire to be a ballerina! I can't believe how many mothers and daughters have already lined up in front of the

National School of Ballet. I had been so sure of myself this morning when I admired myself in the mirror in my pink ballet dress, my hair tied with a new, crisp ribbon and piled up high on top of my head. My stomach is perfectly flat, my thighs slim, my long legs slender, my cheekbones, prominent. I have given up bread, potatoes, rice, noodles and sweets, living almost entirely on tomatoes, cucumbers and hard boiled eggs. I can do a real split, lift my leg straight up and touch my nose, bend backwards to the floor and make a perfect bridge. But now, standing next to Giunica in the long line of mothers and daughters, I notice many other slender, graceful little girls in pretty dresses, their hair tied up in fresh, crisp ribbons, just like mine. Each of us sizes the others up as we practice our splits and leg lifts and back bends, disappointed to discover that we are not the only ones to have mastered these accomplishments.

It is a hot, humid September morning, a week before my tenth birthday, which also coincides with the beginning of the new school year. I pray that I'll be admitted to the National School of Ballet. I pray that I will never have to go back to the school where Comrade Pana pulled my ear, the school where my brother and I were cheated of our awards, the school where my best friend was forbidden to play with me, the school where I was denied my red kerchief.

"I'm studying to be a ballerina now," I imagine myself telling my former classmates. I remember how impressed everyone was when, last June, Marica announced that she had been admitted to the National Academy of Music. The teacher made a big fuss over this "great honor" and asked all of us to congratulate our "talented classmate." Soon after, Marica moved out of our neighborhood, and I have never seen her again. I hope that someday, after I become a famous ballerina like Galina Ulanovna, Marica will sit in my audience and watch my fans throw me big bouquets of red roses!

"Do you have any idea what is expected of them?" the woman in front of us turns around to ask my mother. She is a heavyset, peasant-like woman, who despite the heat is wearing a babushka over her hair. Her daughter, however, is tiny and delicate, a porcelain doll.

"I have no idea," my mother answers. "I'm afraid they were not very specific when I called. I suppose we'll find out soon enough."

The line behind us grows in length as more mothers and daughters join us. Finally, we reach the entryway to the school yard, where a woman sits behind a table and writes down names. A black car pulls up in front of the school, and the chauffeur escorts a little girl in a real ballet tutu straight inside the building. No one says anything.

"That's not fair!" I explode. "Why didn't she have to wait in line, like the rest of us?"

A few other girls and their mothers begin to grumble.

"She had a special appointment," explains the woman official behind the table. "Anyone who is not satisfied is free to go home."

"Everyone's equal, but the big shots are more equal than the rest!" the woman with the babushka suddenly mumbles, loud enough for everyone to hear. "It's not enough that they rob and cheat us every day, they have to teach their children to do the same to our children!"

"You! Get out of the line! Go home! Now!" shouts the woman behind the table.

"Mama! Please!" cries the doll-like girl.

"Get out! Or I'll call the police!" the school official shouts. The peasant woman grabs her sobbing daughter's hand and walks away.

Our turn is next.

"Your name?" the official asks, without even looking at me.

"Irina Eremia."

"Age?"

"Almost ten."

"What do you mean, 'almost ten?' You must be ten to be admitted."

"She'll be ten next week," my mother explains.

"You must be ten to try out," argues the woman.

"School doesn't start until next week. She'll be ten by then. The principal, Comrade Statescu, a former colleague of mine, assured me it was all right. If you would like, I will go in and talk to him."

"Go in the yard and wait until your name is called. And teach your daughter manners. Next time, little girl, keep your mouth shut, or you'll get yourself and your mother in trouble," she warns me, still looking down at her list and not at me. How on earth does she know that I was the one who had complained?

My legs shake as we walk into the yard, which is swarming with women and girls waiting for their names to be called.

"Did you really speak to the principal of the school?"

"Hush! No!" my mother whispers. "But I do know his name. And you, my dear, must learn to control yourself in situations like this. You never want to cut off your nose to spite your face. You almost lost your chance."

My throat feels dry, my stomach empty. I wish I had not been so nervous this morning and had managed to swallow a few bites of toast or sips of milk.

After waiting endlessly, my name is finally called up. Giunica walks me to the door, where another female official organizes the dozen girls into a straight line.

"Parents must wait outside," she barks. "Hurry, hurry, girls, walk right in!"

"Good luck," whispers my mother kissing my hot cheek. "Stand up straight! Chin up! Shoulders back!" I almost trip, pushed forward by the girl behind me. We are crammed into a small dressing room, littered with piles of clothes scattered all over the floor. "Quick! Take off your clothes and line up in the hallway!" the woman orders us.

"Take everything off?" we ask, incredulously.

"Everything!" she orders, "except for your undies."

Scared and embarrassed, I drop down my pretty ballet dress and my nylon slip. Thank God I'm wearing clean undies that have no holes. Though it is hot, I begin to shiver. Barefoot and humiliated, we follow the school official through the long corridor, our arms crossed over our budding bare breasts. We stop in front of an open door. I stare in, over the girl's heads, and see a large room in the middle of which is a long table where three men and two women are seated writing notes. The school official tells us that we must walk in, one by one, past the table where the committee is seated and, unless someone stops us to ask a question, proceed out the back door to the room where we left our clothes. We must get dressed, meet our parents in the yard, and leave as quickly as possible so as to make room for the next group of girls. Those accepted will be notified by mail.

Everything happens with lightning speed. I walk in front of the judges; they stare at me, examine my face, neck, breasts, waist, legs. I can almost feel their eyes touching me, weighing, measuring, sizing up every part of my anatomy. Embarrassed, I want to sink through the floor and disappear. Determined, I want someone to notice me, talk to me, ask me to do a split or a leg lift. But no one says anything. As I'm about to walk out the back door, I hear a man comment: "Good legs, but she's too tall. And developing too soon." I turn around and look at him. Our eyes meet. Yes, he meant me.

◆ ◆ ◆

The sight of my mother's eager, expectant face is more than I can bear. I burst into tears: "Too tall! They think I'm too tall!"

"Who said that? What are you talking about?" she asks me, alarmed.

"One of the judges. He was staring straight at me. And he also said that 'I'm developing too soon!' What's that supposed to mean?"

"Calm down. I don't understand a thing you're saying. What exactly happened? What did they ask you to do?"

"Nothing! They didn't ask us to dance or do anything. We just had to take off our clothes and parade in front of them naked! They wanted to see our bodies! And I don't think they liked mine!"

"Wait here!" my mother says in a determined voice. When Giunica makes up her mind about something, no one can stop her. I watch her go to the door, argue with the official, get past her and walk straight in. An eternity later, she comes back.

"You were right," she tells me. "They think you're too tall. They won't admit you. There's nothing that can be done."

Sobbing, I follow her to the bus stop.

"Why is she crying?" asks another woman who is waiting there with her daughter. "Have they told her anything?"

"It was a trying experience," my mother responds her in a calm, measured voice.

"I don't know anyone on the committee and have no money for bribes," the woman sighs. "Do you think the audition was for real, or was the whole thing a charade?"

"I don't know."

"I don't care!" the little girl cries out. "I don't want to go to that school! I hate ballet!"

"Hush, Rodica! How can you talk that way? They asked you to do a leg lift and they wrote down your name. They smiled at you. You could see they were interested. If you get in, you'll have a wonderful profession and get to live well, travel, buy beautiful things. How can you say you don't want to be a ballerina?"

"I don't!" the little girl stamps her foot.

She's small and slender. Her chest looks flat. She'll probably get in. And I, who want this more than anything in the world, won't.

Our bus arrives. Since it's the middle of the day, it's not crowded. My mother and I find seats next to each other. Usually when that happens I have a million things to tell her, but this time I don't feel like talking. Finally, Giunica whispers in my ear:

"Be glad you didn't get in. That school seemed like a prison. I don't think you would have been happy there."

I refuse to be comforted. I would have been willing to endure anything to be a ballerina like Galina Ulanovna. I am so ashamed. Those men and women looked at me, saw me naked, shook their heads and said "No."

◆ ◆ ◆

They are leaving, Omama, Opapa, Uncle Jack and Aunt Pupi, leaving the country, leaving in three weeks, twenty-one days—the time they have been given to clear out. Tears streaming down her cheeks, Omama opens the door and explains why she has called us so late in the evening, demanding that we come over immediately to hear the urgent news.

The whole family is gathered around the dining room table, conferring in agitated whispers.

"When did it come?" asks my mother.

"Probably this afternoon, with the mail. But I only opened it an hour ago," explains Uncle Jack.

"Stop crying, Mama! This is what you have been hoping for. May it bring you luck and happiness and may the rest of us also be able to join you, soon, in freedom and prosperity," says Aunt Coca.

"How can I leave three of my daughters here? And my darling grandchildren: Irinika! Sorinel! Dinutu! How can I leave without them?"

"Don't worry, mamica, once we're out, we'll help them out too. We must be patient. And calm. And grateful for this chance," says Aunt Pupi, who is always level-headed.

"But they won't ever let Regina and the children leave, not without their father's permission, and how are they going to get it from him when he is…"

"Mamica!" my mother interrupts her. "Let's take one thing at a time. Let's concentrate on getting one part of our family out; later, we'll worry about the other. How much time did they give you?"

"Three weeks or less," my uncle says. "Personally, I think we should aim for a week to ten days!"

My grandparents look at each other, horrified. This time, my grandfather, who is usually quiet, breaks down:

"We have lived in Romania all of our lives. And so did our parents and grandparents. How can we go through everything, pictures, books, china, furniture, papers, relics that have been in our family for generations, and say goodbye to everyone, our friends, our relatives, our lives, in one week?"

"Papicu, we have very few decisions to make," my uncle tries to calm him down. "We're allowed to take practically nothing. Everything that can be sold must be sold. We have no time to waste. Don't you remember what happened in 'Fifty-Eight? After people gave up everything—their jobs, their homes, their possessions—the policy suddenly changed, and they were held back. They had to start life here all over again, as beggars, or worse than beggars, for they had also been branded as having applied to emigrate. I know of several people who killed themselves out of despair."

"It will be a miracle if we manage to make it in the time they're giving us," says Aunt Pupi. "Haven't you seen the list of officials whose stamps and signatures we must collect? Each signature means a bribe, and each bribe means something else we must sell. Each appointment means hours of waiting. I don't know how we'll manage to get it all done even in three weeks!"

"We'll manage in ten days or less!" Uncle Jack pounds his fist on the table. I've never seen him lose his temper before. "There are people who make it their business to help speed people like us along. For a price, of course. We must pay whatever it takes. I don't care if we leave with only the shirts on our backs, as long as we get out!"

"But you must make yourselves some decent clothes," advises Aunt Coca. "That's all they'll let you take anyway. You won't have anything else—no money or jewelry or furniture or china or bedding...Winter is coming. Who knows how long you will have to wait in Vienna before you get your visas for America?"

This is the first time I hear something mentioned about where my grandparents, aunt and uncle are going. Vienna. That's in Austria. A capitalist country. And from there to America. The imperialist empire.

"Why are you going there? Why are you leaving us?" I ask.

My question upsets Omama, who bursts into tears again. She grabs my hand and covers it with kisses.

"I still remember that tiny plump baby hand. And how it used to grab the matzo balls right out of the soup. Irinika! Irinika! How can I go and leave you here?"

The house is in total turmoil. Every day after school, I come over to watch the commotion. I stand aside and observe the people swarming in and out, taking away furniture, rugs, paintings, china, books, vases, statutes, ashtrays, pots, pens, pillows, quilts, sheets, towels and everything else that had once made up my childhood haven. All kinds of people come in—strangers, acquaintances, inspectors, neighbors, friends—to look, to measure, to weigh, to survey, to bargain, to take, to buy, to make good wishes, to ask favors, to say goodbye. Every day Uncle Jack and Aunt Pupi come home in a state of collapse. They are spending their days standing in lines, waiting in rooms for various officials to sign various forms which attest to the fact that no one has been left unpaid and nothing has been left undone.

This afternoon, I surprise my grandfather in the middle of an argument with an inspector—one of many—who has come around to measure the house.

"We have paid everything we were ever asked to pay!" my grandfather is protesting in a loud voice.

"I am telling you, old man, that your house measures two square meters more than it is recorded here. For fifteen years you've been cheating the government of the tax you owe on that extra space."

"But that's not my fault. I'm not the one who measured it in the first place. The government told us how much tax we must pay, and that's how much we paid. What more can be expected?"

"My point is that the house measures two square meters more than what you paid tax on. Consequently, we must now calculate how much you should have been paying for the last fifteen years, figure out the difference, and, of course, the interest on it."

"But that's insane! You're just trying to rob us!" my grandfather shouts.

Alarmed, my grandmother walks in.

"Be quiet, Zaharia, calm down. Let's find out what exactly the gentleman wants. What is it that you would like, sir? Do you see anything around here that strikes your fancy?"

The inspector smiles and points to a blue velvet arm chair.

"That's a very nice piece of furniture," he comments admiringly.

"It's yours, sir. When can you pick it up?"

"This afternoon. You're a very gracious lady." He kisses my grandmother's hand and leaves.

Omama runs to the bathroom and washes her hands with rubbing alcohol. Then she comes back and scolds my grandfather:

"You must control yourself, Zaharia. You heard what Jack said. The smallest complaint, the least problem, and they'll hold us back. That thief could have ruined us! May he roll backwards off the chair and break his neck!"

◆ ◆ ◆

"Goodbye!"
"Goodbye!"
"Goodbye!"
"Goodbye!"

"May you travel in good health!"

"May you arrive in good health!"

"May you find luck and happiness!"

"May you find peace and prosperity!"

"May Jack find a nice wife, and Pupi a fine husband, and may both of you get good jobs and solid homes and have handsome, happy children of your own."

"May Mama and Papa live a long life, together with their children and grandchildren, in health and in happiness."

"May you all stay well, and be healthy, and may the children grow strong, and may they learn well at school, and may we all be proud of them, and may our whole family be reunited again soon, in peace and in freedom, in health and in happiness."

Everyone is crying. Omama, Opapa, Uncle Jack and Aunt Pupi, who are leaving; Aunt Coca, Aunt Rene, my mother, my brother, my cousin and I, who are staying. And not only our family, but every other family who is here at the airport, split up between those who are leaving and those who are staying—everyone is crying, as if this was not an airport but a funeral, and they were saying goodbye to their loved ones forever. But why do they act as if they may never see each other again? Omama promised me that she will visit us or we will visit them. "Soon, we'll see each other, soon, very soon, we'll be together again, before long…" she promised me in the taxi on the way here, grabbing my hand and covering it with kisses.

The people who are leaving are told that they must separate from the people who are staying. A man with a stern voice yells out that "the emigrants" must now prepare to go through customs. They will be subjected to a "close to the skin search." Let no one think that he can hide anything. Anyone caught trying to smuggle out foreign or Romanian currency, precious metals, stones, jewelry, documents, or any paper with anything written on it, no matter how small, even a telephone number, address or medical prescription, will be turned back and delivered to the authorities. I feel frightened, even though I know my relatives have been very scrupulous about obeying all the rules.

The group leaving disappears through a door. The group staying gathers around the large windows, trying to secure positions from where they will be able to see their loved ones as they board the airplane.

"They wanted to take me! But I couldn't do it! God forbid I should be a burden to them!" an old man is crying next to us.

"Don't you have anyone left here?" my mother asks him.

"No! My brothers and sister died in Transnistria. My wife passed away last year, may she rest in peace. And I have heart trouble and rheumatism. How can I saddle my son with a sick old man to care for?"

"I'm sure that after he gets settled he'll send for you!" my mother tries to comfort him.

"No, I'm too sick, too old. I'll never see him again!"

◆ ◆ ◆

I walk away. I circle the large airport waiting room. I stare at the airplanes outside and shut my ears to the crying and moaning inside. This is the first time I have ever been to an airport. What does it feel like to rise up in the air like a bird and fly above the clouds?

Suddenly I see my grandmother and Aunt Pupi emerge back from customs along with another group of women.

"Omama!" I shout and run toward her, wanting to give her one last hug. A security guard stops me.

"Stay away! You must not go there!" With a thick, black cord, he cordons off the section of the room where those who are leaving are gathering as they come back from having been searched. No one is allowed to touch them, talk to them or get anywhere near them.

"They're isolating them like lepers!" the old man tells my mother. "I feel like I'm in concentration camp again!"

For the next several hours we stand, restlessly, in our section of the room, staring helplessly at the other side where our loved ones are waiting to depart. We exchange glances, but we can neither speak nor touch. On both sides, people are nervous, constantly examining their watches.

"Why aren't they leaving?"

"Could there be something the matter with the plane?"

"Is there some kind of problem?"

"Why is it taking so long?"

"What could be wrong?"

No one knows. No one explains. There is no one to ask. Maybe they won't leave, after all, I think. And, to my shame, for I know this would be a disaster, there is a small part of me that does hope they won't go.

Finally, something seems to be happening in the other half of the room. A line forms. A door opens. People slowly begin to move through it. On my side of the room everyone rushes to the windows. The emigrants gradually appear on the open runway. My grandparents look so small, so frightened, so lost, as they slowly move toward the gigantic airplane that will take them on the first flight of their lives to some strange new country, away from everyone and everything they know and love.

"Look at Papicu!" my mother exclaims.

I stare at my grandfather. The fur trimmed collar to his winter coat has been snipped off.

"Even that little collar was too much for them! The pigs!" my aunt murmurs.

Uncle Jack helps Opapa up the steps to the airplane, while Omama leans on Pupi's arm. As they reach the airplane door, each turns around, waves, and finally disappears inside.

"Jack! Jack!" a woman behind me cries. I turn around and recognize a familiar face. I met her last spring when my uncle took me along on a weekend trip to the mountains. Her face is red and splotchy and soaked with tears. Our eyes meet.

"Remember Poiana Narciselor ("the Meadow of the Narcissuses")?" she whispers.

How could I forget it? It was one of the loveliest days of my life. My uncle had invited me to join him along with a group of his friends on an excursion to see the narcissuses—graceful, fragrant flowers that only bloom for several weeks out of the year. Very early in the morning, we took the train up to the mountains and hiked until sundown to the "Cabana Cota 1500," where our group sat at a long wooden table and ate hot, sour borscht and spicy veal paprikash. My legs ached, I could hardly move, and the strong air made me dizzy with sleep. The men spent the night in one dormitory, the women in another. My uncle's friend let me have the top bunk and she took the bottom, and in the morning she braided my hair and buttered my rolls. At the crack of dawn we started our hike, my uncle spurring me on by promising, "just one more step and we'll be there, just one more step, just one more step," until finally, when I didn't think I could take another step, we reached the most beautiful meadow I had ever seen. We laid on the lush grass and ate wild raspberries and gathered big bouquets of the delicate white flowers trimmed with crimson and gold that gave off the sweetest perfume I had ever smelled.

Later, after my rejection from the ballet school, when I cried for days, feeling as if I were trapped inside a rain cloud, it was Uncle Jack's promise to take me back to the "meadow of the narcissuses" that got me to smile again. Staring at the crying woman's red eyes, listening to her soft weeping, I suddenly see her snuggling next to my uncle on the soft grass of the meadow. Her eyes were sparkling then, and she was laughing as she braided some of my flowers into a crown for my hair. I watch the plane take off and disappear into the clouds, listen to the aching cries of painful partings, and smell the wild, intoxicating scent of the narcissuses.

15

Ion: At Death's Door

September, 1963. Orators in striped clothes, with voices cracked by hunger, badger us day and night on prison loudspeakers. They admit their mistakes. They claim they were the pawns of other, dangerous "enemies of the people" who used them for their subversive purposes, taking the "the hot chestnuts out of the fire with someone else's hands." They swear that only now, after years of painful soul-searching, do they realize how much damage they have inflicted upon society. Purified and redeemed, they bid us all to confess, renege, repent! Every day, the confessions multiply; if you listen carefully, however, you realize that you're hearing the same voices over and over again.

Not satisfied with this auditory attack, prison representatives show up in person to pressure me, individually. I am told point blank that if I want to get out, I must confess. I answer them, calmly and reasonably: I have absolutely nothing to reproach myself, since nowhere in the civilized world could "the intention to publish" a political allegory possibly constitute a crime. Immediately, I am made to see the results of my response: my soup gets thinner and thinner, until I spend my dinners fishing for the few specks of gruel that have sunk to the bottom of my bowl.

The incessant broadcasts deprive me of the peace of mind necessary to think, write or listen to literary music. The deafening din does offer one advantage, however: I can speak in a loud voice to my neighbors by pressing the bottom of my tin mug against the wall, the top to my mouth, to direct the sound—a common practice in the "Zarca" section of this prison, where the walls are not very thick. So I manage to pass the time as well as catch rumors.

The neighbor on my right is a former member of the Romanian Peasant Party, dissolved and denounced by the communist regime in a staged trial in 1947. Today, he seems to be in a hopeful, optimistic mood:

"Liberty is in the air, my friend" he tells me, jubilantly.

"Not 'liberty' but 'liberation,'" I correct him. "Even after we're freed from prison, we still won't be free."

"You're right," he agrees. "Liberty and dictatorship are mutually exclusive."

"Unfortunately this doesn't lower the price of our release," I complain.

"Confession and repentance—that's what they're charging us."

"Too high a price for me. Are you willing to pay it?" I ask him.

"I haven't decided yet. But I'm tempted. After all these years in chains, I'm not sure I can last anymore."

"What do you think will happen to us if we refuse?"

"They'll keep us here forever."

"I don't think so," I contradict him. "They are letting us go because of external pressure. They wouldn't do it if they didn't have to. The fact that they're haggling with us, even though we're in their power, demonstrates that world opinion is pressuring them to free us, and that eventually they will free us whether we confess or not."

"I have suffered too much and feel too weak and too sick to count on these speculations, which may or may not be correct. I don't have that much to confess, anyway!"

"I don't have anything!" I declare.

"What did they get you for, anyway?"

"For attempting to publish a political satire in which I made fun of those who consider themselves 'universal geniuses,' governing their people according to their sick whims, and rewriting history according to their crippled imaginations. It was called *Gulliver in the Land of Lies* and began where Swift's novel left off, with a new journey undertaken by the hero to 'Kukunia'—a fictitious state curiously remindful of our own."

Our conversation is suddenly and brutally interrupted. The door to my cell flies open and the guard bursts in, screaming:

"I caught you, fool! You just earned yourself ten days in the 'lock up'!"

I stare at him, dumbfounded, unable to understand how he has managed to approach my cell so quietly. Then, I notice that he is wearing cloth slippers over his boots.

He does not punish me immediately, but tells me that I must wait until the "special punishment cell" is vacant.

◆ ◆ ◆

My food is getting worse and worse, my soup turning into pure water. I will not suffer myself to be murdered in silence. I begin to scream at the top of my lungs so I can be heard throughout the prison:

"Murderers! You're trying to starve me to death because I refuse to confess! Killers! Soon, you're going to pay for your crimes! The tide is turning! Can't you see?"

I am answered with two more portions of "ten days"—to be served, I am once again informed, as soon as the cell is "vacated."

At first I'm relieved that my sentence keeps getting postponed. But my happiness evaporates when my neighbor reveals the criminal intent behind this: the administration is waiting until the depth of winter, when my punishment days, which now amount to thirty, will have to be served consecutively, and will, in effect, amount to a death sentence. As my neighbor is in the process of "enlightening" me, I am once again caught talking with the mug to my mouth, and ten more days are added to my "account."

◆ ◆ ◆

My last "infraction" has coincided with the onset of the autumn rains. For the past seven days it's been raining nonstop. This, and the dread of the punishment to come, plunges me in the arms of my ancient enemy—depression. I summon all my strength, enlist all my resources, and fight with all my might. Poetry still has the power to soothe me:

Incessant rain
Torturous rain
Piercing, plundering,
Ravaging rain
Flooding the earth
Sinking the sky
Drowning my hopes
Of brighter days

Dense, mincing rain
Black wave
Giant shroud
Descending upon the world
To bury my dreams

The winter cold arrives at the beginning of December. Now hunger tortures me even more cruelly, as my body needs the extra calories to fight the freezing temperatures. I subsist on *turta de malai*, the meager baked corn meal mush to which every third day is added a thin slice of bread, around three hundred grams. This I consider a great delicacy, like steak or cheese, and I break it up in tiny little pieces and savor it at carefully planned intervals. Only on my "bread days" do I allow myself the luxury of answering the desperate appeals of the poor, abandoned sparrows caught by the snowfall. But I am too poor and too hungry to share my food purely out of generosity. I need to feel the presence of live creatures next to me. I need to divert my mind, too numb to write.

During several days of fierce frost, I keep up my spirits by embarking on a socio-biological experiment. On four out of the twelve iron bars of my cell I place a little bit of corn meal mush and then wait. After some time the food attracts one sparrow. Surprisingly, however, it does not just grab the food, as I had expected, but first makes certain calls toward its hungry friends. Only when its companions join it on my windowpane does the sparrow have the courage to approach the food. But at that moment, a contradictory social phenomenon occurs: the birds begin to fight over the corn meal mush, even though there is enough for all of them—four crumbs on four bars for four birds. The war is won by the strongest of the combatants, a feisty, quarrelsome male sparrow who chases the others away, one by one.

I repeat this experiment with the same result every time. When it comes to the procurement of nourishment, the sparrow who first finds the polenta always calls his fellows, seeking safety in numbers. When it comes to the division of the food, however, the sparrows can never agree and end up fighting, the strongest always winning. Isn't this, I reflect sadly, also so with man? We, too, realize that we cannot procure our livelihood by ourselves and thus seek the help and fellowship of others. When it comes to the moment of sharing our goods, however, our brotherhood weakens, and suddenly we become selfish and greedy, stepping on our "social contract" to get a larger share of the pie. As the Romanian saying goes: "Sure, brother, we're brothers, but you must pay cash for the cheese!"

◆ ◆ ◆

It is the middle of December, and the weather has worsened dramatically with temperatures way below zero and continuous blizzards. The sparrows visit me more and more often, and even though I have finished my socio-biological studies, I continue my "experiments" for humanitarian reasons. Unfortunately for my feathered friends, on December 17, 1963, I am taken out of my cell and escorted toward the "lock up" chamber.

As I reach my destination, the guard asks me to sign a form that indicates that "I am about to execute the order for my punishment which consists of forty days in the 'lock up' to be served consecutively without interruption." Vehemently, I refuse. I have no intention, I shout, to consent through my signature to the prison administration's plot to assassinate me! Despite the shower of punches mercilessly falling on my mouth, I make such a racket, aided by my "stentorian voice" (as it has been called here by my neighbors) that the frozen walls of the prison seem to ring and shake. I am hoping that my screams and protests will somehow be heard beyond the prison's walls, make public the attempt to murder me, and conceivably reach the ears of someone among my friends "outside." Finally, my jailor gives up on obtaining my signature and shoves me into the "lock-up" chamber.

I now find myself in a monument of "inquisitional art." This chamber, my neighbor told me, was designed by an architect who was also a political prisoner, at the direction of the prison bosses, to suit their sadistic whims. Basically, it resembles a refrigerator: an extremely narrow, extremely high room, which occupies two levels horizontally. Because of the room's height, the little warm air which results from breathing and body heat quickly lifts up, five meters above the cement floor. The room has no bed or chair, but only a retractable wooden board which is maneuvered by the guard from the outside and which is only lowered for seven hours at night. The rest of the time, I have to stand. In order not to freeze, I must walk continuously, all seventeen hours, and my movement only stirs up the air around me, making the cold even more agonizing. The wood plank, which is let down at night to a ninety degree angle, is hardly as narrow as my emaciated body. Exhausted, I throw myself on it, but because I am sleeping in a refrigerator, I wake up frequently, feeling as if I am lying on shards of ice. After one night, I am weak and exhausted. Will I last through tomorrow? Forty days is unthinkable!

Again, I must devise a means of alleviating my suffering. I turn to my imagination, appealing to my old muse, my spiritual mother, who rocked and soothed me throughout my childhood, arming me with health and strength: the Black Sea, on the shore of which once stood my ancestral home:

> Breakers, cry with me!
> White locks, disheveled,
> Lips frothing, foaming,
> Breasts quivering, quacking,
> Backs bending, breaking!
>
> Writhe! Toss! Wail!
> Moan! Bellow! Roar!
> Like the fierce gale,
> Raging through my cell,
> Ravaging my body,
> Unraveling my soul.
>
> Breakers, mourn with me!
> The ice cracks; I sink
> In the frozen abyss...

My verses have taken me through two more days of torture. But now I am forced to stop. Again, my mind is numb. Poetry is too taxing, too exacting, requires too much concentration. I must come up with another way of lighting up the creative fires that will protect me from freezing to death. I search desperately for some dry twigs. Finally, I find them, strike them, spark them; the fire kindles, smokes; gradually, I warm up.

I am not actually writing, but merely sketching an outline for a work of fiction dealing with a period in Romanian history which has long interested me. I will explore this period, I decide, after lengthy deliberation, through two related novels. The first, entitled *Maria Butoianu*, will focus on a fascinating historical figure, a Romanian Joan of Arc, our first female warrior, who took part in Michael the Brave's revolt against the Ottoman Empire in 1594. For over a year Maria battles with Michael's army disguised as a man, demonstrating more courage, strength and physical endurance than any of her fellow soldiers who never once suspect her as a member of the so-called "weaker sex." My heroine will be driven both by her desire to revenge her father and brother's death, as well as by her passionate belief that women are actually stronger than men, better equipped to endure cold, hunger, pain, fatigue and suffering, having been purposely endowed with superior gifts by nature to ensure the propagation of the species. "Haven't the Greeks made the Goddess of wisdom a woman, Pallas Athena? And haven't the Romans invented a similar Goddess as their paragon of wisdom—Minerva? And wasn't Queen Semiramida, creator of the marvelous city of Ninive, the greatest of the ancient Assyrian-Babylonian monarchs?" my heroine will ask, basing her actions on deeply felt convictions. Maria Butoianu will sacrifice her life in the battle against the Turks, inspiring Michael's entire army with her passionate plea: "If we don't fight tyranny, despotism, and oppression, and allow power hungry monarchs to trample over our rights, evil will spread throughout the world." These words will be repeated obsessively throughout my novel.

The action of my second volume, *Pepelea,* will take place between the years 1606 and 1616, a time when our land was ruled by one of the vilest despots in our history, Lady Elizaveta Movila, widow of Ieremia Movila, another odious figure of the past. She will be contrasted and opposed by Pepelea, a wise-cracking, fun-loving, truth-seeking folk hero, representing the wisdom, humor and hunger for freedom characteristic of the Romanian people throughout their sad history. This book, which will also function through symbol and allegory, will juxtapose Lady Elizaveta's cynicism and nihilism against Pepelea's quiet optimism and firm faith in the ultimate goodness of man. The hero's final words, with which the book will end will be: "There is no greater happiness for a real man than the happiness of making others happy, the happiness of spreading happiness throughout the world."

◆ ◆ ◆

New Year's Day, 1964, finds me with Pepelea's phrase on my lips, trying to warm myself with it, like the little match girl in Hans Christian Anderson's story tries to warm herself with her last match. The planning of my two books has kept me alive for another week. But now I have reached the limit of my endurance and can no longer drag my feet around my torture chamber. I have fallen on the frozen cement and am trying to crawl around on all fours. Exhausted, vanquished, I finally give up and remain prostate for some time, completely paralyzed. I know that if I don't get up, I'm doomed to die, but I have no more strength.

Unexpectedly, something extraordinary happens, something unheard of in this temple of sick cruelty. The door visor lifts up, and the guard, disobeying the rules and exposing himself to punishment, shouts: "The latrine! Sit on the latrine!" I crawl to the barrel of excrement, push down the lid, and sit on it.

I interpret the guard's interference as a sign from heaven. I must not give up, I must not give in, not after all I have been through, not now, when liberation is practically knocking at my door. I must have faith in myself, in my body, in my spirit, in my mind. I'm still strong. Years of military and athletic training, avid swimming, skiing, walking and hiking, have built up my endurance. I have triumphed before. I will triumph again. Everything inside of me, all my instincts, all my premonitions are screaming: "You will live!"

Suddenly I remember another such time, when fate took me to death's door but then turned around and brought me back. I cling to that memory, like to a crag off a cliff. I resolve to travel back in time and relive those trying moments bit by bit, plucking enough strength and hope from my past victory to survive my current crisis.

◆ ◆ ◆

It all started with a premonition that turned out to be correct. A month before I was arrested, I had a feeling that soon I will have to pay with my freedom for daring to defy the communist dictatorship. For me, who have all my life loved nature, the outdoors, the fresh air, prison was the worst form of hell I could imagine. And so I embarked on a weekend trip, by myself, to my beloved Carpathian Mountains, perhaps to see them for one last time, and to say "goodbye."

I went to the part I loved most, the ring of mountains known as Bucegi. I chose the most difficult and dangerous trail but also the most charming and grand: a path traversing the mountains, beginning in the Prahov Valley, going up to the Omul (a peak nicknamed "The Man") and then arriving to the opposite side, at the Paraul Mic ("Small Creek") near the locality of Risnov. I would be hiking around thirty kilometers through a chain of mountains that rises up to a twenty-five hundred meter elevation.

I started my journey from the quaint Alpine village, Busteni, over which the Bucegi rise up to the sky. After following a thin strand of water through the Jepilor Valley, the trail abruptly mounted up and cut brusquely into the steep cliff. At that point a large sign warned the reckless traveler that access there was forbidden, as the dangerous trail was no longer in use. Just enough to entice the curiosity of the daring young tourist, I soon realized, as I, too, ignored the sign, started up the trail and was soon confronted by a series of crosses commemorating the young men and women who have died there! Even though I was not a young tourist, I climbed the rotten steps and grabbed the shattered cables of this beautiful trail which defies the steep wall of the mountain and the chasms beneath it. I chose to brave these perils because at the time I felt an irresistible urge to thumb my nose at fate, to throw a defiant glove in the face of destiny. Perhaps I wanted to convince myself that I was not afraid of death.

The more I climbed, the more I realized that I had, indeed, placed myself in mortal danger. The trail was so narrow that at the slightest wrong turn or false step I was sure to roll down into the abyss. Soon I was forced to give up the pretense of being the king of animals and become a humble quadruped, crawling my way up on all fours. Sometimes, when I would reach a slightly wider platform, I would carefully stand up and absorb the fairy tale-like beauty of my view: the town transformed into tiny toy boxes, the pine trees at the bottom of the mountain into an endless green meadow, men and beasts into busy anthills. Only the eagles and vultures looked like themselves as they were roving around my head, waiting for me to slide off the cliff and provide them with dinner.

The path continued to get narrower, the wood steps more hollow and the cables half-gnawed by wild animals. Several times I lost my balance and had to save myself by catching the edge of a craggy cliff, digging my nails in the deepest part of its moss. Then I came upon another row of crosses—four young men who fell into the precipice on summer days. I told myself in a loud voice that fate was now playing cat-and-mouse with me, but that soon it would touch my shoulder in a friendly way, pat me on the back, and assure me that it was all a joke.

After many more hours spent crawling on all fours, threatened by chasms and vultures, I finally reached the giant cliff that guards the entrance to the Buceag Plateau where the cabana where I had planned to spend the night was situated, perched above an awesome precipice. To reach the cabana I had to climb the cliff guarding it, three hundred meters high, on a path cut through rocks in narrow steps covered with slippery moss. To make things worse, the sky suddenly darkened. If it were to rain, I would either slip into the chasm or be struck by Jupiter's lightning for my carelessness and conceit. Still, I kept my cool. I was stubborn enough to believe in myself and in my fate, refusing to think even for a second that I could end up as the vulture's next meal. I had never yet known depression. I had never yet experienced the cage with iron bars, the hunger, cold, immobility and solitude which were to lead me, in the years to come, to more than once lose my will to live.

Vigorously, I went on to attack the last walls separating me from the "forbidden citadel," the lady-in-black threatening me with non-being at every step. I crawled on all fours on the narrow shoulders of the cliff, with my bloody nails digging deep into the moss. Several times I slipped and found myself hanging on a cable, my legs swimming through the air. At a certain point, one of the cables detached itself, and I found myself five meters below the shoulder of the cliff. After swinging several times above the chasm, bathed in cold sweat, I was able to land back on the cliff's narrow shoulder. For several hours I struggled with this accursed cliff, either creeping on my belly or hanging on the cable, until finally, I made it to the plateau, only several steps away from the much-dreamed-of cabana. Its keeper, a sturdy, jovial, young man who had been breathlessly following the last part of my adventure, greeted me with a penetrating stare:

"I could not have imagined that a fully grown man would ignore the warning at the bottom of the mountain! My heart stopped when I saw you hanging on that cable! You were very lucky! Yesterday a student fell into the precipice, and I only learned this from the vultures who were roving around her all morning. Just an hour ago we finally managed to get her body out with ropes."

"And I who thought the vultures were roving around me, waiting for me to serve them dinner!" I answered him, smiling. "Wouldn't it make more sense if you repaired the trail instead of condemning it?"

"I have no say over that!"

"Who does?"

"Others, more important than I. Don't you think it would suit me if they fixed the path? When it was in good repair, my cabana was always full. Now my guests have to come through a roundabout way which has cut their number down to about a quarter of what it used to be!"

"Why don't we go in and drink a toast to my good luck?" I suggested, following him in and ordering two bottles of cold beer which I invited him to share with me. To this, my host added his house specialty, a sizzling steak of wild boar, which was delicious, tender and gamy. Then I entered the common bedroom of the cabana, claimed one of the bunk beds and stretched my tired body between the fresh, cool sheets. I fell asleep instantly.

I woke up before the crack of dawn, got dressed in a hurry and took an easy road along the bank of the river (with the icy water of which I filled my canteen) to the Babelor Cliffs ("The Hags"), which resemble two old women, facing each other, gossiping. I got there in time to catch the sunrise on the high peaks, a magnificent spectacle, full of dramatic optical illusions.

Ahead of me extended an immaculate lake of foam, over which a soft shower of rose petals drizzled and bled into the horizon. Suddenly, from high up in heaven's vault, a volcano erupted, inundating the blue sky and white lake with purple lava and carmine wreaths. Then a rain of falling stars and shattering rainbows exploded in bursts of blue, green, orange and copper. Soon the color storm died down, spears of gold pierced the last remnants of the sea of foam, and the triumphant sun spread itself brilliantly over the entire blue kingdom.

◆ ◆ ◆

The door to my "lock up" opens. The guard orders me to get out and follow him. Legs trembling, I stagger after him to an office where a military colonel is waiting for me. He tells me that today is January 3, 1964, that he is inspecting the prison, and that he would like me to explain to him why I am being punished. I answer that I have been condemned to twenty-five years in prison for writing a book, that I have been punished with forty days in the "lock up" for communicating with my neighbors and more importantly for refusing to renege my political beliefs, and that I consider this punishment criminal and illegal, as it is equivalent to a death sentence. The colonel nods and dismisses me. I am returned to my "refrigerator," but half an hour later am taken out again and escorted to a new cell in the "Zarca" section of the prison. My old cell has been assigned to another inmate. I had not been expected to return alive.

16

Irina: High Hopes

Bundled up in layers of whatever clothes their parents can muster, the children glide over frozen puddles and slide down sloped alleys, pelting each other with snowballs until their icy hands and feet force them to run inside to thaw out. It's so cold this winter that no one can play outdoors for long. Passing by my neighborhood friends on my way to the bus stop, I swing my satchel up and down, proud of its contents: my bathing suit, my swim cap, my towel. While others skate, I swim.

Every day after school, I take the bus to the Winter Sports Palace. I have a special card, which I must show to the guard at the gate before he lets me in. I pass the building where other athletes practice basketball, gymnastics or fencing and walk straight to the building with the big, beautiful indoor swimming pool, where I am training with Coach Iacobini's team. I go down the stairs to the locker rooms to change and then up the stairs to the swimming pool, where I bend and stretch, do sit-ups and push-ups, lift weights, run around the pool and finally dive in and swim, swim, swim. Everything here seems magical, maybe because without my glasses I see it all through a hazy, steamy, blur. I love the gleaming tiles, the undulating, clear blue water, the colorful lane dividers, the numbered platforms, the diving section, where older boys and girls perform amazing feats, the buoyant splashing of the beginners, the graceful gliding of the advanced, the echoing sounds of shouting, screaming, laughing, whistling, splashing, the smells of chlorine, wet and sweat.

My coach, Comrade Iacobini, is a short, middle-aged man with graying hair. He shouts at us until his voice is hoarse, but his watchful eyes can read immediately when one of us has had too much and needs a rest. At first I was disappointed when Comrade Corcec, the handsome young man to whom my mother took Sorin and me to discuss joining a swim team, told us that he himself coached only the advanced swimmers. Comrade Corcec seemed pleased to see us, and I heard him whisper something to my mother about my father, who had been kind to his subordinates, and who was an excellent swimmer to boot. He put one arm around each of us and walked us over to Comrade Iacobini, who scowled, ordered us to dive in and swim a lap for him, then shook his head and muttered, "Normally, we don't take them at this level but if Comrade Corcec insists..."

Later, I found out from some older girls in the locker room that Comrade Corcec coached the best team in the country, that his swimmers often traveled abroad and some of them even qualified for the Olympics. I decided right there, on the spot, that I would work hard and get on Comrade Corcec's team, and someday I would travel with the handsome, dark-haired coach to California and visit the relatives I loved and missed so much!

So all winter long I've been training hard, training every day, trying to listen to everything Comrade Iacobini tells me without getting discouraged and upset when he starts yelling at the top of his lungs: "Irina! Stop dreaming in the water! Are your arms asleep? Did your feet fall off? Kick! Kick! Harder! Faster! Damn It! Kick, Kick, Kick!" Sometimes I notice Comrade Iacobini walking alongside the pool with several other coaches, observing me swim, discussing my stroke. One day, after a sprint, as I catch my breath by the side of the pool, I overhear him say, "This one will do better at meets than in practice. She needs the competition to get it out of her!" During the next sprint, I kick, kick, kick with all my might.

I am now training with Comrade Iacobini's best team. I train twice a day, before and after school. I get up early and go to swim practice. My hair still wet, I run to school. After school, I rush to practice, come home, eat dinner, do my homework and go to bed. My friends are my teammates. We discuss good coaches, bad coaches, strong swimmers, weak swimmers, teams, records, races, awards, training camps and the Olympics.

All of us dream about the Olympics. Romania wins so few medals in the Olympics! And in swimming, never! The Americans, especially the ones from California, where they have swimming pools in their backyards, are the best swimmers. But now we will change all that. We will train hard, we will train twice a day, every day, and we'll get good enough to beat them. We are given brand new bathing suits and warm up suits. Every week, Coach distributes big bars of bittersweet chocolate to give us energy. Our leaders, he tells us, have high hopes for us young athletes. If we dedicate ourselves to our sports, we will bring honor to our great nation.

My best friend, Gabriela, who is a year older than I, always beats me in practice, but lags far behind me during swim meets. Comrade Iacobini was right. Competition does seem to bring out in me whatever it is that a swimmer needs to do to win a race. I've won several first-place medals already and am now training for the big regional meet in May, when I will compete against children from towns outside Bucharest.

In February, I was finally awarded my red kerchief. I am determined to prove that I am worthy of the care lavished on me by my coaches. I plan to make Romania proud when I swim in the 1968 Olympics—I will be fifteen by then—and bring home the gold!

◆ ◆ ◆

I'm now one of the most popular kids on my block, not only because of my swimming victories but also because I have a regular supply of American chewing gum—which our relatives in California send us every month along with the transistor radios, electric shavers, pantyhose and boxes of Kent cigarettes. My mother sells all but the gum at the flea market on Sundays to supplement our income.

Nothing delights my friends more than those long, sweet, colorfully wrapped sticks of gum that you chew and chew and stretch and pop. One stick gets divided into many tiny pieces, which sometimes get traded and passed around even after they've been chewed. One day my teacher caught me chewing gum in class and ordered me to open my mouth. Quickly, I tried to hurl the evidence out the window. She saw this, shouted at me and made me stand in the corner for the rest of the hour. As soon as the break bell rang, all the children ran outside to the yard and went wild looking for my piece of chewed-up gum. Several boys found it and began fighting over it. Our teacher got hysterical over the whole thing. "If someone from America sent you shit, you'd eat it! You'd lick your lips and say it's chocolate!" she screamed.

Suddenly everyone is humming American, French and Italian songs. On the radio, instead of the old Romanian folk music, we are now hearing "Ceau, Ceau!" and "Volare, O, O!" The older girls try to imitate Petula Clark, the older boys Elvis Presley. Everyone struggles to get tickets to American films. No one seems to go to Russian movies anymore. Thanks to our cigarettes and chewing gum, we have managed to get in to see *The Magnificent Seven*, *Fun in Acapulco* and *The Apartment*. Everyone is talking about *The Apartment*. They can't get over what Jack Lemmon says in the beginning of the movie about how he is just an average clerk who lives on a small salary but then names a figure that is ten times what a Romanian professional earns. His "modest" apartment has a television and a stereo and a refrigerator, and all he has to do for dinner is pop a neat little tray from his freezer into his stove. In a few seconds it's ready to eat!

Everyone marvels at the way Americans live, their easy, luxurious, glamorous lifestyles, their huge homes filled with mechanical gadgets, their fancy cars, their extensive wardrobes, their lavish parties held around large private swimming pools where people walk around holding glasses full of clinking ice cubes. We, of course, know more about the wonders of America than most people, since we get letters from our relatives, who are now living in a city called San Francisco. In America everyone, even janitors and garbage men, own their own cars. Americans work very hard and take very few breaks. Some people work two jobs and don't even take time out to have coffee or pastry, the way people do here. Their favorite food is a gigantic ground meat sandwich called a "hamburger," which is a three-course meal in one. To eat it, you have to open your mouth wide to take a bite, but you can finish it in five minutes. Americans shorten and simplify everything, because they're always in a hurry. They don't waste time with manners and ceremony. If they invite you to their house and ask you "would you like some coffee and cake," you better not say, "oh, no, please don't bother," because they'll really take your word for it and won't! They're not very sociable, anyway. They stay home a lot, my uncle writes, but when they go somewhere they drive. Even on vacation, many of them just put their homes on wheels and attach them to their automobiles! I would love to visit this marvelous country, but there is no way I would ever want to live there!

◆ ◆ ◆

The days are longer and warmer now, but I am still training at the Winter Palace. I will continue there until June, when the outdoor swimming complex will open. When I don't have too much homework, I give up waiting for the bus after practice and walk home, breathing the sweet spring air. There's a food stand on the way that sells warm, giant pretzels covered with sesame seeds. Coming home this afternoon, munching on my pretzel, I notice a very thin, ragged man standing on the street corner near our house. He stares at me intently, with eyes that seem to bulge out of their bony sockets. Though he looks like a beggar, his palm is not stretched out; if it were, I would give him the few pennies I have left in my pocket. He stares at me as I bite into my pretzel, my mouth full of sesame seeds, and I am ashamed of myself for filling my stomach while he looks so hungry.

I swing open the gate and, to my surprise, I do not hear it close behind me. I run into the building and rush up the steps. I hear footsteps mounting the stairs behind me. I climb faster, two or three steps at a time, hoping that my mother is home already. It is around five o'clock. My brother now goes to school during the afternoon session. Giunica may still be waiting in some food line to buy milk or meat. Desperately, I pound on the door with one hand, while struggling to unlock it with the other.

"Irina?" a voice behind me whispers. I freeze, then slowly turn my head. It is he! The horrible man!

"Irina?" he says again in a muffled, barely audible voice. "Irina Eremia?"

If I open the door, I think, he'll force his way in after me. Then I'll be all alone with him. I drop my satchel, jump on the stair banister, wrap my arms and legs tightly around it, and slide all the way down until I reach bottom and roll off to the cement floor. I'm bruised, but nothing's broken.

"Are you crazy? Are you trying to kill yourself?" screams my mother, who has just walked into the lobby, her arms weighed down by the two bottles of milk.

"There's a man up there," I try to warn her, barely able to catch my breath. "A horrible man. He looks like a ghost! And he knows my name!"

Without a word, my mother climbs the stairs. I follow at a safe distance. The "ghost" is still there, waiting in front of our apartment.

"Regina Eremia?"

"Yes. Can I help you?"

"I have some news for you. May I come in?"

"Please," my mother answers, and opens the door for him.

◆ ◆ ◆

I have never seen anyone eat like the man eats. The soup, the bread, the stuffed peppers, the mashed potatoes—he gobbles up everything and seems hungry for more. My plate is untouched. Should I offer it to him?

"Aren't you hungry, Irina?" my mother asks me, impatiently.

"No, not really."

"Then please go to the other room and leave us alone here in the kitchen. I'll warm up your food later, after your brother gets home."

I hesitate, not because I'm hungry, but because I'm afraid to leave her alone with the stranger.

"Run along! Get started on your homework!" she says firmly, and I go.

I remind myself that my mother is strong and smart and can take care of herself. If the man attacks her, she'll scream loud enough for me to hear. Then I'll run to the window and call for help.

◆ ◆ ◆

Finally, the kitchen door opens, and my mother leads the man out, just as my brother walks in.

"Who was that?" Sorin asks, as the three of us sit at the kitchen table. "He looks like one of the skeletons we've been studying in physiology."

"He's a man who has suffered a lot. A good man. You can't always judge a book by its cover," she tells us. "He was in the same place as your father. He came to tell us that Neclo is coming home soon."

"From Russia?" I ask.

My mother is silent. My brother looks scared.

"When?" Sorin asks.

"Within the next few months, he thinks…"

"He's coming back from Russia?" I try again.

"No," my mother says, after a long pause. "Not from Russia. Why don't you and I take a long walk after dinner, and then I'll explain everything."

"What about me?" asks my brother.

"You stay here and do your homework. Weren't you just telling me earlier about how much studying you have to do?"

"Can't you tell her here?"

"No, I can't! Get to work! Try to do some lessons ahead. Tomorrow night, I'd like to take you out."

I feel privileged. For once in my life, I will be told secrets first.

◆ ◆ ◆

"He didn't go to Russia," my mother whispers as we walk along the Soseaua Chiselev behind a pair of lovers holding hands. On Sundays everyone—young people, old people, groups of teenagers, families with children—stroll up and down this broad avenue lined with chestnut and poplar trees, but tonight, a work-night, only young couples are to be found here.

The couple ahead of us decides to stop on a bench and start kissing. We are now walking entirely by ourselves. My mother glances over her shoulder, then takes a deep breath and begins. Before I know it, the truth is out, and I am staring in horror at the ugly toad that has jumped from her mouth.

"Your father is in prison. That's where he's really been all this time. He was condemned to twenty-five years for writing a book that criticized the government. The man who came to see us tonight has just been released from the prison where your father is, and told me he, too, will be pardoned and should be coming home soon."

So the kids on the street who had yelled, "Your father's in prison," had not been lying. And Marica hadn't lied to me either. It was my mother who had lied! My father wasn't in Russia. Of course, not! We never got any letters! How could I have been so stupid! "Liar! Liar!" I want to shout at my mother!

"Does Sorin know?" I ask.

"Yes."

"Why did you tell him and not me?"

"Because he was seven and a half—old enough to understand. You were only five."

"So why didn't you tell me later, when I was seven?"

"There was no point, then, in bringing it up. You weren't thinking about him anymore..."

"How did you know that?"

"Look, darling, I am not going to allow this to become an interrogation. I have never lied to you about anything—except about this, because in my judgment, you were too young to be told at the time."

But she's not telling me the truth, even now, I think. What she is saying makes no sense. It's all made up—like the story about Russia. But I'm not a dumb five-year-old anymore. Everyone knows that prisons are for criminals. No one goes to prison just for writing a book.

"Did he do something awful? What did he do? Tell me the truth!" I cry. But even as I say this, I can't imagine that the kind, gentle man I remember—Neclo, my father!—could have done something horrible enough to be put in jail.

"Shhhh! Keep your voice down, please." My mother puts her arm around my shoulder and tries to soothe me. She strokes my hair, my back, and gently prods me to start moving again. "What I've told you, darling, is the truth. But it isn't such an easy, simple thing to understand. If you promise me to be patient and listen and not interrupt me until I'm done, I will do my best to explain everything to you. Can you do that?"

"Yes! But I want you to tell me the whole story!"

"I can only tell you the story I know...Please start walking, look straight ahead of you, and don't act surprised if I suddenly have to change the subject. Do you understand?"

"Of course!" Sorin, she respects, but me, no—I'm the idiot of the family. Still, I decide to shut up and listen.

With her arm around my shoulder and my arm around her waist, her right side glued to my left, our feet moving in perfect synchrony, we walk. As we walk, she talks in a low, measured, careful voice, pausing every few minutes to turn her head, to look back and make sure that no one is following us.

◆ ◆ ◆

"You see these beautiful poplar trees that line the road, my love? We can admire their shiny green leaves and straight, strong trunks, and know nothing about the gnarled and twisted roots, buried deep under the earth, from which they sprang. I wanted you and your brother to grow tall and strong like these trees, and never be held back by the gnarled and twisted roots of the past.

"There are people who get entangled in the past. I have never allowed myself to linger over my memories, or dwell on my childhood, or cry over spilt milk. It's hard to go forward when you're constantly looking backwards (like right now, see how much it's slowing us down?) But your father will soon bring the past back into our lives, and you will need to understand it, if only to move beyond it, as I am sure you will, for you are a very intelligent girl, Irina—which is why I feel I can speak to you now not as I would to a child, but to an adult.

"On that first dreadful morning after they took your father away, when you bounced into our dining room chirping your cheerful little song, I swore to myself that I wouldn't allow anyone or anything to rob you of your sweet innocence. For you were a happy, contented little girl who loved everything and everyone. I wished I could have protected your brother, also, from the awful truth, but Sorin was too old, too smart and too close to his father to be told anything else.

"How well I knew what it meant to be a small, helpless child, weighed down by big worries! You see, my darling, unlike you, I had not been a happy, cheerful child. I was the youngest of six, and I grew up at a time when everyone around me had greater concerns than the sad little girl playing with the broken pieces of leftover toys in her hideaway under the dining room table. It was a remarkable table: a gigantic square of oak that sat on a massive pedestal which ended in four claws. I was fascinated by those claws. I stared at them endlessly and made up all sorts of stories about tigers and lions running through the jungles of Africa.

"Our house in Braila—someday I will have to take you there, it is a charming little city on the Danube—was big and beautiful and very noisy. Your Omama, as you know, is an excellent cook, and everyone else in the family liked to linger at the table. I would eat a few bites and escape to my special sanctuary. I wanted to hide from the anxious voices that were always arguing and contradicting each other about the terrifying things that were happening around us. I didn't want to hear, but still, I listened. 'What if they come and take us?' 'Where can we hide?' 'No, we can't trust them!' 'It's safer here.' 'It isn't safe anywhere.'

"I wished they would stop talking. I wished someone would pull me from under that table and take me somewhere that was safe and peaceful and beautiful, somewhere like my father's vineyard in the hills, where we used to go when I was very young, and he would let me run freely in the fresh air under the blue sky and listen to the songs of the peasant girls. Papa would bring home the sweet new wine and put a drop on his finger for each of us children to taste, and there seemed to be fewer arguments at the table then, and more jokes, stories and laughter.

"But I can barely remember those happy days. What I do remember are the sirens, the air raids, the explosions, and the terrifying cries of men in green shirts who marched through the streets yelling, 'Death to the Jews!' And I remember one bright sunny morning when I was swinging back and forth on our gate and a woman I knew from the neighborhood—I think she lived in the house behind ours—came up to me and gave me a beautiful blue box full of soap and said: 'Here, little girl. Take this to your mother. She'll really appreciate it. There's a shortage of soap, you know.' I ran to Mamica with the treasure, and when she saw it…'Oh, my God,' she shrieked, and then began to wail, as if something horrible were happening before her eyes. Then she drew me by the hand and pulled me into the back yard, where she dug a hole and put the box of soap in it, and then chanted a prayer over it—*Sh'ma Y'Israel*, a special Hebrew prayer—and covered it with earth. I was afraid to ask her anything, and she never could bring herself to tell me anything. It was later, from my sisters, that I learned the soap was made from the fat of Jewish people who were being killed all over Russia and Poland.

"Why am I telling you about these horrible things that happened before you were born? Because it is human beings who made them happen and nothing about human beings has changed. For several years during the war, we had to give up a portion of our house to German soldiers who were stationed in our town. Believe it or not, they were very nice to us, very polite, very thoughtful, even. One sergeant, I remember, would give my father sugar and flour and coal, and he sometimes brought chocolate for us children. And I am sure that many of the Germans who murdered Jews during the War might have been decent human beings at other times in their lives. Most people are a mixture of good and bad—some have a little more of one than the other—but almost everyone is susceptible to greed, envy, spite, malice, coercion, fear, and there are people who know how to exploit these, and situations that bring them out. Haven't you ever seen kids who are normally well-behaved suddenly turn into horrid little monsters when they join a group of troublemakers and follow their lead? Adults are no different!

"I remember the day when your Opapa burst in the door with the news that Romania had joined the allies and the German army was retreating as the Russians closed in. The Nazis had not yet started to round up the Jews in our part of the country. We were saved! 'From now on, everything will go well!' Papicu promised us. What a dream! All day that day hungry, angry German soldiers retreating from the Russian front marched through the streets looting and shooting everyone in sight. Then, after the last of them finally disappeared, the explosions started. Homes, warehouses, factories and office buildings, all of which the Nazis had booby-trapped, burst into flames. People started running out of their houses, running wildly in all directions.

"I ran outside, too, and joined the madness. A neighbor boy grabbed me by the hand. 'Come on, let's go!' he shouted. 'The Germans left lots of good things; we must hurry and get some, too.' I ran after him without thinking, just another follower ready to join the mob. He took me to a burning building and led me to an area where hundreds of people were pushing and pulling and kicking each other over a large supply of sealed boxes. 'What's in here?' I asked him. 'It doesn't matter,' he answered. 'Whatever it is, it's more than we have.' "For the rest of the day I ran with him from one building to the next, grabbing as many boxes as I could, taking them home, putting them down and then going back out for more. I risked being burned or trampled to death over and over again, without the slightest idea about why I was doing it. What an incredible lesson in human nature! During the next ten hours, I saw dignified and prominent citizens of our town—teachers, doctors, judges, refined ladies and elderly gentlemen—with their hair full of ashes, their faces covered with soot, their clothes torn and burnt, pushing each other, stepping over each other, ready to tear each other apart like wild beasts fighting over their prey. And there I was, in the midst of it all, a fierce little animal, struggling for my piece of flesh.

"That night I couldn't sleep. I still felt the flames hot on my skin, the smoke in my lungs and throat, and heard the screams and blows and curses. Finally I fell asleep, only to be awakened by a great roaring sound. All of us ran to the window and saw tanks and every other kind of military equipment coming down the street—the Red Army had arrived. And a new kind of terror started.

"The Russians who were billeted with us treated us about as nicely as the Germans did. But there were groups of wild, drunken soldiers who roamed the streets and were a menace to everyone. My sisters and I had to run and hide constantly. Because we had changed sides so recently, the Russians didn't accept us as allies. They were the victors, and we were the vanquished. They pillaged the city and stole everything they could and sent it back to Russia. They broke into homes and beat people up, demanding that they produce their hidden treasures. Anyone who dared to complain or to ask questions was put on a train and sent to Siberia.

"The war ended, but the months of misery went on. Papicu couldn't find work. He was too old and had been in business for himself all his life. The stress was, finally, too much for him. He had a stroke and was ill for a long time. Finally, we decided to move to Bucharest, where your Uncle Jack was already working, and where we hoped we would find more opportunities. There, seven of us lived in a tiny apartment. We had to use public bathrooms three blocks away and had only bread and potatoes to eat. Opapa was very depressed. 'America sold us to the Russians,' he said.

"Listening to my father moan about how America could have saved us and hadn't, I decided that I would never in my life depend on anyone for anything. No one owes anyone anything, I thought. Everyone must take care of himself. I studied like crazy, and partly because of the chaos after the war, partly because I was blessed with a photographic memory, I managed to get my high school diploma before I turned sixteen. The family encouraged me to study medicine. But from those early years when I hid under the table and listened to people's voices and tried to guess their secrets and pretended I was someone else, I had dreamed about becoming an actress. Because of the war, I had had few opportunities to act in school plays, but I didn't let my lack of training stop me. I applied to the College of Dramatic Arts, where there were dozens of applicants for every spot and, to everyone's surprise, I got in.

"As happy and excited as I was, it wasn't easy for me to adjust to my new life as an acting student. I was so young, so innocent, so inexperienced! I was modest and serious, came to class in one of the two dresses I owned, combed my hair in braids, had no jewelry or make-up, did my work and kept to myself. I knew nothing of the subtle schemes others used to attract the attention or court the favor of those who could pave their road to success for them. No one noticed me. Still, I graduated college with good grades and was offered a decent position at a new theater that was looking for young talent. This position, however, had a condition attached. It would be part of my job to organize a young communist league in the company.

"I thought about my decision deeply. I had mixed feelings about becoming involved in politics, given what I had seen after the Russian occupation. I went to one of my professors, someone who had been especially kind to me. 'My dear, you either ride the wave to the shore, or smash against it and drown,' he told me. I understood. This was not a time for heroes. This was a time for survivors. I took the job, read some books, and began making speeches and organizing meetings at our theater, while also doing everything in my power to develop my craft as an actress. The roles I got were small, but I always looked beyond them.

"One day, even though I was only in the Young Communist League and still far from a full-fledged party member, I was asked to serve on a 'verification committee,' which had suddenly been formed to review the records of party members who were actors. I soon realized that some of the stronger members were trying to kick the weaker ones out the door, discarding them like used, dirty rags. Nevertheless, I went to the meetings and got my first lesson in how the system works."

◆ ◆ ◆

My mother suddenly stops talking. I look around. There's no one else in sight. I listen. The only sound I hear is that of our own footsteps.

"What's the matter?" I whisper.

"Nothing. I just don't want to make things difficult for you..." I realize that Giunica is hesitating about how much to tell me. But for some reason this doesn't bother me anymore. It's getting late and I'm starting to feel tired.

"All right, I'll go on," Giunica says. I guess she has decided to tell me. "Maybe the sooner you know, the better. Such meetings take place every day. Nothing has changed.

"Ours were held in a large empty room. We sat behind a long wooden table. Facing us, at some distance, was a small, hard chair. The actor to be 'verified' was forced to sit for hours and answer the questions that the 'verifiers' shot at him like bullets. All of us had copies of secret files full of information about the actor's background, parents, grandparents, friends, lovers, as well as everything that had been observed or reported about his or her actions, opinions, activities, habits, preferences, weaknesses, vices, failures, mistakes—you name it, it was there! You must realize, my love, that such files exist about all of us. That's why you must be so careful all the time about whom you talk to and what you say.

"I was shocked to see George Vraca, my hero, the greatest Romanian actor of my time, walk in and sit in the hard chair. He stared at us, petrified. His rich, deep voice that had performed *Hamlet* and *Othello* and *King Lear* now stuttered and stumbled over an incoherent string of sounds. I felt tears rolling down my cheek, and had to keep pretending to look through the file so I wouldn't meet anyone's glance. After that, I found ways of avoiding these sessions, mostly by taking on additional roles, until the Party gave up on me and replaced me with more eager volunteers.

"The head of our theater was a man named Finzi, a short, fat slob with frog eyes and a voice that always reminded me of a clock that keeps ticking and ticking in your ears. Not long before, he had been a two-bit actor who considered himself lucky if he got a speaking part. But he was a party member, so he was considered a creative genius and was given tremendous power over the actors and the repertoire. Every actress in the theater competed to get his attention. After some time, he finally noticed me and gave me a decent part in a play. But after the first rehearsal, he insisted on walking me home.

"As soon as we turned the corner, he made me an 'indecent proposal.' I got so mad, I forgot about his power and position, and slapped his fat face. 'Go home to your wife!' I told him. You're old enough to be my father! Aren't you ashamed of yourself?'

"When you get older, darling, remember that there are more diplomatic ways a woman can turn down a man. Slapping may look good on stage, but in life it can have severe repercussions. Finzi was the type of man who could easily have slapped me back and followed the slap with a punch. But the street was full of people. Since he couldn't kick me, he began to croak at me: 'Who the hell do you think you are? Nobody, nobody talks to me like that!' His eyes started rolling in his head as if he were crazy, and I started to run, which made him yell and swear at me until I jumped on a street car and escaped.

"The next morning when I went to work, I discovered that my part had been given to someone else. But I didn't let that discourage me. I continued to work harder than ever. From early morning until late at night, I was at the theater. When I wasn't acting, I assisted at rehearsals. I tried to study the methods of the most experienced and accomplished actors of the time. I memorized every part I thought would be good for me. Sooner or later, I knew I'd have a chance to use what I learned.

Then I got my chance. I had a very small part in a successful play, and the actress who had the lead didn't show up. The performance was sold out. Several members of the Central Committee of the Party were in the audience with their wives or girlfriends. Finzi was jumping up and down like the frog he was. He would be held responsible. Such a disaster might cost him his job. This was a time when there was no room for failure. Any mistake or accident could be labeled an act of sabotage. I went to the stage manager and told him to tell the 'big shot' that I could play Georgina's part. Finzi had no choice but to put me in. I saved the show and, of course, his skin. I proved myself.

"So you see, hard work and determination eventually do pay off—always remember that, my dear. After that, my career advanced. I got better parts, more opportunities to develop my craft. To portray different characters and express their motivations, passions, emotions, to make them larger than life and yet real and convincing, to move audiences, to reach them, to uplift them—to be a great actress…this was all I ever wanted! The theater was my life, heart and soul. Nothing else mattered to me."

◆ ◆ ◆

Again my mother stops, this time to hug me. "Oh, my darling, don't look at me like that! Please don't feel bad for me, that's not the point!"

How does she know I feel sorry for her? I didn't say anything. This is something I've always been careful to hide from her—how sad I think it is that she can't be an actress anymore.

"Realize, Irina, that what happened later with my career is the exception, not the rule. Besides, all is not over yet. Who knows how things may change? I am telling you this now so you'll understand something about my life before I met your father, and why I saw the things he didn't—if only he had listened!

"Anyway, one evening after a performance, a lieutenant came up to me and told me that I was invited to attend the inauguration ball for a new musical theater in Bucharest which was being held that evening. 'Thank you,' I told him, 'but I received no invitation and I came to the theater in a simple dress.' The man smiled and said, 'Look, Major Eremia invited you. Do you know who he is?' 'No,' I said. 'Then you must meet him now.' And he accompanied me to a black limousine where a very handsome man with blond hair was waiting, like Prince Charming, to take me to the ball. All that was missing was the Fairy Godmother and her magic wand to turn my simple dress into a sumptuous ball gown. But my dress didn't seem to matter to him. I really felt as if I were Cinderella. We danced all night long, and then he took me home and said he would speak to me soon, because he wanted to invite me to have dinner with him.

"The very next night I saw him at the theater. He was sitting in one of the boxes, enjoying the performance. He told me later that he came there every evening to watch me, but I had never noticed him. We went out two more times, and then, as we were walking through the Chismigiu Gardens after a lovely dinner at the Athenae Palace Hotel, he looked at me with his clear blue eyes and said: 'I like you and I love you…Do you want to marry me?'

"I was shocked. He was much older than I was, and I didn't know him at all; what did he know about me? I stared at him, unable to say anything. Do you remember your father at all, my darling? He was one of the handsomest men I had ever met—strong, well-built, and had those sky blue, penetrating eyes, an intriguing moustache and a captivating smile. What young girl would not have been attracted to him? He was a decorated war hero, a respected military man, and at the same time gentle, refined and well educated. And he was so romantic! On our walks, he had held me close, spoken to me tenderly, recited love poems, even sung to me! Still, I didn't feel that I was ready to get married. I was very young. I loved my career, and I didn't want anything to stand in my way. He seemed to read my thoughts.

"'Look, I know you better than you know me, because I discovered you, and watched you, and fell in love with you quite some time before I introduced myself to you. I know you are talented. And I know you are ambitious. I would never ask you to give up your career for me. We could be so happy together! I love you! Please don't say no.'

"'This is very hard for me,' I told him. 'I don't know you at all. We've barely met. I need time to think.'

"'Let me come this Sunday to meet your parents. Please don't say no.'

"The following day I went to my rehearsal, and Mr. Finzi was waiting for me. With what courtesy he invited me into his office! Suddenly, he was treating me like a queen.

"'Congratulations! Major Eremia called me last night and told me he is going to marry you. I want to apologize to you. Several weeks ago he asked me what I thought of you and I told him—please forgive me for this—not to waste his time and that I could fix him up with better girls. He wanted me to explain, so I told him that I once tried to flirt with you a little, and that you had been rigid and rude and unreasonable. Of course, I had no idea he wanted to marry you.'

"'But I'm not ready to marry him,' I said. 'We went out three times. I don't know anything about him.'

"Finzi began laughing. 'You want to turn down Major Eremia? He is one of the most respected and powerful men in the army. He is the protégée of the Secretary of Defense. The two of them were the only officers in the Romanian Army during the War who were communists. Everyone expects he will be made a general soon. On top of all this, he happens to be a very cultured, intelligent, charming man—truly one of a kind. You'd have to be out of your mind to refuse him!'

"I went home and told your Omama: 'The major who invited me to dinner has asked me to marry him. He wants to come over this Sunday and meet you and Papicu.' She stared at me in disbelief. She knew that there was no such thing as a Jewish officer. 'Have you forgotten who you are?' she asked me.

"What could I say? The truth was that for me, religion didn't matter. I had other worries than that he didn't happen to be Jewish. 'Mamica, today, such things no longer matter,' I tried to explain to her. 'We live in a society where no one practices religion anymore—which is just as well, look at the horrible things people have done to each other, with religion as their excuse. What I really want to know is if he is a good person, if he is honest and sincere, if he will love me and respect me and support me in my career. Please...Just fix him a dinner!'

"He showed up at the door holding a big bouquet of red roses. During dinner he kept staring at me with such tenderness! And he treated my parents and my brother and sisters with so much warmth and affection, as if he had known them all his life! This meant a great deal to me. He was a wonderful conversationalist—knowledgeable, articulate, but not at all impressed with himself—and by the end of the evening even Mamica and Papicu were won over.

"Then, he formally asked Papicu for my hand, making him all kinds of promises. 'It is up to my daughter,' my father said. 'She's a capable young woman who understands the ways of our new world better than I do.' Suddenly I saw myself as a little girl—maybe eight or nine years old, playing in the front yard of our house in Braila on a very hot summer day. An old, ragged Gypsy woman stopped by our gate. 'Hey, little girl,' she said, 'I am very thirsty, and if you bring me a cold glass of water and also put into my palm a few pennies so I can buy myself some bread, I will tell you your fortune.' I rushed in the house and got her the water, and she drank it and then took my palm and studied it for a while. 'I want you to remember this, my little one. When the time comes for you to be married, you are going to marry a man in a military uniform.' I ran inside and told this to my sisters, and they all burst out laughing. 'She didn't know you are Jewish. Jewish girls don't marry military men!'

"As I remembered this, I thought, Oh, God, maybe this man is my destiny. And I accepted him and we got engaged and two months later we got married. It was a fairy-tale wedding attended by the most powerful men in the country. We had a lavish feast, gorgeous flowers, a small orchestra, country singers, dancers, Gypsy violinists..."

◆ ◆ ◆

"Did you wear a white wedding gown with a long train and a veil over your face?" I can't resist from asking. I have seen a beautiful picture of such a bride in a glossy American magazine I once saw. How exciting to think of my mother dressed in such a costume.

"No, darling," Giunica laughs. "That would have been considered bourgeois and old-fashioned and would have been out of the question for someone in my position. We had a civil wedding, and I wore a pretty white dress, but a cocktail dress, you've seen it in my closet, I'm sure." I'm disappointed. I was hoping she had the bridal gown stored in a secret chest where she was saving it for me to wear some day. I sigh and let Giunica continue with the story that seems to hold no hidden treasures for me.

"Our honeymoon was the most wonderful time of my life, when I finally got to know and understand your father. We went up into the mountains and hiked from cabin to cabin for many kilometers. I saw that he was a great man with a large heart and a big vision. During the war, he had become convinced that communism would save Romania from the Nazis and create a better life for everyone. He admitted to me that there were many things about our government that he didn't like, but he was working to change all that. He attributed a lot of the problems to the Soviet control, but he was full of confidence in himself and in his friends.

"I thought he was too confident. Maybe this was because he had always been liked and accepted, and never expected anyone to mistreat him. He was older than I was and had fought in a war, yet I realized that he was much more naive. I had lived a life of persecution, and so I knew something about the meanness that can hide under the smoothest smile. I didn't want to discourage him, but even then I couldn't resist expressing some of my reservations, and I cautioned him to be careful. He frowned. He said he had no idea I was so cynical. I realized that the only way to make him respect my opinion would be to speak his language well. So after I came home, I studied Marxist political theory more seriously. Soon, I was able to participate in his discussions with his friends and hold my own with them.

"The better I got to know them, though, the more nervous I became. I realized that many of those he trusted were jealous and two-faced, and that he was incapable of picking up the subtle clues. To make matters worse, the man who worried me most was his favorite brother, Gica.

"Maybe you remember your uncle—I always thought he looked something like your father, but was the opposite of him in character. Gica was older than Neclo and deeply resented his success. He had become a communist before your father did, but unlike him, had never been willing to risk his life for the party. It didn't take me long to see that he was an envious, selfish, dissatisfied man. A malcontent—that's how I pegged him. I will never forget his behavior when Neclo earned a special distinction, which was recorded on his party card, for his underground work against the Nazis. A banquet was held in his honor, and Gica refused to attend. My mother-in-law, your Bunicuta, one of the kindest, sweetest women I have ever met—called him and begged him to go. But Gica was adamant. 'It's not fair that he should be honored and not I,' he said flat out. 'I was the one who joined the Party first.'

"Your uncle was unhappy with his job. He was a major in the regular police department, and this was not what he wanted. He would have liked to work for the Securitate, where he would have had much more power. He was always scheming to get himself a position there. And he was constantly pumping your father for information about everything he knew. Of course, your father refused to see anything but good in him and got angry whenever I warned him to be careful about what he said to him. If he couldn't trust his own brother, he asked me, whom could he trust?

"When I got pregnant with Sorin, I was excited, but also anxious. I was getting some good roles, but I was still far from where I wanted to be. To tell you the truth, it had been Neclo, not I, who wanted children right away. Forgive me for saying this, darling, but when I looked around, I wasn't so sure I wanted to bring up children in the world I saw. It was a cold, cruel world. Your father and I lived like kings, but I could never relax. I was always worried. I felt as if I were playing a part on an enormous stage that could at any moment collapse under my feet. Almost every day I heard about some new person who got arrested. Several great actors and actresses were sent to prison on ridiculous charges. It was impossible to trust anyone or believe what anyone said. People spoke to each other more in whispers than in real voices, and told more lies than truths. Everyone struggled to keep his job, his position, his family safe. If that meant taking advantage of another, informing on another, getting someone else arrested, that was fine. Better he than I—that was the attitude then, and it hasn't changed. It's how most people think.

"Your father was still quite sure of himself and always arguing with Ceausescu, who couldn't stand it when anyone disagreed with him. He was Neclo's worst enemy, absolutely hated him for his superior knowledge, education and charm. Ceausescu was a boor, but I didn't underestimate him. I saw he was a very clever man who made up in shrewdness for what he lacked in schooling. His wife, Elena, was the only person he trusted, and they worked as a team, an evil team, Macbeth and Lady Macbeth—I took you to the play last summer, remember? Unfortunately, your father would not allow me on his team. Together, we might have withstood them…

"Despite all my doubts, I was thrilled when your brother was born, and I held him in my arms—a new life, a new generation. But now knowing that my baby would be safe and protected, that no harm would ever come his way, became more important to me than anything—someday, you'll be a mother, too, and you'll know even better what I mean…Two years later, you came along. A wonderful little doll. How I wanted to give both of you the happy childhood I never had!

"Your father got promotion after promotion. Finzi was right. The Minister of Defense valued and respected him. Bodnarash was a man of culture with aristocratic tastes and appreciated having someone around who was well-read and well-bred. At his house, he was waited upon at every meal by servants in white gloves. He found Ceausescu repulsive and kept him at a distance but also was very careful not to make an enemy out of him. Unlike your father, he was a foxy man, a former spy, a diplomat who always knew just how far he could go without endangering his own position. As long as he could, he supported Neclo, and helped elevate him to general and then to Vice-Minister of Defense.

"So everything seemed to be going well with us, but around us everything was getting worse and worse. I had this terrible fear inside me all the time. I knew we were surrounded by spies—our maid, our chauffeur, your tutors, everyone who worked for us, I was certain, had to report regularly on every step we made. It was as if there was a shadow that followed me around, a horrible ghost, that might pounce on me from behind at any minute and choke me to death…"

◆ ◆ ◆

Once more my mother is forced to pause, but this time it's because my feet, which have been dragging for some time, are refusing to keep moving. It is very dark and eerie here. The road is deserted. The benches are empty. The lovers have gone home. We're the only two people left.

"What's the matter, darling? You're shivering. Are you cold? That light sweater isn't warm enough. You should have listened to me and brought your jacket."

"I'm not cold. I'm tired. And my feet are sore."

"All right. Let's sit down on this bench," Giunica says. Finally she's convinced that there's no one around to spy on us. She takes off her wool coat and wraps it like a blanket around both of us. Cuddled up next to her on the bench, I feel a little better.

"Go ahead," I whisper.

◆ ◆ ◆

"I don't know whether I've already mentioned this or not, but Ceausescu was the right hand man of Gheorghiu Dej and he controlled the Securitate. Suddenly, out of the blue, Ceausescu's confidant, Gogu Popescu, a top man in the Securitate, gave Gica a position in his department, promoting him to colonel. This was exactly what Gica had always wanted. How had it finally come to pass? It seemed obvious to me that something fishy was going on. Gogu Popescu was Nicolae Ceausescu's trusted man, and Nicolae Ceausescu was Ion Eremia's worst enemy. Why would they be promoting an Eremia, unless they were planning to use that Eremia, whom everyone knew was a coward and an opportunist and a fool, to bring his younger brother down?

"Gica dropped by our house night after night, sometimes close to midnight, around the time when, after a full day at the theater and then with you children, I was collapsing into bed, exhausted. It was just as well. I couldn't stand watching Gica pour venom into your father's ear. To me, your father was like Othello, and Gica was like Iago. He was constantly bringing him stories—horror stories about the various things he saw in the secret cellars of the Securitate. He would upset your father and refuse to leave until he was sure to have ruined his sleep, so that the next morning, irritable and tired and, with his defenses shot, he would go to this or that friend's office and say things he shouldn't say.

"'Why does Gica keep this job if he hates it so much?' I asked your father. 'And why do you have to believe everything he tells you? Don't you see that he's just provoking you and agitating you with all his tales and lies? And even if some of them are true, why does he have to tell you all the gory details? What does he think you can do, anyway? Can't you see that he's being used to set you up? Everything he says comes from Gogu, and everything you say goes back to Gogu and then to Ceausescu, who is just waiting for the right moment to pounce on you. And when he does that, do you think any of your so-called friends will lift a finger on your behalf?'

"But my husband was addicted to his brother. He told me I was irrational and paranoid, and one time, he even brought up our ethnic differences. 'You Jews are more cynical about your fellow creatures than we Romanians,' he said. Neclo was as open-minded and unprejudiced a man as they come, yet in a moment of anger, he, too, could say 'you, Jews,' and 'we Romanians.' For the first time in my life, I understood what my mother had meant when she said that marriage was easier between people of 'the same kind.' Maybe your father preferred to spend so much time with Gica, his Romanian brother, because Gica was 'his kind.' Maybe he felt closer to him than to his Jewish wife. Maybe he loved him more. I still wonder about that sometimes.

"I am not saying that Neclo didn't love me. And I have no doubt that he adored you, his children. But there are men, my darling, who value their wives above everyone in the world and turn to them only for advice, and never need anyone else, or trust anyone else. When you get married, I wish you such a man.

"That winter we went to Predeal, our favorite resort in the Carpathian Mountains—I don't know if you have any memories of it, we used to go there every summer and leave you to stay longer with Omama after your father and I had to go home. Now everything was covered with pure, white snow. All you could see were the rooftops of the wood cabins and the big cross on the church. It was so quiet. The only thing that broke the silence was the occasional howl of the wolves.

"The village was on a hill, and our cabin was at the very top and had a view of the entire valley. When we arrived, the staff was waiting to greet us. A fire was burning in the terracotta stove. A fragrant hunter's stew was simmering in the kitchen, and an old bottle of red wine on the table was ready for us to open. Your governess took you and Sorin to your room to put you to bed—you had already had your dinner in the car and were almost asleep. The orderly who had helped us with our bags was having his meal with the cook. Neclo and I sat down to dinner. Across the table, I saw a big pair of blue eyes that looked as if they wanted to convey something but dared not. We ate silently. When we finished, your father said, 'Why don't we go for a walk?'

"The orderly was already at the door, waiting to accompany us. 'No, no, you rest,' we told him.

"We could hear the squeak of the snow under our boots. The sun had gone down, and it was very chilly, but it felt so good to be outside and by ourselves. We held hands and talked. Your father seemed happier and more optimistic than

I had seen him for a very long time. Bodnarash had just called him into his office that day and told him that he was planning to suggest to the Central Committee that your father be put in charge of restructuring the most important department in the army. He asked him for a list of ideas and suggestions. Neclo felt that now he would really be able to make a difference, that he would have the power to stand up to Ceausescu and his cronies.

"'Be tactful,' I begged him. 'And careful. I know you will write notes, and there is no locked cabinet in this place.'

"'You always worry about everything.' He smiled. 'My little worrier,' and he drew me close to him and kissed me. Then we began running and chasing each other in the snow, and for the first time in a long time I felt young and happy and hopeful. That night, as I curled up next to your father, I closed my eyes and imagined we were safe.

"We got up very early next morning, before you and your brother woke up, and went skiing. It was a beautiful, sunny day, and the snow was shining around us, and we were laughing and teasing and joking. We came back before lunch, since we had promised you children to spend the afternoon with you playing in the snow. As we got close to our cabin and took off our skis, what did I see but Gica's car, parked right there, in front of our lovely little haven. The white snow all around me turned black.

"'What's he doing here?' I asked.

"'He decided to visit us. So what? He's my brother. What do you have against him?'

"When I came in, Gica came up to me smiling, already prepared for my grim expression. 'Don't worry, Gina, please, I'm not going to barge in on you. Gogu Popescu is here, too, and I'm staying in his cabin.' Then he turned to your father: 'Maybe you can drop by tonight. I'm setting up a game of chess for you and Gogu. He thinks he's unbeatable but I'm sure you'll cure him of that!'

"'All right, just for an hour or so, while Gina's putting the kids to bed,' your father agreed. 'If we don't finish the game tonight, we'll get together again tomorrow.'

"I felt like a balloon that is ready to explode. I couldn't say anything. I walked outside and tried to breathe in the cool winter air.

"We were supposed to be in Predeal for a two-week vacation. But suddenly, after five days, Neclo got a call from Bodnarash. He was asked to return home.

"During our ride back, he sat silently, very preoccupied. I didn't dare ask any questions. The next night, when I left the theater, he was waiting for me at the door. I knew instantly that what I had been dreading for so long had finally taken place.

"'I told the chauffeur to leave so we can walk home alone,' he said. 'Bodnarash called me in this afternoon and told me that he has been ordered by the central committee to put me on a leave of absence for the next six months. Evidence that I am an enemy of the party has been presented to them. An investigation has been launched against me.'

"I knew what that kind of investigation meant—especially for a man like your father, who would rather die than lie. My knees began to shake. He thought I was shivering from the cold. He put his arm around me, as if to warm me.

"He told me that Bodnarash asked him if the accusations were true and that he had replied, 'You know that I have risked my life for the party, but I now realize that we are headed in the wrong direction. You know this as well as I do. How long can we continue to pretend?' I stared at your father in disbelief. He really expected the Minister of Defense to stick his neck out for him. What a fantasy!

"'Look, Gina, there is nothing I've said or done that I'm ashamed to own up to,' your father continued. Then he pulled me even closer to him and looked straight into my eyes. 'For myself, I'm not sorry about anything. But I am sorry about you. You too...You will be put on a leave of absence from the theater until the investigation is over.'

"I was speechless. What could I say? I had managed to work my way up in the theater through my own efforts. He had never done anything to help me with my career. On the contrary, after my marriage, it was more difficult for me to get good roles because my lifestyle caused so much jealousy. It also kept me isolated from my fellow actors, who were intimidated by his position. Yet my career was infinitely more precious to me than his position, his income, his status...I could live without all of it, if only I could be allowed to act! I had the same feeling I used to have as a little kid—helpless, hopeless, no one to rescue me. I had to rely on myself, I had to pull myself up. At the same time, I felt as if I were going to collapse. I hung on his arm, and he almost dragged me home.

"The black days had just begun. They interrogated him every day, from early in the morning until late at night. He didn't tell me anything. I didn't ask him anything. Both of us realized that the more I knew, the more vulnerable I'd become.

"I began to think that soon they would come to arrest him, and then me. You would be left orphans. There was nowhere to run, nowhere to hide. I wasn't allowed to show my face at the theater. At every knock on the door, I jumped.

"One day your father came home in the middle of the day. He had a big smile on his face. He looked positively radiant. For a second, I allowed myself to feel that sweet sensation of hope I had denied myself for the past six months. Maybe he had been acquitted. Maybe he had been cleared. Life would go back to normal. The doors of the theater would open for me again.

"'They have made their decision, Gina!' he cried. 'And I am happy! Happy! Happy! I am finally free of them. Do you realize what it has meant for me to have been part of that horrible masquerade? They took all those years out of my life, all the best years of my youth, when I had convinced myself that I was dedicating myself to something noble and gigantic! But in reality I had joined a group of thieves and thugs. Oh, God! If you exist, thank you for liberating me and helping me to open my eyes and see the truth!'

"He was dismissed from his office. He was discharged from the army. He was free. I understood his feelings. But his life was different from mine. What about my dreams, my goals, my hopes? And what about our children? What would happen to them?

"'You, my darling are a very strong woman,' he answered when I confronted him with that last question. 'I realized how brave you were during our honeymoon, when I saw you had no fear of heights, or of steep and narrow paths. If they arrest me, I know you will manage to take care of yourself and our children. Don't worry, they won't arrest you. You haven't said anything, done anything. And to distance you from me even more we will file for divorce.'

"This we did, though we continued to live in the same house, as many couples in such situations do because of the housing shortage. And I was fired from my theater. Not only fired but told not to come around or try to stay in touch with anyone there. I understood. How could I blame them? I knew what was at stake.

"I found a job in a small shop and labored there as an ordinary worker for long hours to make a little bit of money. I wasn't willing to give up the theater, however. Before work, after work, during my breaks, I made the rounds and knocked on every door I knew. Finally, I applied to a new theater that had just been created as a training ground for young directors. The man who was doing the hiring had been a college classmate, and I knew him as someone who had great courage and integrity. He hired me to be his assistant, on condition that my name never appear on the program and that I keep quiet about my job. I was satisfied. The salary was small, but I loved the work; my employer was satisfied, too, because I relieved him of many of his duties.

"Papicu came every day to take care of you kids. He was old and had many health problems, but he stood in line for hours to buy bread, milk and whatever else he could find in the empty stores. Your father also spent a lot of time with you at first. After a few months at a demeaning job inspecting food stores, he told me he wanted to quit and work part-time writing other people's books. He said he wanted to go to the library, read, research, maybe write something of his own. I knew this had always been his ambition, and I didn't object, even though we had a hard time surviving on the little we made. My brother and sisters helped us out as much as they could.

"Neclo seemed reasonably content at first, but then, gradually, I noticed that he was getting more and more agitated. Suddenly he would get up and leave right after dinner, to go to his sister Agripina's, he said. Then he began leaving early in the morning and coming home very late at night. I was afraid to ask anything.

"One day I came home and found him there playing with you, at a time when I had gotten accustomed to him being away. I tried to talk to him but found it impossible to engage him. He was distracted and irritable.

"I was in a deep sleep around one in the morning when I heard a terrible noise, as if our house had broken apart. I jumped up and opened the bedroom door and was confronted by about twenty men armed with machine guns. They weren't wearing any uniforms and they had broken into the house. I thought they were some kind of bandits who would kill us all. Only after they handcuffed your father and told him he was under arrest, did I realize that they came from the Securitate. I blocked the entryway to your room, where, mercifully, you and Sorin were still asleep, and told them: 'You will have to shoot me before you go in there and scare my children.'

"The leader of the men came over and told me that if I kept quiet and didn't make a racket, he would leave your room for last. They tore through the rest of the house and apparently found what they wanted without having to wake you up. Around five in the morning, they took your father away in a big truck along with a mountain of books, notes, notebooks and I don't know what else. As soon as they left, I tried to call my parents, but the phone lines had been cut. I did my best to clean things up in the dining room and hallway so you wouldn't be shocked and frightened when you woke up.

"Only later, from various sources, did I find out what the police had been looking for, that your father had written a book that was a satire about our government, that he had been going to his sister's house to work on it and had read portions of it to Gica, and that Gica had found him an old, childhood friend, a sailor, to take the typed manuscript to France. But the sailor was an agent of the Securitate and Gogu's men set up a trap to get the original, handwritten manuscript as well. Your father had buried it in the cellar, and I think that it was Gica who they got to call him on the day of his arrest and ask him to dig it out and get it ready. Gica went to prison, too, for he had served his purpose, and it was easier to lock him up than shut him up.

"So that's the story, my darling. Your father was an honest man, but unfortunately, the world isn't made up of honest men. He trusted people who betrayed him and put others ahead of himself and his own family. No one else was willing to do the same for him. I wish I could have told you a prettier story with a happier ending. But this was a true story, not a fairy tale or a fantasy, like the ones I used to tell you when you were little. Do you still remember, 'Chucha, the Little Chocolate Girl?'"

◆ ◆ ◆

Giunica seems to be waiting for me to answer her question. I am too tired to think, too tired to speak. I just want to go home and slide under my blanket. All I know is that we have walked all the way here and that we must now walk all the way back. The thought of the distance we have already covered but must cover again makes me want to cry!

"Don't cry, my love," Giunica tries to comfort me. All the bad things are behind us, and only good things lie ahead. And there's one more secret I want to tell you. Every morning after Neclo was arrested, when I woke up to see your dear little faces, yours and Sorin's, I couldn't help but smile and count my blessings. And then, for the rest of the day, every day, I held my head high and my shoulders square—as I keep telling you to do, though you sometimes don't listen and slouch and look down at the ground instead of up at the sky. (Never be ashamed that you are tall! Always be proud of who you are.) 'Why Mrs. Eremia, what do you have to be so cheerful about?' people used to ask me, amazed, during the first couple of years after your father's arrest. 'A lot,' I would say, and I meant it, because I knew that my two real treasures were waiting for me at home. As long as I had you and Sorin, nothing else mattered. As for the rest, my love, each day for me is a new adventure, a challenge to be conquered, a battle to be won in the war of life."

◆ ◆ ◆

It is past midnight, and we have finally made it back to our apartment building. Our streetlight is out. I almost trip over the broken pavement, torn up by the exposed roots of the big tree in front of our house—those gnarled and twisted roots my mother talked about…I want to look at them in the morning. I've never really noticed them before.

Every window is dark, except for the small, square attic window on the third floor, the window of our apartment. It seems to be open, and I think I see Sorin's head poking out. He must be scared and worried about us. Never before has my mother taken one of us out so late. Did he imagine we were hit by a bus or killed by a robber? I feel sorry for my poor brother, sitting at that window, alone in the dark, seeing terrible things, thinking terrible thoughts, with no one to comfort him or hold his hand.

I squeeze my mother's hand. As long as she's with me, I'm not scared to climb the stairs in the dark.

◆ ◆ ◆

"Swimmers take your marks…"

I mustn't think about my father now. I mustn't think about the Germans or the Russians or the Party, or Gica and Ceausescu and the book, or the man who just got out of prison and came to tell us about his friend who will be coming back soon.

"Get set…"

I must think about my stroke. Three pulls, then one quick breath. I must think about my turn. Touch the side or be disqualified. I must win this race!

"Go!"

I spring. I dive. I glide. I kick, kick, kick with all my might. My arms are like oars, pulling hard, pulling smoothly, evenly, scarcely splashing at all. I'm in charge of my body and my fate. I must win, win, win!

I hear the muffled sounds of whistles blowing, spectators cheering, coaches shouting. No one is splashing ahead of me. No one is splashing next to me. I touch the side of the pool, breathing hard. I did it! I came in first! My mother is waiting with my towel. She is smiling. Next to her stands Comrade Iacobini. He, too, is smiling.

"Congratulations! This is your best time yet!" He beams.

Then my coach puts his arm around me, lowers his voice and whispers: "I have high hopes for you, dear. Very high hopes!"

17

Ion: The Supreme Miracle of the Universe

In this Transylvanian citadel, set on a plateau at five hundred meters above sea level, protected from the cool winds of the north and the dry winds of the south by thick chains of high mountains, winters are usually mild and springs enchanting. The freezing temperatures of last December were, to my bad luck, highly exceptional for these parts. Nature has now compensated this spring with an unusually rich flora. I know this from the intoxicating fragrances which I inhale greedily and the abundant foliage of the trees on the hill near the prison which I stare at hungrily every morning when I go to the latrines in the courtyard to empty out my bucket of excrement—my only chance to experience the delights of the world outside the prison walls. Even though I'm only allowed a few crumbs of spring, I'm happy, whispering cheerful melodies to myself, joking and chattering with my neighbor on the left with the mug to my mouth, and sometimes even without a mug, for the jailers seem to have softened a bit—a clear sign to me that the moment of our liberation is coming. The loudspeakers have redoubled their broadcasts and the party missionaries multiplied their visits. I remain a stubborn infidel, impossible to re-educate or reform.

Among these party emissaries, I happen to stumble upon a decent man, who was once a soldier in my unit and remembers with fondness the times he served under me. He lives in Bucharest, in my own neighborhood, and brings me extraordinary news: my wife and children are alive and well. Ecstatic, I ask the neighbor on my left, who has decided to confess, to contact them, in case he is released ahead of me.

Now I experience spring not only outside, but also inside, for I feel deep within my soul that very soon I will see my loved ones again. Of this, even poor Luca has become convinced. Since I was moved to a new cell after my miraculous rescue, Luca has become the neighbor on my right. Every day I speak with him through the wall. He is ill and demoralized. His heart bothers him, and he is tortured by the thought that now, when getting out of this hell finally appears plausible, he won't make it to the end.

"You must have faith in your powers of resistance," I try to encourage him. "A few months of normal living, a good doctor, a bit of medicine, and you'll be as good as new."

"Thank you for your kind words. But I'm not terribly optimistic. I feel like a soldier who is mortally wounded, watching himself slowly bleed to death."

"It isn't my optimism which is exaggerated but your pessimism, my friend."

"Oh, thank you, pal, I wish I could believe you, but I'm incapable of lying to myself. The pliers inside my chest are squeezing my heart tighter—especially in the morning when I have to take out my bucket to the latrines. Even this is too much for me. I don't think I can last much longer."

"Why don't you request the doctor to see you and demand to be exempted from this task?"

"And who will empty my mess out for me?"

"Me. Your neighbor."

"Then they'll know we've been communicating through the wall, and we will both end up with ten days in the lockup!"

"Just ask the doctor to exempt you. Let them decide who'll take out your bucket."

"All right," he agrees after a long pause. "I suppose it won't hurt to try."

◆ ◆ ◆

Finally, three days after our conversation, Luca informs me that he did receive a medical visit. The doctor told him that he would do his duty and request medicine for his heart condition. But since this condition is chronic, he cannot have him transferred either to the infirmary or to a hospital. As far as exempting him from physical effort, that isn't a decision he can make, since such matters as the "prison's clean up program" are the responsibility of the administrative staff.

"In other words, he refused to help you."

"I can't blame him. It really isn't his responsibility."

"It is the responsibility of every human being to help another in need," I explode, outraged by the doctor's cowardice. "Don't give up just because the scoundrel wouldn't put himself out for you. Request that the administration choose another person to perform a task that is beyond your strength."

"I can't. First of all, such a request would never be granted. Secondly, it would make me the laughing stock of the prison, the butt of jokes and insults!"

"But it's your only way out!"

"There is no way out. Sooner or later, the matter will resolve itself, anyway. One day I will collapse on the cement and die my soldierly death covered by my own excrement. Finished. End of discussion," says Luca with resignation in his voice.

◆ ◆ ◆

His macabre premonitions have come to pass. As I sit in my cell, waiting for my turn to the latrines, I hear Luca's heavy breathing and slow steps down the hallway followed by a thud, a splash, and the guard's hysterical screams and curses:

"You son of a bitch! You fouled up the hallway with your filth! You're gonna sweep it up with your tongue! Lap it up! Get up, you stinking moron!"

After a long silence, the jailer starts shouting for the other guard on duty.

"Hey, you, Paprikash! Bring your Hungarian ass over here! I think the old man just kicked the bucket. We better carry him straight to the morgue!"

◆ ◆ ◆

It is the beginning of August, 1964. Spring passed before I knew it. I spend the rest of it in solitude. After Luca's death, I once again suffered a bout of depression. I no longer communicate with my neighbors. They change quite frequently now, sometimes even daily, and their pointed questions along with their profusion of curses addressed toward "the fascist, fanatic, despots who run our country," lead me to distrust them. I refuse to fall into their trap. I keep silent. I keep my mouth tightly shut during my incessant visits by party missionaries. Again, I am punished with hunger.

Starvation and loneliness have once more weakened my resistance and reopened old wounds. I am tortured by questions and doubts.

Was I wrong? Is it possible that human beings will never be happy? Isn't it foolish to give up your own happiness in order to fight for the happiness of others? Have I wasted my life? Have I made my loved ones suffer for nothing?

◆ ◆ ◆

The guard bursts in this morning and orders me to get out of my cell. He leads me to the small yard of the "Zarca" prison section. A number of convicts are gathered here, waiting. The prisoner standing next to me introduces himself, and I recognize a good friend of the unfortunate Lucretiu Patrascanu. I ask him whether he knows what is going on. He answers me that he works in one of the prison's metal shops and that there he heard that all political prisoners in the country have been granted amnesty. As we wait, hoping to soon hear confirmation of these news, Belu Zilber tells me his story.

According to Zilber, Stalin turned against Patrascanu when the latter had the naiveté to declare in a speech that he considered himself first of all a Romanian, and secondly, a Communist. Outraged, the Russian dictator agreed to support Dej in his scheme to eliminate his charismatic rival. It was Zilber's signed testimony, along with that of Moscony-Sircea, that enabled the military jury to give Patrascanu the death sentence for espionage in a public trial. Zilber is still obsessed with the trial and tormented by guilt for his complicity in his friend's death.

"I simply could not resist the torture...Two days and two nights at Malmaison we were hung upside down, like lambs on the spit, and beaten continuously with iron rods on the soles of our feet. When we fainted, they threw buckets of water over us until we came back to our senses, and then they started all over again. Even Patrascanu finally "confessed" after they tortured his poor wife, Elena, in front of him. The same was done to Moscony-Sircea and Torosian, who also eventually succumbed."

"But Patrascanu and Torosian withdrew their 'confessions' at the public trial, declaring that they had been dragged out of them under torture. Why didn't you and Moscony-Sircea do the same?"

"From weakness, cowardice, fear of death...more than anything else because we believed it wouldn't make any difference," answered Zilber with tears in his eyes.

"It may have. This was a public, not a secret trial, in front of the whole world, and perhaps if you and Moscony-Sircea, the only witnesses against him, had also withdrawn your testimony, Dej wouldn't have dared to go as far as the death sentence."

"I don't think so. The trial would have been suspended, and we would have been tortured some more along with our wives and children until we gave in."

What more can I say? I feel sorry for the poor man, who continues to be tortured even now, so many years later, by his own conscience. I remember the answer that Trotsky gave, when he was a political refugee in Mexico, to an American journalist who asked him why his friend, Buharin, admitted at his open Moscow trial all the odious crimes Stalin accused him of: "I have known, in my battles against the Czar, several men who were able to resist all the tortures to which they were subjected by the czarist secret police. But I don't believe anyone could withstand Stalinist torture, which stops at nothing, including the crippling of the victim's wife and children in front of his eyes."

◆ ◆ ◆

Finally, the prison dignitaries have made their grand entrance in the courtyard. Colonel Craciun, once a train conductor, now the almighty director of our prison who tried to assassinate me with the lock-up last winter, begins an impassioned discourse. He tells us that the magnanimous leaders of our country have decided, out of the goodness of their hearts, to forgive our sins and set us free. He expresses his fervent hope that we will prove ourselves worthy of the generosity of our illustrious leaders and mend our ways after our liberation. Then, the orator does me the honor of personally addressing me: he launches into a venomous tirade about my "mule-like stubbornness, desperate fanaticism and blind hatred of communism," and punishes me with gloomy predictions of a dismal future.

After that, without any further explanations, all of us are sent back to our cells.

◆ ◆ ◆

It's been two days since I have heard the amnesty decree, but I'm still incarcerated alone in my cell. Belu Zilber is now in the cell next to me. Other convicts are walking freely up and down the hallways. They ask us why we are still here when so many of the others have already given up their striped clothes and are on their way home. We tell them we don't know. Several of them stop, on their way out, and ask the guards to give us some sugar cubes and cookies which they received in packages from home. I savor these treats—it has been years since I have eaten such delicacies, whose taste I had long forgotten.

This afternoon Zilber taps to me in Morse code, signaling that he wants to communicate something confidential.

"I have just come back from the prison director's office. He asked me to make a request to emigrate to Israel. Moscony-Sircea was also there and had already agreed to make a similar request to leave for France, where he has some relatives. What do you make of this?"

"They want to get rid of all witnesses in the Patrascanu trial."

"That's right. And I refused. I told Craciun that I don't want to leave the country, since I have no one outside. The truth is that though I know I'd be better off in Israel, where I do, in fact, have relatives, I swore to myself after Patrascanu's execution that I will not rest in peace until I exonerate his name."

"That's very noble of you."

"It's the only way I can live with myself."

"You may have to wait a long time before you can do anything."

"It doesn't matter. I have nothing else to live for. But I'm afraid that they will try to get rid of me now and say I died of a heart attack like Luca. I've heard that money has been distributed for the train tickets. I haven't received any. Have you?"

"Not yet. But I'm sure I will."

"If you are released before me, promise me you will visit one of my relatives when you get to Bucharest. If I don't appear within a week, please go to the Israeli embassy and ask them to intervene in my behalf."

"I'll do that, of course. But I don't think they'll keep either of us much longer. They had to pardon us. They have to let us go. They're just torturing us a little longer to punish me for refusing to confess and you for refusing to leave for Israel."

Zilber is less confident than I am. He asks me to memorize his relative's address. This is one thing, alas, I can do for him with no trouble!

◆ ◆ ◆

We have both been released! Belu Zilber and I find each other among the group of prisoners walking out the prison's gates. I shake hands with the man small of stature but big of heart who once again vows to set things right posthumously for his friend, Lucretiu Patrascanu.

A moving spectacle unfolds on the way to the train station. I see others, less fortunate than I. Several convicts are being carried on the backs of comrades. They have become paralyzed during the course of their imprisonment. Among them I recognize a former high school classmate, condemned many years ago for being a member of the young wing of the National Peasant Party. We look at each other and cry.

All of us keep turning our heads back to make sure we are not being followed. Are we really free? Aren't the guards going to run after us and put us back behind bars? We wait anxiously for the train, the ground of Aiud burning the soles of our feet. When the train finally arrives, all of us charge in at once, still frightened that our jailers will change their minds.

The other passengers look at us in shock. They keep on staring at us with eyes full of pity. We look frightening, like concentration camp survivors at the end of the war. At first, I think that only the others look so bad, and that I, the man of iron health, am still in good shape. But when I catch a glimpse of myself in the compartment mirror, I too am shocked. I also look as if I've just stepped out of Auschwitz. The people on the train, who don't look particularly well-fed themselves, offer us all the food they brought with them, ignoring the hungry stares of their children. I accept only fruit—which I haven't tasted for many long years.

None of us can keep our eyes off the windows, mesmerized by the enchanting Transylvanian sights. We pass through Tirnave Mari, by well-known vineyards with hills covered with vines. Then we pass by Sighisioara, the beautiful medieval city full of towers and walls from the ancient citadel. We follow the Olt River through lush, green mountains, past Brasov, another beautiful, ancient city. Now my heart beats faster as I recognize familiar sights which are very dear to me. There are two ways to hike up to the top of the mountain that rises 2000 meters high above the village, Timisul de Jos, where the train makes a short stop. One is the familiar road, with winding roads and sharp turns. The other, more challenging, is a steep vertical climb up the "seven iron steps" walled into the cliff—from which this trail derives its name. How many times have I braved the Seven Iron Steps trail, my knapsack on my back, all the way up to the top of the mountain, drunk with the beauty of the scenery and pride in my nerves and muscles! Now, in my present state, would I manage to climb one single step?

After another hour of traveling through my beloved Carpathians, I emerge, made younger and stronger, by my intense immersion in this magic kingdom. I am now getting close to home, where an eighty-year-old mother, a wife and two children have perhaps given up hope of ever seeing the man who six years ago vanished off the face of the earth, swallowed by a gigantic man-eater. Is my mother still alive? Will my children remember me?

I close my eyes to write in my thoughts the conclusion to my book with the paradoxical title, *The Subterranean Tower:*

I'm alive! I'm sane! I confessed nothing! I signed nothing! My spirit is intact!

My will is even stronger, and my mind more agile than when I first entered the infernal realm of cold, hunger, loneliness and immobility. From an apprentice in the art of writing, I became a skilled worker. I learned to sing without sound and write without paper. In a miraculous transformation, immobility turned into creativity, torture into ecstasy, the desert into a rich internal world, hell into heaven. The miracle I experienced is not my own, personal triumph. It is the triumph of the human species, of man's extraordinary powers of self-preservation, of his remarkable ability to adapt to new situations, of his indomitable will, of his infinite imagination.

Like most men of my generation, I have experienced the horrors of World War II. I am familiar with death. I have seen bodies on the battlefield treated like rocks or stumps that must be kicked out of the way. I have seen men shattered into pieces, thrown up in the air like broken dolls tossed in the trash, men without heads, men without arms and legs, men with bellies torn open and emptied out of guts, men strangled by their own insides. I have heard the desperate call for help, the agonizing cry of pain, the croaking sound of death. I have seen and heard man in his most tragic state, when dying and mutilated, a mere crumb of life, a live rag, a dismembered cockroach, he continues to crawl about, even when everything around him shows him that he is nothing but a crushed insect, in an absurd desire to save himself, to live.

Despite everything, man remains the most marvelous, the most accomplished creature yet wrought by nature. Man is the supreme miracle of the universe. For this reason, we must never lose faith in his greatness, in his right to be cherished, and yes, to be loved.

18

Irina: Hello Children, Goodbye

My name is in the paper! A small article in the sports section lists Irina Eremia as the winner of the fifty-meter crawl at the Junior Swim Olympics. At school, I'm the celebrity of the day. Everyone congratulates me, even the teacher who has had few words of praise for me all year. What a great way to end fourth grade! A long, glorious summer vacation stretches out ahead of me.

Mornings I train at the Youth Swimming Complex—one of the most beautiful places on earth. Every time the guard lets me through the majestic gates, and I skip down the paved walkway lined with colorful pansies, past the fountain with the giant flower petal squirting water on bronze cherubs, past the lush green grass in front of the two shallow pools where groups of beginning swimmers practice kicking, to the wood bungalows on the stretch of sand behind the Olympic pool where I change into my bathing suit, I feel like a queen entering the grounds of my palace. The complex has five swimming pools: the two large, shallow wading pools where I love to splash and tumble after practice; a thirty-five meter pool that we use for warm-ups, a short but very deep pool where divers practice their aerial feats from platforms of various heights (just watching them makes me dizzy); and the spectacular fifty meter Olympic size pool, where we train and compete. This is my kingdom!

I work out until lunch time, and then I'm free to lie out in the sun, frolic on the grass with my friends and splash around the shallow pools. I'm left with plenty of time after I get home to ride my bike around my neighborhood and play ball, hopscotch and jump rope until dark.

I have put the story my mother told me during our long walk in the park out of my mind. Whenever I remember, a nauseous feeling sweeps over me and I get dizzy, as if I were standing on the edge of a precipice. So I close my eyes and refuse to look down.

My mother thinks that Sorin and I have too much free time this summer. With some of the money earned from selling the goods our relatives in America sent us, she has hired us an English tutor. Twice a week, a tall, thin, withered old man whom we have nicknamed "Bubook" comes to teach us. The moment we hear the doorbell, both my brother and I make a run for the bathroom and struggle with each other to get in. The winner (usually my brother) locks the door, forcing the loser (usually me) to take the dreaded lesson first. What an insufferable, horrible language! The sounds of English are not clear and melodious like the sounds of French or Romanian. To speak it properly, you must keep your lips taught and talk between your teeth, as if your mouth were full of cookie crumbs. Nothing is written the way it sounds, and no letter is pronounced the same way twice! For example, what sounds like an "I" could end up being an "A" or an "E." What sounds like an "S" could turn out to be "Z" or even "Th." And a "Th" is sometimes pronounced like "Z" and other times like "S" and must be spat out with your tongue stuck out between your teeth, as if you were a baby just learning to speak. My brother, who has never been able to roll his "r"'s properly should take comfort in English, which is really a language for people with speech impediments.

Bubook does not have a lot of patience and often loses his temper and begins to shout and pound his fist on the table. This is how he derived his nickname. One day, he had a fit over my pronunciation of the impossible, tongue-twisting phrase, "blue book."

"Not bubook!" he screamed. "Not bubook! Bubook! Bubook! It's blue book. Say blue book, blue book, blue book!"

"Bubook! Bubook! Bubook!" I insisted. My mother, who was pretending to read the newspaper, couldn't restrain herself and burst out laughing. Finally, even Bubook cracked a smile, after which all of us started calling him by his new nickname, behind his back, of course.

Bubook speaks Romanian with a foreign accent, and at first I thought he was English, but two weeks ago my mother told us he was Russian, like Madame Olga. He had studied in England as a young man, and because of that was later accused by Stalin of being a capitalist spy and sent for ten years to a labor camp in Siberia. My mother told my brother and me this sad story because we were both furious with Bubook for eating up all of our cheese *placintas.*

Whenever Bubook comes, my mother serves him a snack which he devours greedily as if he hasn't eaten for days. Monday, however, she just happened to finish baking a batch of cheese *placintas* while he was there. Politely, she placed the tray of hot pastries on the table in front of him, expecting that he would help himself to one or two. To our shock, Bubook consumed the entire tray as we stood helplessly by, our own mouths kept busy by the insufferable English tongue twisters! Giunica had to reveal our tutor's tragic past to calm us down, for we vowed to lock ourselves in the bathroom together and never come out the next time Bubook showed up for a lesson!

◆ ◆ ◆

My mother has promised to bake another batch of placintas as soon as she has the time, and this Sunday, since there is no swim meet and nothing to sell at the flea market, we stay home and make them together. What a treat! Giunica rarely allows me to help her in the kitchen, usually sending me out to read a book or ride my bike.(She says she wants her daughter to aspire to better things than becoming someone's cook or maid!) My brother, too, is happy because he gets the Romanian translation of *Sherlock Holmes*, which my mother bought for both us to share, all to himself.

While my mother is rolling out the thin sheets of dough, I use the big wooden spoon to stir the cheese, sugar and eggs as vigorously as I can. I am so wrapped up in my task that I almost don't notice when the phone rings and my mother runs in to get it. Intent on counting my strokes (which must add up to three hundred), I don't make my usual attempt to guess from her tone who is on the other end of the line. But suddenly I notice that her voice, which I can hear clearly through the thin walls of our apartment, sounds very strange.

"Feed him only light foods! No! Absolutely nothing fried!" She sounds very worried, very agitated as she gives this advice, which is more like a command.

"This is a dangerous time for him. His stomach is very weak. The wrong food could kill him. I've heard of many such tragedies!"

Who is she talking to? Who is sick? Curious, I prick my ears.

"I want to see him alone first. Later, I'll prepare the children. I'll be over in a few minutes."

I now know that something extraordinary has happened, but a feeling of dread keeps me glued to my chair. I continue stirring the cheese filling, though I have lost track of the count.

My mother calls me into the living room, where my brother sits, reading. She has changed into her pretty blue summer dress and has put on some make-up. She looks ready to go out. I don't really want to know where.

"What should I do with the cheese filling?" I ask her.

"Put it in the ice box. And the dough, too, please."

Sorin's eyes are glued to his book. He doesn't seem to know where she is going either. But Giunica tells us anyway.

"Your father's back. He's at his mother's—your Bunicuta's house. I'm going over to see him now."

My brother and I are left alone with our shock. Neither of us can find anything to say. Since my father disappeared, we have never mentioned him to each other, nor have we ever discussed the stranger's visit or what my mother told each of us during our separate long walks with her. It seems too late to start talking about him now.

◆ ◆ ◆

Bunicuta lives two blocks away from us. We hardly know her, though, and haven't been to her house since we were little. She visits us only twice a year: in December, when she brings us stuffed cabbage and fruitcake, and in April, when she gives us sweet pastries and colored eggs. Only after learning about my father did I understand why this other grandmother behaves so strangely—treats us so differently from Omama, whom we consider our real grandmother.

Her daughter and son-in-law don't want her to have any contact with us. They don't want any of the neighbors to know that we are related, or that their little boy, Lucica, is our first cousin. Many times I used to catch Bunicuta stopping to stare at me and my brother as she passed us by while we were playing on the street, and once I noticed she was crying. Our eyes met, and she smiled at me through her tears, then went quickly along her way. I just thought she was strange.

My mother's eyes are red when she comes back from Bunicuta's house. She gulps down several glasses of water before she sits down at the dining room table and asks us to join her. Then she tells us:

"I saw him. He has suffered a great deal in prison. He misses you and is anxious to see you. But I've asked him to wait another two weeks. He is thin and frail. I think he should put on a few pounds before you meet. This will give him a little time to adjust and you to prepare."

Judging by the expression on Sorin's face, I think that he is as scared as I am. "Why did he go to Bunicuta's house instead of coming here?" my brother asks.

"As soon as he got off the train, he looked for us at our old house. He was told that we had moved. So then he went to his mother's house. She called me almost immediately."

"Is he going to stay there?"

"Only for a couple of days. His sister and brother-in law were barely willing to allow him even that," my mother says bitterly. "Tomorrow I'm going to see various officials and try to obtain an apartment and a job for him. I'm also going to make sure he sees a dentist immediately. He must have his teeth fixed or he'll never be able to eat properly. And he must have a complete medical checkup right away. His brother, the doctor, should be able to help me arrange that."

"So he's not going to move in with us?" Sorin asks.

"Not now. Not right away...I'm not ready yet...For the time being, your father and I are divorced...Later, we'll see."

Sorin seems unable to stop the questions. "What did they do to him in prison?" he asks, this time in a small, frightened voice.

My stomach tightens up. I'd like to leave the room. I don't want to know. But I make myself stay.

"He was kept in a cell by himself. It was very cold, and he got very little to eat. He was not allowed to do anything. He kept sane by composing poems and stories and memorizing them. That's all I know. When you see him, don't ask him questions. Whatever he wants to tell you, he'll tell you. We must help him forget about the past and concentrate on the present."

My mother has now regained her composure. Her head is full of plans. She seems to know exactly what she needs to do. Energetically, she makes one phone call after another. She explains, pleads, cajoles, argues, shouts and threatens.

"Aren't you ashamed of yourself? Who put you through medical school? Who got you your first job? That you forgot about us all these years, I don't give a damn! But him, you have no right to forget. Don't give me any excuses. You must arrange for him to be examined immediately. Yes, you can. There's no such thing as impossible. Tomorrow. You're going to have him seen tomorrow!"

◆ ◆ ◆

Lenuta, who lives in the new high-rise across the street from me, is a small, thin girl who is always hungry. She is only a year younger than I but looks much smaller. Her father works in a factory. Her mother is sick a lot, so she doesn't go to work like other women and is always home in their messy one-room apartment. Lenuta does odd jobs to earn a few extra pennies: she stands in food lines for neighbors, carries their heavy bottles of milk or beer and sometimes even washes their dishes or sweeps their floors. She must be very poor, I guess, since only the neediest families allow their children to work. Whenever I have any goodies, I share them with her.

This Tuesday afternoon it's hotter than usual, and Lenuta and I decide to cross the Piazza Dorobanti to Lupoica Park, where we can play in the shade.

There, we chase each other around the statue of the she-wolf suckling Romulus and Remus until, exhausted and sweaty, we collapse on a bench under a tree. There's only one other person, a man, sitting on the bench, so there's plenty of room for the two of us.

Suddenly, as Lenuta and I giggle and tease each other, I notice that the man is staring at me in a very strange way. "What's your name?" he asks me.

"Irina," I answer without thinking, though my mother has warned me countless times never to talk to strangers. The man looks at me intently. His eyes, which are buried deep in their sockets, are very blue, very sad, and, I think, very kind. He fumbles through his pockets and digs out something wrapped up in a paper napkin. It is a small brioche.

"Please take this and share it with your friend," he begs. "It's very fresh." The piercing blue eyes suddenly fill with tears. Is he going to cry if I don't take it?

Lenuta, always eager to eat, smiles and stretches out her hand. I feel a surge of panic. I grab her hand, drag her off the bench and start running home as fast as my legs will carry me.

"What's the matter? What did he do? Why are you scared of him?" my girlfriend shouts.

"You're not supposed to take food from strangers!"

"I don't think it was poisoned. He was just a lonely old man."

"I've got to go now. I'll see you later," I tell her, running into my building. My head aches. I want to be alone.

◆ ◆ ◆

My brother isn't home. I call my mother at her office, hoping to hear her reassuring voice, but I'm told she is out on some "personal errands." I look around for a book. A good book. I'm not in the mood for *Sherlock Holmes*. I pick up *Jane Eyre*, a book highly recommended by the librarian who now encourages me to read English rather than Russian translations. But I can't seem to get past the first page. I read the same words, again and again. Finally they begin to connect, and I am captivated by the story of the suffering orphan girl until I am roused by someone knocking softly at the door. Lenuta knocks that way, gently, timidly. She probably can't find anyone to play with, I think. Annoyed, I open the door determined to tell her I'm coming down with something, which isn't a lie because my stomach aches and I feel nauseous.

But the visitor is not Lenuta. It is he—the man on the bench.

We stand in the doorway staring at each other.

"I couldn't wait another minute. Your mother asked me to wait, but now, after fate brought us together, I just can't wait anymore. You know who I am, don't you?"

I look at him and can't say a word. My mouth simply won't make any sounds.

"I'm your father. Neclo. Have you forgotten me?"

Suddenly, he begins to sing: "Somnoroaaase, pasareeeele..."

I notice that his head has been shaved. His deep-set blue eyes are watering. He reaches out to hug me with two long, thin, bony arms. I turn away.

◆ ◆ ◆

My father is now sharing a room across town with his sister, Agripina, who has also been released from prison, but he comes over to see us every day. Sorin and I are terrified my friends will notice him, so we have made an agreement. When he shows up unexpectedly and I'm playing outside with the neighborhood kids, Neclo doesn't say anything to me, but just walks discreetly up to our apartment. I find an excuse to leave the game of volleyball or hopscotch or jump rope, and follow him upstairs.

He is standing, waiting at the door, smiling apologetically. Sorin isn't home. He's never home anymore.

"I'm sorry to take you away from your game, but I wanted so much to see you...Would you rather I came back later?"

"No, no...it's all right," I lie. He's so thin, so frail. How can I say anything to hurt him?

"Let me fix you a snack," I say, going into the kitchen.

"No, thank you, I'm not hungry, don't bother, please!"

I refuse to listen and force him to eat.

We sit together in the living room. He asks me questions about school, swimming, friends. I answer as best as I can, but it's hard; he doesn't know anything about any of it. Where do I start? Then, he talks about himself. He recites poems he made up when he was...down there. His eyes light up, and he gets excited. He tries to share with me what seem to him to be light, entertaining poems about his childhood, or adventure stories about a woman during medieval times who dressed up as a man and went out to fight the Turks. But all of it is sad to me, and frightening, for I can see him sitting there, by himself, in that dark, terrible place. He talks and talks (for such a long time he had no one to talk to), and I hum silently to myself and imagine I am very far away.

Today I keep him waiting a bit because my friends threaten never to have me on their team again if I walk off before we finish our game. When I finally get upstairs, where he's waiting, forlorn, by the door, he bursts out:

"You really don't need to hide me from your friends. Just explain to the kids that your parents are divorced and your father has visitation rights. There's nothing shameful in that!"

I hear someone's apartment door open and close. Quickly, I unlock the door and let both of us in without saying a word. What can I say to him? That everyone knows I don't have a father? That it's hard to account for the sudden appearance of someone whom everyone knows does not exist? Where am I supposed to say he's been all these years? I've lived on this street for a very long time! Why hasn't he ever visited me before? How am I to explain that to the kids in the neighborhood?

Though I keep my mouth shut, I'm not good about hiding my feelings. I must have a very unhappy expression on my face, for my father looks at me with eyes full of pity.

"My poor little girl!" he exclaims. "I'm causing you so much grief!"

"No, you're not! It's all right." I try to reassure him, but I don't sound very convincing.

After he leaves, I run outside again to play. Coca, our building manager's little girl, who lives on the second floor, begins to interrogate me:

"I heard a man talking to you on the stairs before. He said he was your father! Is that true?"

"What the hell are you talking about?"

"The man who said he was your father! I heard him talking to you on the stairs."

"How do you know he was talking to me?" I realize that I must take the offensive, I must intimidate her. Otherwise, she'll start the rumors.

"You're crazy. Maybe you've heard something on the radio! Or maybe you're just hard of hearing!"

Luckily, Coca is not the smartest girl on the block. No one who flunked second grade could be too sure about anything! Before, when the other kids would shout after her, "stupid! stupid!" I always felt sorry for her and refused to join in. But this time I feel threatened and I defend myself any way I can:

"What do you know, stupid! Don't go around telling stupid stories about me or you'll be sorry!"

◆ ◆ ◆

Finally, Sorin and I have managed to convince Neclo to call us before he pops in. He calls us from his mother's house, where he visits first, since he has to be out of there before four o'clock, when his sister and brother-in-law, who don't want to see him, get home. If the coast is clear, we tell him it's O.K., he can come over, but if it isn't, we ask him to wait until there are no more children on the street. We hate having to do this, especially if it's close to four o'clock and we know that he'll have to wander around the neighborhood and then try us again from a public phone. Neclo pretends to understand. But we're not really sure he does. Still, we can't help it. We're so anxious. We know what it's like to be ridiculed!

My mother gets home very late these days. She stays at the office until nighttime to make up for the hours she misses during the day running from one government official to another, trying to fix things for my father. This involves a lot of fighting, begging, bribing and threatening, I gather from her phone conversations with my aunts:

"He took the pack of Kents, thanked me, and said, 'The list of people waiting for apartments is many kilometers long and your ex-husband's history doesn't exactly put him at the top.' So I told him off. 'My husband and I are divorced, Comrade' I said. 'I have nothing to gain from this. I'm only doing my duty as a compassionate citizen. The Party pardoned the man and let him out of jail. Now it can't just leave him begging in the streets! You took everything away from him. Now give him something back! Give him an apartment! Give him a job! Give him the opportunity to rebuild his life. The world is watching, Comrade. The world expects the Party to do the right thing!'"

◆ ◆ ◆

Sundays, Giunica makes dinner for the four of us. She tries to cook my father's favorite dishes and engage him in light, pleasant chatter. When she is around, everything is sunny and cheerful and almost relaxed. But when I'm alone with him, it's very hard for me. I try to explain to her just how painful it is. But she's tired and irritable and has little patience. "Be kind to him. Help him. He has suffered so much," she repeats again and again. And that is just the problem. Everything about him—his voice, his smile, his walk, his gestures, and most of all, his eyes—are reminding me constantly of how much he has suffered. And I would like, more than anything in the world, to make things better for him. But I can't. I try, but I can't.

He has a certain look, a hungry, greedy, needy look that cuts into me like a knife. I catch him staring at me, dwelling on each of my features, studying my every movement, and I panic. I feel as if I'm going to be engulfed, swallowed up, devoured by him. I turn my head away. When finally I'm ready to look at him again, his kind, gentle blue eyes are spilling over with love and tears. I can't bear the tears. Or the love.

◆ ◆ ◆

I hate November! The weather is dreary, rainy, cold, but there's still a long wait until the first snowfall. Fifth grade is hard. For the first time I have different teachers for different subjects. I must listen to long, boring lectures, concentrate, take notes, study for tests and worry about midterms and finals. In Geography I have to learn the latitude and longitude of every country in Europe, its climate, rivers, mountains, seas, lakes, its major cities, its industrial centers for light and heavy industries, the main products it imports and exports. In Botany I must learn all the parts of an onion, a potato, a tomato and various other plants, fruits and vegetables, and be able to sketch them on the blackboard. In Math there are insufferable word problems about trains, cars or airplanes coming toward each other at various speeds from opposite directions. At what point will they hit each other and explode? If it weren't for History, where I'm learning about the ancient Greeks and Romans, and Romanian, where we read stories and write compositions, school would be unbearable.

My father, who still doesn't have a job, comes over every day after I get back from swim practice and helps me with my lessons. I try to do math, geography and botany with him because he doesn't lose his temper, even when I don't pay attention and drift off and he has to repeat himself and explain things over again. This Sunday I have finally agreed to go with him to the park. Neclo has been so kind and patient that I can no longer refuse his request to visit the places where he used to take me as a little girl.

He picks me up early, while everyone in the neighborhood is still asleep and the streets are deserted. I allow him to hold my hand, as in the old days, and we walk together to the park that was once called Parcul Stalin but has now been renamed Parcul Herastrau. As we pass through the shaded walkway, I can't stop staring at the big poplar and chestnut trees, imagining the gnarled and twisted roots growing deep beneath the ground from which they sprang. I remember what my mother said about it not being good to get entangled in the past. She said that I should try to understand it, but then put it behind me. But how can I do that? We haven't even reached the children's playground, and already Neclo has started his, "do you remember?" routine.

"Do you remember how I used to bring you here to feed the deer?"

"Yes...I think so."

"And do you remember the time the deer took the bread out of your hand so fast you got scared and started crying because you thought you'd lose a finger?"

"I guess so."

"And do you remember how we used to go rowing on the lake and Sorin and you took turns at the oars with me?"

"Unhuh..."

"And do you remember this bronze turkey and duck? How you and Sorin used to love to climb them!"

"Yeah...we have some pictures sitting on them."

"Look, there's your seesaw! Too bad Sorin wouldn't come! Remember how much the two of you loved it? You both weighed the same, since Sorin hated to eat and was slight for his age, while you loved everything and were a plump little Galuska; I could put Sorin on one end and you on the other and then sit down on this bench and read a book while you kept each other entertained going up and down for the longest time! And look, your favorite swing. It's still here, nothing has changed. How you loved that swing, and how you'd turn red in the face and stomp your foot if any other child dared to get to it before you did. 'Make her get off, Neclo, that's my swing!' you'd cry, and curl down your lip and pout. And then, when you'd finally get on it, you'd throw your head back and laugh and shout: 'Push me up high! High to the sky! I want to fly! Make me fly high!' Do you remember?"

"Yes, but I'm too old to swing on it now!" I say, beginning to lose my patience.

"Of course you are!" he exclaims, smiling, but I have a feeling that he's not quite sure about that. He doesn't really believe I have grown up that much. He would like me to get on that swing.

"You used to make up your own little songs and poems. Do you still do that, sometimes?"

"No, I'm too busy for that now," I tell him, though that isn't entirely true, for I still like to make up poems in my head and sing to myself, but I would never admit this to anyone.

"You were such a happy little girl, always humming and singing and laughing!"

I guess I'm not so happy anymore. I guess I'm much more serious now. I'm eleven years old and have to worry about geography and botany and swim races and what to tell my friends about the strange man who comes to visit me every day. Looking at the deserted playground, full of fallen, yellowed leaves, at the rusty swings and at the muddy sand, I feel more like crying than laughing.

Suddenly, a little girl, all bundled up in a heavy blue coat, much too bulky for November, her head covered in a babushka, her plump cheeks red from the cold, her nose running, waddles toward the swings, followed by her grandmother.

"Slow down darling, slow down or you'll trip and hurt yourself," shouts the old woman, gasping for breath. "She's such a restless kid! Can't leave her alone for a minute!" The woman complains to my father, rolling her eyes up to heaven. "I had to take her out early this morning to give her poor parents a break. All four of us cooped up in one small room, and she up at five banging on the walls. Her father would have taken the belt to her if I hadn't rushed her out!"

"Puss me, puss me," the little girl commands the tired old woman, pointing to the swing I once thought belonged to me.

"Sit down, Grandma, I'll push her for you!" my father offers.

"God bless you, son," the old woman says, collapsing on the bench.

My father lifts the little girl up on the swing, then gives her a gentle push.

"Harder! Harder!" commands the spoiled child.

He pushes her harder. "Is this hard enough? Or should I push you harder?"

"Harder! Harder! Wheee!"

"Do you want to fly? Way up high? High up in the sky?" my father asks the little brat.

"Wheee! Wheee!"

He pushes and pushes, and she laughs and laughs. I don't envy her at all. I'm happy for my father. He has finally gotten what he wanted. Soon, we should be able to go home.

◆ ◆ ◆

This week, my father has not come to visit. At first, I was relieved to have a break, especially since it finally snowed, which gave me an excuse to play outside after swim practice and put off doing my homework. I simply could not resist those first soft, shiny sheets of pure white, which made me long to jump in the snow, as into a freshly made bed. Unfortunately, my geography teacher, who never once called on me when I had my lesson perfectly memorized, probably guessed by my face that I was unprepared, and called me up to the podium. I knew nothing about Albania and stared dumbly at the map, unable even to point out the right spot, much less say anything about its latitude, longitude, climate, neighbors, rivers, mountains or major industrial centers. In the one matter I could guess, I guessed wrong, declaring that "Albania" was a capitalist country. I ended up with a big, fat "Four!"

Now I miss my father and am beginning to worry about him. I know that it's icy and cold and hard to get around. But why hasn't he called? My mother explains that he's not feeling well and needs to rest quietly for a few days. I'm not sure I believe her. Is it possible that he's angry with me?

◆ ◆ ◆

It is the middle of the night, and my mother is shouting into the phone. Slowly, I wake up to what she is saying:

"How dare you did that without consulting me? No, I don't believe you! No! He doesn't belong there! You're just trying to get rid of him! No, that's the absolute worst place! I want him out of there tomorrow!"

My mother hangs up. My brother walks in from the living room (where he now sleeps on the couch), rubbing his eyes.

"What happened?" he asks.

"Neclo has not been feeling well. He hasn't been eating or wanting to get out of bed. I visited him and told him I thought he had just been doing too much and needed a little rest. I stayed up late tonight to make him a big pot of lamb borscht, which I know he loves. I was sure that would whet his appetite. But his brother, the doctor, had no patience. Nicu thought that Neclo was having some kind of mental breakdown, and that it was dangerous to keep him at home. So tonight he had him committed to a mental hospital!"

"Why would it be dangerous for him to be at home?" asks Sorin.

"Nicu says your father is suffering from depression and might try to kill himself. I think that's a bunch of nonsense. A place like that is the worst possible thing, because there, even a sane man could be driven crazy! And I don't trust any of the people who work at that hospital. I'm getting him out tomorrow."

"What can we do?" Sorin asks in a shaky voice.

"You go back to sleep, both of you. Don't worry. I'll take care of everything."

I, of course, can't go back to sleep. I'm trying to understand what Giunica said, but it's hard for me to make any sense of it. My stomach feels queasy, and I'm afraid.

"Do you think that maybe Neclo is mad at us?" I ask.

"Mad at who? What are you talking about?"

"At me and Sorin. Maybe he was just mad at us and didn't want to come to see us."

"Of course not, darling! He loves you! You're everything to him! If he didn't come to see you, it's because he hasn't been feeling well!"

Giunica doesn't understand. I close my eyes and try to fall asleep.

◆ ◆ ◆

Tonight my father calls and asks to speak to Sorin and me. (He is still in the mental hospital. The doctors insist that he needs to be supervised. My mother doesn't believe them and is fighting with everyone to get him out.)

Neclo doesn't sound as though he is angry with me. On the contrary, he is very warm and loving.

"How are you feeling?" I ask him. I can tell my voice is shaking.

"I'm all right. It's good to hear you. I've been thinking a lot about you, and how sweet you have been to me. I've caused the three of you nothing but trouble, and you've all been bending over backwards for me!"

"I hope you get better!" I shout into the phone, not knowing what else to say.

"You are my dear, kind, beautiful little girl. You will grow up to be a wonderful woman. I love you very much! Can I speak to your brother now?"

Relieved, I hand the phone over to Sorin.

◆ ◆ ◆

In the middle of the night, the phone rings again. I hear my mother's frightened voice. I know something terrible has happened when she says, "I'm getting a taxi and coming over immediately."

I'm afraid to ask anything when she gets off the phone. I follow her into the living room, where she wakes up my brother. Then, she tells us:

"Your father is having emergency surgery. He tried to jump out the second story window of the hospital. Luckily, he landed on a tree branch, which arrested his fall. But the branch perforated his stomach. I'm going to see him right now."

"Is he dead?" I ask.

"Idiot!" my brother shouts. "Didn't you hear? He's having emergency surgery!"

"Why did he do it?" I ask. "Why did he jump out the window?"

"Nicu says he was having hallucinations. He thought some men were chasing him, trying to take him back to the prison. I don't know what to believe. He never should have been committed to that place! God knows what kind of drugs they gave him! And maybe somebody pushed him, for all I know."

After Giunica leaves, I lie in bed, torturing myself. I don't believe anyone pushed him. I think he really did try to kill himself. When he called earlier in the evening and asked to speak to my brother and me, he was really telling us goodbye. He didn't want to live anymore. He thought that he was too much of a burden on everyone. He thought no one wanted him or loved him. And I could have prevented him from feeling that way! How many times had he begged me to let him come and watch me swim? Or to go with him to a movie? Or to give him a hug, or a kiss? And I refused him, always!

And how about the time he came to visit, and I lied and said I was on my way out to a special swim practice and pretended to walk down the stairs and toward the bus, but only hid around the corner until I thought he was gone and then walked back home? Somehow he knew I had lied, and half an hour later rang the doorbell, with that sad, apologetic smile on his face and a package of chocolate éclairs in his hands. He didn't say a word, not one word of reproach, just pretended the incident never happened. No, I don't think any stranger pushed him. I pushed him. I'm the murderer!

◆ ◆ ◆

It doesn't look as bad as I thought, I decide, as I follow my mother and brother through the shady courtyard of the hospital. But when I enter the brick building and see the men with strange, vacant eyes walking around in pajamas, and hear wild screams from behind the closed doors, I am frightened. My heart beats quickly when we reach my father's room—a private room my mother obtained with the help of her Kent cigarettes.

Neclo is wearing the plush, royal blue robe my mother bought for him. He is sitting up on his bed, smiling at us. I am so relieved to see that he looks neither sick nor sad.

"Children! I'm so glad to see you! Come, sit next to me, don't be shy!"

Sorin and I sit at the edge of his bed and hand him the box of chocolates we brought him.

He rips it open and then offers us the candy. We each take one, but he keeps insisting we have more. We refuse. We want him to have it. He needs to get strong.

Then he reaches inside the drawer of his night stand and pulls out two bananas, one for each of us. I haven't seen bananas since I was a small child.

"Here, I've saved these for you! Your mother has been coming to see me every day and stuffing me with all kinds of delicacies—ham, Swiss cheese, oranges, tangerines, bananas. I don't know where or how she manages to get these goodies. And she stays here and watches me like a hawk to make sure I eat everything up myself. But these, I managed to save for you!" Triumphantly, he hands us the bananas.

"No," my brother protests. "Giunica brought them for you. You can use the extra vitamins."

"It's O.K.," my mother says, smiling at my father. "If it makes Neclo happy to see you eat them, don't disappoint him." I peel the skin and bite into the soft, sweet fruit. Suddenly I see myself, a plump little girl running through a very large house toward a giant who has just opened the massive front door. The giant lifts me up and kisses me. His moustache tickles my cheek. Then he puts me down, digs into his pocket and takes out a strange-looking fruit which has the softest, sweetest taste of anything I have ever yet put in my mouth!

My father watches us eat, smiling.

"I'm so lucky!" he suddenly exclaims. "I suffered a relapse of an illness I developed when I was in prison. But I'm fine now. I'm so grateful it's over! There's so much to live for!"

"Of course there is!" my mother says. "You better hurry up and get well, because your daughter needs lots of help with her math and geography!"

"And I've started to play chess again," my brother adds. "I entered a tournament at school. As soon as you come back, we must play."

"And there's a new American movie at the theater right by our house. Giunica knows someone who can get us tickets!" I jump in.

"Thank you, children. You and your mother are trying so hard! My three, good angels!"

I turn my face away. I don't want him to see the tears.

◆ ◆ ◆

The Umbrellas of Cherbourg is the first movie my father and I actually sit through together. Tickets are not so scarce anymore, and Neclo has taken me to several movies already. In the past, however, he just walked me to the theater door and then picked me up two hours later. Though he has always made up some excuse about having errands to do, I knew that the real reason he didn't stay was that he couldn't afford two tickets. But now he has a job. He is working in the electronics department of a factory as a dispatcher. Though he had hoped to find work as an engineer, for he has a degree in "polytechnic" from the military college, he is relieved at least to be able to support himself. The work is tedious, he says, but the other workers are very kind to him and go out of their way to help him.

"Did you like it?" Neclo asks as we walk out of the theater together. I'm not so nervous about being seen with him anymore. He has put on weight, and his old clothes no longer hang on him. He looks like a regular person now.

"Yes, it was beautiful. But…" I stop, not wanting to hurt his feelings.

"Tell me! I want to know your honest impressions!"

"Well, I liked the music and everything, but it bothered me that the characters were singing instead of talking to each other. Normal people don't just burst into song every time they see each other!"

My father laughs. He puts his hand in his pocket. We're passing by a pastry shop, and I can tell, from the clinking sound, that he is counting his loose change.

"After you," he says, opening the door.

"No, I don't really want anything," I object.

"Oh, come on, you can't turn down one small scoop of peanut ice cream!"

"Honestly, I'm not in the mood for sweets," I lie.

"Don't be silly, I've got money," he tells me, guessing my thoughts.

"Only if you'll have something, too," I demand. For usually he claims he's not hungry and just sits, sipping a glass of water, then insists on buying me a second scoop.

"I'll have a coffee," he promises, smiling.

◆ ◆ ◆

I love the first week of March when, to celebrate the beginning of spring, women and girls wear *martisoare*, pretty little charms made out of painted wood in the form of flowers, birds, animals and dolls hanging on delicate red and white threads. Everyone exchanges them as gifts and then proudly displays their collection pinned on the lapels of their sweater or jacket. The snow is melting, the sun is shining and the gypsy women's baskets are full of snowdrops—the white, bell-shaped flowers that are the first to poke their lovely heads out of the snow.

On March 8th, Women's Day, my brother and I always use our allowances to buy small presents for our mother. This year, I buy her nail polish. My brother gets her perfume. In the evening, my father shows up with a big bouquet of red roses.

"Where on earth did you find them!" my mother exclaims, obviously delighted.

She disappears into the pantry and comes back with a bottle of champagne and four glasses.

"I've been saving this for many years," she says, wiping the dust off the bottle. Then she raises her glass and proposes a toast:

"To our family! May only good things happen to us from now on!"

"To the most beautiful woman on earth!" my father declares. "Thank you for raising our little boy to be such a strong, smart young man, and our little girl to be such a lovely, accomplished young woman."

My brother and I both turn red with embarrassment. But then the cork pops. The champagne spills. We laugh.

I sip some of the fizzy, bubbly drink in my glass. It tickles my nostrils and makes me sneeze. Again, we laugh. Is this what it's like to be a real family?

◆ ◆ ◆

"Today, March 19, 1965, is a very sad day for our country," begins the principal of our school, who suddenly, during our last period, has summoned all of us into the courtyard. "Our President, Gheorghe Gheorghiu-Dej, is dead."

Everyone gasps in shock. No one had any idea he was sick.

"We will mourn together the son of our people who dedicated his life to the good of his beloved country. We will always remember his devotion to socialism, to Marxist-Leninism, to peasants and workers, to students and children, to all the citizens of this great land. Everyone can go home now and weep!"

No one dares to ask any questions. Quietly, we disperse. The streets look less crowded than usual. From open windows, I hear radios blaring funeral music. I search people's faces for signs of tears. I don't see any. But everyone seems to be worried and nervous and in a great hurry to get home. They probably want to listen to their radios, I think.

Giunica, Sorin and Neclo are gathered in our living room around the radio, just as I expected. But all that can be heard is funeral music.

"I suspect that somebody poisoned him," my mother is saying. "He was going too far with his reforms."

"But the announcement said he died of cancer," my brother objects.

"Why did no one know he was sick? Why was that kept a secret? People just don't drop dead from cancer in one day!" my mother retorts.

"No one will ever know. But I'm certainly not going to mourn for him!" exclaims my father. "He was responsible for hundreds of thousands of innocent lives!"

"Neclo!" my mother stops him, looking at me with a worried expression on her face. This is the first time my father has ever said anything forbidden in front of us.

"Don't worry, I won't tell anyone," I assure my mother, angry that after everything that has happened, she still thinks I'm too young to hear things.

"The question now is who will take his place," my father says. "For the time being, let's be optimistic and hope for the best. Who knows what will happen? Maybe things will change..."

Maybe he'll be called back and asked to become part of the new government—is that what he means, I wonder? Will we get to live in our old house again?

"Don't build up any illusions!" my mother warns him. "We'll find out soon enough."

◆ ◆ ◆

Nicolae Ceausescu will be Romania's next leader, and my mother, brother and I must try to leave the country. Everything has happened with lightning speed. I'm still in a state of shock. When, the day after Dej's death, Ceausescu's name was announced over the radio, my mother and father looked crushed. At first, I couldn't understand it, because Nicolae Ceausescu is the youngest member of the Politburo and seems much nicer and gentler than any of those other stern old men. And he looked so sincere and cried so much at Gheorghe Gheorghiu-Dej's funeral. Everyone else—our friends, neighbors, people on the street—seem to be quite happy and hopeful about him. But my father said that you can't judge a book by its cover and that Ceausescu is "a wolf in sheep's clothing" who will bring our country to disaster. Furthermore, he is Neclo's worst enemy, personally responsible for what happened to him. Only evil can be expected from him.

My parents have decided that we must quickly take advantage of the relaxed Jewish emigration quotas and apply to join our relatives in America. There is no way, my father explains to Sorin and me, that he will be able to leave with us. Not only is he not Jewish, but his past, his background, his knowledge of government secrets, as well as Ceausescu's personal hatred of him, makes it unlikely that he will ever be allowed to leave Romania. In fact, we must try to keep our identities separate, for if our connection with him were discovered, our application would never be granted. Given the present confusion and anxiety of officials, maybe we will be lucky and our papers will slip through without anyone making any inquiries into the past of Regina Eremia Abramovici's ex-husband. In fact, my mother adds, Aunt Coca has a friend, a colonel, who works in the passport department and who has already offered to help her and her two sisters get out (for a price, of course). Before, nothing came of it since Giunica didn't want to take us away from our father, and my aunts refused to apply without us. Now she realizes that we have no other alternative.

We must not tell anyone anything. No one must know, not even our closest friends.

"What about Comrade Iacobini?" I ask. "And Comrade Mitrofan, my new coach? They're working so hard to train me for the Olympics! And they expect me to go to a special swimming camp this summer!"

"Absolutely not!" my mother gasps, frightened. "No one from swimming must know anything. They would try to hold us back, for sure. If you talk to anyone about this, you'll ruin our chances and our lives!"

"Of course I won't talk! I'm not that stupid!" I tell her angrily.

"Calm down," my mother says. "We have no idea right now how long it will take for our application to be granted. It could be weeks, months, years. Try to forget about it for now and go on as usual."

Yes, I decide. There's no point in worrying about this. They'll probably find out about my father, our applications won't be granted and we won't have to go.

◆ ◆ ◆

We're going! With the help of my aunt's friend the colonel, our application was granted after only a month! We have six weeks to sell everything, pack our belongings into several suitcases and depart forever. Aunt Coca, Aunt Rene and Cousin Dinu are leaving with us. My father, of course, must stay.

I am not allowed to say goodbye to anyone. Not even to Bubook, who might like to hear that we'll finally get to practice our English, or to Comrade Iacobini, who first taught me how to swim. Or to Comrade Mitrofan, the handsome young coach who is now working so hard with me on improving my stroke. Not to any of my friends, not to Gabriela or Mioara or Doina or Lenuta, not to any other kids in my neighborhood or in my class or on my swim team. What will everyone think happened to me?

I cry and cry. I'm so ashamed. I feel like a traitor. I'm abandoning my father, my friends, my swim team. I must leave everything that means anything to me behind. I can't take any of my books, my scrapbooks or my swimming prizes. I can't even take my dear old doll, Ancuta, whom I've kept always, because they would suspect I'm hiding gold or diamonds in her belly!

My suitcase will be filled with the several dresses and coats which my mother is having made for me and which are supposed to be "roomy"—meaning baggy and shapeless—so they can last me for some time. I refuse to sit still while the seamstress tries to take my measurements. I know I'll hate everything!

◆ ◆ ◆

"Don't cry, my darling." My father tries to comfort me on our last night in Romania—a night our family spends together at his new place, which is filled with as much of our furniture that his small, single apartment can fit. Everything else has been sold or given away. We will take only suitcases filled with clothes—two per person. Our own apartment has been taken over by a policeman and his pregnant wife. They moved in this morning.

"I don't want to go," I cry. "Why can't I just stay here with you?"

"You are going to a great country," my father says, "and you'll be very happy there. Have I ever told you that my own father, when he was a young man, always talked about emigrating to America? He was constantly trying to save money for the trip, but he had eight little mouths to feed and never managed to make it. Now you, his grandchildren, are finally going to live out his dream. Do you know anything about the country where you are going to live?"

"Yes, I know that everyone there drives cars, and I hate cars because I always get car sick! And people are always in a hurry and they eat huge sandwiches, which must be swallowed in three big bites so as not to waste time!"

"No, my sweet, you really don't know much about your future country. You'll have a wonderful life there. America is the best country on earth. Come here, Sorin, I want you to hear this, too."

Sorin, who has been pacing nervously up and down the room like a caged lion, finally sits down on the edge of the bed. He, too, looks unhappy, but unlike me, he doesn't complain.

My father now lowers his voice to a half-whisper, and begins:

"Did you know that almost two centuries ago the American people fought a revolution?"

"No! I thought America was a capitalist country!" I answer, surprised.

"Dummy! Sorin exclaims. "Communist countries are not the only ones that have revolutions!"

"I'm not a dummy, you're a dummy!"

"Hush, children, don't fight. Yes, the American people fought a revolution to establish their independence from Great Britain. This was perhaps the only revolution in the history of the world that was not stolen or perverted or corrupted by power-hungry tyrants. The noble ideals of its leaders were immortalized in its constitution, which has ensured the freedom and happiness of its people generation after generation.

"Children, in Romania you have no future. Here you will always be considered the offspring of the class enemy. In America you will grow up to be everything you want to be!"

"Do you promise me that you will remember to return my swim stuff?" I ask him, more concerned right now with what I'm leaving than with where I'm going.

"He's already promised you three times," my mother snaps at me, irritated. "Is that all you can think about?" Once again, she goes through her purse, trying to make sure we have everything and that all our documents are in order.

"That's all right, darling, I don't mind." My father looks at me with compassion. "Irina, I swear to you that the moment your plane gets off the ground, I will go straight to the swimming complex and return everything."

I'm worried about the swim clothes. Last week, everyone on my team was given a brand new bathing suit, sweat shirt and warm-up suit with the name of our team on it in large, bright letters. All the other kids wore their new outfits the very next day at practice. I said I was saving mine for the race next Sunday. Now, when I don't show up, and they find out that I have abandoned my team and snuck out of my country like a traitor, they'll at least know I'm not a thief.

◆ ◆ ◆

We huddle together in a corner of the airport, not wanting to be noticed. My mother looks worried, my brother glum; I sulk. My father tries to smile and cheer us up.

"The sky is clear. You should have a nice flight. Kids, this will be your first time on an airplane. I think it will be an interesting experience for you. I know you'll enjoy it!"

But even as he says this, his hands hold ours tight, refusing to let go. Then the loudspeaker begins to blare, "The emigrants must now enter the sealed area," and my mother is forced to say it first:

"Goodbye, Neclo!"

"Goodbye, Gina!"

"Stay well! May you be able to join us soon!"

"Goodbye, Sorin! Goodbye, Irina! Don't forget to write! As soon and as often as possible! My mailbox will be my best friend!" Neclo's chin begins to tremble, and he can no longer stop the tears.

I throw my arms around him and, for the first time since his return from prison, kiss him on the cheek.

"I'll write! I promise! I'll let you know everything! I'll write you every day!"

"They'll write, I'll write, all of us will write," my mother shouts as the guard starts marching us toward the area where the "untouchables" are gathered.

"Take good care of yourself, Neclo!" yells Sorin just before we enter customs.

◆ ◆ ◆

Nervous, excited and heartbroken, I climb the steps to the airplane that will take me away from my father, the land of my birth and all the places I know and love. At the door, I turn back and wave at the weeping crowd gathered at the airport window to take one last look at their departing loved ones. I spot my father, his face glued to the glass. He is smiling and waving at us, his trusting blue eyes full of hope and tears.

Epilogue

Ion and Irina: Letters

December 16, 1965

Dear Neclo,

I was very happy to receive your letter. I am glad to hear that you are well and healthy and that "your spirit has been uplifted" by your trip to the mountains where you "tasted the splendors of our majestic Carpathians."

Still, I want you to know that I am very angry with you for putting your life in danger! Why hike up such difficult trails? Why take such great risks? I want you to promise me that you'll never do that again. You must stay in one piece, at least until I see you again!

America is nothing like what I expected. There are no skyscrapers in San Francisco. Most people here live in little houses made out of wood (like Romanian peasants!) which are painted blue, green, yellow, orange—the kinds of colors used to illustrate children's books. The streets are bare of trees, and the little houses which are glued to each other in even rows have little plots of grass growing in front of them that look like graves. Maybe people bury their pets there.

No one here likes to walk, and I don't blame them, because many of the streets are slanted uphill and you run out of breath after half a block. The whole city is built on a hill, which gives you the opportunity to see many pretty views of the ocean, the bay, The Golden Gate Bridge and the Bay Bridge, but I would gladly give all of that up for a flat street where I could ride a bike!

I go to school from 8 to 3, a much longer day than what I'm used to. But don't think that American children learn all that much during these hours. The teachers here spend most of their time trying to convince their students to please stop jumping up and down in their seats, to please spit out their gum, to please stop throwing spit balls and paper balls at each other, to please not pull their neighbor's hair or kick him from behind! Here, it isn't the students who are afraid of the teachers, but the teachers who are afraid of the students! And if you saw some of these students, you, too, would be scared! The white girls wear their hair all ratted up in these enormous puffs which they hold together with this sticky substance called "hair spray." The black girls, who have very thick, bushy hair, wear theirs even higher and stick these pitchfork-like combs in them that are often used as weapons. All the girls wear thick, black eye liner under their eyes, blue eye shadow on their lids, and look as if they've been punched in the mouth and are bleeding from all the bright red lipstick they smear themselves with! The boys either puff their hair up in a pompadour held together by grease or let it grow longer than the girls. They swagger around in tight pants looking like lunatics who have just escaped from a mental ward.

Things are getting a little better now, but in the beginning, I had a very hard time. The first day of school, I was so nervous that I threw up in the bathroom before leaving our apartment. Giunica promised me that if I just tried to smile at everyone, everything would turn out well. Then (through Uncle Jack, the interpreter) she told the principal that I did speak a little English and that I probably could also understand Spanish. The neighborhood where we live is full of immigrants from Mexico and South America, and there are some Spanish-speaking teachers at my school. Giunica had heard that Spanish was a lot like Romanian and Italian, so she thought that if I had trouble understanding English, they would at least be able to communicate with me in Spanish. All day long, people tried to talk to me in two incomprehensible languages, and all I could do was stare at them bewildered, and grin idiotically. At the end of the day, the principal called Sorin in (who, because he paid more attention to Bubook than I did, can speak some English now). She told him to please explain to my mother that she had brought me to the wrong school: I needed to be enrolled in a special school for the mentally retarded! Sorin, of course, had a great laugh over this, and told Giunica that he, himself, even in Romania, had always suspected that to be the case!

Now, I am starting to catch on a bit. Every day, after school, I go over to Omama's house (our apartment is only two blocks away from hers), and Uncle Jack, after he comes home from work, sits with me and translates every chapter in my Social Studies book from English to Romanian. School here is very easy. I was allowed to skip sixth grade (to be with my age group, since kids here start school at the age of six, not seven, like in Romania). But I am finding out that what we're learning here in the seventh grade, I had already learned last year, in the fifth. So, even though I speak very little English, I did get pretty good grades on my report card—not as good as my brother, who got straight A's (we are graded here from A to F instead of from 10 to 4), but still, nothing to be ashamed of: I got "A's" in history, math and music, and "B's" in English, Physical Education (where I'm learning this awful game where you have to hit a small ball with a big stick; usually I end up hitting the air or myself!) and a B- in "Home Making."

I have to tell you a little bit about "Home Making," where for the first time, someone tried to teach me how to cook. At school, I made noodles with tuna (a hard, salty fish that comes out of a can), jello (a wiggly, fruity dessert) and beef stew. I brought everything I made home for my mother and brother to taste. Giunica claimed to like everything but left most of it on the plate while Sorin refused to touch it saying that since he's the best player on the soccer team, he can't afford to get sick to his stomach. But I know that if you were here, you would have eaten everything all up and told me how delicious it tasted! I wish I could wrap up my dishes and send them to you in Romania!

Since I've been taught how to cook, I thought I would experiment in the kitchen myself when no one was home. I decided to make an omelet, and tried to follow a recipe I got from school. It called for "butter" and the only butter I could find in the house was something called "peanut butter." Even though this is a brown and sticky substance, I thought that since it was "butter" it would melt. But instead, it burned, and caught on fire along with the eggs, and despite all my efforts to dispose of the evidence, Giunica and Sorin could "smell" my disaster even before they walked into our apartment.

I didn't have much luck with sewing, either. Our class has a number of sewing machines and I happened to sit at the nicest, newest one. The teacher explained how to use it, but I, of course, didn't understand a word. Never having seen anything like it before, I pushed all the wrong buttons, and ended up breaking the machine. It's a wonder that I got a "B-" in the class, and not an "F"—especially considering that the first time I tried the blouse I made, the sleeves fell off!

The children here think I'm weird, and make fun of me. Since I haven't yet mastered the insufferable English language, I can't even talk back to them! It doesn't help that Giunica, who thinks that the soft, spongy American bread is fattening and unhealthy, makes my sandwiches on these thin crackers called "saltines" which crumble the moment you bite into them. She also refuses to let me rat my hair, wear eye shadow, lipstick or nail polish. I finally convinced her to allow me to shave my legs, like the rest of the girls here! Uncle Jack took me to the store and bought me three dresses so I don't look so different from everyone else.

I miss you and Romania and all my friends so much! I'm so homesick! The weather here is dreary and foggy and windy all year round. There is no real summer or winter. People put fake Christmas trees in their windows! It must be cold there now and the streets must be covered with snow. Sometimes, before going to bed, I close my eyes and pretend that I'm still there. I imagine myself skipping down the three flights of stairs from our apartment, stopping to chat with my friends on the street who are having snow ball fights and building snow men, and then walking down the road I know so well to the Winter Palace for swim practice. I visualize each store, each tree, each house along the way. Will I ever come back? Will I ever see those dear sights again?

Please tell Bunicata that I enjoyed the lines she added to your letter, and that I miss her very much. (Not as much as I miss you, don't worry, even though I know that you miss Sorin more than you miss me!)

I want to wish you, Bunicuta and the rest of the family there a Happy New Year.

I hope that next year, we'll celebrate New Year's together.

Love and kisses,
Irene (my new American name)

P.S. I'm enclosing two poems I wrote in Italy, while we were waiting for our visas, and a drawing of my new street. I hope you like them!

March 15, 1966

Dear Neclo,

Please forgive me for not having written for so long. But when you hear about all the things that have happened to me, I know you'll understand and stop feeling so hurt. My life has been so eventful since I last wrote (in August, when I congratulated you on your birthday).

When school started in September, I took Drama as my "elective" class, and the teacher encouraged me to audition for a part in the school play, a comedy called *Long Live Christmas*. I tried out for the part of the Christmas Fairy, who at one point in the play must lift up her arms in the air and say, "Spirits of Christmas, come!" "Spirits of Christmas, come!" Everyone who auditioned pronounced these words in the normal way Americans are accustomed to hear them pronounced. But I took a deep breath, and elongated all my vowels, the Romanian way: "Spee-reets of Chreest-maas, cooome!" I also "rolled" my "r"'s, which the American's don't know how to do. So, unlike the other children, I didn't sound like an ordinary person, but more the way a real fairy might sound. So, I got the part!

At our "premiere" my heart was beating so hard I thought it would jump out of my chest. I was dressed in a long, silky white gown, and I wore a shiny gold crown on my head, and shiny slippers on my feet. I was made up by one of the children's mothers who is a real make up artist. When I found myself on stage, the lights pierced my eyes, and I could see nothing without my glasses. For a short time I forgot who I was and really had the feeling that what I was saying was also what I was really thinking. My part must have been very funny, because everyone in the audience was roaring with laughter. When, at the end of the play, I took my bow, I got more applause than any other actor. I was so happy! What wouldn't I have given to know that you, too, were there in the audience, for then I would have performed only for you, and I would have gotten even more applause.

When, after the play, I went backstage, even Mary, my rival congratulated me. For a long time no one talked about anything else at school other than *Long Live Christmas* and its Christmas Fairy. I was on cloud nine! I felt as if I were dreaming a beautiful dream and I never wanted to wake up.

After all this, another exciting event happened. Every year, all the junior high schools in the city hold a speech contest. The subject this year was "Peace." My drama teacher entered me in the contest as the representative of our school.

I chose a selection from *The Diary of Anne Frank*. This time, I had to rehearse much more than for the play, and my selection was very long, very beautiful, and very sad. Giunica spent lots of time coaching me on how to interpret it.

I was very frightened when I got to the contest. I felt that my entire school depended on me. My drama teacher had worked with me a lot, but I don't think her hopes were too high as our school had never won before—we are considered one of the worst schools in the city. I was intimidated by the judges: five lawyers, two actors, and a real stage director. If I had even a ray of hope in my heart, it extinguished when I saw and heard my competition. Still, when my turn came I tried to do my best. After a while, I forgot my nervousness, and began to feel as if I were really Anne Frank.

Afterwards, if anyone had taken my temperature, I am sure it would have been over 105 degrees! My drama teacher and school principal who had come with me, smiled and told me I did well, but I thought they were just being kind. When the awards were called out, I hoped I would get at least honorable mention, so that our school could finally walk away with something. But my hopes were dashed when other children's names were called for honorable mention, third and second place. Then, I noticed that the gentleman reading out the names of the winners paused and looked very embarrassed. He gawked at his announcement, as if he were trying to make something out, and seemed confused. My heart started beating faster and faster as he stuttered and stammered and finally came out with: "First place goes to Arimaia Airenia from Horace Mann Junior High School." Thank God he mentioned the name of my school, or I would never have been sure enough he meant me to stand up and risk making a fool of myself!

My drama teacher and my principal had both turned bright red. I could hardly walk up to the podium, my knees were shaking so hard. Neclo, I received the loveliest trophy I have ever seen in my life! It's about fifty centimeters tall, and looks like it's made out of gold!

My beautiful dream lasted for the rest of the semester at school where I became everyone's hero. This was the first time that our school had ever won a speech contest! At the assembly at the end of the semester, our principal mentioned me during her speech and told everyone how moved she had been by my interpretation of Anne Frank, and how proud the school was of my achievement. Then, this same principal who, only a year ago suspected that I was mentally retarded, sent a beautiful letter to Giunica, thanking her for her "daughter's contribution to the school."

Dear Neclo, I told you that I felt as if I were living a dream, and like every dream, mine finally ended and I was forced to wake up to reality. Giunica has found a job working in a furniture store, and was lucky enough to discover a house for rent in a much better neighborhood than our old one. It was a real find, and though the rent is a stretch, we will manage to make it. We moved before the beginning of the new semester, and I have had to transfer schools. We now live in a real house, with a backyard, two bedrooms, a living room, dining room, bathroom and kitchen, and even a garage, which we don't really need for no one knows yet how to drive. Everyone at my old school was very sad to see me go, especially my drama teacher who had worked so hard with me. I was heartbroken. Finally, I had become accepted, respected, and even considered a celebrity. Now it was all over.

Neclo, it's been so hard for me to start everything all over again. This new school is much harder than my old school, the students much smarter, and the teachers more demanding. Despite my straight "A" report card and the wonderful letter I carried with me from the principal, I was not put in the class with the smartest kids because of the school where I came from. And now it turns out that instead of being ahead of everyone in my class, I'm starting out behind, and struggling hard to catch up.

One nice thing seems to be happening, at least. In the old school I had no friends. Here I've met several girls already with whom I have a lot in common and I am beginning to develop some friendships. I am determined to work hard, get good grades, and prove myself again just as I did before.

I think that you can understand now why I wasn't able to write you for so long. Please don't be mad at me! I miss you and I love you, and don't you ever think that you could love me more than I love you!

Many kisses,
Irina (pronounced "Aireena" in English)

P.S. I am enclosing the letter sent to us by the school principal. It is addressed to "Irina Eremia's parents" so you should, of course, read it. I'm sorry, but I haven't had any time to write any more poems.

January 25, 1973

My Darling Daughter,

I was very touched by your last letter, which by far made up for the six months of silence which preceded it. Don't worry, my child, I do understand how busy college life is, so full of pressures, worries, exams, so empty of spare time! Your letter was so warm, so sweet, so loving, how could I possibly stay angry with you?

That suddenly, in the middle of the night, you felt the urge to write your Neclo a letter and open up your heart to him, moved me deeply. There you were, in your little college room in Berkeley, sitting at your desk, conversing with your father who lives so many thousands of miles away from you, sharing with him your innermost thoughts and feelings. Neither time nor distance has been able to diminish our closeness! I'm so grateful for that!

My lovely, talented, beautiful child, what a profound realization you shared with me in your letter! I have been hoping and praying that you would have this realization much earlier in life than I did. You wrote to me that you suddenly realize that more than anything else in life you want "a meaningful existence," and that you know that a life of material comfort, domestic happiness, and even professional success will not be sufficient to provide that meaning for you. You say that the only way you think you will ever be happy is by creating something from your imagination, something that will live long after you are dead, something that will make a contribution to humanity. My darling, I am so glad you reached this realization now, when you are only twenty. I was in my mid-forties, and in very hard circumstances when I came to the same conclusion.

My sweetheart, I have read, over the past eight years, your speeches, essays, short stories and poems. I know you have talent. But talent must be cultivated. You can only become a writer by writing. And if you are a writer, you will never be happy, unless you are writing. So, write, my darling, write every spare moment you can find, write short stories, essays, articles, poems, anything you can. Don't be satisfied with just doing your college assignments. I know it's hard, but still, you must somehow strive to find the time. You must not let your talent go to waste, you must not silence that voice within you that is crying to be heard, or as you yourself sense, there will always be a part of you that will remain unhappy and unfulfilled.

I speak from experience. Other than having children, nothing has brought me more joy in life than the process of writing. Ever since I managed to have my pension restored for my many years of military service, a pension which though modest, has spared me of the need to work, I too, have been writing. I hope to have my book, *Popa Stoica* (remember how I used to tell you and Sorin stories about him when you were young?), published soon. I am dedicating it to you, my two beloved children.

Let me now turn to the second matter you discussed with me in your letter: the matter of love. You seem to have found a wonderful man, a man of "integrity and high moral character," you say, a man who "loves" you, "values" you, "believes in your talent" and treats you with "respect and consideration." You, too, value this man's qualities and find him "attractive, capable, intelligent, and kind." In spite of all this, you doubt whether you want to commit yourself to this man. You write that there is a part of you that "craves excitement, adventure, romance." You worry that your relationship is too "safe and predictable." You quote from Dostoevsky who writes that suffering is a necessary and noble aspect of the human condition. Are you suggesting that you want to turn down this man because he hasn't made you suffer enough?

My dear girl, I can tell you, again from my own experience, that suffering—loneliness, want, misery, frustration—doesn't ennoble man, but only debases him. We are made for happiness. If happiness stares you in the face, don't turn your back on it and go search for suffering! If you have been fortunate enough to meet a man of pure mind and heart (and believe me, darling, such men are rare and precious in this world), don't walk away from him out of some misguided notions about the meaning of love.

I know, my dear, that you are a romantic. I was too, at your age. Based on the novels you read, you imagine love to be something stormy and tempestuous, full of agony and ecstasy. That may be true, my sweet, of a certain kind of sexual passion that may lead to fleeting moments of pleasure and lasting years of pain. True love between a man and a woman is based on friendship, understanding, respect, support, self-sacrifice. The man you describe sounds exactly like the right kind of man for a sensitive, pure soul like you.

So my darling, this is my advice, given only because you have asked for it, from your father who loves you and wishes he were near you instead of so many miles away. I trust you and believe in you and know that you are smart enough and wise enough to choose what is right for you.

I support your decision to apply to graduate school in English rather than to law school. I understand that it is the less practical alternative, as your mother and brother point out, but one that is much better suited to your temperament, your interests, and your talent. Reading and studying the works of great writers can only help to turn you into a better writer, and that, we now both agree, is your goal in life, isn't it?

I am well and healthy. My wife Nicoleta and I have a harmonious marriage, and our domestic tranquility makes up for some of the material difficulties of our lives. I am happy to hear that Giunica, too, is content in her marriage. We were not made to live alone!

I love you, and miss you, and look forward to your next letter.

Your devoted father, Neclo

March, 1984

Dear Neclo,

I am so sorry that it has been so many months from my last letter! There was so little I could tell you during our brief phone conversations about the exciting event that has changed our lives.

Neclo, your grandson, Andrew, is beautiful and my love for him is deeper than I could ever have imagined was possible, but I had no idea that one tiny little human being could turn two big ones into slaves. He is a feisty, hearty little boy. When he laughs (which is most of the time) his whole body shakes with mirth. But when he cries, he makes such a racket you can hear him from miles away! He loves people, action, movement, noise. He hates sleep. The moment I start walking toward his room, before I even open the door, he begins to scream and kick. At the first sight of his crib, he goes into hysterics. I have to rock him in my rocking chair and sing to him "Trestioara de pe lac" and "Somnoroase Pasarele" (not having grown up here, I don't know the American lullabies), until those big blue eyes (as blue as yours) finally succumb to sleep. Then gently, gingerly, I lower him in the crib (this is a crucial moment) and then stealthily, like a thief in the night or a soldier in an ambush, creep out of the room praying that the floor won't creak or the door won't squeak! If he sleeps for three hours at a stretch, I'm lucky. Eventually I give in, defying the advice of all the doctors, books, articles, friends and grandparents, and take him into bed with us. Triumphant, the little prince stretches himself out over the entire bed, relegating Ronn and I to the edges, and then proceeds to roll and toss and kick and tumble for the rest of the night.

My job, teaching writing at U.C.L.A., is very demanding. After a night with Andy, I stagger to my classroom like a drunken sailor and have to struggle not to fall asleep during my own lectures.

I have to be honest with you, Neclo. I have worked hard all these years to have a profession, to feel I can support myself (Giunica always ingrained in me that a woman must never depend on a man), to feel proud, successful, accomplished. But the reality is, I hate leaving Andy every morning and worry about him all day, and resent having to grade papers in the evening when I would much rather chase him around the house on all fours!

Still, as much as I love Andy, I know I am not the kind of woman who could devote my entire life to him. And yet he's so small, and so precious, and his babyhood is flying by so fast! I don't want to wake up one morning and realize that he's all grown up and doesn't need me any more and that I somehow missed his childhood.

Neclo, the urge to write is as strong in me as ever. I am suddenly realizing that I have only one life and I cannot do and be everything! I cannot be a teacher and a mother and a writer all at the same time. Something has got to go. What is going this year is writing, for which I have absolutely no time. And so, I am now starting to think that I should give up my job at U.C.L.A., and divide my time between raising my son and writing.

This will be very hard for me to do, because suddenly I will lose my status.

How ridiculous this preoccupation with what other people think of me! It suddenly dawns on me how powerful my need has been all my life, ever since I was a child, for approval, recognition, awards, "10s," "As," degrees, pats on the back! And yet I know that in order to be true to myself, I must stop being dominated by these needs.

Last year, after my bout with Hollywood, I decided that I would not sell my soul for any price. All the attention I got after I won the Goldwyn award was wonderful for my ego. I felt like that little girl again, who won the trophy for reciting from *The Diary of Anne Frank*. But after two years spent meeting one producer or studio executive after another, all of whom claimed to "love" my writing, but had some other, "catchier, more commercial" idea of his own he wanted me to write about, I decided that I would not give up my freedom to say what I want to say for anything in the world.

I do think, Neclo, that I am finally ready to answer that voice that has been crying to express itself for all these years, while I was busy researching term papers, studying for exams, running to meetings, preparing lectures, teaching classes.

Neclo, I want to congratulate you on your publication of your book, *Pepelea*, and I look forward to seeing *Maria Butoianu* in print.

Sorin and Susy came over for dinner last weekend. They are both so busy, he with his dermatology practice and she with her family practice, that our moments together are rare. Andy is wild about them.

Giunica has become a celebrity in San Francisco, as a result of acquiring a famous music hall, once called "The Fillmore West" and now renamed "The San Francisco Landmark." She is working with a famous music producer, Bill Graham, to bring all kinds of rock 'n roll groups to perform in her auditorium. There was a big article in the *San Francisco Chronicle* about the glamorous European lady who now owns the hottest concert hall in the city!

I love you and miss you and wish you could be here, with us!

Love and kisses, Irina

March 24, 1990

My Darling Child,

I am very sorry to have worried you and your brother so. Six years ago, when I suffered my first serious bout of depression in almost twenty years, and Sorin came to my rescue with the medication I needed, I thought I was completely cured and did not believe I would ever have to live through such a nightmare again. Unfortunately, right before the revolution that freed our people from the two criminals who ruled us, I was stricken with the illness again. This time, nothing seemed to work.

I have to confess to you, my darling, that I had been under great stress. My book, *Maria Butoianu*, which had just appeared, contained veiled portraits of the two monsters who have destroyed our country. The first day the book appeared, lines running several blocks long formed around the book stores. Then, suddenly, the books were taken out of circulation. At the same time, I had secretly been working on the manuscript of a book which I had composed in my mind during my imprisonment, twenty-five years ago. Nothing is veiled or disguised in this book. Suddenly I became terror-stricken that my house would be searched, that I would be arrested again, that I would be interrogated and tortured and isolated and beaten and starved. I re-lived everything I went through the first time, as if it were happening to me right now. Only this time, I felt I no longer had the strength to endure!

I was deep in the jaws of my illness when the spontaneous uprising, which I had predicted a quarter of a century earlier in my book *Gulliver in the Land of Lies* finally took place. But I was so sick that neither the great news, nor Nicoleta's devoted care, nor your insistent phone calls succeeded in pulling me out.

Now, suddenly, I feel better my darling. The fog began to lift when your brother's efforts to arrange my visit to Los Angeles (a visit which I simply could not believe would really take place) ultimately resulted in the passport, the visa, and the plane ticket which I now hold in my own two hands. Finally, I will get to meet my grandchildren, Andy and Lauren, whose beautiful pictures I kiss every night before going to bed. And finally I will see you, my dear children, and hold you in my arms, and hear your voices, and sit inside your homes, and feel part of your lives!

To see you, in flesh and blood, finally, to see you, I live only to see you!

Your loving father, Neclo

Essays

When Children Ask About Heroes

Before I embarked on *Subterranean Towers: A Father-Daughter Story*, there were many things about my father I did not know. I did not regard him as a hero, or consider him a survivor or think of him as a poet. I had no idea how much of myself I would find in him and of him in me, and then come to recognize in my own children, particularly Andy, who resembles him in so many ways. I could not have predicted all the issues in my life that these discoveries would help me to resolve. Still, even after I thought the book was finished, there was one important question, perhaps the most important of all, which remained unanswered. I had posed it to myself in my introduction: My father was robbed of our childhood. We were robbed of our father. Was it worth it? Or was the price of heroism, perhaps, too high?

I did not feel obligated to answer it. How many times in my years of teaching had I heard myself preach the commonplace that every lecturer on contemporary literature must occasionally repeat for the sake of that sometimes dissatisfied student: "The task of the writer is to explore the complexities, contradictions, absurdities of the human experience, to challenge us with hard questions rather than soothe us with simple answers."

So I was content to leave matters in this regard where they had stood when the airplane carrying my mother and Sorin and me disappeared into the clouds, and my father and I went on to live our separate lives, he in Romania and I in America, and then came together again and decided to celebrate our reunion with our joint memoir, and so conquer life with art. Then, one evening, just as I was about to print out the final version of the manuscript, twelve-year-old Andy burst into my study and surprised me with a simple question, which required a mere "yes" or "no" answer: "Do you think Grandpa Neclo is a good example of a hero?"

That night I dreamed my "Neclo" dream again. Or more accurately, my recurrent Neclo nightmare. I dreamed it in several versions at various times ever since that warm June day in 1965 when I last looked down from the soaring airplane at the man with the tear-stained face and determined smile who was waving goodbye to the "sleepy little birds" he had just set free.

He calls to tell me he is due to arrive next week. I wait for him at the airport, watch the other passengers leave one by one, but my father is not among them. I run up to the last stewardess off the airplane. "Isn't this the flight from Bucharest?" "No, this is the flight from Budapest. The Bucharest plane landed yesterday." I grab my calendar out of my purse. To my horror, I realize she is right. My father's plane was due to arrive yesterday. What could have happened to him? He has no money. He doesn't speak the language. Frantically, I search for him everywhere. Finally, a janitor tells me: "Yes, there was a man here from Romania. He stood all night, by the door waiting for someone to pick him up. In the morning, he took the plane back home.

The dream was never difficult to decipher. I knew it had to do with guilt. The guilt I felt when my father came home from prison and I could not give him what he had lost and so desperately wanted back: the child I once was, the closeness we once shared, the trust, the ease, the spontaneity, the simplicity. The guilt I felt for leaving him behind, for enjoying freedoms he couldn't share, for tasting joys denied to him, for not writing often enough. His unanswered letters perpetually hung over my head.

When my father came to America, he brought me several of my early letters to him, which he thought my children might enjoy reading some day. He had no idea what an effort they had required. They always began with an apology. They always ended with a promise. And they always attempted to make up, by their cheerful tone, lively descriptions, detailed narrations, intimate revelations and constant avowals of love and longing, for the long intervals of silence between them.

As I reread these letters, I marveled at the artful coyness with which the twelve-year-old girl, so different from the one I remember myself to be, tried to amuse, charm, please, impress and ultimately reassure her father that she loved him. I, who know her, also know that behind her light, gay tone was the image of a lonely man sitting by a door, or a window or an empty mailbox, waiting for her to fill the empty spaces in his heart with stories of her conquests, victories and triumphs. Never did she sit down to write him a letter (often driven to it by the recurrence of the dream) without feeling the heavy burden of expectation that this image of him aroused. The other image of him, of the great man in the white uniform with shiny gold buttons, who she had once fantasized would return to his family, victorious, like Odysseus returned to Penelope and Telemachus, to vanquish their enemies and set things straight, had almost faded from her mind. The ghostly creature who had returned in the hero's place needed her to help him heal. He had brought back no trophies, only scars. The fragile, hurt, vulnerable father she had left in Romania was a man who had lost everything: his home, his position, his freedom, his wife, his children.

◆ ◆ ◆

Heroes are winners. They vanquish the villains. They defeat their enemies. They beat their opponents. They fight for us, their people, their dependents, their supporters, their team, their fans. They return triumphant from battle, holding the shining relics of their victories: gold and silver, medals and trophies, flags and emblems, grants, treaties, declarations and proclamations. They have the vision to seek, the courage to risk and the power to get us that which we needed but could not get—land, bread, homes, honors, comforts, luxuries, freedoms, rights, privileges, opportunities. To win these prizes for us, they risk their lives, and when they succeed, we cheer and applaud and shower them with gifts.

When heroes don't win, they die, but their causes triumph. We honor their sacrifices with statues and monuments. We immortalize their deeds by remembering their names. We know that in heaven, their souls will reap their just rewards.

These, of course, were the heroes of old. They lived in worlds where heroes could win. Today, a few of their descendants live in the world of sports.

After World War I and World War II, after Auschwitz and Hiroshima and the Gulags and all the killing fields from Vietnam to Afghanistan, Argentina to Rwanda to Bosnia, the very notion of heroes seems to be an obsolete, archaic notion, one that is incompatible with the realities of our time. In his acclaimed book *The Survivor*, Terrence Des Pres argues that now that "the final solution has become the usual solution and the world is not what it was," to speak about heroism "in places where people die by thousands, where machines reduce courage to stupidity and dying to complicity with aggression," is both meaningless and absurd: "If by heroism we mean the dramatic defiance of superior individuals, then the age of heroes is gone."

My father's experience, repeated for more than half a century by various individuals, at various times, in various parts of the world, is at the very core of this anti-heroic attitude. The cause that led my father in his youth to risk torture, death and imprisonment, along with thousands of other "true believers," was communism. His team won, he was declared a "war hero" and rewarded with that white uniform with epaulets and medals and shiny gold buttons that as a young child I saw as the symbols of his glory. But the prize he brought to his people turned out to be a scourge. The good guys he helped triumph proved no better than the bad guys he helped defeat. He tried to protest and change things, but what chance did one man have against an entire political system that dominated not just his own country but half of Eastern Europe? What did his self-sacrifice win and for whom? Did it change anything? Benefit anyone? Or was his courage stupidity, his idealism, madness?

Several days before my father was due to arrive in the United States for our reunion, I watched an interview on *Sixty Minutes* with a Romanian journalist who had collaborated with Ceausescu's regime. Asked why she had consented to violate the standards of her profession and spread the tyrant's lies, the Romanian replied, "I had to survive, all of us did what we could to survive." The American anchorwoman wouldn't let her off so easily. Politely she suggested that some people prefer to die with honor rather than betray their principles. "Don't you think you owe your people an apology?" she asked, as the Romanian journalist hung her head in shame.

"Oh, shut up!" I shouted at the TV (shocking my children, who thought people talked to it only during football games), irritated by the reporter's self-righteous attitude. Did she have any idea what sacrifices were involved in staying true to one's principles? Did she know that such choices often result in hurting not just oneself, but also one's nearest and dearest: a beloved wife, a cherished mother, an adored child? Did she realize that the rare individuals who are willing to pay the price of courage in life, not in old movies, are often perceived not as heroes but as fools? For more than a quarter of a century, my father's own brothers and sisters (some of whom were demoted from their jobs in reprisal for his acts) considered him not a hero, but a failure who had destroyed his brilliant career, ruined his marriage and broken up his family. What had he gained, they asked, by stubbornly adhering to his principles? Just look at his former colleague, Ceausescu, not nearly as bright or capable or handsome or charismatic, who has risen to lead the country and elevate every member of his family to a position of power!

Now history has turned the tables in Romania, and for the first few weeks after the "spontaneous revolution," the world media, in one dramatic account of it after another, were temporarily bringing back the age of heroes. How could they resist the high drama, the larger-than-life characters, the Shakespearean plot of the Ceausescu saga that for many Americans had just now put Romania on the map? The faces of Nicolae and Elena Ceausescu (Macbeth and Lady Macbeth) briefly graced the covers of as many national magazines as would, a few years later, those of O.J. and Nicole Simpson (Othello and Desdemona).

The 1989 revolution in Romania became the climax of that absorbing drama—The Fall of the House of Communism—that unfolded so rapidly before our astonished eyes at the end of the 1980s. It was a romantic play that filled spectators with faith and optimism. Glasnost had triumphed in Russia. The Berlin Wall fell. A dissident playwright in Czechoslovakia and a rebel union chief in Poland became the triumphant leaders of their long-suffering nations. Capitalism proved stronger than communism. Francis Fukuyakma declared that we had reached "the end of history." As the Iron Curtain rose, the spotlight fell on Romania, which offered the most dramatic spectacle of all. A once wealthy nation brought to utter ruin. Hungry, frightened citizens moving like shadows on dark, frozen streets, scavenging for food. Neglected orphans rocking themselves for comfort staring into space with desperate eyes. A pair of wicked tyrants terrorizing their subjects from their magnificent palace filled with stolen treasures. Suddenly, young martyrs throw themselves in front of tanks and bullets, and the oppressed masses join them in a miraculous revolt. The vicious tyrant and his vile consort try to flee through the labyrinthine tunnels beneath their palace. After a fierce chase, they are captured, tried and finally executed. Their grotesque bodies lie side by side in a pool of blood in the muddy snow. The liberated slaves dance in the streets of their ravaged cities and toast the "heroes of the revolution" who have led them to freedom.

To a world starved for glory, it seemed like this time, the "good guys" had won. In what looked like a remake of an old black and white movie, it was easy to cast the winners as heroes, the losers as either villains or traitors. As I watched the American correspondent stand in judgment of her Romanian counterpart, it struck me that the American's attitude had almost nothing to do with principles and everything to do with the fact that the Romanian had played for the losing team. An old Romanian expression came to my mind: "It is easy to suffer twenty-four lashes on someone else's behind."

Would the slick, self-confident American correspondent have risked her own life, her own family and her own career, or even less important things—her membership in her country club, her position on the board of her children's school, her reputation in her neighborhood—for the sake of her principles? I wondered. How many people are willing to risk anything of real value to themselves for an ideal, a standard? Why should they, anyway?

I have struggled with this question for most of my life. For if I am the daughter of a man who would not abandon his principles for any price, I am also the daughter of a woman who had to suffer the consequences of her husband's acts of conscience, bravely pick up the pieces of her family's shattered life, stubbornly teach her children how to survive and strive and hold their heads up in a hostile environment, lick their wounds, put bread on their table and then start a new life from scratch in a foreign country, alone, with two children.

My father's commitment to such abstract notions as truth and justice robbed her of the career she loved and left her to struggle single-handedly with the mundane realities of feeding, clothing and educating my brother and me. Unlike my father, she had no faith in the nobility of human nature, the loyalty of friends, the kindness of strangers or the generosity of Providence. She perceived that life in communist Romania was a battle, and you had to be as tough as a soldier in mortal combat in order to survive. If you didn't keep your feet firmly planted on the ground, your head on your shoulders and not in the clouds, your eyes peeled in all directions—to the left, to the right, ahead of you and behind you, she used to say—your thoughts clear and your wits sharp, you would quickly fall into one of the myriad traps laid all around you, or step on a mine and blow yourself up. In this treacherous world, designed by villains far too powerful for anyone to confront openly, there was no room for heroes: only for victims or survivors, losers or winners.

This philosophy, forged out of her experiences as a Jew who lived through the Holocaust and as the wife of a political prisoner in a police state, is that of "the survivor," the only philosophy that, according to Terrence Des Pres, would have made sense under the circumstances. "Survivors do not choose their fate and would escape it if they could, but at the same time, by their irreducible presence, by refusing to go away and simply be a victim, they prove that no matter how bold and massive the machinery of power becomes, it does not prevail."

According to Des Pres, "the survivor" is the only type of hero possible in the world born out of the tragic events of the twentieth century. And indeed, as I grew up, it was my mother whom I saw as the captain of our family team, the champion of our cause, a larger-than-life heroine who triumphed over every obstacle in our way. Unlike my father, she did not choose her own fate, but had it forced upon her. Her passionate devotion had been to her children, her husband, the theater, not to the future of mankind. But even though she had not wanted to fight the system, once that system turned against us, she did everything in her power to protect us from its wrath. Like a lioness she fought for us, and after my father was released from prison, she fought for him, too, using all her energies and resources to help him reconstruct his life.

That she herself simply had to do the best she could with the hand that others dealt her has remained, despite her many later successes, her cheerful disposition and her innate optimism, a hidden source of a sadness I have always detected in my mother. The two great passions of her life—for the theater, for my father—had to be buried forever. I will never forget those painful days after our arrival in San Francisco—a city not known for its theaters—when it finally became clear to her, after one futile interview after another, that her diploma from the prestigious Romanian Academy of Dramatic Arts was now worthless and that an immigrant with two children had no chance of making a living as an actress.

But if she had been cast in the role of survivor, for her children she wanted more. She wanted us to be winners. My mother's life experiences, her encounters with Nazis and Communists, actors and officers, directors and politicians, seekers of fame and seekers of power, had left her with one conclusion: life was a game, and the winners were those who figured out how to play it. "Always know your priorities. Always focus on what is important to you," she advised us, trying to teach us how to make a success of our lives. "Remember, in life you either hold the reins and gallop to your destination or allow yourself to be harnessed to someone else's carriage."

Watching her struggle to adjust to our new life in America, find work, learn English, help us develop interests and pursue activities, shop, cook, clean, juggle, shuffle, balance and organize, I marveled at her inexhaustible energy and drive. From her first job selling furniture in a small store in the Mission District, a task she performed by telling herself that she was an actress playing the part of a saleswoman, she became a successful businesswoman and property owner and eventually even a minor celebrity in San Francisco. An article in 1987 in the *San Francisco Chronicle* tells about the former Romanian actress who, along with her second husband, acquired Bill Graham's old Fillmore West:

> Riding a bus to work one day, Regina noticed a "for sale sign" on the Fillmore building, figured it would be a good deal and decided to buy it, sight unseen. She had no idea that in the 60's it was home to bands like the Grateful Dead. Seven years later, Regina reads *Rolling Stone*, watches MTV and reigns over a plush night spot that she has remodeled to the tune of half a million dollars. She began bringing a bunch of hot new bands. Some of the concerts have been selling out much to the surprise of the community.

My mother could easily have written one of those how-to-succeed books that teach driven members of my generation time management, goal setting, focusing and prioritizing. My no-nonsense brother, a successful doctor, seems to have inherited her pragmatic approach to life. About me, on the other hand, her head-in-the-clouds daughter, she continues to worry. For if it was my mother who was my role model as I grew up, it was my father whom I seemed to take after. This was even more of a problem for me than for her, since I associated her qualities with survival and success, his with absence and failure. At every crossroad of my life, I found myself torn between their contradictory voices: one impelling me to think with my head, the other with my heart; one urging me to act in accord with my interests, the other to follow my ideals.

In graduate school I realized that my idealistic father and my pragmatic mother held diametrically opposed views of life that are as ancient as Greek philosophy. "Two irreconcilable ways of viewing the world go back to the disagreement between Plato and the Sophists, Virgil and Ovid, Dante and Petrarch," explained George Kennedy in *The Art of Persuasion in Greece*. "There have always been those, specially among philosophers and religious thinkers, who have emphasized goals and absolute standards and have talked about truth, while there have been many others who find the only certain reality in the process of life and the present moment." My favorite professor at UCLA, Richard Lanham, in his book *The Motives of Eloquence*, examined the conflict in Western literature between what he defined as the "rhetorical" and the "serious" views of life: "The Western self has from the beginning been composed of a shifting and perpetually uneasy combination of Homo Rhetoricus and Homo Sinceritus," Lanham wrote. "It is their business to contend for supremacy." The serious view of life is based on the notion that "every man possesses a central self, an irreducible identity." The rhetorical view of life, on the other hand, "conceives reality as fundamentally dramatic, man as fundamentally a role player...For homo rhetoricus the world is a stage, identity a function of situation, of needful role and needful audience. Rhetorical man is trained not to discover reality but to manipulate it."

Throughout my years of high school, college, graduate school, teaching and parenting, my nature has impelled me in my father's direction, but not without doubts and misgivings. Should I express my disagreement with my professor's literary theories and take the chance that he'll fail me on my orals? Should I oppose the new curriculum at the faculty meeting and risk antagonizing the head of my department? Should I encourage my husband to stick to his guns even if it costs him a partnership in his law firm? What do I advise my little girl, who has just transferred to a new school and finds herself confronted with her first moral dilemma: The girl who most welcomed her turns out to be the child nobody else likes. "Everyone makes fun of her, Mommy! I think she's nice, but I know if I keep eating lunch with her, they won't like me either. What should I do?" Hardly a life-and-death matter, and yet for her, a school year's worth of happiness may be at stake. What should I tell her? Do I advise her to follow "the right way" or "the smart way" at this and other complicated times in life when the two do not coincide?

I was one month short of thirty (having thus managed to meet my own deadline) when I had my first child. I had by then acquired enough life experience to convince me that much of what my mother had told me about the world was true. Politics were played everywhere. I had been exposed to the politics of graduate school (getting on the right side of the right professor to get the right job), the politics of academia (keeping rather than getting a job was the prize there), the politics of the large law firm (survival depended on one's ability to align oneself with the right team of senior partners). After Andy's birth, I became familiar with the politics of parent groups, the politics of school boards, the politics of the playground and the politics of schoolchildren.

Among the high achieving urban professional parents who are my peers, competition is high. Rushing with the other frenzied parents from play dates and parties that should help our children develop social skills, to sport leagues that should sharpen their competitive skills, to enrichment classes that should improve their academic skills, I realize that I am part of a generation that is obsessed with success. All of us have heard the "experts": The road to happiness is paved by self-esteem, and the road to self-esteem is paved by success. At meetings, conferences, parties, the same questions seem to be on everyone's minds: "Is my child reading soon enough?" "Adding fast enough?" "Scoring high enough?" "Performing well enough?" "Will my child be one of the winners of the race?"

How should I raise my children? Should I teach them that we are but actors on the stage of life, the quality of our performance the measure of our worth? Had my father conceived of himself as an actor in a drama, playing for applause, he would not have gone to prison, and I would not have grown up fatherless. Had my mother shared his idealism, I might still be in Romania, the product of an orphanage. Perhaps we only get one game to play. Why shouldn't we play to win? If here is all there is, why not collect our prizes here?

◆ ◆ ◆

Players play to win. They study the rules. They estimate their chances. They size up their opponents. They evaluate their strengths and their weaknesses. They plan out their strategy. They calculate their moves. When the odds are not in their favor, they bluff. They manipulate appearances to create the illusion of strength. They are clever rather than courageous, witty rather than wise, prudent rather than passionate, doubtful rather than hopeful, cynical rather than optimistic, diplomats with golden tongues rather than warriors with golden swords. They are master realists, master image makers, master pretenders.

The rhetorical rather than the sincere view of life has prevailed in the contemporary world, where players rather than heroes seem to triumph. Our media worships the celebrity, the winner of public attention through acts of notoriety rather than of nobility. It is not surprising that popular performers are the stars of our culture, for as Richard Lanham points out, rhetorical man is above all, an actor.

> His reality is public, dramatic. The lowest common denominator of his life is a social situation. He thinks first of winning, of mastering the rules the current game enforces. He assumes a natural agility in changing orientations. He hits the street already street wise. He dwells not in a single value structure but in several. He is committed to no single construction of the world, much rather to prevailing in the game at hand.

The player has taken the lead away from the hero in Hollywood films. Unlike his spiritual father, James Bond, the player undertakes missions not on "her majesty's secret service," but on his own. He represents himself. He serves his own cause. He promotes his own interests. He knows that anyone who serves anyone else is a fool.

The player, unlike the hero, keeps his prize and spends it on himself. Although he gives us nothing, we admire his skill, his nerve, his ability to beat the odds. Watching him, we hope that maybe we too will sometime get lucky, or by studying his moves, start learning how to win.

"Who is your hero and why do you admire him?" is the topic of the essay my son must write for his application to private secondary school. This is the first time in his eleven years that Andy has been asked to answer such a question. For me, this would have been a cinch at his age, stuffed as I was from early on with the glorious deeds of the "heroes and martyrs of our great socialist revolution." An easy question it would have been for my husband as well, for at age eleven, Ron could have just leafed through his fifth grade American history book to find an explorer or a conqueror or a general or a president worthy of admiration. But for the wised up, sophisticated kids of the electronic age, who have already learned that cowboys and conquistadors were often ruthless killers, that presidents may well be hypocritical, self-serving politicians, that admired athletes are sometimes criminals and favorite stars, drug addicts—a generation of kids raised on the "hard facts of life"—such a question is a tough one indeed.

At the open house for this much-sought-after private school that promises in its brochure to teach rigorous academics alongside such equally important skills as goal setting, organizing, prioritizing, socializing, time management, team playing and networking, I sat among the worried parents brought there by fear of drugs, gangs and violence at our local high schools, and listened to the headmaster's speech connecting problems of today's youth with the absence of heroes, meaning and values in their lives. He suggested that the two California girls who not long before had shot themselves, leaving behind treasure-hunt maps to guide their classmates to their bodies, may have sacrificed their lives for the sake of notoriety, perhaps mistaking it for a kind of immortality. Growing up without models of heroic action, in a society where the merely sensational increasingly wins the spotlight, many adolescents seek to distinguish themselves through desperate acts.

I couldn't have agreed with him more. But now his speech, the essay topic he designed and the question my son asked me are forcing me, the daughter of the man who followed his conscience and the woman who suffered the consequences, to resolve my lifelong conflict. *What do I think about heroes?* For my children's sake, I must finally make up my mind.

I started seeing my father as a hero only after I encountered him in the underworld of his prison chronicle. For weeks after I received it, I was afraid to read the manuscript, afraid to fall into what I suspected would be a black hole filled with monsters who would later attack me in my sleep. After all, the glimpses of what he must have suffered that I caught in the fragments I had read during our trip to San Diego had brought the "abandoned Neclo" nightmare back.

"Now you know why I won't read Holocaust memoirs," my friend Tova, to whom I confessed my misery, exclaimed. Tova, like many of my friends, is a child of survivors, and we share many common traits: old world European parents, close but conflicted family relationships, guilt over our parents' suffering, a sense that we have a mission to make our lives matter, that we must compensate for their losses through our success. One thing I do not share with Tova is my interest in Holocaust memoirs which she, like every one of my second-generation friends, refuses to read. Now, I do finally understand why. It is hard enough to confront the terrifying events that are part of our collective history; it is so much harder to face those which have affected us personally, shaped our childhoods, become part of the fabric of our memories.

My father's prison memoir, I suddenly realized, belongs to the literature of survival. Having made this connection between his manuscript, which I didn't want to read, and the memoirs of Holocaust survivors, which I couldn't stop reading, I reminded myself of my arguments in favor of this genre: Holocaust memoirs expose us not just to the worst horror in the history of humanity, but also to the men and women who somehow lived through it and continued to live after it. Such books are not depressing but uplifting, because ultimately they teach us about—and here I rely on those book-jacket phrases—the triumph of the human spirit, man's capacity to endure and prevail…I reminded myself that my father, in spite of all he suffered is neither a bitter man nor an angry man—I know many people who have been through much less and are both—but on the contrary, considers himself a lucky man. And so talking to myself, I picked up the manuscript and allowed myself to follow him on his journey, which turned out to be not a descent into darkness but an ascent into light.

◆ ◆ ◆

Heroes are not players. Heroes see the game and want to know, Why? They know they have a choice: to play, or not to play. If the game is twisted, the outcome, mad, they have the courage to say, "I will not do this." Their choice proves everyone that everyone has choices. Anyone can choose to stop or change the rules or make up a different game. For heroes see beyond the game. And what they see has meaning. Without their vision and courage, everyone's board would be empty, every move, pointless, every game, worthless.

My father's memoirs began at the point when the game ended. From early adolescence when, following his father's strategy for success, he entered the military academy, and until the moment when he refused to retract his objections to the regime, my father tried his best to stay in the game. He was a good boy. He obeyed his father and did what was expected of him. He was poor and had to make his own way in the world. His choices were limited by his circumstances. He wanted to be a writer. He had to become an officer. He dreamed that someday he would work out a compromise. During the war, an event occurred that temporarily pulled him out of the game. A man's life was in danger. He was in a position to save it. He risked his own life and did.

As a result, he became involved with a new team of players. After the war, this team won, and he was rewarded for having played on their side. He was smart and charming and ambitious, and he won many prizes that helped him forget that he was still following a course set by others, and that it was still not the course he ever really wanted to take. Soon, however, the game began to sicken him. What happened to him is what happens to people all over the world. Through a combination of circumstances, he found himself performing tasks he hated, smiling at people he despised, saying things he didn't believe, pretending not to see what he saw. And he had a wife and children and a position and a lifestyle and obligations to them all. For a while he followed the routine, trying to make the best of things, even though he felt trapped and stuck in a rut. So a producer, writer or director in Hollywood continues to churn out the films he despises because, according to the rules of his game, "hard" movies win, and "soft" ones don't. So an adolescent may continue to exclude the kid his "clique" and its "star" have designated "the nerd," fearful that to be seen sharing lunch or even a conversation with him will cost him his place in the group. So a mother in West Los Angeles might continue to pressure her stressed-out child to follow the "game plan" for success observed by the offspring of all her peers, because to do otherwise would appear to be an admission of family failure. So most of us stay in the rut, follow the prescribed course, keep up the routine, shrug our shoulders, look at each other and sigh, "This is so terrible, so absurd, so unfair! Unfortunately, this is how it is—what else can we do?"

My father chose to interrupt his routine and break out of his rut. The game he was playing was a bad game. It was bad for him. It was bad for everyone. He refused to play it anymore. In a few short sentences, he explains how he made the decision that changed our lives:

> I had every reason to be happy with my life; a lovely wife, two beautiful children, a successful career. But every day I drove in my limousine past long lines of desperate, starving, terrified people, endlessly waiting at stores whose shelves were bare. My wife begged me to keep my mouth shut and think about my own family. Did I want my children to grow up orphans? So many were arrested, so many disappeared. Why flirt with self-destruction? What could I possibly hope to accomplish, anyway. I could have chosen to look away, to bury my nose in the very important papers on my desk. But how could I?

Of course he could very easily have continued to do what most people in his position usually do: bury their noses in their papers and look away. They say, "I had no choice," which in reality means, "I didn't want to pay the price," because that price consists of a loss of some kind—a loss of employment, status, prestige, social approval, material possessions, and in repressive societies, of life.

Jonah Goldhagen, in his controversial book *Hitler's Willing Executioners*, tries to demonstrate that the Holocaust was implemented in Germany with the help of massive numbers of ordinary citizens who in the tens of thousands of concentration camps enthusiastically inflicted suffering on millions of victims. This notion is hard to swallow for Clive James, a critic in the *New Yorker*. He responds by reminding us of the kind of world the Nazis created. This was a world in which those who helped or protected the Jews were the losers and those who tortured and murdered them, the winners. "The Nazis honored anyone who attacked them, punished anyone who helped them, and educated a generation to believe that its long-harbored family of prejudices had the status of a sacred mission." In this world, too, the players, and not the ideologue, triumphed. Opportunists like Goering, "who would have forgotten all about the Jews if he could have done a deal to save his skin," and Himmler, who "did try to do a deal on that very basis," were no more dedicated to national socialism than Dej and Ceausescu were to communism. Each man served the cause the player always serves: his own. Refuting Goldhagen's argument that most Germans participated in the Final Solution out of their sadistic hatred for Jews, Clive argues that German behavior was natural given the system of rewards and punishments their leaders designed. To Goldhagen's question—why didn't the population rebel?—he replies: "The answer is obvious. Because you had to be a hero to do so."

James doesn't expect such heroism from most human beings. Just look what happened, he shows us, to a Catholic priest who dared to stand up for the Jews. "When he protested the deportations, he was put on a train himself—to Dachau. Those men were made examples of to discourage others. They were made to pay for their crime." How many people can be expected to brave such consequences? The implication here is that their severity made such choices impossible for ordinary mortals.

In my father's memoir, we encounter several such "ordinary mortals": the doctor who refused to inform on his cousin; the pianist who, unlike his friends, refused to sign a false confession of his guilt; the priest who refused to turn against his Hungarian friend, and my father's own father who, several decades earlier, jumped into the fire to stop an explosion that would have destroyed his city. The crueler the consequences of such choices, the harder they are to make and the stronger the temptation of those who don't make them to argue that no such choices existed. But that one man or one woman who is willing to make the choice and suffer the consequences proves that this answer is a lie. His or her actions demonstrate that always there is a choice and a human being capable of making it.

Not until I read his memoirs did I realize that my father's arrest, the years he spent in prison, his suffering and his separation from us were the outcome of a conscious and deliberate choice. Regardless of the role his brother played in the intrigues that led to his "apprehension" for his "crimes"—and although my father concedes that Gica may have been boastful, perhaps envious, definitely indiscreet, he refuses to believe that his brother willingly betrayed him—Ion Eremia's decision to speak up against his government had been his own. The end result of such a decision was inevitable. Sooner or later, the consequences would have been the same.

My father was not a helpless innocent who fell into a trap laid by powerful villains—as my mother, in her pain, perceived him—but a brave, determined man who decided to sever the knots that entangled him in the villains' net. No one and nothing could deprive my father of the freedom to make this decision, a freedom which Viktor Frankl, in *Man's Search for Meaning*, following a long line of humanist thinkers within the Judeo Christian tradition, considers to be the defining attribute of our humanity. Frankl, an Auschwitz survivor, believes that even the inmates of extermination camps had choices:

> There were always choices to be made. Every day, every hour, offered the opportunity to make a decision, a decision which determined whether you would or would not submit to those powers which threatened to rob you of your very self, your inner freedom; which determined whether or not you would become the plaything of circumstance, renouncing freedom and dignity to become molded into the form of the typical inmate.

Viktor Frankl's position has been challenged by Terrence Des Pres in *The Survivor* and even more vehemently and directly by Lawrence Langer in his 1995 book, *Admitting the Holocaust*. For Des Pres, the only choice for a Jew in a concentration camp, a prisoner in the Gulag or any person caught in a place where "the outcome of power is hostility to life itself" is to exert one's will, resist the murderers and live. In such a situation, to die is to lose, to live is to win. According to Des Pres, all survivors are winners. For Langer, even this much choice is an exaggeration of an even bleaker reality. According to Langer, Jews caught in the Holocaust had no alternatives whatsoever, only "choiceless choices," all pointing toward the same destination: death. As far as he is concerned, not only were there no heroes, there were also no survivors, only victims—the dead corpses and the living corpses, for Holocaust survivors may look alive but are in reality, "the walking dead." "Choice had little to do with their fate, which took them beyond the frontiers of moral endeavor," Langer tells us.

A world without choices would be a world without heroes, a world without men like the German Catholic priest or the priest in my father's neighboring cell, a world where decisions like the one my father made when he refused to confess his guilt after six years of torture, the promise of liberty and the threat of death, would be inconceivable. But such decisions can be made and were made even in concentration camps. Even in Auschwitz there were heroes.

◆ ◆ ◆

The hero is a man or a woman who behaves as decently in an extraordinary situation as in an ordinary one. His or her standard of behavior toward other human beings is set from within and not from without. The hero's soul recoils at cruelty and injustice, regardless of the circumstances or the consequences.

When one reads the personal stories of Holocaust survivors, one is struck by the range of choices and behaviors that were exhibited in the unique realm of the concentration camps. As in any world inhabited by human beings, as in the prison worlds described by my father, different prisoners followed different courses of action. Here too, a game developed, with an object, a strategy, a goal and a prize. Here too, people had to decide whether to play the game or quit, whether to follow the rules, break them, or create a new set:

> Is it possible to put a price on life? Can a definite price be set on life, or is it priceless? The way you answered these questions determined the way you behaved toward other people. Those who asserted, 'I want to live at any price,' would put even their own parents into the car that was going to the crematorium. On the other hand, parents who wanted to live at any price put their small children into valises and cast the valises aside. Those who asserted, 'My life is priceless,' dragged out prisoners who were hiding during the selection so they themselves would escape danger. The real challenge was to overcome the animal instinct of survival at all cost, as reflected by the cynical proverb, 'better a living dog than a dead lion,' and to avoid being sucked into the pervasive bestiality.

This vision of life at Auschwitz presented by Sara Pritzic, one of its survivors, is not the rhetorical one. The player's logic—this life is all I have, so let me play to win—would have considered any strategy that led to success, meaning survival, a winning strategy. But in this passage, this eyewitness informs us that such a strategy would also have had its consequences, and when used to its limits, the consequences could be even harsher than those of not playing the game or quitting altogether. Following this line of thinking, we realize that the Germans who played by the rules of Hitler's game, or the Romanian party officials who played by the rules of Ceausescu's game, also paid a price, and that price could be considered even higher than the one paid by people like my father or the German priest or the members of the Saunterkomando who one day blew themselves up along with one of the crematoriums at Auschwitz.

If life isn't priceless, what is? Pritzic never gives it a name, but I think most of us know what she means. The prophets, poets, artists, philosophers and religious thinkers of all ages have struggled perennially to find the right words or notes or shapes or images by which to express it: our soul, our spirit, our heart, our dignity, our humanity, our divinity, our immortality.

There is a line, Pritzic suggests, that even in the worst of all possible worlds cannot be crossed without abandoning that essential thing that defines human beings as human. To cross the line means to surrender to "the animal instinct," to allow oneself to be "sucked into the pervasive bestiality," to trade "the life of a man" for "the life of a dog." The hardest challenge for individuals caught in such worlds is to decide where exactly to draw that line, in the absence of support from law and religion, which in civilized societies create and sustain it. And this is why Viktor Frankl observed that the world of the concentration camp "tore open the human soul and exposed its depths," leading him to conclude that there, as everywhere, there were only two races of men, "the race of decent man and the race of the indecent man."

Which category one fell in would have depended on where exactly one drew one's own line between decent and indecent behavior. There were those who drew no line at all, abandoned themselves to the animal instinct, and surrendered all decency and humanity. There were those who preserved a line but maintained some flexibility about where to draw it, and drew and redrew it depending on their circumstances. They were more decent to some than to others and allowed themselves more latitude in some situations than in others. According to Primo Levi, most survivors, himself included, drew their line in a place that put them in a kind of "moral gray zone." Then there were individuals, and this was a very small minority, who gave themselves no flexibility or latitude at all. My father was this type of an individual.

The privileged position in which he found himself as a member of the upper echelons of the government allowed him even less flexibility about his line than an ordinary citizen, since his moral responsibility for the well-being of the general population was so much greater. To watch from his limousine as his people sank farther and farther into slavery was to act like a captain who jumps off a sinking ship into a comfortable lifeboat, from which he calmly sees everyone else drown.

The captain might have a wife and children for the sake of whom he has chosen to save himself. If he were a truly decent man, however, he would not consider their needs greater than the needs of the passengers and crew in his charge.

My mother did not have the same sense of responsibility to the Romanian people that my father did. For her, to follow my father and abandon her children would have meant to step over the line, step over her heart, crush her own soul. For my mother, it wasn't her own life, but the lives of her children that were priceless. But even there, she had to draw a line. For had she been willing to abandon herself entirely to the maternal instinct and do anything and everything to guarantee her children's survival, she would have only been one moral notch above those who ruthlessly abandoned themselves to the survival instinct.

Yet my mother, too, being a decent human being, drew a line that she could not cross even for our sakes. While the injustice of her children's privileged position did not violate her sense of decency, signing a statement that denounced her husband as a traitor did. Had she agreed to denounce my father, not only would her children have been spared from persecution, but my mother would not have been robbed of her acting career, which, next to her family, meant more to her than anything else in life. However, neither her passion for the theater nor her love for her children could have led my mother to destroy her own soul.

Mothers as loving and devoted as my mother hid the children of other mothers during the Holocaust, risking the lives of their own children because they could not bring themselves to turn away the children of others to be killed. Those women treated the children of others in the way they would have wanted their own children treated in similar circumstances. They set a higher standard than those who put their own children first. Had everyone followed that standard, the Holocaust would not have happened. The cook Viktor Frankl describes, by practicing the "golden rule" at Auschwitz, reminds everyone about the ideal meaning of human decency:

> He stood behind one of the huge pots and ladled soup into the bowls which were held out to him by the prisoners, who hurriedly filed past. He was the only cook who did not look at the men whose bowls he was filling; the only cook who dealt out the soup equally, regardless of recipient and who did not make favorites of his personal friends or countrymen, picking out the potatoes for them, while the others got watery soup skimmed from the top.

This man would not take advantage of his position as cook to cheat some in order to favor others. He would not have done it if he had been serving soup to his customers in a restaurant. He would not do it when he was serving soup to prisoners in a death camp. In fact, just like my father, he felt a special obligation by virtue of his privileged position to do the "decent thing." Men like my father or the cook draw sharp, rigid, inflexible lines for themselves and do not stretch them or bend them or cross them. Regardless of the situation, such men cannot act indecent without feeling inhuman.

◆ ◆ ◆

The heroic impulse is triggered by empathy and compassion. Heroes can look at others and recognize themselves. Heroes can feel the pain of others as their own pain. Heroes can do for others what they would do for themselves. Heroes have the courage to turn their compassion into acts of kindness. Heroes value human life more than human objects, and human beings more than human theories. Heroes are humanists. Heroes are the lovers of mankind.

Before I read my father's book, I thought of him as a man who sacrificed his life and his family for the sake of his ideals. And it is this notion of heroes as individuals who consider abstract ideas to be more important than live men and women that has led contemporary thinkers like Terrence Des Pres to view them as "symbols of nihilism" rather than of humanism. For after all, Hitler and Stalin were also idealists. According to Jonah Goldhagen, Hitler remained an idealist to the end, even when his theories went against his own self-interest. Idealists like Stalin or Hitler—or Jim Jones or the Unabomber for that matter—cannot accept human beings as they are and cruelly mistreat them in order to "improve" them. Like any abusive lover or parent or like the scientist in Hawthorne's short story, "The Birthmark," who cuts out his wife's birthmark in order to make her perfect and kills her in the process, such individuals end up destroying life in order to cure it of its imperfections. And as Dostoevsky demonstrated in his "Legend of the Grand Inquisitor," when he exposed the contempt for humanity that lay beneath the Grand Inquisitor's utopian schemes, such men are driven not by their love but by their hatred of their fellow creatures and their desire to enslave them in order to control them. "Men are feeble, vicious, insignificant and rebels...weak, eternally vicious and eternally ungrateful," argues Dostoevsky's Antichrist who, like the communist dictators he foreshadows, tries to tempt men to give up their heavenly freedom with his promise of earthly bread.

My father's memoirs led me to realize that his decision to speak up against his government was inspired by the quality in him I most treasured, the quality that created that unbreakable bond between us during the first five years of my life: his loving kindness. My father was a man who could not see someone in pain without trying to do something to alleviate the suffering. He could no more stand by in silence and watch men suffer when he was a powerful government official than later, as a powerless prison inmate, he could refrain from expressing his indignation at "Gorilla's" attempt to crush the pianist's hands, or from offering to take the poor, sick Luca's turn at emptying out the latrine.

"Human kindness can be found in all groups," writes Viktor Frankl. "I remember how one day a guard secretly gave me a piece of bread which I knew he must have saved from his breakfast ration. It was far more than the small piece of bread which moved me to tears at that time. It was the human something which this man also gave me. The word and look which accompanied the gift." During extraordinary situations, the milk of human kindness becomes the magic potion that turns ordinary individuals into heroes. Gifts of kindness had an infinitely greater value, Holocaust survivors tell us, than their mere physical worth. In a place where few ate and most starved, few lived and most died, where a plate of soup or a slice of bread could make the difference between life and death, every act of selfless generosity marked a defeat for the animal instinct of survival and a victory for man's soul. "Sometimes I think that the patients are a kind of doctor who are healing my soul," writes a Jewish doctor to her son before her ghetto is exterminated. "Schukin, a patient of mine, said he'd come once a week to the fence and give me bread. Do you know Vityenka, after he came, I began to feel once more that I was a human being—it wasn't only the yard dog that still treated me as though I were." It is that same milk of human kindness which Lady Macbeth had to dry up in herself in order to kill that flows to dissolve the barriers between human beings created by the survival instinct and fortified by its exploiters.

The man who, last fourth of July, got out of his car, abandoning the jungle of the L.A. freeway along with its "every car for itself" law, and sacrificed his entire afternoon and evening as well as that of his tired wife and hungry children, in order to help a family he had never met—"I'm a mechanic," he explained, "how could I just drive by and leave you in the lurch?"—had a rich supply of that milk. I couldn't help wondering if this isn't the kind of man who, in a situation of extremity, would have the courage to let the kindness flow. Primo Levi's life was saved by a man named Lorenzo, who wasn't very different, perhaps, from the man who stopped to help my family on the freeway.

> We belonged to two different castes of Nazi universe, and therefore when we spoke to each other we were committing a crime, but we spoke anyway. I don't think I ever asked him for help. Two or three days after our meeting he brought me an alpine troop mess tin. He brought it for me every day for six months. I shared the soup with Alberto. In the violent and degraded environment of Auschwitz, a man helping other men out of pure altruism was incomprehensible, alien, like a savior who comes from heaven. One day he handed

> me the tin and said the soup was a bit dirty. He did not explain.... A year later, as an apology, he explained that his camp had been hit by an air raid, a bomb had fallen close to him and exploded in the soft ground. It had buried the mess tin and burst one of his eardrums, but he had the soup to deliver and had come to work anyway.

A man runs across a field in the middle of an air raid, carrying a tin of soup that he is saving for another. A bomb explodes next to him, but he ignores it, focused on preserving his soup and getting it to his destination. Levi has just painted for us the perfect image of the hero. Like the survivor, this man struggles to win a life, but the life he strives to win is not his own life. Like a star football player, he runs across a field, allowing nothing to stop him from carrying his prize to the finish line. But unlike the football player, he has the freedom to break away from the position he has been assigned, change the game, switch teams and carry the ball for the other side. Like the player in recent Hollywood films, he breaks rules and defies the rule makers. He too is focused, driven, intent on reaching his destination with his treasure. But his courage, his determination, the compulsion to succeed that makes him ignore the air raid, the explosion and the risk to his life is set not by something outside himself, not by the prize, not by the applause. Lorenzo never even told Primo Levi of the danger he went through, nor that Levi wasn't the only man whose life he saved. "We are in the world to do good, not to boast about it," he explained.

Lorenzo's act was impulsive, irrational, did not evolve from any plan or strategy, and followed a structure and rhythm set by himself alone. Yet, although he refused to accept any gifts of gratitude in return—not money, not even a "thank you"—his act had its rewards. That time during the war, when he lived to save lives, Lorenzo later told Primo Levi, he was happier than he had ever been. A restless, rootless man who had no home, no family, no goals before, he found purpose and value and self-worth through his act. After the war, he went back to his rootless ways, found no new purpose, structure, nor anyone to love or reason to live and drank himself to death. His heroism was but a moment in time, recorded and preserved and immortalized in Primo Levi's book.

◆ ◆ ◆

Heroism is poetry enacted. Heroes actualize the beauty of the human soul. The heroic act is an instant expression of human goodness, a celebration of human love, a realization of the human yearning for unity, harmony, perfection. The heroic act is a hymn to the grandeur of the human spirit.

Alone in his dark cell, having lost all the structure, purpose and goals of his life, the people he loved, the cause he wanted to serve, my father, like Lorenzo, loses the inner satisfaction he gained when he defied the authorities, stood up for his beliefs, wrote his book and acted like a hero. He looks back at the year when he wrote *Gulliver* as the happiest time of his life. For during that year, he had freed himself of both the rewards and obligations that kept him a slave to the material privileges of his position. But now he is once again at the mercy of his senses, this time because of deprivation rather than satisfaction. He is a slave to hunger, cold, immobility, solitude and the cat-and-mouse game he must play with the guard to obtain the slightest relief from his misery. His present seems unbearable, his future nonexistent. He questions his choices, the value of his gesture, and asks himself whether the price wasn't too high. Was "he" worth it, he asks himself, meaning both he and she, that abstract, general being that represents all the human beings he dreamed made up his team. Was he a fool, he wonders, when he tried to be a champion of mankind?

Then, as he despairs, with a few taps on the wall, the astronomer imprisoned in the cell on his left throws him the rope with which he will save himself. He takes the astronomer's advice, sets up a daily routine and follows it religiously—those external structures which enabled him to "earn his daily bread," but which kept him from developing his creative self, will now enable him to fulfill his youthful dream and become the writer he has always wanted to be. Unlike the writer in the outside world who must always worry about the value of his work which depends on external recognition, my father writes with the certainty that his work has an intrinsic value of his own. He must write to live and live to write. And so prison becomes a kind of paradise, for here he has everything he needs: solitude to dream, time to shape, space to fill and a reason to fill it. In the darkness of his cell, Ion Eremia experiences the brightest moments of his life.

How can human beings feel happiness in a world of horror and pain? How can one feel one's spirit soar even as one's body shrinks? How can we speak about "the triumph of the human spirit" or "man's capacity to endure and prevail" at the same time that we speak about concentration camps or frozen gulags or secret dungeons?

Virginia Woolf, who was confined not to a prison cell or a concentration camp but to the sick room, has explored the reasons for this paradox in her essay, "On Being Ill."

> There is a virgin forest in each; a snowfield where even the print of birds' feet is unknown. Here we go alone...In health the genial pretense must be kept up and the effort renewed—to communicate, to civilize, to cultivate the desert, or work together by day and by night to sport. In illness this make believe ceases. Directly the bed is called for, or sunk deep among pillows in one chair, we raise our feet even an inch above the ground on another, we cease to be soldiers in the army of the upright. We become deserters. They march to battle. We float with the sticks on the stream; helter skelter with the dead leaves on the lawn, irresponsible and disinterested and able, perhaps for the first time for years, to look round, to look up, to look, for example at the sky."

Viktor Frankl describes this same phenomenon, in less poetic terms, as "the intensification of the inner life," which offers sensitive people a "retreat from their terrible surroundings to a life of inner riches and spiritual freedom."

If one acknowledges the possibility of such an occurrence, one must also acknowledge the spiritual nature of human beings. Those who, like Lawrence Langer, ridicule such ideas as "natural innocence, innate dignity, the inviolable spirit" as the "stable relics of faded eras" also deny that such experiences are possible. Langer sees them as lies and fabrications clothed in ill-fitting terms borrowed from writers long dead and worlds long gone. They spring out of the cowardly need of self-deceiving individuals to "restore pattern to an apparent chaos that flatters no one" by relying on the "cultural correspondences" that have falsely "sustained the mental comfort of Western man."

And indeed, in the same way that Robinson Crusoe brought with him the practical and scientific knowledge that enabled him to create a civilized life for himself on his island, so my father brought to his dark cell a rich humanistic culture that has for centuries attempted to elevate man by feeding his soul's yearning for beauty, harmony, symmetry and meaning, with music, poetry, philosophy and religion. Only by resurrecting the civilization within himself was my father able to impose shape and form on the formless, shapeless hours, days, nights, weeks, months, years, that stretched out indefinitely before him. His memoirs are just another link in the cultural chain that has affirmed the existence of a "higher self" in human beings and has inspired them to manifest it again and again throughout the centuries. Without this chain, my father may not have survived. I doubt that any of us would.

The heightened moments of awareness of life's essential beauty and goodness which appear throughout my father's memoirs, as they do in the memoirs of many Holocaust survivors, and which I, too, remember experiencing even during the hardest times of my childhood, have been poetically defined by Virginia

Woolf as the "little daily miracles, illuminations, matches struck unexpectedly in the dark" that enable human beings to go to bed every night and want to wake up again the next morning. Woolf's lifelong struggle with painful losses and clinical depression made the reality of such moments crucial to her existence. This is how she accounts for them:

> I feel that I have had a blow, but it is not...simply a blow from an enemy hidden behind the cotton wool of daily life; it is or will become a revelation of some order; it is a token of some real thing behind appearances...From this I reach what I might call a philosophy; at any rate it is a constant idea of mine; that behind the cotton wool is hidden a pattern, that we—I mean human beings—are connected with this; that the whole world is a work of art, that we are parts of the work of art.

This intense awareness of a connection between the self and others and the self and the outside world grants meaning and value to the human experience. Religion ascribes a divine source to the harmonious pattern and urges human beings to celebrate it by stressing such concepts as "universal brotherhood" or "the golden rule." What prophets celebrate through religion, poets celebrate through art, and heroes celebrate through action. Shelley's famous romantic definition of the poetic also applies to the heroic. Poetry, according to Shelley,

> lifts the veil from the hidden beauty of the world, and makes familiar objects be as if they were not familiar...The great secret of morals is love; or a going out of our own nature and an identification of ourselves with the beautiful which exists in thought, action, or person, not our own. A man, to be greatly good, must imagine intensely and comprehensively; he must put himself in the place of another and of many others; the pains and pleasures of his species must become his own.

The priest who turns his "special privilege" into a special prayer coughed in Morse code is a poet whose moving song draws the isolated prisoners into a perfect moment of unity and love. Although the prisoner in cell four collapsed and died, his heroism inspired the prisoner in cell five to struggle to record and preserve it in the hope of some day conveying its hopeful message to the world.

My father entered prison a hero who was willing to experience the "pain of his species as his own pain." He emerged from prison a poet who is willing to experience his personal triumph as "the triumph of the human species." His journey through the underworld led him to an even greater appreciation of his own humanness, which he sees as a reflection of everyone's humanness. The barefoot, half-naked ex-con who barely has enough energy to drag himself from the prison to the train station is not a beggar, but a prince. His soul is filled not with bitterness for his wrongful suffering but with gratitude for his spiritual growth. The creature who may appear as a "live rag, a dismembered cockroach, a crushed insect," also has the greatness of spirit to turn "torture into ecstasy, the desert into a rich internal world, hell into heaven." Ion Eremia returns to his family convinced that his losses were worth his gains. Human beings deserve every sacrifice that affirms their humanity. They who are capable of heroism are also worthy of their heroes.

How can anyone maintain hope and courage in a place as bereft of humanity, as cruel, ruthless and horrific as that engraved on Auden's "Shield of Achilles"?

> That girls are raped, that two boys knife a third
> Were axioms to him who never heard
> Of any world where promises are kept
> Or one could weep because another wept

The noble acts of heroes are the "miracles, illuminations, matches struck unexpectedly in the dark" that enable us to continue to believe, even after we have witnessed the gas chambers, the secret dungeons and the mass graves, in the possibility of a world "where promises are kept" and "one could weep because another wept."

I hope my children will grow up in a world that values heroes. For when we abandon them, we are abandoning the best within ourselves.

Why American Kids Fantasize Suicide

Tonight we didn't rush to grab a front row seat in the school auditorium, hoping to snap a better picture of our own young stars. It wasn't our kids we were expecting, nervously, to appear on stage, but a team of experts. Of course, this wasn't the first time we had ordered pizza for dinner, yelled at our spouses for being late, negotiated with the sitters about the TV and the kids about the homework, so we could spend an evening sharpening our parenting skills. Still, none of the lessons on how to handle bottle weaning and separation anxiety, toilet training and sibling rivalry, the homework battle and the battle for independence, had prepared us for tonight. Tonight we would be taught how to handle the death of an eleven-year-old boy who, after receiving an E-mail rejection from his summer camp girlfriend, had hanged himself.

"He was very creative," my daughter said. The morning his death was announced, she had called home, crying. Students, teachers, staff—everyone was heartbroken. She and the boy had never been friends, but at our small, private school the kids had grown up together. The English teacher, especially, was having a hard time. "He was an incredible writer," my daughter explained. "He made up fantastic stories about spaceships and aliens and life on other planets." Later, I noticed that whenever her friends talked about the boy, it was his imagination that they seemed to blame for his act. No, he hadn't been very sad or very lonely. Just very creative.

"Maybe he thought he'd be traveling on a cool spaceship to another solar system. I drew a picture of it for the therapists," I heard one of my daughter's friends say as we drove home from school.

"Or maybe he imagined he'd have an out-of-body experience and then jump out of it at the last minute," my daughter suggested.

When he put the noose around his neck, they seemed to think, he intended to embark on a new and exciting adventure, which may have turned out differently from the way he had imagined it.

That night, unable to sleep, I got out the file of clippings I had begun to make more than a year before, when my daughter's eighteen-year-old babysitter had confided that once, during a troubled period in her early teens, she had put a gun to her head and pulled the trigger. The gun belonged to a boyfriend's father. She thought it was loaded. Luckily it didn't fire.

The smart, talented daughter of close friends, she shattered my notion that self-destructive behavior only takes place in dysfunctional families. After our conversation, I began noticing the articles in my morning paper about the suicides of young Americans and had cut some of them out.

There was the story about the ten-year-old who, after his teacher gave him a note for his parents about his swearing, yanked a gun out of his backpack, begged two friends to shoot him, then put the muzzle to his temple and fired. "Children are turning to suicide more and more as a way to find an answer," I read in the article, which reported that the national suicide rate among ten to fourteen-year-olds had increased one hundred twenty percent since 1980 (*Los Angeles Times*, 3/9/97).

There was the story about the seventeen-year-old boy who hanged himself from the porch of his family's house, the sixth young man from the South Boston area to kill himself in 1997. There was the story about the horse-loving, soccer-playing young woman and her song writer boyfriend who had carried out a suicide pact (*Los Angeles Times*, 3/19/96). The young man had been doing a project on suicide for his creative writing class. He was "death-happy," one of his friends explained. He was not sad, but viewed death as fun, "more like, 'I can't wait to die.'" The young woman's note to her mother said that she wanted "to be free" and "to fly."

Was it possible, I wondered, that imaginative, adventurous kids today fantasize killing themselves the way in earlier times they fantasized joining the circus or running off to sea?

That an act of self-destruction could be conceived as an act of the imagination shocked me. I had always associated the imagination with survival. The daughter of a Romanian general who was imprisoned for writing an anti-communist book, my imagination had enabled me to soar above the dark, gloomy places of my childhood. It had soothed me from sadness and healed me from hurt. It was my shelter from cruelty, my refuge from rejection. I still remember the children who chased me away from their snowman, pelting me with snowballs, yelling, "convict's daughter, go away!" And I remember how I comforted myself with thoughts of Thumbelina, the heroine of my favorite fairy tale. I shut my eyes and imagined that I was flying on the back of a swallow high up in the air, over the mountains of eternal snow to the warm countries, where the flower fairies greeted me with a set of wings.

Why didn't the dead boy use his imagination to fly away from hurt?

Our meeting began with the director of our school reading a heart-wrenching letter from the boy's parents. They asked us to disregard media accounts that labeled their son a suicide when, in reality, his death had been a tragic accident, a "prank gone bad." The news reports, they told us, made their agony even more unbearable. Their son could not have wanted to die. Their son loved life. Their son was loved. They hoped we would remember him for his joyful smile.

As she read, the director, a mother of two teenagers, broke into tears. It was hard for any of us not to cry. These parents had stood among us at drop-off and pick-up, school assemblies and holiday festivals, science fairs and enrichment classes, family picnics and birthday parties. This boy had regularly played, eaten and slept over at several of our homes. Last Saturday night he had danced at cotillion with a number of our girls. Sunday afternoon he had sat in his secondary school test-prep course among a group of our boys. His best friend's father drove him home. He gave his buddy a "high five" and said, "I'll see you tomorrow." His parents were downstairs watching television when he went up to his room and turned on his computer. Later, his father went to his room to say goodnight. His son's last message to the girl he had met at camp was flashing on the screen. "You won't hear from me again," he had E-mailed her. "What do you mean, you're going to commit suicide or something?" she had E-mailed back. The boy was in the bathroom, a bathrobe belt looped tight around his neck.

When I was twelve years old, I emigrated to America. I didn't speak a word of English. During those early days of desperate longing and painful readjustment, I comforted myself with *David Copperfield*—a Romanian translation I had carried with me in my suitcase. None of the rejection and humiliation I was experiencing could compare, I told myself, with David's ordeal with the murderous Mr. Murdstone! I took my book with me into the schoolyard and, ignoring the looks, smirks and pointed fingers at the odd new girl who always wore the same pleated blue skirt and starched white blouse, shared my lunch with David Copperfield. How reassuring it was to discover that my hero had overcome his misery by identifying with his heroes, pretending to be Tom Jones or Roderick Random or "Captain Somebody of the Royal British Navy who never lost dignity from having his ears boxed with the Latin Grammar."

David Copperfield was precious to me because my father had read to me about him when I was very young. Like my father's voice, the voices of my literary friends were warm and loving. They tutored my imagination with images of beautiful places and noble deeds. At times of doubt and trouble, they did for me what good friends always do: lifted my spirits and filled me with hope. They reminded me that others had faced failures and injustices as bitter as my own and managed to survive and overcome. And they also led me, as such friends always do, to form new friendships, teaching me early on that our best friends are those who bring out the best in us.

Had the boy who hanged himself ever read *David Copperfield*? Did he have any nurturing literary friends?

After the reading of the letter, the leading expert on the panel began dispensing his professional expertise, offering a profile of the type of "young person" most likely to commit suicide. If only the profile had suited the boy we knew! If only "the young man" had not been just a boy, at least two years short of puberty; if only he had been quiet and inarticulate, friendless and withdrawn; if only his parents had never been seen hugging and kissing him, chatting and laughing with him, praising and applauding him! Then we might have believed that at the root of this tragedy was the worm that the expert told us caused all self-destructive acts: low self-esteem. Then we could have assured ourselves that we, who do everything in our power to make our children love themselves, need not worry about them tonight.

When my son was in third grade, I bought him *David Copperfield.* Another mother noticed the book on his nightstand and laughed at me. "Aren't you going a bit too far above his reading level?" she asked in a sarcastic tone.

Among the professional parents who are my peers, the competition begins the moment our children are born. We are as driven to excel at parenting as at business, medicine and accounting. Faithfully, we follow the gospel preached by the experts: The road to happiness is paved with self-esteem and the road to self-esteem is paved with success. Frantically, we rush our kids from play groups led by experts paid to develop their social skills, to athletic leagues coached by experts paid to sharpen their competitive skills, to enrichment classes taught by experts paid to challenge their academic skills.

Our children have little time for long, slow books like *David Copperfield.* They have few empty hours to daydream, few open spaces to roam freely. Their energies are channeled into structured activities designed to promote the proper profiles for the proper resumes. We begin marketing our children from the womb.

Reading was one of the most hotly debated issues of our early parenting years. How soon, how fast, how fluently one's child read—there were few greater sources of anxiety and contention at our school meetings. For us, reading is a highly prized skill which can be tested, quantified, rated on a scale, compared against a norm and interpreted as a measure of a child's intelligence, a teacher's dedication, a school's competence. Books are stepping stones in a child's career. For it is books, which must fiercely compete with movies, records, games and software for our children's attention, that will ultimately lead to the important prizes: an improved vocabulary, a higher verbal ability score, a stronger ERB,

SAT, LSAT or MCAT score, a classier prep school, a more prestigious college, a better paid job, a life of wealth, power and privilege.

In this world view, books are not good friends, but good contacts, the kind to be used to get even better contacts up the ladder of success. All of us are in a frenzy to introduce our children to as many of them as possible. The value of a book, like the value of a good "connection," is based on its utility rather than its character. A book with a more sophisticated vocabulary, which might speed up a child's ascent into the top reading group, is a more desirable association than one from the lower orders.

Whether taught through the "whole language" or the "phonetic" approach, the process now called "reading acquisition" has nothing to do with the acquisition of wisdom. Our generation makes no connection between the "life of the mind" and the "life higher," the way our predecessors might have done. "There is something—a hope—a help out—it lifts me on top of my hungry body—the hunger for the life higher"—cried a poor, young "greenhorn" in a story by Anzia Yezierska, an immigrant writer at the turn of the century who got her education in night school. For her, as for her sweatshop heroines, literacy represented not just a passport out of the slums but a ticket to a higher plane of existence: "When I only begin to read, I forget I'm on this world. It lifts me on wings with high thoughts."

If our generation of educated parents spends more money on books than any generation before us, it is because we realize that in a meritocracy, books are good business. Parents in my world go about securing good verbal scores for their offspring the way parents in Jane Austen's world went about securing good dowries. And if we view our children's "literacy" as a promise of their "annuity," we also regard their creativity as an emblem of their nobility.

"Creativity" is the second most esteemed word (next to self-esteem) in the vocabulary of "parenting." If good reading skills are the bread and butter that will guarantee our children's survival in the competitive next century, good creative skills are the cake and jam. Nothing excites us more, stirs us to action quicker than talk about creative thinking and creative problem solving, creative teachers and creative programs. For all of us know that if the literate will make a good living, the creative will make a great one. The good student will know how to make a buck; the creative one will know how to make piles of them. Creativity starts up companies, invents new products, begets celebrity. Creativity leads to Microsoft and Dreamworks, *Star Wars* and Starbucks.

The "creativity" we are determined to foster in our children as we rush them from dance classes to art classes, from music programs to theater programs, has no relationship to that faculty that writers and poets in previous centuries defined as the human imagination. Shelley, the great romantic, believed that being imaginative entailed "a going out of our own nature, and an identification of ourselves with the beautiful which exists in thought, action, or person, not our own. A man, to be greatly good, must imagine himself intensely and comprehensively; the pain and pleasures of his species must become his own."

For us, unlike for Shelley, creativity is related not to goodness but to efficiency, not to empathy but to boredom. We would say: A person, to be greatly successful, must continually come up with marketable ideas and products. Consumers get bored quickly and can be hooked and captivated only by the new and different.

Shelley's notion of the imagination as "the great instrument of moral good" is alien to the contemporary sensibility. Equally foreign is Shelley's concept that such an instrument needs to be fine-tuned and that literature, art and poetry might "strengthen the faculty which is the organ of the moral nature of man, in the same manner as exercise strengthens a limb." Our obsession with strengthening our bodies by zealously exercising each of our muscles does not extend to the "organ of the moral nature of man." We might spend our last penny on computer software and athletic gear and our last free minute driving our children to math tutors and tennis coaches, but we would never dream of enlisting the services of a poet, like Shelley, to "awaken and enlarge the mind itself to the truth and beauty of friendship, patriotism and persevering devotion" or to "broaden the circumference" of our children's imagination to the "hidden beauty of the world."

Was the boy who killed himself aware of any hidden beauty in the world? Was he aware of the hidden beauty of human beings?

Confused and uncertain, anxious and frightened, with all the humility we had acquired since we began our parenting training, we begged our hired experts for wisdom. Our own school psychologist, whom our children love and trust, sat tearfully among us. Even the parents in the audience who were bona fide members of the profession relied on the imported team members for answers: It was they, after all, who were being paid for their services tonight—the ultimate validation of expertise.

"What do we tell our children to make sure they'll never do the same thing?" a nervous father blurted out.

"I told mine the boy was crazy," another shot back. "Only crazy people kill themselves. That's plain and simple and easy to understand. Is there anything wrong with that?" he demanded of the experts, unable to proceed without reassurance.

The delicate issue of how to teach our children that life is worth living had never been covered by any of our parenting courses. Our lessons on how to raise that well-adjusted "whole child" with an integrated social, emotional and academic self who would always land in the top portion of every chart and graduate in the top quarter of every class had never contained a section on the soul. A soul, perhaps, might prove to be an encumbrance. Those trained to dedicate their lives to production and consumption are more likely to succeed without souls.

"He thought the death thing was cool," my daughter told her babysitter about the boy who killed himself. "He wore black a lot and was really into Marilyn Manson and Kurt Cobain."

Out of my daughter's presence, the babysitter confessed that during the period when she tried to shoot herself, she too had been "into the death thing," had worn black and idolized Kurt Cobain, a rock singer who had killed himself. She told me she had kept a journal at the time, and offered to show it to me, if it would help me understand.

I copied down the phrases that scared me most:

> "...I'm listening to Kurt. I miss him. Death is the only truth I know of. We can't be living for our death, it's unnatural, it's sick. But I have yet to find a solid truth to live by or maybe the point of life is to learn to live without a truth. If so, then maybe I'm wasting my time trying to find myself because there's nothing to find. I'm merely a mess, merely a mistake. A mistake from the world's worst ecologic disaster that made human life possible.
>
> "...My tutor told me that if I just get good grades, if I just perform in what I am asked I can be happy, but I can't accept that, I have to find a different world, I have to find happiness that approves with my ideal life. My parents, my tutor, society, everyone doesn't understand that I need to find that other world, that place of rapture, because if I don't, if I don't find a land of freedom, a land where we can all be prosperous, I'll have to kill myself.
>
> "...So I've set a goal. I want to reach ecstasy and be free of life's difficulty..."

Did the boy who killed himself also want to "reach ecstasy and be free of life's difficulty?" Was he trying "to find a land of freedom" by hanging himself?

My father resisted hanging himself through six torturous years of solitary confinement because he was able to find a "land of freedom" even in a dungeon. It was the imagination that sustained him as he sat alone on a stool in his dark cell for sixteen hours a day, back bent, eyes on the ground, scrutinized every five minutes by the piercing eye of his jailer. The dead boy looked into himself and found his fate, sealed in endless night; the political prisoner looked into himself and found his soul, bathed in sunlight.

But the prisoner had not entered his painful trial entirely unprepared. He was able to use his imagination in a way that conquered circumstance rather than capitulated to it; his imagination had been nurtured by a lifestyle, a culture and a tradition that elevated his spirit and fortified his will to live.

My father was not raised in a large home by professional parents who sent him to enrichment classes and private schools. He grew up in a bungalow in the seaport of Constanza, the son of a mechanic who perished in a fire, leaving his wife to raise eight children on a widow's pension. Yet how much richer was his childhood than that of his American grandchildren! His boyhood was not spent between freeways and shopping malls, or glued to computer screens and television sets, but between the surf and the sand of his beloved Black Sea, swimming, rowing, climbing rocks and cliffs. His youthful imagination was not engaged by violent video games and horror movies but by ships and waves, by the stories of fishermen and the adventures of sailors. At school, he did neither long research projects nor short reading comprehension exercises; he memorized an endless number of poems, passages from Homer and Virgil, Dante and the Bible, soliloquies from Sophocles and Shakespeare, Racine and Moliere.

Deprived of all the natural world, forbidden to look up through the bars of his tiny window at a patch of sky, he soothed himself with lyrics about green meadows, woods and pastures, about the unbounded green of hills and valleys celebrated in every line of Romanian folk music. The book he stored in his mind, the book that saved his life, became for him another link in the cultural chain that has sustained our faith in life and in human beings throughout the centuries.

Contemporary culture is ready to break this chain. Public statements about life's essential beauty or man's innate goodness are as passé as Elsie Robinson's "I will hold beauty as a shield against despair." We no longer expect writers, artists and filmmakers to sustain our mental comfort. We have replaced the dowdy old friends who have flattered us with brash new friends who are bold enough to insult us. They exercise our brains and keep our imaginations fit on a diet designed to confront rather than console, unmask rather than uplift, deconstruct rather than rebuild, reduce rather than enrich. Whether we watch a "lowbrow" TV show or read a "highbrow" literary novel, the contemporary imaginative experience entails an identification of ourselves with the mean, the bad and the ugly.

At the beginning of the century, the fervid imagination of a romantic, eleven-year-old middle class boy, like Joyce's Stephen Daedelus, might have been stirred by alluring scenes from *The Count of Monte Cristo*: "In his imagination he lived through a long train of adventures, marvelous as those in the book itself, toward the close of which there appeared an image of himself, grown older and sadder, standing in a moonlit garden with Mercedes who had so many years before slighted his love."

At the end of our century, the imagination of an impressionable eleven-year-old boy, brooding over his first love, is stimulated by the lyrics of Marilyn Manson: "white trash get down on your knees, time for cake and sodomy/time for cake and sodomy/(i am the god of fuck, I am the god of fuck)/vcr's and vaseline, tv-fucked by plastic queens/cash in hand and dick on screen, who said god was ever clean?"

In the months before his death, the imagination of my daughter's eleven-year-old classmate was hooked and captivated by this man, who emerges on stage with rope burns around his neck, cuts himself with broken glass and blares: "Little kids/Who don't understand the world/I understand your pain/Come out of yourselves and bleed to me/I'll suck your pain away." This popular teen idol, who named himself after Marilyn Monroe and Charles Manson, has become a commercial success with such hit songs as "Cake and Sodomy," "Misery Machine," "Suicide Snowman," and with a hot selling T-shirt emblazoned with the slogan, "Kill God, Kill Your Mom and Dad, Kill Yourself." From him, a restless young mind can learn that the "the world is an ashtray," where human beings "burn and coil like cigarettes." In his haunting lyrics, melancholic adolescents seek refuge from the pain of rejection and betrayal: "Prick your finger it is done.../the moon has now eclipsed the sun/the angel has spread its wings.../the time has come for bitter things." And then, at times of doubt and trouble, at moments of anguish and heartache, the vulnerable young can draw inspiration from the words and deeds of that other hero, the self-martyred Kurt Cobain: "Look on the bright side/There's always suicide."

Once upon a time, the world loomed large with promise for the restless young mind; the possibilities for escape seemed countless. Hordes of dissatisfied youths could sail the oceans with Captain Hornblower, hide on desert islands with Robinson Crusoe, roam the jungles with Tarzan of the Apes, unravel tragic secrets with Jane Eyre; adventurous teens could hunt for the treasures of Robert Louis Stevenson, soar in the hot air balloons of Jules Verne, ride through the forests of Walter Scott, conquer the West of James Fenimore Cooper, wander through the moors of Emily Brontë, flirt in the drawing rooms of Jane Austen, glide down the rafts of Mark Twain, jump on the railroad cars of Jack London. As a girl, I ran off to all these places, my imagination as unfettered by my gender as by my race, creed, nationality or date of birth. "Those of us who read carried around with us like martyrs a secret knowledge, a secret joy and a secret hope," wrote Annie Dillard in *An American Childhood*, her tribute to the literary mentors of her youth. "There is a life worth living where history is still taking place. There are ideas worth dying for and circumstances where courage is still prized. This life could be found and joined, like the Resistance."

Today, Dillard's "Resistance" is being driven further and further underground. Few young people are lucky enough to find it and join it. Mass media have done everything in their power to destroy it. Never in the history of the world has the imagination of the young been the object of such relentless assault. Large armies of well-equipped experts continuously invent new strategies for defeating their opponents in the fierce battle for the conquest of youth. They have deposed parents, teachers, relatives and neighbors and replaced them with a set of electronic rivals who are now molding our children's imagination and shaping their vision of the world.

Is it possible that girls and boys are destroying themselves in such numbers because their imaginations subsist on a diet of destruction? Is it conceivable that creatures who envision themselves as empty vessels occupying an abysmal space may also envision death as an odyssey to a superior planet? It was this view that convinced the Heaven's Gate cultists to destroy themselves in order to "ascend in a cloud of light" to that "higher plane" they could not find here on Earth.

Our panel of experts relied on statistical correspondences—the accepted form of authority for my generation—to restore our mental comfort. Their speeches began with the awe-inspiring phrases by which we had raised our children: "Research shows..." "Studies prove..." "Surveys demonstrate..." They led us down the familiar road to the familiar destination: Only deviations from the norm engage in aberrant behavior. The chances that a typical, well-adjusted young person will fall into the aberrant category are minimal. Most parents in the room need not feel alarmed—unless their offspring have defective genes or dysfunctional families.

Our panel of experts used facts and logic to demonstrate that none of us had caused the tragedy at our school or could have done anything to have prevented it. They tried to reassure us with talk about "normal reactions," "common worries" and "predictable fears." But nothing they could tell us about curves and norms could make us feel less threatened or less responsible.

Nothing the experts ever told us had truly convinced us, even as we followed the plan, that any of it was right or made sense. Although all of us are experts preparing our children to fill top ranks in the army of experts, we don't like the system we are a part of. We wish we knew how to escape it. We wish we were brave enough to defy it. But what if our children are forced to pay for our intransigence? If we don't conform, they might suffer. If we rebel, they might get punished. It's their future, after all, that's at stake.

De Tocqueville predicted that the tyranny that might evolve in a democracy would be far more brutal and oppressive than anything that could ever be conceived in a dictatorship. "In democratic republics tyranny leaves the body alone and goes straight for the soul," he wrote in *Democracy in America.* Still, the impulse to resist tyranny remains deeply embedded in our democratic selves. We are not entirely ready to surrender our freedom of thought and become part of what De Tocqueville warned might someday become "an innumerable multitude of men, alike and equal, constantly circling around in pursuit of the petty and banal pleasures with which they glut their souls, each one of them withdrawn into himself, almost unaware of the fate of the rest."

Ultimately, none of us who knew the stricken family could go home convinced that the atypical young person from the aberrant category had anything to do with the unique boy who had grown up with our children and played in our homes. And none of us who sat at his memorial several days later, and heard his teachers and friends talk about the lively, interesting, curious, adventurous, passionate, and yes, imaginative being who was no more, could walk away absolved of guilt or free of fear.

The Conspiracy of Consumption

Can freedom survive post-modern despotism?

> The great paradox of this economic revolution is that its new technologies enable people and nations to take sudden leaps into modernity, while at the same time they promote the renewal of once-forbidden barbarisms.—William Greider, *One World, Ready Or Not: The Manic Logic of Global Capitalism*

> Despotism often presents itself as the repairer of all the ills suffered, the supporter of just rights, defender of the oppressed, and founder of order. Peoples are lulled to sleep by the temporary prosperity it engenders, and when they wake up, they are wretched.—De Tocqueville, *On Democracy*

I never thought I'd come to envy my father, a former Romanian political prisoner, for his years of solitary confinement in a communist dungeon. A deep, dark hole it was, the cell where my father was held captive in complete isolation, forced to sit for sixteen hours a day on a backless chair. The chair where I was being held captive last Sunday afternoon, when I caught myself wishing to trade seats with him, was an overstuffed, down-filled, chintz-recovered armchair. It had just been selected for extermination by my three torturers—a space planner, a professional organizer and a remodeling expert. One by one, they worked me over, determined to destroy my resistance. The communists went for propaganda to Karl Marx, the Nazis to Adolf Hitler. My remodelists use an equally clever, though not as yet renowned a theorist—Maxine Ordersky. In her manifesto, *The Complete Home Organizer*, Ordersky presents her ideology as a cure to the most debilitating illness of our time:

> Today it's easy to own a lot of things. We're an acquisitive society. Family members each require different gadgets and gizmos to enhance their own lifestyles, hobbies and routines. Technology is obsolete, before warranties expire. So we upgrade. The more we buy, the more we have to store. The more elements to store, the greater the likelihood of disorganization. If you have to search frantically for something whenever you need it or, worse, have to search for everything you store regardless of how immediate your need, then your possessions own you...your possessions are controlling your life instead of the other way around.

It didn't take much brainwashing to convince me that my family was being oppressed by its possessions. We were few; they were many; they were marching onward toward victory; we were spinning backwards toward defeat. The triumvirate promised that if we let them take charge of our household, they'd deliver us from bondage. Their vision was seductive: new built-in work centers for each of our four computers with special desks, counters, shelves, cabinets, drawers, files, pullouts and hideaways; new built-in closets for each of our four wardrobes, with adjustable slots and pegs for rapidly changing fashions; new twin bathrooms large enough to accommodate a young woman's hair and bath products and a young man's weight training equipment; a new state of the art kitchen with sufficient room for the future cappuccino, bread, pasta and ice cream makers, and the fifth desk for the fifth computer for quick access to recipes, restaurants and take out stores.

The new order would be enshrined by the common bulletin board above our separate mail cubbies—the guardians of harmony in our household. Never again would my husband and I accuse each other of having swallowed a bill, form or invitation. Peace would reign in our new kingdom. The lion would lie with the lamb. My son and daughter, no longer at each other's throats over the bathroom counter, would take turns reading out loud in the evenings from my favorite Russian novels, as we gathered blissfully around our blazing new fireplace.

Let us take control, the triumvirate swore in one voice, that of their prophet, Ordersky, and "you'll be the one in control of yourself and your life style!" All I had to do was to give them my trust. All my husband had to do was to give them a check. (Not because he's the head of the household, but because he's the quickest to find a pen that writes.)

It was only when I asked the leader of the pack how long it will take to reach Jerusalem that the facade cracked. The three contradicted each other, agreeing only on the fact that the "interim stage" will be tough, rough and miserable; historically, such "transitional periods" require a few sacrifices, a little belt tightening and a lot of patience. No further explanations were needed. I knew all about "transitional periods," having grown up in one, and also happened to be well-versed on the Reign of Terror and the Chinese Cultural Revolution.

Noticing me grit my teeth with renewed resolve, the organizer-in-chief tightened the screws. "The newest studies show that youngsters with proper work environments earn fifty percent higher grades and test scores than those from disorganized households."

It was at that moment when I began to yearn for the clear bareness of my father's cell.

◆ ◆ ◆

> It turns out that those who inspired the revolution aren't at home in anything except change and turmoil...For them transitional periods, worlds in the making, are an end in themselves...And do you know why these never ending preparations are so futile? It's because...man is born to live, not to prepare for life.—Boris Pasternak, *Doctor Zhivago*

My father landed in prison for calling his country's transitional period a lie. It was a lie he had once believed, just as he had once believed in the socialist paradise, universal brotherhood and the withering away of the state. He had joined the party as an officer during World War II, convinced that it would help save his country from Nazi bondage. In the first decade of communism, as he rose from colonel to general to Vice Minister of Defense, he had accepted the logic of the transitional period: all the sacrifices and the compromises would eventually lead to a better world for his children. Then one day he faced reality: the transitional period was not a finite road uphill, toward that pure, white summit that he, an inveterate mountain climber, had envisioned, but a plunge downhill, toward a dark abyss. The rights that had been surrendered would never be returned. The freedoms that had been relinquished would never be recovered. The transitional period was not an ascent toward freedom but a descent into bondage. His children were growing up into a world of slaves.

Outraged, he wrote a book exposing the country's leaders as thugs and swindlers who had robbed their people of their most precious possessions. Their tactics were the ones usually employed by the tyrants of history and the bullies of playgrounds. Even a child can understand that a treasure that would never be surrendered without a bitter fight can be won over by a seductive promise. "Let me have your dump truck for a minute and tomorrow I'll let you drive my electric jeep!" And a tyrannical child can figure out that one such treasure can beget another; once his, what was once freely held can now only be bought; the dump truck may be sold back for the price of the fire engine which may be sold again for the price of the lunch money. With each concession, the price increases, as does his power over his victim. And ultimately, power is the treasure that tyrants of all ages hunt as they devise their vicious cycles of promise, surrender, frustration, deprivation and coercion—and call them "transitional periods" to paradise.

◆ ◆ ◆

> What is the nature of the storm upon us? A new structure of power is gradually emerging in the world, forcing great changes everywhere it asserts itself…The Robespierre of this revolution is finance capital. Its principles are transparent and pure: maximizing the return on capital…—William Greider, *One World, Ready or Not: The Manic Logic of Global Capitalism*

The possessions oppressing my family and the remodelists who came, like Soviet troupes, to liberate us, are agents of the same power that now rules over every aspect of our lives. Gradually, we have surrendered our freedom to an army of experts, products and services which have entrapped us in a vicious cycle of production and consumption that is plunging us deeper and deeper into bondage. Increasingly, we must toil to buy what we once freely owned and gradually bartered away. Most of our energies and resources are devoured by the process of upholding the rule of experts, products and services, extending their domain and expanding their power.

Although our generation has been accused of being materialistic and acquisitive, we did not fill our homes with gadgets because we have an avaricious love of things and enjoy counting them, like gold, in the middle of the night. We did not fill our lives with services because we are spoiled and lazy and prefer to pass on our loads to others. Our transitional period to Paradise began with the usual promises. Our computers would free us from many of our administrative burdens; time previously spent researching and revising could be devoted to reflecting and creating. Our children would improve their reading, math and thinking skills; new games and software would broaden their horizons. Our entertainment centers would draw us together for hours of family unity and shared fun. Our trained experts would help us have smoother relationships; raise better adjusted, more highly educated children; live fuller, deeper and more meaningful lives.

De Tocqueville has observed that if human beings were made the way tyrants wished to remake them, they would not need such lofty promises as "liberty, equality and fraternity" to join revolutions. Tyrants recognize that our deepest hungers and our most powerful aspirations are not for the tangible things that can be bought and sold, but for the intangible things, which nourish those aspects of ourselves that define our freedom. Consequently, the riches with which they entice us are precisely those of which they aim to deplete us.

Tyrants promise harmony but bring discord, promise unity but create isolation, promise knowledge but foster ignorance, promise education but create propaganda, promise to enrich lives and expand choices but reduce lives and limit choices to those they can control and manipulate. They promise essences but enmesh in surfaces. They promise meaningful truths but mire in trivial details. Tyrants never allow us to really live but condemn us to endless living arrangements, and entrap us in infinite transitions.

The tyrants oppressing my family entered our household through the interim phase door, disguised as friendly allies who would strengthen our forces, then leave us on our own. We did not know that they would move in and take over. We did not foresee that each product would bind us to another product, each service to another service, and that soon they would reduce our activities to an incessant process of buying and selling, producing and consuming.

When we brought our technological aids into our children's lives, we did not know that we were surrendering our custody rights. We did not know that our electronic rivals would usurp our places as role models, companions and educators, and that soon we would have to compete with their paid services for our children's time, attention and respect. We did not know that they would isolate, separate and divide us, or that they would become the infiltrators of hostile and subversive messages in our midst.

When, while expecting our first-born, we attended a La Maas class and later took our new baby to Gym Buree, we did not know that we were relinquishing what parents have always taught their children and children have always taught themselves to an interminable battalion of trained experts. We did not know that the companionship once provided by neighborhood kids, the advice freely given by relatives, the sport events, creative activities and social gatherings once organized by parents and children themselves would now have to be purchased from moderators, trainers, entertainers, instructors, teachers, tutors, coaches, advisors, therapists and other specialists. We did not foresee that our time with our children would be dedicated to transporting them from one provider of services to another or that our roles would shrink to that of procurers of services. Nor did we anticipate that our homes would be invaded by the products of products and the services of services—the newsletters, brochures, forms and bills that now devour our non-shopping, non-schlepping family hours.

When we welcomed our technological allies into our home, we did not know that we were abandoning our right to exist without them. We did not know that we were surrendering our freedom to amuse, stimulate, interest, delight, relax and engage ourselves and each other with our own ideas, stories, memories, dreams and fantasies. We did not know that soon we would not be able to think without their presence, talk without interruption, gather without their involvement, that no activity could be performed without their services, and that we would never again be free of their interference in our lives. Our work hours would grow in order to pay for them, our rest days would shrink in order to hunt for them, service them, upgrade them, organize them and store them; our conversations would center around them; our thoughts would be filled with them.

Since we can't beat them, we've joined them. Overpowered by products, we envision ourselves as products and regard our relationships as an exchange of services. We buy books, attend lectures and hire instructors to teach us how to maximize our capacity to "multitask," and enhance our ability to "sell," "package" and "promote" ourselves to employers, clients, lovers, spouses and friends. "Professional women whose taste and background should enable themselves to package themselves with great skill seem to be missing the point," explains *New Women's Dress for Success.* "The best garments for moving into the executive suite are suits in muted conservative colors that scream money and class."

Compulsively, we work on perfecting our appearance, appeal, efficiency, productivity and marketability. At cocktail parties we tell each other that we're looking for "low maintenance, high quality" relationships and trade tips on how to "package our kids" and "pitch them" to the elite schools and colleges that will turn them into the most commercial commodities of the 21st century. No one seems to remember that a human being who can be bought and sold on the market is by definition a slave.

◆ ◆ ◆

> In the end men will lay their freedom at our feet and say to us: "Make us your slaves and feed us" for they are weak, vicious, worthless and rebellious...Yes, we will make them work, but in their hours free from toil, we shall organize life for them, like a child's game with children's songs, a chorus, with innocent dances...—Dostoevsky, *The Brothers Karamazov*

Tyrannical systems depend on the Faustian bargain described by Dostoyevsky's Grand Inquisitor: the bartering away of heavenly freedom in exchange for earthly bread. Every system of oppression relies on the same basic assumptions about human nature and employs the same basic strategy to enslave it: the survival instinct is stronger than the civilizing one; our appetites are stronger than our aspirations; the beast will devour the man. The strategy of tyrants is to create conditions in which survival instincts conflict with civilizing drives. "I was about to set off a morality versus the need to eat controversy," confesses Larry Flynt, in his memoir, *The People vs Larry Flynt*. "A pastor's group sent Dayton Press executives an outrageous letter, condemning them for their decision to print the magazine. How could they stoop so low as to force their church members to choose between their moral convictions and their need to make a living?"

Human beings are able to create civilizations because they are motivated by other forces than their own basic survival. De Tocqueville observed that "a principled devotion to something beyond the self is the sum total of human greatness." The bonds upon which civilizations are based are an expression of those passions, potentials and aspirations that define human beings as human. The Greeks defined "freedom" as freedom from the necessities of life. Free men, unlike slaves or animals, could devote themselves to those things which, as Aristotle wrote "were neither necessary or merely useful: the life of enjoying bodily pleasures in which the beautiful, as it is given is consumed; the life devoted to the matters of the polis, in which excellence produces beautiful deeds; and the life of the philosopher devoted to the contemplation of things eternal, whose everlasting beauty can neither be brought about through the producing interference of man nor be changed through his consumption of them." For the Greeks, the freedom of mortals depended on their ability to contemplate, create and preserve immortal, everlasting things.

"Man is not man because of what he has in common with the earth, but because of what he has in common with God," wrote Abraham Herschel. The goal of tyrants is to reduce man to what he has in common with the earth, degrade him to the level of an animal who can be harnessed, saddled and whipped or—as in the contemporary world—into a gadget that can be manufactured, programmed, packaged, mass produced, rated, sold, bought, used, discarded and replaced. Slavery reduces human beings to human tools that exist in order to perform and are valued in terms of the utility and efficiency of their performance. Slaves live to produce and consume to live and produce. They are deprived of the freedom to contemplate, relish, relate, meditate or create anything that will not enhance their productivity or increase their market value. "When men carry a chain, they think of little, of very little," writes the author of *Spartacus*, "than when you will eat again, drink again, sleep again. So there are no complex thoughts in the minds of Spartacus or in the midst of any of his Thracian comrades who carry the chain with him. You make men like beasts and they do not think of angels." Sheila Conrad, in her article, "What Personal Life:

Downsizing/Restructuring/Reengineering," presents a more updated image of the same condition:

> When I asked someone at a physician-owned medical group how the increase in her already heavy workload had affected her personal life, she quickly retorted, "What personal life? Your personal life goes away...My husband and I spend time together at night—he's on the phone in his office and I'm on the phone in my office. My folks say, 'This is a relationship? This is a life?'

Slaves have no families, no private time, no personal lives.

Tyrannical systems attack the values which sustain families, communities and civilizations—selfless love, the golden rule, harmony, tradition, continuity—and promote the laws of the jungle: self-preservation, domination of the weak by the strong and survival of the fittest. Those aspects of human nature that lead beyond the self to others and the immediate to the permanent must be suppressed, and those sides of human nature that are motivated by basic instincts must be aroused. Ties of love must become ties of appetite; ties of friendship must become ties of self-interest; ties of permanence must become ties of expediency. In *How To Succeed In Business Without a Penis*, Karen Salmasohn, who boasts that her "favorite time of day is NOW," confides that the secret to her publishing success in the "stupendously competitive nighties marketplace" was reading *The Art of War*: "It changed me. A woman does not need a penis to succeed in business. She does need balls. A good set of boobs doesn't hurt either. Sex is a weapon. We should not fight our female side but use it in our fight to attain career advancement." Sun Tzu's *The Art of War* is now an "obligatory work in the Hollywood agent's bookshelf," according to an article in the *Los Angeles Times* about the "dawn of a new predatory age" of unprecedented treachery in Hollywood. And in *Princessa: Machiavelli for Women*—one of the many popular instruction manuals in the ideology of consumption, Harriet Rubin sells her "principessa package" by promising that it will outmarket, outsell and outpower rival packages in a competitive economy: "This book is about the wars of intimacy, where the enemy is close enough to hurt you, betray you, oppose you, whether a spouse, boss, client, parent, child."

Tyranny thrives in an atmosphere of suspicion, mistrust, rivalry and hostility which poisons personal relationships, weakens families and communities and leaves individuals isolated, separated and defenseless. "Everybody lies to me. Trust no one. No more Mr. Nice Guy"—is how Karen Salmasohn describes the moment of awakening which led to her rebirth as a new, successful woman. "Despotism, by its very nature suspicious, sees the isolation of men as the best guarantee of its own survival," De Tocqueville explains. "A despot will lightly forgive his subjects for not loving him, provided they do not love one another." The process of turning human beings into slaves is a gradual process of dehumanization and degradation. We can call ourselves slaves when we each struggle alone just to make it through the day.

Tyrannical systems aim to sever every bond that does not bond to the system. Bonds to friends, lovers, community, nature, culture, morality and religion—the bonds of civilization—must be destroyed and replaced by bonds designed to sustain the structure of tyranny. Just visit our neighborhood's only public meeting ground—the health club—on Sunday, our day of rest: you'll find the kids in the game room, each hooked up to his or her own video game, engaged with his or her own joystick. You'll find the parents on the treadmills, each hooked up to his or her own TV channel, engaged with his or her own headphones. Our club was forced to buy seven separate screens to stop the fistfights between the sport fanatics and the talk show addicts! Despots, like cult leaders, demand total and exclusive relationships. For every system of tyranny pursues the same goal: unlimited power. "Such power," Hannah Arendt explains in *The Origins of Totalitarianism*, "can only be secured if literally all men, without a single exception, are reliably dominated in every aspect of their life."

◆ ◆ ◆

> "How do you feel son?" the priest taps lightly with his fingertip. He must not be feeling well himself.
>
> "Very well, thank you Father," I tap him back. "I'm lucky, I suppose."
>
> "Better not speak of luck, son, when describing your condition in Hell."
>
> "To be perfectly honest father, lately I've come to believe that one can find good even in Hell, especially a man like me."
>
> "What kind of man are you, son? I should hope your life outside was no worse than your life here."
>
> "Of course not, only, from a certain standpoint, I do feel freer now than I did before…"
>
> "That's impossible to believe…" the priest interrupts me, now tapping with his fist rather than his fingertip. "How can you feel free when you are buried alive? I will pray for your mental health!"—*The Subterranean Tower* by Ion Eremia

The Romanian military tribunal that in 1959 punished my father for his intransigence could never have foreseen that the condemned man would someday come to view his sentence as a gateway to freedom. Well-informed as they were, my father's persecutors could never have grasped the secret my father conveyed during his Morse code conversation through taps on the wall with the neighbor in the cell on his left—the Romanian priest who refused to denounce his Hungarian friend.

I was as shocked as the priest when, during the course of his first visit to Los Angeles in 1990, my father confided that he had actually found happiness in prison.

"Believe it or not, my darling," my father declared, on a sunny summer afternoon as we strolled on the Santa Monica pier toward a peaceful ocean, "it was in that cell that for the first time in my life I felt truly free." My children were still very young then, and I had not yet read the manuscript my father had brought with him. I had not yet given much thought to the differences between freedom and slavery, political censorship and commercial censorship, the tyranny of communism and the tyranny of consumption. I did not believe him then. Now, over a decade later, I finally do.

Prison freed my father from an interim phase that stifled his individuality, dissolved his will, limited his imagination and diminished his humanity. His social and economic privileges were bought at the price of his complicity with a cruel and inhuman system that forced him to violate the best in himself: his sense of compassion, truth, justice, beauty. A tool of the system, he had to treat others as tools of the system, as "workers" or "parasites," "friends or enemies," "useful or useless." By rejecting the material rewards and privileges that kept him in bondage, my father exercised the most defining attribute of his humanity: the ability to choose, regardless of the conditions or the consequences, the ties of civilization over the laws of the jungle.

As he sat on a stool in his dark cell for sixteen hours a day, back bent, eyes on the ground, scrutinized every five minutes by the piercing eye of the jailor, my father drew upon human resources that were far more powerful than his persecutors could ever have imagined. The prisoner sang in his thoughts and listened to concerts in his mind; he recited and composed poetry. Through Morse code taps on the wall, he had passionate debates about God and religion with the priest in the cell on his right. His mentor, the astronomer in the cell on his left, inspired my father to structure his time, stick to a schedule and channel his creativity.

Prison became a better writing school than many of the M.F.A programs now spawning throughout our universities. Anyone who knows, like Hemingway, that the only way to relieve the urge to write is by writing, will understand why in the darkness of his cell, my father experienced the brightest moments of his life.

If freedom is, as John Stuart Mill defined it, "a condition of human affairs that brings human beings nearer the best they can be," or as De Tocqueville describes it, "the source of all moral greatness in man for it alone provides the sphere of action required by human individuality," if freedom enlarges, ennobles and uplifts, while slavery stunts, degrades and belittles, then my father's transformation from party official to political prisoner was not a fall from but a rise to power, not a descent into darkness but an ascent into light.

◆ ◆ ◆

In my high tech room, continuously distracted by my ringing cordless, my clicking answer tape, my buzzing fax machine, how I envy my father his freedom! Wearied by my daily battle with the mouse, the continuous struggles to decipher the secrets of the new software, my ever-growing sense of ignorance, incompetence and confusion as I struggle to withstand each invasion of products, services and systems, how I envy the simple tools of my father's trade! I envy his Morse code through taps on the wall conversations with his neighbors, so much deeper, richer and more meaningful than the brief exchanges of taped messages on answer phones and cryptic E-mail notes to my overburdened, exhausted and overwhelmed friends. Most of all, I envy my father's faith in the future, his unshakable belief that his children will someday read his book and share his language, values, ideals, heritage, assumptions, history, imagination, vision, hopes. When I compare the sense of isolation and oppression I experience in my high tech study, with the sense of freedom and community my father experienced in his bare prison cell, I am struck by the wisdom of De Tocqueville's observation: "Under the absolute government of a single man, despotism, to reach the soul, clumsily struck at the body, and the soul, escaping from such blows, rose gloriously above it; but in democratic republics, tyranny leaves the body alone and goes straight for the soul."

In one of the cruelest dungeons of dictatorship, my father was able to find all the elements De Tocqueville understood human beings needed in order to resist despotism and fight for freedom: an identifiable enemy, a supportive group of friends, passion, energy, hope for the future, dedication to a cause greater than oneself. But where can we, victims of the growing tyranny of consumption, find the conviction, commitment and community to fight our invisible, amorphous new tyrants, best captured by William Greider in the image of a "wondrous machine running out of control toward some sort of abyss," a machine "that has no visible hands on board, and no one stirring at the wheel"?

Over a century ago, De Tocqueville struggled to articulate his vision of the type of despotism which might ultimately destroy American democracy:

> I think that the type of oppression that threatens democracy today is different from anything that has ever been in the world before.... Such old words as "despotism" and "tyranny" do not fit. The thing is new and as I cannot find a word for it, I must try to define it...
>
> In the first place I see an innumerable multitude of men, alike and equal, constantly circling around in pursuit of the petty and banal pleasures with which they glut their souls. Each one of them, withdrawn into himself, is almost unaware of the fate of the rest...
>
> ...Subjection in petty affairs is manifest daily and touches all citizens indiscriminately. It never drives men to despair, but continuously thwarts them and leads them to give up using their free will. It slowly stifles their spirits and enervates their souls...
>
> ...Over these kinds of men stands an immense, protective power which is alone responsible for securing their enjoyment and watching over their fate.... It would resemble parental authority if, fatherlike, it tried to prepare its charges for a man's life, but on the contrary, it only tries to keep them in perpetual childhood. It likes to see the citizens enjoy themselves, provided they think of nothing but enjoyment.... Why should it not entirely relieve them from the trouble of thinking at all?

From his quiet, somber Victorian study, as he dipped his penknife into the inkwell and stared thoughtfully at the blank sheets on his desk, De Tocqueville saw straight into the future, saw us as we are today, each trapped in our private corners, stuck to our swiveling massage-a-back chairs, headphones on, fingers glued to our keyboards, eyes fixed on our screens, lulled into meek acceptance of our wireless chains.

Bibliography

Des Pres, Terrence. *The Survivor*. New York: Oxford University Press, 1976.

Goldhagen, Daniel Jonah. *Hitler's Willing Executioners*. New York: Alfred A. Knopf, 1996.

Greider, William. *One World, Ready or Not*. New York: Simon & Schuster, 1997.

Langer, Lawrence L. *Admitting the Holocaust*. New York: Oxford University, 1995.

Frankl, Viktor E. *Man's Search for Meaning*. New York: Simon & Schuster, 1984.

Frankl, Viktor E. *The Unheard Cry for Meaning*. New York: Simon & Schuster, 1978.

Levi, Primo. *Moments of Reprieve*. New York: Simon & Schuster, 1985.

Levi, Primo. *The Drowned and the Saved*. New York: Random House, 1989.

Tocqueville, Alexis de. Trans. George Lawrence. Ed. J.P. Mayer. *Democracy in America*. New York: HarperCollins, 1988.

Woolf, Virginia. *The Moment and Other Essays*. New York: Harcourt Brace Jovanovich, 1948.

0-595-31136-9

CPSIA information can be obtained
at www.ICGtesting.com
Printed in the USA
FSHW020240240119
55228FS